# I Shall Find You

# I SHALL FIND YOU

A Novel

*[signature]*

## Micki Berthelot Morency

# I Shall Find You
# Micki Berthelot Morency

®All rights reserved
© Copyright 2025 Micki Berthelot Morency

Any unauthorized reprint or use of this material is prohibited. No part of this book may be reproduced or transmitted in any form or by any means, electronic or mechanical, including photocopying, recording, or by an information storage and retrieval system without express written permission from the author.

This is a work of fiction. All names, characters, locales, and incidents are products of the author's imagination and any resemblance to actual events or locales or person, living or dead, is entirely coincidental.

Published in the United States May 2025
Published by Island Publishing 2025


ISBN - 979-8-9924745-0-3 (Paperback)
ISBN - 979-8-9924745-1-0 (Ebook)

# DEDICATION

*To Yves,*

The wind beneath my wings

*To my girls,*

You give me purpose

# TABLE OF CONTENT

Praises

Acknowledgement

Author's Notes

Part One

Part Two

Part Three

Share Your Thoughts

# PRAISES

"Micki Berthelot Morency does it again. A double whammy of love and adventure in a dangerous country. A young Haitian-American woman in Florida struggles to find her Haitian roots while a mother in Haiti struggles to protect her identity and find her lover. A must read.

—**David C. Edmonds,** multiple award-winning, author of Lily of Peru and 12 other books of fiction and non-fiction.

A heartbreaking yet tender story filled with love, loss, ugly deceit and unwavering hope. Morency brings the lush island of Haiti and its people alive on the page.

—**Linda Rosen,** award-winning author of *The Emerald Necklace*

*I Shall Find You* is the story of families lost and then found, of enduring love, spiced up with the flavors of Haiti. The interwoven stories of Ketly and Adele show us the strength and perseverance of women as they overcome obstacles others have placed in front of them.

—**Pamela Stockwell,** author of *The Tender Silver Stars and A Boundless Place*

The book explores themes of identity, cultural heritage, and the complex relationship between mothers and daughters. It tells the story of two women. One who was adopted and the woman who gave her up for adoption...But did she really? The writing is powerful and evocative. I love the way the author goes back and forth between the past and the present of the two main characters in the book. The book deals with the importance of finding one's roots. This is the second novel I have read by this author, and she did not disappoint.

—**Sandra Gordon,** Librarian

# ACKNOWLEDGEMENTS

Writers write alone. Writers do not publish books alone. I don't. Many angels have helped me with the publication of this book. I want to thank Connie Spencer of Busybee Publication for her patience, her generosity and her kindness. She took my vision for my book cover and made it a reality. Connie is one of my angels.

When I needed early blurbs to include in the book, my writer friends said yes, even though I know how busy we all are with life. A huge MERCI to Linda Rosen, David C. Edmonds, Pamela Stockwell and Sandra Gordon, a local librarian and an island sister. It means so much to me.

For obvious reasons, some of the mothers I interviewed who had given their children up for adoption do not wish to be mentioned by names. But this book would not have been authentic without their poignant stories. I am forever grateful to you for trusting me with your pains, your secrets and more importantly your courage.

We all have cheerleaders, but my sister Marlene Berthelot is my greatest one. She believes I can do anything and always supports me. I have amazing siblings and I'm grateful for all of them.

To the family I have created, I thank Elizabeth, Katherine, Synthia and Savannah for enriching my life and teaching me love and humility.

And finally, to my amazing husband, Yves. Thank you for all that you do to help me always reach for my star. You are my first critic, my biggest fan and my best friend. I owe you so much. I will love you always.

# AUTHOR'S NOTES

The idea for this book came to me while I was on a mission trip on the island of Lagonave in Haiti. There were many children roaming around, but they each belonged to a mother who, despite their apparent poverty, did not want to lose *not* even one of them.

Then I thought, what if she did? What lengths will she go to find her lost child? As a mother, it wasn't hard for me to find out.

I think giving up a child for adoption is the most unselfish and toughest act for a mother. Adoptive parents have big hearts full of love to give to a child. It's a win-win when a child lands in the right family. As mothers, we always want the best for our children.

Parents all over the world want their children to fare better than they do, regardless of how successful they are. It's almost fundamental. I spoke with women who had given their children up for adoption by choice and by force. One thing they all had in common was that they lived their lives wondering what happened to their children. Always hoping that their offspring were happy and living their best lives.

They never forget!

# PART ONE

# CHAPTER ONE

## ADELE

*July 2009 - Florida Present Day*

When you work in trauma, like I do, you leave your own at the door every day. I take a couple of deep breaths as I stir cream into my coffee and sip, the caffeine kickstarting my workday. A flurry of activity at the nursing station ushers the afternoon shift. Soon, the emergency room door opens with a whoosh followed by three paramedics running alongside a gurney with a strapped man covered in blood but still kicking and cussing. I sigh. It's never an average day of work for a trauma nurse, but some come at me faster. I place my mug on the counter and rush to join the team already tending to the patient. Two of the city's finest follow the gurney into the unit, hands resting on their guns. Within minutes, multiple stretchers burst through the door. I throw myself into the synchronized chaos of the unit.

Hours later, my replacement calls to ask me to cover the first part of his shift. My empty house pushes me away, although my body screams for a bed. My husband left this morning on another business trip and did not say goodbye. He hasn't called since.

I take a deep breath to dilute my anger and walk down the hall. I pull a pair of blue surgical gloves from the gaping box on the wall without breaking my stride. When I shove my hands into them, my middle finger pokes a hole through the left one. I toss the ruined glove in the trash receptacle in the corner and reach for another one.

The two police officers stand outside the cubicle where the patient handcuffed to the bed rail, is resting after being sutured to close a laceration on his forehead. One cop is so average his name must be John or Bill, but the other one was indeed *fine*. He and his partner stand where they can see the action but not be splashed by wayward blood or run over by a crash cart. I snort. Officer Fine's tamarind eyes crinkle in a quick smile.

"Oh, *Miss*," Tamarind Eyes says, following me inside, and pointing to his prisoner, "he needs a blanket. Says he's cold."

His accent pulls my eyes to the name embroidered on his shirt. *Vilsaint*. "You're Haitian?"

"Yeah," he says. "How can you tell?" A smile blooms on his wide lips, revealing straight white teeth. "Is it my sexy accent?"

How unoriginal. I roll my eyes and say in Creole, "Most Haitians call nurses *Miss*. I've met lots of them here but not many are cops." I clear my throat. "I'm Haitian, too. Well, Haitian-American." I shrug.

"Yeah! But…you have no accent. Must have come here real young?" His furrowed brow demands an answer.

"I was." I throw the words over my shoulder while checking the IV bag and recording the vital numbers from the monitor. The handcuffs clatter with every movement from the patient. "He's not going anywhere. Do you need to keep these on?" I ask, knowing the answer, but still do every time.

"I'm sorry." He shrugs. "Policy."

I grunt, closing the chart and placing it back in the slot at the foot of the bed.

"When were you in Haiti last?" he asks, rocking back and forth on the balls of his feet, fingers tapping his gun belt. "I go every year. Heading there again in December."

"You are?" I turn so fast I knock a box of tissue and a foam cup off the tray table. I bend down to pick them off the floor.

"Geez! You okay, Miss?" He squats down to help. "Was it something I said?"

I swallow, hoping to hide the anxiety seizing my chest. "Umm...I've never been, but I'm going in December, too."

"Okay." He nods.

"I bought my ticket already." I cross my arms over my chest. "I'm really going this time."

"O-kay." He stretches out the word and chuckles. "I can see your mind's made up, Miss. Why haven't you ever been?"

"Long story." I turn to leave to get the blankets. A code blue yanks me down the hallway toward the trauma bay.

Later that afternoon, two different officers flank the cubicle. I hesitate for a second, trying to hide the disappointment that must show on my face with a fake smile. "Officer Vilsaint asked for these." I extend my arms with the blankets toward the closest one.

"Oh, yeah. He's off duty," the pimply-faced young cop says, reaching for the pile in my hands, while peering into my eyes. "He said Green Eyes...I mean... you would bring the blankets. Thanks."

I back out of the space feeling a sense of loss. I want to talk to Officer Vilsaint about Haiti. For as long as I can remember, I've been told by my adoptive mother that my life would be in danger if I travel there. The stories I've read and heard about Haiti frighten me sometimes. Officer Vilsaint can shed light on the realities of the country he must know well.

My replacement shows up a few minutes after midnight. After signing out, I wait by the door for Dan, the security guard who escorts the female staff to their cars in the employee garage at night.

"Hi Dan." I wave to him. "I swear this is the hottest July ever in Florida and I've been here all my—." I stop walking.

Dressed in a pair of fatigue-shorts and a black sleeveless top, Officer Vilsaint leans against a Ford Bronco. The cone of light from the streetlamp highlights the light brown hue of his skin. A grin hitches the corner of his lips.

"Hey, JR, what's up?" Dan says, shaking Officer Vilsaint's hand.

"Man, we missed you Saturday at the game." He lets go of Dan's hand. "We got crushed."

Dan raises himself on his toes and flicks his wrist with an invisible basketball. "I'll be there next week, my man." He turns toward the parking garage.

"Hey Dan, I'll walk the *Miss* to her car," JR says, still leaning on the truck.

Dan looks at me. "Oh. You two know each other?"

"We met today," I say. "The officer brought a patient in earlier."

"Well, you couldn't be in safer hand. JR's my buddy and a good guy. Goodnight." Dan steps over the curb and disappears through the emergency room doors.

I stand a few feet away from the officer. "What are you doing here?"

He glances at his feet in the flip-flops before looking up. "I love long stories, and I'd love to hear yours, Miss."

"Officer—"

"Name's Jean-Robert. My friends call me JR."

"I'm Adele and I'm very tired. Perhaps you can give me your number. I'd like to ask you a few questions about Haiti before my trip."

"Tell you what, Miss Adele. I'm on my way to Denny's. Care to join me?" He sways from side to side; hands shoved inside his pockets. "That way when you get home you can go straight to bed."

For several seconds, I chew on my bottom lip. "Okay. I didn't eat much today, and I really want to talk, so I'll meet you there." I turn toward the garage. His footsteps slap the pavement behind me. "And only because you're a friend of Dan," I say, raising my voice over the symphony between the crickets and the tree frogs.

Once inside my car with the door locked, I free my hair from the crunchy and run a comb through the tangled curls. I scrub my face and my armpits with a handful of wipes, apply gloss to my lips and spray some Estée Lauder Eau de toilette behind my ears and my exposed skin after changing into a white T-shirt and a pair of jeans and sandals. It's not like it's a date with the man. But in about five months, I'll be making the trip to Haiti, so I need all the additional information I can get to be successful in my search for my biological parents.

At Denny's, I park my car next to JR's truck and walk inside. He's facing the door from a booth against the back wall of the almost empty restaurant. The sounds of utensils hitting plates break the silence. The few patrons whisper in a low hum in the dimness of their tables. I pick up my feet and tread toward JR before sliding onto the bench next to him.

"I almost put out an APB on you." He squints at my face. "Whoa! You look fresh and smell good." He sniffs the air like a search and rescue dog. "You have a shower and wardrobe in your car?" He chortles.

I roll my eyes. The waitress with too much bounce in her steps at this ungodly hour, skips toward us, balancing two pots of coffee in one hand.

"Good morning," I say, pointing to the regular one. My body is screaming for caffeine.

"Good mornin', Sugar," she replies in a deep southern accent as she fills a mug on the table.

We order our breakfast. I pour cream in my coffee mug and reach for the spoon. The small mountain of empty sugar packets in front of JR tells me how he likes his.

"Aha!" He raises his eyebrows. "No real Haitian drinks coffee without sugar. Unless it's with herbs to treat *sezisman*. You know…shock," he says in English.

I suck my teeth and say in Creole, "I know what it means. My mom taught me the language she'd learned from her many trips to Haiti. I'm thankful to have that part of my culture. Besides, I grew up with a Haitian family next door whose daughter is one of my two best friends."

"So, your mom's not Haitian?"

"No. My adoptive mother, Marge, was a missionary nurse who went to Haiti for years. I was a couple weeks old when she found me outside of a clinic in Lasalle." I shift in my seat, my heart beating loud and fast. "You know where that is?"

He nods. "Yeah, it's about an hour and a half by car from Port-au-Prince. I've explored the countryside since I've been going there. It's beautiful." He leans forward. "So why haven't you been back?"

"Well, mom has told me since I was very young and started asking," I blow air out loudly, hoping to expel the fear, and anger I experience whenever I talk about Haiti, "that I can never go back there."

"Why ever not?" JR frowns. "That's *your* home."

"Apparently, some people objected to my birth and had made threats." I raise my shoulders to my ears and keep them there. "That's all I know. Mom never went back after bringing me here."

"Wait a minute." He sits back. "And you just bought a ticket to go without knowing the who, where, and what. Haiti's a beautiful place, but it has an ugly underbelly like every other country."

"Well, a month ago I hired a private investigator to look for my parents. He comes highly recommended. He lives in Miami, but he'll be in Haiti to guide me when I land in December." I bring my shoulders down with a long sigh.

"Oh, you're going by yourself?"

I sip lukewarm coffee and ignore the question.

"You need to take that threat seriously," he finally says. "Who wouldn't want you to be born? Why? Who left you outside of the clinic? What do you know so—?"

"Stop." I hold my right hand up like a traffic guard. Suddenly the trip is not as simple as I'd imagined all these years.

"Safety in numbers," he says all cop-like. "How about some girlfriends going with you or, your boyfriend?" He slurps his coffee, looking at me over the rim.

I ignore his fishing expedition and sip my own now bitter coffee.

"Of course." He breaks into my silence. "I'll be more than happy to help if you want me to, if your PI can't deliver. I'm a detective."

I sigh, too tired to thread words into my feelings. "It's complicated and a long story."

"I love long stories, remember." JR puts his elbows on the table and rests his chin in his palms. "I don't have to go back to work until three this afternoon."

I laugh. "So, when are you leaving in December?"

Before he can answer, the waitress brings our food. The smell of bacon, coffee, apple pie and warm bread fills the air. I dig in.

"I usually spend Christmas with my mom in Haiti." JR bites into a piece of buttered toast. "This year, though, I'm spending New Year through my birthday."

"When's your birthday in January?"

"Oh, for my birthday *zétrenne*?" He laughs.

I shake my head to stifle a smile. "Man, I just met you. Why would I buy you a birthday gift?"

He puts his fork down on the plate. Suddenly, his eyes glow wet. Oh dear. He looks like a sad little boy not getting a toy or something.

He clears his throat and dabs his lips with a napkin. "January 2010 will be the first anniversary of my Papa's death of a heart attack while he was on a trip in Haiti. I wanna be there, you know, for my mother."

"Oh. I'm so sorry." I gulp some water to wash down a mouthful of hash browns. "That's a deep loss."

"Thank you." He pushes his plate away. "I'm grateful for my mom. And I had Papa for so long."

It's as though he knows what I'm thinking. At least he grew up with both parents. "So, how old were you when you came to America?"

"Sixteen. Been here fifteen years already." He wipes his fingers with the crumpled napkin. "After Papa died, my mom stayed in Haiti. My two married sisters live in Philly. So, it falls on me to check…you know…on mom. I welcome it. I love to be home."

I nod. "I fear I'll never have a sense of home wherever I am in the world until I make this trip. Why are some people so afraid of going there, JR?"

"Propaganda!" He waves his hand as if shooing flies. "Yet, there are many flights going to Haiti every day from the US, Europe, and Canada."

"Then, who are the passengers when the state department advises Americans to stay away. Why the warning?"

JR peers at a point over my head. The silence stretches through another coffee refill. Now I'm not sure I want to hear what he has to say. The advisory warns prospective travelers about possible kidnappings, curfews, and political unrest. Is my mother right about the danger I may face if I go there?

He clears his throat. "I don't know how much you've read about Haiti, but it's a proud country inhabited by a proud people. We became the first free black republic from slavery in 1804 by defeating France." He lifts his mug, wrapping his huge hands around it. Our eyes meet and I see the pride he's talking about. He squares his shoulders and leans against the back of the seat. "You can imagine how our freedom made slaveowners all over the Americas nervous. Ever since that time, Adele, there has been a campaign to destabilize and demonize Haiti and Haitians."

I lean forward as if his passion about Haiti will anoint me as well. "So, who are the people on these flights, then?"

"NGOs. Non. Governmental. Organizations." He makes air quotes with his index fingers. "They are non-profit."

"I know what NGO stands for."

JR nods. "Anyway, they run the country." He continues, ticking numbers on his left fingers. "Healthcare, education, agriculture, housing, roads, religion..." He narrows his eyes. "What do you suppose this dependence has done to the people of Haiti?"

What a picture this man I just met is painting for me. I have read a lot about Haiti, but certain things, I imagine, you must experience firsthand. Sometimes books can misrepresent truths. It's about who is telling the story and what message they want the tale to impart.

"But don't some of them do good work, JR? I personally believe in empowering people to do for themselves than giving handouts."

"I don't know." He shrugs. "Some do, I suppose."

Then he talks about growing up in Haiti. How much he hated to leave but had no choice since he had to follow his family. He paints a picture of the verdant countryside, friendly people, and a simpler life. I want him to keep talking, despite my anxiety revving up. We clean our plates and drink too much coffee.

"Wow! You know your country." I smile. "*Our* country."

He meets my smile with a serious look. "Why are you making the trip now despite your mother's warnings?"

How many times have I tried to go to Haiti? Only to have to cancel the trip because of my mother. Not this time. "Well, I'd pledged to meet my bios before I turn thirty. My twenty-ninth birthday's this month."

His eyebrows shoot up. "Oh, the whole month of July? That's a whole lot of birth days."

I shake my head as if he's an unruly child. "I celebrate it on the twenty-second, which is the date my mom found me." I stare into the bottom of my coffee mug as if it contains leaves that tell secrets. "How about you? What's your birth date?"

"January eight. I'm going on December thirtieth to return January eleventh…in case you want to go at the same time, which I think you should seriously consider on account of the threats and all and don't forget I'm a cop."

"Okay, okay." I roll my eyes. "I'll think about it."

He smiles. "What has really stopped you from going there, *Miss Adele*?" His gaze rests upon the circle of lighter skin on my ring finger before moving up to my face. "Your green eyes and double dimples are good clues, obviously they came from one or both of your parents."

"Wow. You're good, *Sherlock*." What a genius, I think, refraining from rolling my eyes again. At the rate this is going, I'm going to be cross-eyed before we finish breakfast. I slip my left hand under the table. I'd forgotten to put my wedding ring back on again. It gets in the way of work. "To be honest, I'm scared," I whisper.

"I'm good at unraveling mysteries. I can help you find your biological parents."

"I have retained the services of an investigator."

"Can't hurt to have more help. With me you'll be really safe, Miss."

These are the words I want to hear from my husband. I want Ben to plan the trip with me and experience the joy, the anxiety, and even the danger of making the journey together. This stranger seems to understand my need to do this. How hard can it be?

"You and I are meant to go to Haiti together," he says. "That's why we met today."

"But…but…" I look for something logical to add. "I…I have to think about all this."

"That may be part of your problem, Miss. You think too much."

"You have no idea," I mutter, even though, apparently, he does.

"Look, in my line of work I value and protect life." He leans over the table, muscles bulging in his neck and shoulders, his eyes dancing in the yellow light from the lamp hanging over the table. "But life is to be lived as if every day can be our last."

This time I roll my eyes and suck my teeth. "You're corny, Detective JR."

He throws his head back and laughs. "Hey, I'm a poet."

"You're a trip," I say, "but you're no poet."

"Okay, so I'll take you on a trip, then."

I stand. "Good night. Gotta get some sleep. It was nice to meet you. I'd like to talk some more about Haiti." Excitement has wiped sleep clean from my tired body. I reach for my wallet.

JR palms the check. "I'll get this. You pay next time." He winks. His white teeth dazzle in the glare of the light.

I nod as if I know there will be a next time. We exchange numbers and I walk toward the door, feeling his eyes on my back like fingers.

"I was going to Haiti anyway," I whisper as if to convince myself. Mom and Ben cannot possibly object now if I have the protection of a police officer and a private investigator. Joy lightens my steps.

Then my cell phone rings in my purse. The joy vanishes. Something you never want to happen when it is your husband's ringtone.

# CHAPTER TWO

# KETLY

*April 1980-Haiti, Twenty-nine years earlier*

Madame Simone raises the fork to her mouth, and I swear there are three grains of rice and one bean on it. At this rate, I'm going to spend the whole night watching her eat while standing on my swollen legs like a sentry. Holding my stomach in for hours hurts my back as if someone's stabbing it with a machete. I shuffle from foot to foot to relieve the cramps while I maintain a grin that threatens to shatter my cheekbones. I swallow twice to moisten my teeth before I open my mouth again in the smile I practice in the mirror every morning.

I look at the clock over the credenza. It's seven twenty-six. I have been standing here for over an hour. I lean slightly forward to relieve the tightness in my lower back and silently hum the songs Mama sang to me when I was a child.

It has been ten months since I left my village. I miss Mama, but my job in Port-au-Prince allows me to support my family. I miss school, but I plan to go back one day. I'm going to be a *Miss*. I close my eyes and rub my stomach. Something flutters. My heart skips. I swallow a lump of joyful fear. Madame Simone's cough brings me back into the dining room with its crystal chandelier splashing slices of light in the middle of the mahogany table.

"Ketly...what are you? A statue?" she says. "I'm not paying you to daydream." She pushes her glass toward me. "I need more ice in my water."

"*Oui Madame.*" I pick up the glass and shuffle toward the kitchen in the back of the house, grateful to move and shake the needle pricks in my legs.

"Hey, Ketly." I turn to look at Madame Simone. "Monsieur Henri will be home soon. Tell the cook to have his meal ready."

I bow. When I return with the ice, Henri's sitting at the other end of the long table. "*Bonsoir* Ketly," he says, his eyes dancing with mischief and promises. "*Comment vas-tu?*"

My face starts to open into a genuine smile until I look in the direction of Madame Simone. Her squinting green eyes remind me of the lizards that crawl on the walls outside as she points her index finger at her son. "Henri, you're late." She tucks a long strand of silky brown hair behind her ears. Her gold pendant earrings catch a ray of light and glitter like sparks. "Go get his dinner, Ketly."

Henri stares into my eyes and I want to dive into his green ones and curl up in a ball. I want to go to sleep in his heart where I can read his thoughts, touch his feelings and drink in the love I know is there. Instead, I stare down at the floor, afraid Madame Simone may read my mind.

"Stay, Ketly," Henri says. I look up. He smiles again, pulling his eyes away from mine and turning to face his mother. My right foot moves slightly forward as if I'm being pulled by the force of his love. "I'm not hungry Maman. I had something to eat with some friends tonight."

"Oh, was your new girlfriend there?" The unmistakable approval in her voice stabs at my heart. This time I look at Henri by moving my eyeballs to the side without facing him.

"Maman, how many times do I have to tell you?" His arms shoot up in the air. "Natasha and I are just friends. And you need to stop telling people we're a couple because we're *not*."

Henri blushes as if his red polo shirt has bled into his skin. His eyelashes flutter down like hand fans. When he looks up, he smiles at me. "Ketly, why don't you go to bed? It looks like Maman's done with dinner. I'm sure you've been on your feet all day."

I stay put knowing Madame Simone must have the last word. "Henri, don't meddle with how I run my household. I need Ketly upstairs to turn down my bed and freshen up the bathroom."

Henri opens his mouth. I shake my head in a fluid movement as I shuffle toward the spiral stairs to prepare her room. She may need me to shoo away a fly off her bare shoulder later or something. I snort, slamming her bedroom door shut after me.

∞∞∞

This morning, I purr as I stretch my arms over my head. The tips of my fingers scrape the bare cement wall behind me. But this room in the squat building that houses the staff at the back of the main house provides refuge from Madame Simone. She demands my time, as though every second of my life belongs to her. I pound the pillow into a ball and place it under my head, my body vibrating with anticipation.

Earlier at breakfast, Henri had rubbed his palms together and tapped his lips with his index fingers twice. Our signal that we will meet later. Now I need more rest on my rare day off. Madame Simone left hours ago to meet with her *haute societé* friends. She'll be gone all day.

The sweet smell of ylang-ylang floats on the tail-end of the early afternoon breeze pushing its way through the open window into my tiny bedroom. From my twin bed, I can see the pregnant clouds gathering in the sky. The rain will soon follow. I wish I could run through it like I used to in my village when I was a little girl. Being away from home, dropping out of school, living on my own in Port-au-Prince, working to support myself and my family, I'm no longer a child.

The cotton fabric of my dress sticks to my skin. I roll off the bed and pull it over my head. Curly pubic hairs peek over the elastic of my red bikini panties. I cup my breasts and weigh them in my hands like the *pamplemousse* I buy at the market to satisfy my cravings for citrus fruits lately. I turn around in front of the full-length mirror on the back of the door. The crack in the middle bisects my body making me look short. My skin glistens like wet charcoal under a sheen of sweat. I gather my thick braids in both hands and secure them on top of my head with two long hair pins. The breeze kisses the back of my neck. Thunder growls outside and raindrops pelt the tin roof almost in a beat. I step over my dress on the floor and crawl back on the bed, close my eyes and listen to the rhythm of the rain before sleep pulls me under.

The sound of the door hitting the wall wakes me up. The rain has stopped. Slivers of sun peek from behind the mountains. I blink several times to bring the person standing on the threshold into focus as I grab for the sheet to cover my nakedness. My hands come up empty. In my sleep, I must have kicked it off the bed.

Madame Simone fills the doorway. "*Oh, Mon Dieu*! Ketly! What…what is this?" she points at my belly. "Are you sick? Do you have a tumor in there or is it what I think it is?"

Fear glues my tongue to the roof of my mouth. I swallow several times while I try to remember the many ways, I've practiced telling Madame about my condition and my plan. My mind's blank now. I reach for the bed sheet on the floor and wrap it around my body. Immediately, I feel less vulnerable, and anger replaces my fear. She has no right to barge into my room without knocking even if it is her property.

"Are you going to answer me? You tramp." She hisses. "Who did this to you?"

# I SHALL FIND YOU

I sit up straighter on the bed. "I'm due in July, Madame...umm...I plan to take the baby to Mama in Lasalle after a couple weeks. I'll be back. I won't be gone long. I promise."

"So, you're what...six months along?" she asks. Her face gathers like she smells something foul. "You're seventeen. You're a child yourself." She shakes her head; brown curls bounce on her head. "Now country girls are just as fast as the city ones. Huh!"

A shadow appears behind her in the doorway. "Who's the father of your bastard, Ketly?" Madame Simone yells.

"What's going on here," Henri asks, forcing his mother to step aside as he walks toward my bed. "You're all right, Kek...Ketly?"

"Oh, Henri." I sob, unable to move from the bed. I pull the sheet all the way to my chin, holding it tight with one hand to stop the shaking, the other hand reaching for him.

Madame Simone's eyes narrow, her mouth opens wide while her hands flutter in front of her face as if she can't catch a breath.

"Oh, no," she screams. Henri stops. "You're not keeping *this* child, you whore! I know a doctor. I'm going to take care of this mess. How dare you?"

I cradle my belly as if to protect my unborn child from such evil words. Tears fall on my clenched fists, dripping down on my belly. I stare at Henri. Sweat coats his forehead while fear dances in his wide green eyes. I feel trapped. I can't breathe. The baby kicks hard. I jump off the bed and grab my dress off the floor as I shove my feet into a pair of leather sandals.

"Maman, I have something to tell you," Henri says in a loud voice, perhaps to make sure I hear him. His fingers glide down the sheet on my back, grabbing a handful of the fabric. I pull and fly by Madame Simone like a ghost and plunge into the cover of the night. Henri can't protect me and our baby from his mother. Not yet.

# CHAPTER THREE

# ADELE

The best time for me to think is while driving and I have a lot to think about. The phone call from Ben earlier at the restaurant to tell me he's not coming home as scheduled still irks me more than usual. Now I wish Ben was home because suddenly I have this need to see him, to share my happiness with him. I'm going to find my biological parents. I can really feel it tonight. The quietness of the streets soothes my nerves.

I pull into a space in the empty public beach parking lot and step out barefoot on the warm asphalt. I roll up the legs of my jeans and walk into the water until it's above my ankles. The moonlight spreads like a crinkly silver blanket over the surface of the water. I kick the waves as I stroll, wishing I could walk to wherever I want to go in the world without barriers. All the coffee I drank at Denny's earlier has chased the sleep out of my body.

Throughout my idyllic childhood filled with toys, trips, birthday parties and love, I've always missed that piece to complete the puzzle of my life. Meeting the people who brought me into the world. Over the years, I've watched documentaries, listened to the news, and read stories, and many books about my birthplace. Haiti is usually portrayed as a place people escape from, not a place an American child has been planning to go to since she understood that it was an important part of her identity.

I turn around and the red and yellow neon lights are miles behind from where I started my walk. I head back, thinking about JR as my ally on this upcoming journey. Minutes later, I pull into the driveway of my childhood home and let myself in with the key Mom insisted I keep, after I left to marry Ben three years ago. I spend time with her whenever my husband is away. I've been seeing a lot of Mom lately. The clock on the wall says it's almost four in the morning. I tiptoe down the hall and peek into her room.

"Addy?" Mom calls out from under the sheet. "You work late today?"

"I'm sorry, Mom. Did I wake you?"

I walk into her room and brush the graying blond hair off her forehead and kiss it. "It's almost morning," she says, her blue eyes twinkling in the beam of the nightlight.

"Well, I need a shower and a bed." I lightly squeeze her papery hand. "We'll talk later. Go back to sleep."

The shower, the two glasses of wine, and the fatigue all fail to douse my excitement and usher in sleep. Nothing can stop me now from going to Haiti. I have a PI and a bodyguard. I smile. My eyes stop on the bookshelf. My collection of books and academic awards fill every inch of the wall surface in the small bedroom where I spent the first twenty-six years of my life. It looks exactly like the way it was when I lived here. Like I never left.

∞∞∞

When Mom started getting sick the summer before my senior year in high school, I decided for the first time to go to a different school than my two best friends. I couldn't leave Mom alone despite her insistence that I went away to college as planned with Ninnie and Lisa.

I ball up the pillow, put it against the headboard, and sit up. Sleep is not on the horizon. I reach for my knitting basket on the floor and smile at the bright green yarn I'm using to make a vest for Beulah. She loves green.

At age ten, Mom took me with her to volunteer at the senior center in town. I didn't know it was impolite to gawk and point at an old lady dressed in green from head to toe. I thought she was a black leprechaun. Beulah became the grandmother I never had. Mom was the only child of parents who were only children who died when she was young. Mom grew up alone.

I can't wait to tell Beulah about meeting JR and how I'm going to change my itinerary to go with him to Haiti. For safety, of course.

"Mm-huh." I grunt. "I guess I'm going with JR," I whisper as if to convince myself.

My hands clutch the needles, but they never move from my lap. I can't concentrate on a single thing. I look up to the ceiling and the whirring sounds of the old fan grate on my nerves. My eyes stop on the painting on the wall. *Coconut Woman.* A pre-wedding gift from my husband. The painting depicts a yellow-skinned woman, her head tied with a red scarf and curly black hair escaping in spirals over her forehead. Her eyes mirror the setting sun in the background.

Suddenly, I want to talk to Ben. I want to tell him about meeting JR and how hopeful I am that I'll find my parents. Ben is an early riser. I reach for my cell phone on the nightstand and dial his number. After five rings, it goes to voicemail.

"Hi Babe, I...I'm sorry I snapped at you when you called me earlier about extending your business trip. I have some news about my plan to go to Haiti I want to share with you. Can't wait to see you, Ben. Well, not just for that. I miss *my* hubby." I meow. "Call me back anytime. Love you."

# I SHALL FIND YOU

I turn to the single window in the bedroom. The disappearing night, and the incoming new day meet like old friends who share the same journey. New friends can also be bound by a singular goal. Like finding my roots. But what if they don't want to be found? I shudder as I swing my legs off my childhood bed and place my feet on the cool tiles. I stand and stretch my coiled muscles. My fingertips almost touch the light globe below the fan.

The idea of going to Haiti with JR lessens my fears. Unlike the PI, he's a police officer. But what can the secret about my birth possibly be? Does Mom know? Why does she never want to talk about it with me?

When my cellphone rings, I grab it before it wakes up my mother. "Hi, Ben. You got my message, Sweetie."

"Hi, Miss Adele."

My hands shake as if I'm touching something forbidden. It's JR.

# *CHAPTER FOUR*

# KETLY

*April 1980*

    I run until the pain in my side pinches like pincers forcing me to slow down. I stop at the bottom of the hill and bend over and throw up. The darkness takes hold of my panic and crushes it under my feet as I run away from danger. I sit on a short wall in front of the cemetery and away from the circle of light of the lamppost. I lost one sandal. The sharp rocks that litter the road shred the bottom of my right foot. I slip the dress back on and wrap the bed sheet tight around my shoulders, not because I'm cold, but by a need to be held.

    A red car drives up toward the hills where people like Simone hide from the poor souls they steal from daily. Shortly after, a second car slows down, and I drop behind the wall and hold my breath. When I can no longer hear the engine gurgling on the ascent, I climb back up. I need to get to Auntie Yvette's house but it's miles away into town. I switch the remaining sandal to my injured foot and take a step. Pebbles burrow into the open skin.

    I moan in pain. "Oh, God, please help me."

I sit back, put my head down over my chest and wail. For the death of my papa, for the loss of my innocence, for my dreams that are leaking out with my tears to be sucked into the ground like the dead people behind me.

I shiver as if fleshless fingers are sprouting from the earth and grabbing for me to join them in their forever beds. I tighten the sheet around me and scoot to the edge of the wall. I'm having a baby in less than three months. Will Henri be there like he promised? Now I wish I'd told Mama about my condition, but Henri thought we'd go after the baby is born and he'll ask her for my hand in marriage when he turns eighteen in December. Am I too naïve to think that a rich boy like Henri will marry me? But I know he loves me. I blow my nose on the sheet and swipe at the tears running down my face.

A string of hysterical giggles bursts into the air around me breaking the silence. I turn around to see if zombies are lurking around only to realize that the sound is coming from my open mouth. I clamp both hands over it until I see the headlights with the heart-shape design.

I stand, putting my weight on my good foot and wave. The white Mercedes with tinted windows rolls on the shoulder and before it fully stops, I hop to the passenger side, open the door, and slide in. "Oh Henri—"

Alphonse shakes his head and blinks. "I'm sorry it's only me."

"Where's Henri? Why are you driving his car?" I yell.

"*Monsieur* Henri sends me looking for you. He couldn't leave his mother," Alphonse says, staring into the darkness through the windshield. "When you drive someone like Simone every day, you see and hear things, Ketly. She won't give up. Why didn't Henri tell his mother before? I offered to help you because I knew this would end badly. You don't know these folks."

"Alph," I say, placing my hand on his forearm to stop him, "I will never understand why you'd want to raise another man's child?"

"Because I love you Ketly, the way Henri never will."

I squeeze his arm before folding my hands in my lap. "Alphonse, Henri loves me. No one will convince me otherwise. *No one.*"

"Kekette, let me take you to my mother's house. She knows how I feel about you."

I shake my head. I don't have the answer Alphonse wants.

"You have any plan?" he asks. "Simone threw all your stuff in the trash after you left and started beating on that boy. In almost five years I've been driving her; I never see her hit Henri once. She threatens to kill herself if he leaves her tonight and you know Henri's a good boy. He sneaks out to give me his car keys and this envelope for you after calming his mother down, with God knows what promise." He pulls his lips inside as if to stop more words from spilling out.

"What did Henri say, Alph?" I ask, ripping open the yellow envelope. I reach inside and pull out a wad of money. Alphonse's eyes open like a yawn. I throw the money on the car floor, shove my hand back into the envelope, it comes out empty. I put the money back inside. "Tell Henri, I don't need his money." I throw the envelope on the back seat. "I need *him.*"

Alphonse turns his wiry body toward me. "If you won't let me help you, Ketly, you'll need that money for yourself and the baby." He exhales. "You girls from the countryside have no idea what life's like in the city. Maybe *Monsieur* Henri wanted to get into your cotton panties, and you think it's love." He hits the steering wheel with his fist several times.

I move closer to the passenger door, away from his scary words. He steps out of the car and walks over to my side and opens the door. I fall into his arms and sob. We stand in the darkness, my belly between us. Alphonse runs his palm up and down my back until I hiccup as if the well of my tears has run dry.

"I'm sorry, Kekette. I shouldn't have said that. I will help you no matter what. Just tell me what I can do."

I step back from him and reach for the door handle behind me. Inside the car, we say nothing. I look straight ahead into the darkness as if I can see my future in the twinkling stars.

"Where am I taking you?" He starts the car.

I tell him.

We leave the quiet hillside, driving on the curvy two-lane road flanked by oleander, hibiscus, and bougainvillea hedges in front of high walls that hide mansions from prying eyes. A dog barks with indifference behind a gate only to clear its throat, unconcerned about trespassers. I close my eyes and try to form coherent, decisive ideas to no avail. I inhale Henri's Bleu de Chanel cologne from the leather seat.

The smell unleashes a torrent of feelings that gushes with pain and pleasure. I look in the back seat and blush as if Alphonse can see or hear our cries of passion etched into the soft beige leather. I bite my bottom lip and press my legs tight together to quelch the avalanche of emotions threatening to drown me.

Sometime later, my head hits the headrest, and I open my eyes. "Sorry," Alphonse says. "I had to brake fast. Some people are still looking for the day's meal so late into the night."

Kerosene flames from the lamps flicker under the peaked roof of the public market. Sleepers crowd the alleys between the stalls on straw mats, burlap sacks and cardboard spread on the dirt-packed ground. After we pass the market, the streets become quiet. Alphonse slows down in front of a row of businesses where Simone's biggest department store occupies several blocks. I peer at it through the window and sigh.

When I left work yesterday after carrying Simone's purse, her briefcase, her lunch bag, her glass of wine, and her hat to the car, I'd made my way to the bus station. Now I'm surprised, she didn't ask me to carry her fat behind downstairs as well. I look at the building long after Alphonse has driven past it, knowing I will never set foot inside again.

As we get closer to Aunt Yvette's house, the smell of fried food, standing water and dog feces forces its way through the closed windows of the car. Like a pair of nosy hands, the headlights reveal holes in mud walls, peeling paint on wooden windows, rainwater oozing out of muddy footprints. A rooster flies in front of the windshield and crows in protest. I scream.

The car stops in front of a small cement block house in the narrow alleyway. Two cane-backed chairs face each other on the small porch as though in conversation. The house is dark. Alphonse squeezes out of the driver's door and walks to my side with the envelope in his hand. I shake my head. He helps me hobble over the two front steps. I rap my knuckles on the door several times before I hear footsteps getting closer.

"*Sé ki moun?*" Aunt Yvette asks.

An errant sob pops into my throat. Suddenly, I feel beaten like the weight of my despair is pushing me into the ground. "It's me, Auntie. Ketly."

The door flies open, and I stagger inside, followed by Alphonse. Slivers of moonlight squeeze between the single window and its jagged frame. Auntie grabs my arm and deposits me in one of the four mismatched chairs around the square table. She strikes a match and removes the glass shade from the lamp and lights the blackened wick swimming in the kerosene.

"You're safe…for now." Alphonse squeezes my shoulder. "Good luck, Kekette."

"Tell Henri I'm here."

Alphonse nods. He places the envelope on a chair in the corner and closes the door behind him.

Auntie sits facing me, every line on her face, a road on her life journey. "I'm sorry to barge in on you like that, but I have no place to go." I sniffle and stare into her old wise eyes. "At least Simone knows the truth now." I tap my belly. "No more secrets. I can go on with my life."

Auntie tut-tuts between the gap left by several missing front teeth. "I was expecting you sooner. I've worked for Simone's family before she was born. She's only begun with you. I warned you." She shakes her head. "Simone always gets what she wants."

"Well, I'll kill that baby and myself before I let her get her hands on my child." I stand on my bleeding foot and let the pain fuel my anger.

"You may have to do that, child, but don't you see, either way you gon' live with everlasting pain."

I sit back in the chair, tired but not defeated. "Simone can't take my child from me. Henri and I will fight her."

Her head moves from side to side, a lone tear cascading down before disappearing into the folds of her skin. "Bébé, you can't stay. Simone already knows you're here, and I don't want any trouble with that woman and her goon. I'm sorry, Kekette. When I told your mother, I'd help you get a job in the city, I warned you to be careful."

How is one careful with falling in love? Something snaps inside me like a twig. I grab my belly and rock back and forth in the chair. Where's Henri? I need Henri. I can't possibly do this alone. I push the chair behind me and stand, staring at the front door. For flight or fight, I'm no longer sure.

# CHAPTER FIVE

## ADELE

I fumble the phone before catching it again. My hands shake. I will have a hangover later. I should have stopped with the second glass of wine after my shower. I glare at the intrusive instrument. "Can't you tell time? It's too early."

"I wanted to make sure you made it home safely last night, or well, this morning," JR says. I sit on the bed and brush my messy hair with my fingers as if he can see me. "Hey, who's Ben?"

"Umm…you know what time it is, JR?"

"You already told me it's too early. So, who's Ben?"

"Ben's my husband," I say with a touch of satisfaction because I resent the way my heart suddenly races, and my forehead feels damp with sweat.

"Oh! Hope I didn't wake your children. You have some of those, too?"

"Why the inquisition. I don't owe you any explanation."

"True. And it wasn't an inquiry. Go back to hubby. *Bonne journée*."

"Umm...I'm actually over my mom's. Ben's on a business trip. I usually hang out with her every chance I can. She's diabetic, hypertensive..." I stop.

Why am I telling the man all this? We share a birthplace. I want to know more about it. That's all. Yet, I talk about my mom and how I never had a dad, and I miss that very much. My two best friends, Lisa and Ninnie shared theirs with me at father-daughter dances when we were in grade school. Mom gave me everything. She did double duty as mom and dad but in the end she fell short. I wanted to be a daddy's girl.

When I take a breath, JR asks, "Is hubby going with us to Haiti?"

With us. As if he knew I'd decided to go when he goes. "Yes, but..." I take a deep breath. "I haven't told him that I've bought...umm...my ticket yet. It's' a touchy subject."

"Christmas, New Year and Mardi Gras are the times Haitians travel to Haiti the most. At least by next month he'll need to get his ticket if you want him to go with you."

"I always wanted him to go, but...anyway, we'll see. Maybe he'll surprise me by going as a special present for my birthday."

"*Maybe?*" he says.

"So, are you having a party in Haiti for your birthday? January eighth, right?"

"Maybe. I believe life should be celebrated every day, remember. I live as if every day was my birthday. Maybe it's my line of work as a cop."

"So, you're a deep thinker." I tease. "A philosopher?"

"As a matter of fact, I try not to think too much. Second reason for my call, there's a Haitian band playing in Tampa this Saturday, you wanna go...umm...listen to some music?"

"Oh, my husband will be back from his trip. Besides, I...I don't think it's a good idea."

"See, first you think too much. Second you want to go but worry about what people will think. That's not living, Adele. Since when is it a crime to listen to music? Bring your hubby if he's back in town and your girlfriends, Lisa and Ninnie. The more the merrier. I really would love to meet them."

Over an hour later, I end the call. I open the vertical blind at the window to read. It's too early to wake up Mom. She needs her rest. My eyes land on the painting again. I wonder why I never moved it to Ben's house after our wedding. *Ben's house.* Never felt like mine. He'd built it before we met. Ben is a man used to getting what he wants.

∞∞∞

Three years ago, Ben's relentless pursuit broke down my emotional barriers with daily phone calls and surprise lunches at my work. The night after our first dinner date, he'd kissed my cheek on this very doorstep.

"I'm going to marry you, soon, Adele," he said, before skipping to his car.

His quiet love had ironed out the kinks in my self-esteem after being dumped by my college sweetheart Andrew, for another woman. I loved the way Ben had to have me. Our romance bloomed over the months and Ben promised to be my ally in my plan to go to Haiti. But he never intended to. Instead, he'd been hiding behind the state department advisory and my mom's anxiety.

The sun peeks through the blind like a snooping neighbor. I make my way to the kitchen for some coffee. The thumping behind my left eyeball demands Haitian caffeine. Before sitting down in the breakfast nook with a steaming cup of Café Rebo, I take the basket from the counter with the envelopes and the checkbook. The red past-due stamp on the water bill catches my attention. It appears Mom started to write the checks and stopped and went to bed. I need to take over this duty as well. I sigh.

She is the best mother a child could want. But at an early age I knew that I needed to be a great daughter because Mom chose me. I have seen pictures of dying children in Third World countries and I'm grateful to her for saving me because obviously my biological parents couldn't care for me.

I write two checks, one for the water bill and the other for her Visa card and stuff them inside the envelopes. The checkbook's empty and I still have one more bill to pay. I walk into the spare bedroom we use as storage to get more checks. I pull the handle on the top drawer of the file cabinet where she keeps her financial records. It's locked. I frown. Why is that drawer locked now? What can she possibly keep in there? I stop midway between the spare room and the kitchen. Last month, I saw a letter from her bank about closing their safe deposit service.

"Oh my God," I whisper.

She must have closed her box. I walk back and stare at the black cabinet as if it holds the secrets to my life. Mom and I had openly talked about her finances and last wishes years ago. She even showed me where she kept cancelled checks and statements in that top drawer. Could there be documents from the safe deposit box about my adoption or my parents in the cabinet now? Is that why she locks it? I must get in there without her knowing. If I don't find anything, then she won't have to know.

The key is probably in her bedroom, and I need to wait until Sunday when she goes to church to find it. I join my hands in prayer. God, please give me the patience. I know I've been slacking off with going to church, but you see I give Mom my tithe envelope every Sunday. Please forgive me, but I'll do just about anything to find my biological parents before my next birthday.

# CHAPTER SIX

## KETLY

*April 1980*

Auntie pushes me back in the chair and pulls her pouch of leaves and balm from the wooden shelf behind me. She lifts my injured foot onto her lap and brings the lamp closer. She pokes with her finger. I groan. She rests my foot on her chair and walks to the back of the house. I must have dozed off. Now she carries an aluminum basin. The smell of burnt charcoal follows her into the room. She places a cup in front of me.

"You need a good night's sleep, child. Drink this tea. Tomorrow's a new day."

"Thank you, Auntie," I whisper. "Henri will come for me tomorrow."

I sip the hot brew. The leaves and the fruit of the Soursop tree are believed to possess sleep-inducing components, but it's the sugar that hits my bloodstream like soft hands rubbing my tummy from the inside.

The warm water soothes my injured foot. She cleans the wound gently with some boiled leaves. After drying it, she rubs a minty smelling compound on it and reaches into her pocket and pulls out strips of fabric to wrap my foot. When I finish my tea, Auntie leads me to the back room with the double bed. I climb on and make myself small by hugging the wall with my belly. Later, when she settles down next to me, the mattress sinks, and I feel myself rise slightly and roll toward her. I grab the pillow like an anchor, close my eyes and remember the first time I saw Henri.

∞∞∞

I had stepped off the bus that carried me from Lasalle to Port-Au-Prince and stared at the people, and cars in the middle of the wide street moving fast as if they were in a race with each other. Excitement made me dizzy as I waved the blue headscarf that would identify me to my contact person. The medium height man in tight navy pants and a white short-sleeve shirt, standing by a big black car motioned me to cross the street. The car air conditioner sucked the heat from my body and replaced it with goose bumps on my dusty skin.

"*Bonswa m'sieur*," I said to the driver, as I climbed in and settled in the passenger seat. "I'm Ketly. Folks call me Kekette."

"I'm Alphonse," he said, squinting at me.

I smiled and looked down at my lap. "My papa fell off his donkey in the field, hitting his head on a rock and died three months ago. As the oldest, I had to leave school to help my family. I'm grateful for the job. Is Madame Simone nice?"

"Hmm!" His eyes bore into mine. "Girl, you can't use nice and Simone in the same sentence."

I rubbed my arms to warm them up, wishing Mama had come with me. There wasn't enough money for two bus fares. At the main house, my gaze followed the footsteps coming down the spiral staircase. A plump woman with skin so white, it looked like she'd turned it inside out, stopped halfway down and stared at us. Her green eyes shone like pieces of glass in the sun. Behind her stood a young man about my age with the same eyes except he was taller and thinner. The woman glared at Alphonse.

∞∞∞

"Kekette, *Ketly*?" Auntie's voice intrudes into my happy reverie. "Wake up. You cryin' baby," she says before leaving the bedroom.

I open my eyes and look around me. The sun's on the wrong side of the room. My baby kicks as if to remind me where I am and what I'm facing this Sunday morning. If ever there was a day, I needed Jesus, it's today, but I have no clothes for church. At least I won't miss Henri since I don't know what time he'll come today. I know he will.

Pots and pans bang outside in a chorus and the sounds mingled with the smell of coffee and salted fish fuel my hunger. I try my weight on my bandaged foot and the pain is dull and bearable. On a low chair in the corner, are a pair of white cotton panties, the size of summer shorts, an open front housedress, a toothbrush with a dot of toothpaste and a piece of homemade soap.

I gather everything and make my way to the washroom that shares a wall with the outhouse. I wash the grimes off my skin and my hair before settling into one of the cane chairs on the porch after breakfast to wait for Henri. We'll go for a ride and walk on the beach and revisit our plan and make love. My body tingles.

The minutes roll into hours and by late afternoon, I've only left the chair to relieve my bladder. I smell the coconut oil from the food before feeling her presence behind me. My stomach growls in hunger but my heart fills my chest with pain. I swipe the tears off my cheeks but not before Auntie comes to stand in front of me with a tray.

She bobs her head so hard; her scarf slides down to cover her eyes. "That boy ain't coming today…or maybe never," she says, pushing it back. "You need to eat somethin'. You can starve yourself but you gotta feed that baby in there."

I push the tray away, suddenly feeling nauseous. "Henri won't abandon me. You don't know him like I do. He'll come."

"You're a fool, if you think Simone's gonna let him be with you. Go back to your village and have your baby in peace."

I stump my feet on the dirt floor. "Henri loves me. He'll marry me. You'll see," I say it loudly as if I need the words to take roots in the hole in my heart and fill it with hope of a happy future.

"Mm-huh," Auntie snorts. "I pray Simone will let you be, cause if I know that woman, she won't want Henri's child loose out there to spoil her family lineage with black skin and kinky hair. People like her value skin tone and hair texture as much as they worship money."

"Now you're telling me all this about Simone and Henri, Auntie."

"Well, didn't I tell you to stay away from city boys? You're a beautiful and smart girl, but I never thought Henri would fancy being with you."

I open my mouth and close it. The words I want to speak are for my own comfort. I can keep them inside because deep down I fear Auntie may be right. I swallow the sobs when she pats my head and walks back inside the house with the untouched food. As darkness paints the blue out of the sky, I rock my body so fast to keep the mosquitoes from feasting on my blood, but the movement also keeps the scary thoughts from invading my brain.

The next day, the roosters wake me from a fitful sleep. After washing up, I camp on the porch again and wait. Monday morning brings students spilling out of doorways into the alley on their way to school. Their colorful uniforms give the scene a carnival atmosphere. Girls walk in small groups, the boys bringing up the rear as they bump into each other to get closer, their eyes never rising above the girls' waist. I smile, remembering going to school in my village and the boy who gave me my first crush like it was a contagious disease. In only a few months in the city, I can no longer remember his name, for Henri occupies every nook of my heart and mind. I know he will come today. What am I supposed to do on my own with a baby?

My eyes scan the entrance into the alley as if I can divine his car to appear. Soon the sun pierces through the morning haze and pushes its way onto the porch. I close my eyes and raise my face to the blaze as an offering, relishing its warmth on my skin. Floaters move around in the bright red pool under my eyelids, until my bladder demands my attention. On my way back from the outhouse, I stop when I hear Auntie's raised voice. A warning.

"I told you, Ketly ain't here," she says. "Haven't seen her in weeks. Why, she's gone missin'?"

A deep voice mumbles. I peer around the curtain in the window and gasp before clamping both hands over my mouth. Shadow towers over Auntie, gesturing his long arms and whispering. In all the months I work for Madame Simone with the man hovering around her like her shadow, I've never seen the eyes behind his dark glasses or heard his voice. I whimper in fear. Shadow as everyone calls him, then turns and leaves but not before a twitch raises one corner of his fleshy lips.

Auntie steps outside. "I told you Simone knew you were here." She wrings her gnarled fingers. "We're going to the bus depot, now. Go back to your mama. I pray you'll be safe there."

"But... I'll go wait for Henri at the entrance to the alley. Maybe he got lost yesterday."

"Come." Auntie pulls me into the back room. She reaches for an old headscarf under her pillow and grabs her pair of dark glasses on the dresser. "This man could be waiting out there. I don't think he believes me. Please be careful." She ties my head like hers and I slip the glasses on. "And if that boy don't show, you come back, you hear. I'll go with you to the station." She places a bowl of stew on the table and closes the doors and windows. "Eat."

I eat fast, scraping the bottom of the bowl with the spoon before wiping it clean with the last piece of bread. I kiss her wet cheeks. "Thank you, Auntie, for everything. I love you."

I buckle the sandals she gave me that are too big for my feet and head out, going through alleyways until I arrive at the only place a car can enter the corridor. I have no idea how long I sit on the ground with my back against the trunk of an oak tree fighting sleep and the heat. Sweat runs down my face and I let it flow, too scared to move. I watch for Shadow until my eyes dry up from not blinking enough. Alphonse starts to walk past me into the alley.

"Alphonse," I whisper.

He stops and peers at me. "Kekette? What are you doing out here in this heat?"

"Did Henri send you?" I ask.

"No. I wanted to make sure you were okay. I heard Simone tell Shadow to come here. Yesterday he went to the homes of all the girls you ever talked to at work. She'll send him here soon."

"Oh, he's been here. I hope Auntie convinced him I was never with her. Sometimes the best place to hide is in plain sight. I'm waiting for Henri."

"Please go to Lasalle, if he doesn't come. I'm…worried about you." With his head down, he walks away from me.

People mill around the street vendors looking for bargains. I see Shadow in every face, but the thought of going back home in my condition clinches my stomach with shame. I've been sending money to help feed my brothers and keep them in school. Now I sit on the street like a beggar with nothing but my unborn child and the love in my heart.

The familiar honk of the car parts the mob and pulls me to my feet. I limp to it and bang on the window as it begins its entry into the alley. Henri stops the car and jumps out, taking me into his arms. "Oh, Mon amour, I'm so sorry." He kisses my dusty face as he opens the passenger door and helps me inside, locking it.

I settle into the soft leather and let the frigid air dry my skin. Henri reaches for my hand while driving, stealing glances at me.

"Where have you been, Henri?" I pull my hand away. "I've been waiting since yesterday." I swallow the angry words.

"Oh, Kekette, I feel so bad, but I had to wait for a safe time to leave. Maman has been impossible." He reaches for my hand again and kisses my palm. "I don't ever want you out of my sight."

"I need you Henri." I rub my belly. "*We* need you." I look at the back seat with the food containers. "The food smells good." I lick my lips, suddenly ravenous. The pile of books grabs my attention. I can't wait to dive into them. Reading always brings me peace and joy. "I'm famished."

"I have enough for an army of three." Henri smiles and pats my belly. "Didn't want us to stop at a restaurant, you know…in case." He shrugs.

"Shadow…he was here," I say, looking through the back window. "Please…please make sure we're not followed." Fear paints my words.

Henri squeezes my hand but not before I catch him looking at the rearview mirror. "Maman can't possibly know where I'm going, sweetheart. You'll be safe."

We drive in silence leaving the city behind heading south. In Carrefour, we stop at a shopping plaza. I pick out clothes, two pairs of sandals, underwear, toiletries, and a big bottle of Bien-être eau de toilette. Henri comes from the back of the store carrying a light pink satin blanket and adds it to the pile.

"For my daughter," he says.

I punch his arm. "Oh silly!" I giggle. "What if it's a boy?"

"It's a girl. We'll name her Juliette."

"*Juliette*," I murmur. "I love it."

The cashier looks back and forth between me and Henri and frowns as if she can't unravel a riddle. Henri throws his arm around my shoulders, leans over, and kisses my lips. We smile. We eat some food at the park behind the plaza before getting back on the road. I doze off until Henri pulls in front of a hotel on the beach.

"Where are we?" I ask, looking for Shadow before stepping out of the car and shading my eyes with my hand to take in the multi-story hotel.

Henri takes my hand and whispers, "I'll explain when we get upstairs."

Inside our suite, I open the door to the balcony overlooking the white sand beach. Henri locks the suite door and takes me in his arms. We stand like that for a long time, the breeze trying but failing to force its way between us. He swallows my trepidation with his kisses. When he lets go of my lips, I say, "I need a very long shower."

I pull him into the bathroom and close the door, sealing us from the cruel world, intent on keeping us apart. I start taking off my clothes. "Join me?" I purr, sticking my tongue out at him. He steps out of his clothes so fast he is in the stall before I finish unbraiding my hair.

The water sprays pound against my body and light a fire under my skin. Henri pours shampoo over my hair and with both hands, massages my scalp until I have to lean against his chest to remain upright. After rinsing my hair and my body, he kneels on the tile floor and brushes my stomach with his lips kissing from my belly button to between my legs. I grab his shoulders for support and try to slow my breath. Our baby kicks and I feel pressure before the explosion releases the tension. I pull Henri up and kiss him with a demand for more.

On the bed, he spoons my body, and I lift my top leg and rest it over his. He enters me, and we rock back and forth in a dance where the music comes from our beating hearts. My world is complete. Henri is with me. Henri is within me. My orgasm brings forth feelings of a bright future, but when Henri comes, he grabs my hair, and in his cry, I hear fear. I know the sound well as it lives within me. I turn and face him, kissing his trembling lips.

"What's wrong, Mon amour?" I ask. "I've never been happier than this very moment. We're together. *Je t'aime*."

"Oh, Kekette, I'll love you forever. No matter what happens," he cups my face and squeezes it so hard I have to look into those green eyes, "don't you *ever* forget that I love you."

I kiss his cheeks, his chin, his forehead, his eyelids. "I will *never* forget," I whisper.

"This place belongs to my friend's family. I trust him. You'll stay here until you have the baby. I've made arrangements this morning with the doctor. He knows where you are. Don't worry about anything. You know the plan."

"Yes. Tell me again." He kisses my forehead instead, making his way down the length of my body.

When I wake up from a long nap, the sun has dipped below the horizon casting the room in a golden glow. Henri brushes the hair from my face and says, "Here's the plan again. Listen carefully. When I turn eighteen in December, I will inherit a considerable sum of money left to me by my paternal grandmother. I'm marrying you and will build you a big house that we'll fill with babies. Maman will no longer control me." He sits up. "But now I have to go back before she suspects anything."

I snatch his fingers as though they're a lifeline. "Henri, please don't leave me here alone." I place our palms over my stomach. "What if something happens."

He pecks my lips. "Shh! There's a phone next to the bed. Call downstairs and ask for Gaétan. Everything's arranged. I'll come every day after practice. I'd rather spend the days with you, but I can't break my routine. They'll call Maman. Remember in about five months, we'll be free. Besides, you have tons of books." He grins. "Pace yourself."

We laugh.

The following afternoon as dusk approaches, I throw the book I've been reading all day on the bed and pace the room. Henri should have been here hours ago. The sound of the phone breaks the tomblike silence of the hotel suite.

"Mademoiselle," the receptionist says, "Alphonse's here to see you. Should I send him up?"

I drop the phone and take the stairs two at a time holding my belly with both hands. I stop when I see Alphonse in the lobby. Terror grips my insides.

"Where's Henri?"

"Kekette, let's sit down."

"No! Tell me, Alph."

He takes my arm and drags me to a sofa in the corner of the lobby. "They set Auntie Yvette's house on fire," he whispers. "She…she didn't make it out on time."

I holler. The shaking starts at my head and travels through me until I open my mouth again and let out the weight of the pain in broken sobs. "No, no, no," I yell. "Who…why…" I grab Alphonse's shirt. A button pops off and skitters on the tile floor. "Oh, Alph, why, why would anyone hurt Auntie. She didn't do anything wrong. It's my fault. I killed her. *O Bondié*, she warned me. I didn't listen." I let go of his shirt, pushing him. "Alph, please stay away from me. Go, go, go. I don't want to lose you, too." The pain slices through me like pieces of glass.

A man in a three-piece suit comes over. "Mademoiselle, please let me take you to a side room for privacy." Suddenly, I notice the silence and the eyes staring at us. "May we get you some water?"

The man closes the door after us, and I drop my body into a wing chair in the small room. Alphonse stays on his feet.

"Kekette, Madame Simone tricks Henri this afternoon and ships him to France with the clothes on his back. Well, they have houses everywhere. Henri thought he was seeing his mother off at the airport because she told him she had some medical issues and would be gone for a while except he was the one being sent off. He said to tell you he loves you and to remember the *plan*." Alphonse shrugs. "I told you; Simone won't give up."

I double over in the chair, waiting for nausea to pass. A picture of Auntie imprints itself behind my eyes. Auntie and Mama have been friends since they were kids in our village. Auntie was family. Why did Simone kill her? How do I protect myself and my child from such wickedness?

"What do I do now, Alphonse?"

"Let me take you to the bus depot. Go to Lasalle. Shadow will find you wherever you are in this city. And don't stay in Lasalle too long, either. Your family won't be safe. Go to that island you told me your papa was from. Simone wants to get rid of your child—Henri's child, one way or another."

"But…why? I won't ask her for anything. I won't tell anyone. I'll let Henri decide what he wants to do once he inherits—" I stop when I see the incredulity on Alphonse's face.

"I know you're very young, my dear but look around you." His arm sweeps over the splendor of the resort with its manicured lawn and gardens. He takes my hands and squeezes, staring into my eyes. "People like Simone want nothing to upset the balance of their social plan. She already has someone from her circle for her son. She wants nothing to smear his image of a socialite boy. She might not be able to find him a good match, if he has a bastard tar baby running around town calling him Papa. Don't you understand?"

I pull my hands away. "Let's go, Alph."

The truth is too ugly. We collect my belongings from the room upstairs, and I follow Alphonse to the car. I pinch the skin on the back of my hand hard to make sure I'm still alive. I feel nothing. It's as though even the baby has deserted me. I'm empty. I close my eyes to this very evil world, and I hum, and hum the beautiful hymns of my childhood.

They bring me no solace. I don't know yet how to protect my unborn child.

# CHAPTER SEVEN

## ADELE

I jerk my hand away from the hot steering wheel. I forgot to place the visor on the dashboard when I parked in mom's driveway last night after my walk on the beach. Meeting JR yesterday at work seems like an answer to my prayers for help to find my birth parents. I crank the air conditioning to the highest notch, hoping my make-up will dry the way I've applied it before leaving the house. I steer the car toward downtown.

I'm still not sure if I'm going to the club with JR tomorrow night, so why's my heart skipping beats every time I think about it. He's a police officer, so it can't be any safer. Anyway, it's all part of my research into my culture. I already planned several outfits in my head this morning and discarded them. What does one wear to a Haitian live band event? Ninnie will know. Besides, I need my friends to go with me to keep things light.

As if I don't have enough thoughts bouncing in my head, a migraine creeps behind my left eye and is now knocking on my temples. My husband travels a lot. I'm going to Haiti with a cop. Mom has a locked file cabinet in the house. I close my eyes at a red light, trying to rein in my thoughts, a honk behind me pushes my right foot hard on the gas pedal. My head pounds. What a jerk.

The two musketeers and I missed our monthly get-together last month because they were out of town at separate times. No way we'd miss July. I hand my keys to the valet and walk into the cool bistro on Beach Drive. Dusk dusts the skyline with grey and pink streaks.

"You're late," Ninnie says, looking at her phone resting next to her bread plate.

"Well, some of us actually work on the clock and need sleep," I say, planting kisses on their foreheads.

"That's exactly what I said to her, Addy," Lisa says. "Ninnie makes her own schedule at that agency where she works."

Ninnie sucks her teeth the way her mother Nadine does when making a point. "Oh, Liss, please! And this from the woman who's in her PJ's till late afternoon."

"Oh yeah! I have two small kids, Ninnie. You have no idea."

"Okay, ladies," I say like the mother of rambunctious children. I wave the waiter over. "Please bring me some coffee." I massage my temples. "Oh, and I'll also have a long island iced tea."

"Uh-oh! Mixed drink!" Ninnie laughs, taking a long pull from her Heineken bottle. "What's the *pro-blame*?" she says in Haitian Creole.

"Why can't you drink from a glass?" I ask, annoyed beyond reason. "Like any civilized woman."

"Why you always ask the same goddamn question?" Ninnie retorts. "What? Ben's still not scoring a touchdown after three or so years?" She hitches her eyebrows almost to her hairline. She looks comical. I swallow the giggle bubbling in my chest. That sister.

"Oh, Ninnie!" Lisa says, blushing beet red under her curtain of strawberry blond hair.

"What? What did I say?" Ninnie swivels her neck as she rolls her brown eyes. The silver beads at the ends of her long braids jingle.

The waiter brings my drink and sloshes it onto the tablecloth as he stares into my eyes, then he turns to the others and squints. "Sorry! You ladies have rainbow eyes," he says, pointing at Lisa, "hers are blueberry blue," then at Ninnie, "Werther's brown and you, umm…sorry for spilling your drink, but you have the brightest green eyes I've ever seen on a…umm—"

"Black person?" Ninnie says, flattening her lips and scrunching her face. The kind of expression I recognize from when we were toddlers. "How many Black people do you know up close and personal?"

The waiter wipes the table, pushing a strand of sun-bleached blond hair from his red face and skips away.

"Ninnie," I scold. "Must you make a scene everywhere?"

"Same wild girl since kindergarten," Lisa adds, shaking her head. "Remember, Addy?"

I nod. Nothing's changed. I smile as I remember.

∞∞∞

I grew up in a three-bedroom house nestled between Lisa and Ninnie's. I thought we were sisters who lived with different mothers in almost identical houses. At age four, I didn't know my mom was a single white woman, Ninnie's parents were Haitian immigrants, and Lisa's were Irish Catholic and divorced. We spent most of our time at Ninnie's because her house had a pool, and her mom Nadine was a great cook. The second week of Pre-K, a boy stared at the three of us playing in the sand box. "She's white. She's black." He pointed at my friends. "What are you?" he asked me.

"I'm white like my mommy," I said.

# I SHALL FIND YOU 47

He laughed. "You're a freak with yellow skin and M&M green eyes."

Before I could react, Ninnie jumped on him and pummeled him with her red plastic shovel as Lisa tried to pull her off the boy.

"Addy's not a freak," Ninnie screamed. "Take it back."

When I got home from school, I asked mommy whether I was black or white. She'd pulled me into her ample bosom and said, "Addy, God loves all his children regardless of skin color."

"But…but why don't I have a color like Ninnie or Liss?"

"Because you have your own special color, sweetheart."

"Who gave me the color, Mommy?"

"One day I'll tell you, Addy."

Now, twenty-five years later, I'm still waiting for Mom to tell me. "Please come back in five," I say to the waiter, standing on the side with his pen poised over the pad. "Thank you."

I focus my attention on Ninnie. "About that touchdown, Boy tries hard, pun intended," I giggle. "I need to let go of my fear about opening myself like that again to somebody after Andrew. Everything'll be fine."

"I hope so," Ninnie says. "Girl, I wouldn't marry a man who can't pop my cap. Unh-unh! Nooo!"

"I didn't marry Ben for sex. At least that's not the only reason. Am I right, Liss?"

"Absolutely," Lisa says. "A marriage contains many other components. Sex is just one of them."

Ninnie lets out a screech. Heads turn. I glare at her. "Mm-hm!" Ninnie clears her throat. "Well, I'm sorry for my unlady-like behavior." She winks at us. "But for me sex is a big and I mean *B.I.G* part of all my relationships." Lisa and I roll our eyes at the same time. Ninnie taps the glass with my drink. "Okay, what's going on?"

"Well, I met this guy last night at work. He's a local cop who happens to be Haitian. Sooo, we got to talking after work." Ninnie opens her mouth. I shake my head and continue before it stops making sense to me. "He promises to take me to Haiti with him—I mean not *with* him, but we go at the same time. You know I've already bought my ticket." Lisa sits up straighter and leans in. "Ben never commits into going with me. So, this is almost like divine intervention, and I don't even believe in such things hardly anymore."

"Oh, Addy, I keep telling you God walks among us," Lisa says. "You have to believe, and he'll deliver your wishes."

"Liss, honey, god must follow white people because he can't see the dark ones," Ninnie says, "many of us don't even have wishes. We have dire needs."

Lisa reddens like an over ripe tomato, stammering. "I...I'm sorry. But—"

"Oh, Jesus, Ninnie," I say, reaching for Lisa's hand. "It's all right, Liss. We've been learning from each other since we were babies, right? Yet we still have a long way to go, but we'll never get there if we don't all try. Sometimes, though, it feels like God is partial to some, but faith is faith."

Ninnie raises her hand like a witness on the stand. "Wait. A. Minute," she says, staring at me, "stop preaching, girl. What's his name and what do you mean we got to talkin' after work? You went out with the man? Oh, that's juicy."

"*Eugenie*, get your mind out of the gutters," I say, using the name she hates, but that belongs to her grandmother. This sister can smell pheromones from other continents. "We didn't go *out*. We had breakfast at Denny's after my late shift. His name's JR."

"So, you're going on a trip with a stranger?" Ninnie says. "Is it safe? I mean…that's not like you Addy."

"Yes, I was thinking the same thing," Lisa chimes in. "How about the private investigator you hired a couple months ago?"

"Y'all come down. JR's a friend of Dan, a retired police officer and one of our security guards at the hospital. See." I gulp a mouthful of my drink. "They play basketball every week. So, he's not a serial killer. And the PI so far has not come up with much. Granted all I gave him was the little bit I know. That I was born in July 1980 in a village called Lasalle. That's all mom has ever told me."

Lisa nods. "Ok. I trust your judgement, Addy."

"Go on." Ninnie says, arms crossed over her generous chest.

I take a sip of cold water from my frosty glass to abort a blush. "JR knows Haiti well. It was so easy to talk to him. Nobody has ever told me this much about my birthplace. Mom would probably rather talk about sex than her time in Haiti as a missionary. And I wonder if she has ever had sex. *Ever*."

"Marge must be hiding some deep secrets," Ninnie says, "because our mothers don't talk about sex." She sucks her teeth. "Mom used to tell me I came from the sky. Can you believe this crap?"

I smile. "Speaking of secrets, Mom now locks the file cabinet at home. I believe it may contain the information I need before making the trip. Without it, it would be like looking for two needles among millions. I need to find the key."

"Why don't you just break the damned lock?" Ninnie says. "I don't have your patience."

"Clearly," Lisa says, moving her gaze to me. "Find the key, Addy. There might not be anything in there…so Marge won't need to know you invaded her privacy." She cuts her eyes at Ninnie, Haitian-style, the way we'd taught her when we were kids from watching Nadine.

Ninnie leans back in the chair and burps. Lisa blushes as the waiter makes his way to our table. I want to strangle her, but I need her. "Listen, JR invited me to go…listen to a Haitian band tomorrow night. Can you guys go with me? It should be fun. Remember in high school when Liss got a car. We'd lied and gone to Tampa to a *Haitian Bal*."

"Of course," Lisa says. "Ninnie was dating this Haitian guy, and she dragged us there and he didn't show up, so we didn't stay."

"His broke ass couldn't get in," Ninnie says, laughing.

We join in laughter. "Okay, who's going this time. It's on me. I don't want to go with JR alone. But I want to soak in more of the culture before my trip. You know."

"Wait. Isn't Ben coming home tomorrow?" Lisa asks.

"I wish. Then he could go with me. He's coming back Sunday. Change in plan."

"I can't go," Lisa says, pouting. "My mother-in-law's birthday party's tomorrow."

"I'll go," Ninnie says.

"Great. We'll pick you up."

"I'll meet you there. In case I want to stay a bit longer…if I'm having too much fun." Ninnie winks.

In the car, I crank up the music and lower the AC. I'm glad Ninnie is going. I love Haitian music, yet I don't go to live parties. I can't wait. I won't stay too long. I want to surprise Ben and pick him up at the airport on Sunday afternoon and tell him about my plans. But first, I need to find the key to the locked file cabinet.

# CHAPTER EIGHT

❋❋❋

# KETLY

*April 1980*

The two-hour bus ride from Port-au-Prince to Lasalle fails to give me enough time to prepare an apology to Mama. Auntie's murder twists my insides until breaths struggle to come out. I groan in emotional and physical pain. I stroke my belly over the dress Auntie had given me to wear the day I left her house to wait for Henri, searching for her scent underneath the laundry soap.

"Oh, Auntie Yvette, please forgive me." I close my eyes and pray.

And now with this pregnancy, I've disappointed Mama in a way I am not sorry for because Henri will make it right. She will understand. I bury my face behind the glasses to avoid being recognized. The headscarf comes down to my eyebrows and I round my back, slumping my shoulders before getting off the bus at the last stop.

My belongings are tied in a bedsheet from the hotel; I lose myself within the throng of people in the market. I didn't need to exaggerate the limp from my sore foot. I walk around until I find a shady corner to sit in and wait for the cover of darkness. I watch every corner for Shadow. Simone is not going to be satisfied with only separating me from Henri, she wants me and the baby to disappear. Auntie would not tell them where I was. Simone killed her. The baby kicks as if to remind me that I am carrying my problem along.

At dusk, I stand and stretch the kinks out of my back and legs. My deep burgundy ensemble blends into my skin and the darkness. A young man I went to school with approaches. I look at the ground.

"Can I help with that bundle, Auntie?" he asks.

"Thank you, son, but I can manage," I say, making my voice quiver. "God bless you." I relax, feeling safe in my disguise.

At the edge of the river, I take off the sandals. The cold water sucks away my breath the way Henri did yesterday as he nibbled on my toes in the hotel room. I squat and drench my dry throat before washing my face and swishing a handful of water in my mouth.

Slowed by the load I carry on my back and in my belly, I arrive at Mama's late. I knock on the back door and wait in the dark corner of the kitchen.

"Who's it?" Mama asks.

"Open the door, Mama," I whisper.

"Kekette," she whispers back. The door opens and I slip through pulling the bundle behind me.

Our eyes meet in the middle of the room. I hold my belly as if I'm presenting her with a gift. Tears blur my vision. Mama walks to me as if in a trance, opens her arms and her embrace comforts me like a blanket. I bury my face in her neck and inhale the smokey smell of charcoal from her skin and the love and security from her arms. Like Auntie's.

We sit at the end of the bed. I lean closer to her ear and whisper, "I'm sorry, Mama. I didn't tell you about my…situation before. Henri and I wanted to tell you together." My heart hurts with the next news. "Oh, Mama, they killed Auntie Yvette and it's my fault."

"*Ki sa?*" Mama pushes me away from her to look into my eyes but still holding my arms. "What! *O Bondié*." She raises both arms over her head. "Who killed Yvette? Why? What are you talking about, Kekette?"

And I told her about Henri and our love. Simone and her hatred. Shadow and his quest to harm. When I finish, she pulls me to her bosom to smother my sobs. "Shh, shh, bébé, you can't take the burden of the devil into your heart."

We cry for a long time before she stands. "I'll make you something to eat and we'll have to go. Not because I'm scared of Shadow. I'll be ready for him, but others can get hurt, more importantly you."

"Mama nobody can know I'm here. Not even the boys."

"Your brothers are over your uncle in Beauville for Easter break."

I remember my summers in Beauville when Papa was here taking care of the family. It seems like a long time ago that my brothers and I tried to ride Uncle's goats. I miss that carefree life. I miss my childhood. I miss Papa.

"Ketly," Mama leans toward me until our heads touch. "I can't send you away in your condition, but once the baby's born, we'll figure out a safe place. Your young man will find you if…I mean when he comes back."

I shudder. "Mama, Henri will come in December like I told you. We have a plan."

Much later, she sits across from me at the table watching me eat. Tears bathe her face as she rolls the beads of her rosary. I know she's praying for Auntie Yvette's soul and my safety.

"No one in this village and beyond needs to know you're back here and pregnant. People sometimes talk not out of malice but out of fear and necessity. Let's go."

# I SHALL FIND YOU

We walk under a blanket of stars until I had to stretch. Mama takes my hand in hers the way she used to when I was a little girl. The nocturnal symphony of the village is the only sound between us. The moon lights our path through rocks and holes toward Auntie Irene's house in the next village.

Soon, she opens the door and lets us in, hugging Mama before smashing me into her chest. She and Mama look more like twins than sisters, except Mama's younger.

Sometime later, Auntie Irene says, "So sorry about Yvette. She was kinfolk."

"I don't want to bring you any trouble, Auntie." I breathe in deep to stop my nose from running.

"Hush, child." She swats the stuffy air in the room, her eyes staring at her machetes hanging on the wall, like the ones Mama keeps in her house. "Go in the back and lie down. You need your rest."

In the back room, I let myself cry for all the losses that follow me. Auntie's death. Henri's exile. My dream of becoming a Miss. All I have now is my unborn child. I'll do anything to make sure she wins the war against her grandmother.


The weeks go by as I lose myself in the books that take me to places around the world like Paris where Henri lives. I stay hidden in the back room like a prisoner. People come all day to buy tobacco and herbal medicine from Auntie Irene. I spy on them from behind the sheet hanging in the doorway. On clear nights, I lie on my back in the middle of the tobacco field and count the stars wondering if Henri can see them as well.

The weeks go by as fast as my imagination takes flight all day long. By late June, my baby's still upside down. I pray it'll turn. I need Henri. Why do I have to do this alone? When he comes back, I want the three of us to live in Paris. I'll never trust Simone. I stare at a shiny star winking at me the way Henri does before kissing me. I lift my hand off the ground as if to touch it.

"*Ce sera la belle vie, mon amour.*" I hum a love song into the night before making my way back.

Two weeks later, a sharp pain across my belly wakes me up with a start. I scream from the narrow bed. Auntie steps into the room with a kerosene lamp raised above her head. "Child, you can't holler like that. It'll bring the neighbors."

"I need Mama," I whimper. "She's always here by now, Auntie."

"She be here soon. It's storming outside."

She covers the straw mat in the corner of the room with white sheets and helps me lie down. After washing her hands in the plastic bowl on the table, she kneels in front of me and reaches for my knees. My belly contracts like a fist and delivers punches everywhere inside.

"Oh, Auntie, I'm going to die. I need Henri. He promised to be here when the time comes," I wail. "It's not fair."

She strokes the inside of my thighs. "Keep your legs open. Don't wanna smother the baby. And Henri ain't here. This baby coming with or without him." She pulls her hand out of me. "I gotta boil water."

I grab the hem of her long nightwear. "Please don't leave me alone here. I'm scared."

"Close your eyes and pray," she says before going outside. I listen to the rain as it pelts the tin roof.

When I open my eyes again, Mama says, "I'm here, but God was here first."

Sweat drenches my sleepwear and the sheet underneath my body. The pain tapers off when Mama sings gospel songs, as if the baby stops to listen to her soothing voice. I hum with her. She slides in behind me and cradles my head on her chest. I settle into her. I remember Auntie Yvette telling me to fight for my baby.

Minutes later, Auntie pushes her hand inside me one more time, the scream catches in my throat before bursting out of my mouth at the same time I squeeze my legs trapping her arm in a vise.

"Listen here, Ketly," Auntie says in a stern voice. "The pain comin' whether you ready or not. You hear me. Remember the happy times. I bet there were some," she mutters.

I close my eyes, and I remember.

∞∞∞

One month after I arrived in Port-au-Prince, I was already tired to the bones from the way Simone treated me like a lazy donkey that needed constant prodding. In the morning, I rode with her to the store so I could carry her stuff, but after work, I took public transportation then walked the long way up the hill to her house.

One afternoon, when a car stopped behind me, I knew it was Henri. We had been talking with our eyes every morning while I waited for Simone to finish her breakfast, his green ones shooting messages like falling stars and my dark ones storing them deep into my lonely heart.

"Get in," Henri said after pulling over to the side of the road. "Pretty girl like you shouldn't be out in the dark alone."

Grateful he could never see the blush under my skin, I said, "Umm…Madame Simone wouldn't approve. Besides, I'm almost there."

He got out of his car and took my hand in his, pulling me into the deep shadow of a flaming tree. His skin pierced the darkness and glowed like a lantern; mine disappeared into the night as if I was invisible. The kiss was tentative yet urgent. I leaned into him and opened my mouth wide and at that moment, my heart thudded in my chest and a soft cry escaped my lips when we pulled apart.

∞∞∞

The cry becomes louder, and the metallic smell of blood invades my nostrils. "My baby, my baby." I push away from Mama's embrace and reach my arms out like a supplicant. "What is it, Auntie?"

"Take a breath," Aunt Irene says. "Your daughter fine. A fighter." She places the baby in my arms. My heart soars. Mama brings the lamp closer, and I stare into the greenest eyes I've ever seen. The women recoil and make the sign of the cross.

"Oh, Kekette," Mama says. "Her eyes…umm…can she see?"

"She can see." I smile. "She's got her papa's eyes."

Mama sighs and sits back on the edge of the mat. "What's wrong, Mama? You look...sad."

"Bébé, the man you described as Shadow." She looks at me. I nod, my happiness leaking out of my heart. "He was in our village asking people about you. Yesterday he was waiting in front of the clinic staring at our house when I came home from the market. By the time I grabbed my biggest machete and went back outside he was gone. He only wanted to send a message this time. I'm sure he'll come back."

I exhale. My newfound love for my child feeds my anger. "Mama, when do the American missionaries leave our village?"

"They leave in three days. Why…what are you gonna do, Kekette?"

"What's the baby's name," Aunt Irene asks, "you know people be calling her Lizard Eyes." She hands me her tattered midwife record book, and I write: *Juliette Marie Murat née le 14, Juillet 1980*. I clutch Juliette to my chest and hum a lullaby while I finalize a new plan in my troubled mind.

∞∞∞

# I SHALL FIND YOU

The first time I saw Miss Marge; I was about six or seven. She gave me one of the many vaccines I would receive at the little clinic across from the house where I was born. I hollered when she plunged the needle into my upper arm. Miss Marge picked me up from the bench and placed me on her lap.

"Don't cry *Ti cherie*," she said in heavily accented Creole, "this will keep you healthy."

I buried my face in her long cottony hair the color of dried corn husk. She smelled like gauze and alcohol swabs. She handed me a red *piwouli* and sang a song I didn't know. "I wish I had a pretty little girl like you, Ketly," she said, kissing my cheek.

I settled against her and sucked my lollipop. Miss Annette who lived in the two-room house behind the clinic and had been its *Directrice* since before I was born poked her head from the back room and said, "Marge, we have hundreds of kids in this village to see." She stared at me and said, "Ketly, go home." She called another child.

Miss Marge never missed a year. All the time she'd been coming she was still unmarried and childless. Everybody loved her, especially the kids, but she always had something special to give me before she left. I told her I wanted to be a Miss like her one day.

Now, three days after her birth, I swaddle Juliette in the pink blanket Henri had bought for her and whisper to Mama to hurry. The village sleeps. In the moonlight, I blow gently on Juliette's face, so she'd open her green eyes. I want to etch my baby's face into my memory like the pictures of the village children Miss Marge brings back every year for their parents. Sometimes the child is no longer here, but the parents relish the souvenirs.

I look up to see Mama staring at me with wet eyes. "Ketly, for the last time, let's go to Terreville with the baby. Simone wouldn't know where your papa came from. It's such an isolated island."

She must have seen the resolve in my dry eyes. "Mama, I think Simone wants my baby perhaps more than she wants me. She won't stop. How long before someone here tells them where Papa was from. Not too many places to hide a green-eyed baby in these parts."

I hold Juliette so tight against my chest, her heartbeat synchronizes with mine. I step into the night. Mama carries the cardboard box behind me. We follow the moon in silence. At the clinic, I place the note I'd written to Miss Marge that afternoon at the bottom of the box and place Juliette on top. After kissing my daughter, I put the box under the window of the clinic in Lasalle, my heart breaking into tiny pieces.

"I'll see you soon, my love. Your papa and I will come for you." I pinch her arm before joining Mama behind an avocado tree. Juliette lets out a wail, then stops. I hold my breath and pray. "Please, baby, cry," I whisper as if she can hear me.

With the second wail, the window opens. Miss Marge appears holding a flashlight and looking around before staring down. When she carries the box inside the clinic and closes the door, I let out my breath and collapse into Mama's arms like a pile of dominoes.

The next morning, disguised in my old woman outfit, I peer through the gap between the door and the frame of my childhood home as the missionaries gather outside the clinic waiting for the bus that will take them to the airport in Port-au-Prince. I see no sign of Juliette. I rein in my panic with slow breaths. Miss Marge climbs our porch and hugs Mama.

"Give my love to Ketly whenever she comes this way," she says. "I wish I had time to see her in the city. I pray she's happy, Clara."

"Oh, she's doing fine," Mama says a bit too loudly. "As a matter of fact, she sent me money this week."

"Good, I'll see you next year, my friend," Miss Marge says, hugging Mama again.

I slip out the back door with my belongings away from the crowd waving and yelling "Bon voyage" to the missionaries. I crouch under a tree among the local beggars and watch. I don't know what she needs to do to carry a child out of the country, but I know Miss Marge will protect my baby.

The hiss of the closing door of the bus shreds my heart. The roar of the engine carrying Juliette to safety starts the healing. Miss Marge will keep our baby safe until Henri, and I can get her back. With my belongings wrapped in the same hotel sheet that no longer smells like Henri's Bleu de Chanel, I turn my back on my child, my home, and my family to make my way to what I pray will be a safe haven.

# CHAPTER NINE

❀❀❀

## ADELE

The ringing phone intrudes into my semi-consciousness. I was in a dream with Ben and JR dressed in dueling costumes with brandishing swords while Grace laughs as she points at her son repeating the phrase. "I told you so, Benjamin. I told you so."

Like a refrain.

My heart beating in my ears, I reach for my cell. "Addy," Ben says. "I almost hung up and called Marge. Are you out with the ladies?"

"Hey, honey." I yawn. "I had dinner with the girls earlier. I'm at Mom's. Had this dream though." I look at the screen. "It's after one in the morning."

"Just got back to my hotel room. I had a late dinner meeting. Was the dream about me?" He moans. "Can't wait to see you…Monday. Let's play hooky."

"Monday!" I sit up in bed. "You told me you'd be back early Sunday. You're changing your return day *again*? Aren't we having dinner with your new clients Sunday evening?"

"I rescheduled it. Look, honey, I ran into some college friends tonight. I can't pass up the opportunity to play golf tomorrow with them and there's a get together later. I'm networking. You know."

"I'm off this weekend, Ben. You're gone a lot. We need to talk." I shake my head. "Oh, never mind."

"Don't be mad, Addy. I bought you a gift. You'll love it. Hey, have some fun with your friends tonight." He laughs. "See you on Monday."

I push End on the screen and turn on the lamp. We say we love each other but we seem to always be at odds with our agendas, our interests, even our culture. Maybe I should have waited a bit longer before saying yes to marrying Ben. But wasn't it love that made him ask and made me say yes or did we both have something to prove? I take a sip of water from the glass on the nightstand and hug the pillow to my chest thinking about that day.

∞∞∞

We'd been dating for about eight months when Ben asked me to meet his parents. He'd squeezed my hand before stepping out of the car on the red brick driveway. My eyes traveled the length of his lean body with naughtiness. Ben uses the service of his personal trainer successfully. It shows everywhere on his well-toned physique.

His long-sleeve blue shirt tucked inside a pair of dark grey linen pants and sock-less loafers, Ben looked every bit like a model for a yacht magazine. His high-yellow complexion held on to the kisses of the sun on his skin. The recent textured crop cut flatters his strong jaw. A dark curl rests on his high forehead. His bold fragrance wafts into the air. Stirrings warmed my skin.

I squeezed his hand back. Beads of sweat dotted his forehead despite the cool October breeze. "Are you okay, honey?" I asked.

"Oh. I'm fine. Umm…mom can be a bit…difficult, but her barks are worse than her bites." He kissed my cheek. "But you'll love Dad."

We walked into a foyer the size of a hotel lobby. A medium-height woman with an updo and dark brown skin so stretched out, it shined, glided down the stairway, her head held high, her slender hand floating over the polished banister. I expected to see a 'Mrs. Universe' sash across her royal blue gown. On the last step, she opened her arms, beckoning to Ben. He leaned into her and kissed her cheek.

"Benjamin, we waited for you to complete our Thanksgiving list this morning," she said, ignoring me standing next to him. "We have a tradition, Son."

Ben moved away from her and wrapped his arm around my waist. "Mom, this is, Adele."

I extended my hand. "Nice to meet you, ma'am."

She stared at me, dark eyes narrowing into slits. "Hello, it's Mrs. Barrett," she said, shaking my hand with three fingers. I waited for her to wipe her hand on the back of her dress. "Benjamin, you didn't tell me she was…so exotic."

I dropped my hand and balled it by my side.

"Hey, you guys are here," said a booming voice preceding a tall man coming from the hallway wearing a big grin. He had skin that would rather burn than tan. His lively grey eyes, like Ben's smiled with mischief. He ran his hand through a mess of dark blond hair, pushing it away from his face. "We've heard so much about you, Adele," the man said. "You're just as beautiful as Ben said. Come in, come in." He took my hand and led me to the living room followed by Ben and his mother.

"Thank you, Mr. Barrett," I said. "Bennie tends to exaggerate sometimes."

"Please call me Senior." He tilted his head toward his wife. "She's Grace. Not *Your Grace*." He laughed. I laughed with him.

I loved Senior. Grace glared at me with a furious look on her face. "Please don't call him Bennie. *I hate it*."

"Mom, please. Don't start," Ben said in a small voice.

I shook hands with many guests and repeated my name but did not register any of theirs, except the woman dressed in an olive-green sequined gown, flaunting all her body parts. platinum blond hair framed her oval face with the piercing cobalt eyes that stopped on Ben. She pulled her bottom lip between her teeth in a slow motion.

"Adele, this is Paige O'Malley," Grace said. "Paige's family have been longtime friends of ours. Benjamin and Paige were engaged."

Ben glared at his mother. Why didn't he ever tell me about this? I told him about Andrew the week we met. What else was he keeping from me? At the table, I sat across from him and watched in disgust as Paige practically climbed onto his lap. He moved pieces of food on his plate, but his fork barely made it to his mouth.

Much later, the guests said goodbye to Ben's parents, and I was the only one left— and Paige. We moved to the family room with cups of gourmet coffee. Ben stood, shuffling from one leg to the other like a little boy in need of a bathroom.

I exchanged looks with Senior. He smiled. Grace peered at Ben and squinted when he reached into his pocket and pulled out a small box. He knelt in front of me on the couch. Taking my left hand, he opened the box and slid a four-carat ring on my finger.

"Adele Marie Pearson, will you do me the honor of marrying me?"

Before I could answer, Grace stood and screeched. "Oh, Benjamin. *No!*"

I held Grace's stare. Perhaps my smile had more to do with victory than love, and said, "Yes, *Bennie*. Yes! I will marry you."

∞∞∞

I'm still smiling at winning that round over Grace three years ago. But did I really win? My insomnia is a constant companion lately. I change into a loose dress, strip the bed, and start my Saturday cleaning of my mother's house. The drawer is still locked. Mom is already in the kitchen. She's made Haitian coffee earlier and pours me a cup. I inhale the rich smell. The smell of home. I imagine people sitting around a campfire in small villages, drinking coffee and telling stories while children chase each other at play. I want to go see for myself.

"You want breakfast now, Mom?"

"A bit later, Addy. Thank you."

I pull the vacuum cleaner from the hallway closet and push it to where Mom sits by the bay window sipping coffee with a book open in her lap.

"Mom, why don't I take you to the hairdresser after I'm done today. My treat." I need to get her out of the house. The key must be in her bedroom. I look everywhere else. "You feel better enough for church tomorrow, right?"

"I do feel better, Addy. You take such great care of me. But I'll pass on the hairdresser." She runs her hand through her thinning hair.

"Okay. Let me know when you want to eat. We're going shopping later. You need some fresh air, and I need a new dress. I'm going to a party tonight."

She opens her mouth to speak. I turn on the vacuum and it swallows her questions. My husband told me to go have fun with my friends. JR and Ninnie are my friends, right?

# CHAPTER TEN

## KETLY

The ferry looms large against the backdrop of the ocean. Frothing waves crash against the seawall, splashing the cement platform and dusty feet with warm sea water. I tilt my head back, shading my eyes to take in the top level of the boat. The movement and the sight of the people leaning over the rail cause my stomach to flip. But since I can't swim to the island, I swallow my anxiety and walk toward the gangplank.

No sign of Shadow. Vendors and panhandlers mingle in a dance to separate you from your money either way. People lounge around on benches, on the ground or walk about in groups. I plaster a smile on my face and walk to a petite woman dressed as if it was Sunday. Even in high heels, she disappears behind a group of people pushing her to board the ferry. Sweat mists her powdered face making her red lipstick look wet. With a baby nestled in the crook of her right arm, she struggles to make a little boy hold on to the hem of her floral pleated dress.

"Eddy, stay with me," she says, shrugging up a big vinyl bag on her left shoulder. "Watch your step, son."

"Good afternoon, ma'am," I say, dropping my bundle on the ground. "Can I help?"

"Oh," she says, looking me up and down.

The boy gawks at me, squinting into the blazing sun. A gust of wind brings in the smell of rotten fish and fried food on the same breeze, reminding me I haven't eaten since I left Lasalle this morning. "Eddy's cute." I smile at him.

"I'm Alice...Poitier," the lady says. "Hold Eddy's hand and stay where I can see you. Thanks."

I squat and stroke his chubby cheek. "How old are you, sweetie?" He raises three fingers in the air. I take his hand. "You're a big boy." I stand and peek at the bundle in her arms. "A girl?"

"Another boy," Alice says, pouting, like a little kid disappointed with a gift. "Simon."

"Maybe next one."

She shrugs. "Maybe."

The softness of Eddy's palm brings fresh tears to my eyes. When will I hold Juliette's hand? Longings hollow part of my heart, but anger fills the rest. I hope it doesn't corrode my insides and make me barren. I follow Alice into the boat.

"You're okay?" Alice asks. "What's your name?"

"Oh, umm...Marie," I take a seat in a row of bolted orange chairs on the bottom deck.

She squints at me, waiting for the rest of my name. Just about every female child in Haiti has Marie in front of her name in reverence to the Virgin.

"Where are you staying on the island, *Marie*," Alice asks, when I ignore her and place Eddy on my lap. "Never seen you on the ferry before. I go to Port-au-Prince often on account of Eddy's vision."

# I SHALL FIND YOU

I glance at the boy bouncing on my lap. "What's wrong with his eyes?"

"He's fine." Alice swats the air with her hand. "He'll probably need glasses. Where are you staying on the island?"

"This is kinda my first trip to the island…umm…Mama said we came here when I was maybe Eddy's age." I know Alice won't stop her inquisition. Her eyebrows are penciled as permanent question marks. "My papa is…was from there. I don't remember much except the soil in Mapou where I'm going is red and his family home sits across from the Baptist church."

"Ha! What's a young girl like you going to Mapou for? There's nothing there but poverty, dirt, and Jesus." She snorts. "But Jesus is everywhere, so you don't need to go that far to find him." She slits her eyes at me. "You must be hiding from someone or something, right?"

Eddy stops moving and rests his head between my breasts as he succumbs to sleep. I inhale his talcum powder smell mixed with innocence and squeeze him to my chest and exhale.

"I already found what I was looking for without knowing that's all I wanted." I sniff, unable to blow my nose. "But I lost him and our... I'm going to wait for him to come find me in Mapou."

"In Mapou?" She laughs before turning serious. "Where's your baby, *Marie*?"

I sit up so fast Eddy opens his eyes and looks at me before slipping his thumb in his mouth and settling back.

"Umm…what baby? How…," I stammer, my heart beating loud as I look around for potential danger.

She points to the wet spot on my dark green blouse. Suddenly, the sour smell of breastmilk fills my nose. Despite the padding, I am leaking milk like a cow. Alice hands me some cloth diapers from her baby bag.

"I can't talk about it," I whisper.

She strokes my arm. "But you're a baby yourself. How old are you anyway?"

I stand and stretch Eddy on two chairs. "It was nice to meet you, ma'am. I'll pray for Eddy's eyes." I heft my stuff off the floor to leave.

She grabs my arm. "Listen, I live in Galette, the so-called capital of the island." She rolls her eyes. "If I can help in any way, just come down from Mapou anytime. My husband's the director of the Lycée, the mayor and sometimes the bank manager. You can't miss me."

"Thank you, ma'am."

I climb the spiral staircase to the open deck on top. The ferry pulls away from the dock. At the stern, I watch my past recede in the churning waters until the sea swallows everything. I turn toward the bow, waiting to see land again.

Two hours later, the ferry docks. The wharf teems with people pushing, talking, and unloading bales of goods onto the streets. Mopeds scatter around like ants making the three cars stand out like statues. Small fishing boats bob and sway in the rushing waves that die on the rocky beach. Sea birds fly overhead before diving down to pick morsels off the ground.

I watch an older man, dressed in a taupe three-piece suit with a straw hat perched over his forehead scoop Eddy off the plank. He must be Alice's papa. They have the same russet skin tone and small frames. His dry face opens with a big smile. The July heat seems to have spared him by doubling down on my bare head. I wipe a trail of pomade grease running behind my neck with the back of my hand. The man leans over and kisses Alice on the lips, the two children pressed between them. I look away.

# I SHALL FIND YOU

"Marie, *Marie*, come over here," Alice yells, waving her plump arm at me. I almost look behind me. "This is my husband Raoul. We'll take you to Mapou later, but first we'll stop by our house for refreshments."

I shake Raoul's hand. "I don't want to impose. I'm sure I can walk to Matante's house. I mean how hard can it be?"

Alice lets out a piercing laugh. The baby in her arms wails. She pats his head. "Take a good look at the *city* around you." She swivels her head for me to take in the small scale of everything as if I'm blind. "The road to Mapou is unpaved. I can't imagine walking there, although people do."

We climb into a white and blue car with fins on the back like a shark. Raoul places Eddy on his lap and the boy grabs the wheel with both hands and giggles. Alice sits in front with the baby, and I slide into the back. My nose touches the window as I peer outside. A gaggle of children runs after the car, laughing and shoving each other. Their joy unmasks my pain. Raoul drives as if we are in a parade.

Soon he pulls under a carport attached to the biggest house on the block with a cement roof. I stand in the doorway and take in the large living room with a white tile floor and wicker furniture covered in floral prints. A warm breeze from the open windows blows the filmy curtains inside the room. The atmosphere invites me to sit and take a load off.

"I'll have the maid take you to the washroom," Alice says. "We'll eat soon then we'll drive you to Mapou before dark."

The cook piles the table with bowls and trays of food. I fill my plate with rice and beans, stewed goat, fried plantains, legumes and catch Raoul looking at the plate. I cast my eyes down at the table.

"It's okay, Marie. You're a growing girl still." He smiles.

I blush.

After lunch, Alice puts the boys down for their nap and changes into a white summer dress with straps tied in bows on her shoulders, her house slippers click-clack on the floor. I gawk at her feet. I've never seen slippers with high heels before.

"I had them made," she says, looking down at her small feet. "I'm too short."

We settle in the rocking chairs on the verandah. "You're beautiful, *Marie*," Alice says, facing me. "What happened? Young girls like you don't leave Port-au-Prince to come here." In her dark brown eyes, I see recognition. "I'm not from here either. Whatever you're going through, it'll get better."

"But...but you have a husband, a nice home, your boys...I have nothing, Alice." I shrug, feeling despair settle upon my shoulders.

"You remind me of my younger self, *Marie*. Maybe one day I'll tell you, my story. What's your name?"

I stop rocking, feeling a sudden need to unburden my soul to this stranger. "My name's Ketly...Ketly Murat and I'm seventeen," I whisper, the words colliding in my throat to spill out.

I'm so far away from Lasalle and Port-au-Prince, no one will ever find me, except Henri, because Alphonse will send him. I talk about my daughter, the death of my father the year before, falling in love with Henri, and Simone's war to keep us apart. When I get to Auntie's murder, I hold my stomach to keep the food from coming up. I stand, closing my eyes to slow my heartbeat. "I need to leave now Alice. I don't want to expose your family to danger. This man is a murderer."

"Sit down, child. Shadow won't make it off the ferry before Raoul knows. Everybody already knows you're here and you're *our* friend. This island takes care of its own. They know everyone who belongs. I'll put the word out. I hope he comes."

I frown at Alice. "What?"

"Shadow will experience island justice if he comes here. He'd never make it back alive."

I shiver in the heat. What kind of place is this? I need to leave already. "Henri will come for me in December as planned."

Alice clears her throat and reaches for my hands. "Ketly, listen to me. I pray Henri comes for you, but"—she squeezes hard; I wince, "if he doesn't, this is an opportunity for you to find yourself before you become someone else. If not Henri, one day you'll meet a good man and create a family."

I pull my hands away, and Alice almost comes off her chair. "Henri will come," I yell more to convince myself than to drive the point home to her. "He'll find me here."

Silence stretches long like the shade from the breadfruit tree branches scraping the walls of the house. We size up each other. She nods. We talk about dreams, losses, hope and the love for our children that sustains us.

Hours later, the sun makes a slow descent behind the mountains when we climb back into the car and set out for Mapou. With no road signs, the car trudges upward. Our only reference is the church I remember. I haven't seen Matante in almost thirteen years. By the time Raoul pulls in front of the small house with faded green paint on the door, I've worked myself into a frenzy. I feel like I was being buried alive. Port-Au-Prince seems like it's on another planet.

I open the car door and step on soil so red it looks like dried blood. An older woman parts what looks like a bed sheet from the doorway and shades her eyes even though the sun has set leaving colorful streaks in the clouds. Two women on laden donkeys stop in their tracks to ogle the car.

"Who you, *pitit*?" the older woman asks.

I climb the two steps that lead to a small porch and put my arms around her round shoulders. "Matante Hilda? I'm Ketly. I came here with my father Joseph…Murat when I was very young."

*"O Bondié,"* she exclaims. "Kekette, you look just like my late brother." She looks in the direction of the car where Raoul and Alice stand surveying the swath of land as far as the eyes can see. "Where are my manners?" Matante says, "Come in, come in. I'll make cinnamon tea. I have some biscuits."

"We can't stay long," Alice says, "but tea would be lovely."

I know they don't need tea or biscuits but it's impolite in these parts to refuse hospitality. I bet Matante has never been to Port-Au-Prince. Seated around the wooden table with the flame from the kerosene lamp throwing dancing shadows on the mud wall, we regale her with stories of the city as we sip our tea and nibble on stale biscuits. When my new friends stand to leave, I want to follow them. Alice takes me in her arms like the big sister I never have and whispers, "My door's open. If Henri…can't come, you and I will find another way to get to Juliette."

I kiss her round cheek as if I want to soak in that promise, lest she forgets she's made it. But somehow, I know Alice will be an ally in my plan to reunite with my baby.

# CHAPTER ELEVEN

## ADELE

After cleaning the house, I pull mixing bowls from the cupboard, the flour and eggs from the fridge and start to work. Humming a Haitian song from a Tabou Combo CD Ninnie had given me last year for my birthday, I swing my hips from side to side as I chop onions and sweet peppers for an omelet.

"It sure smells good," Mom says, kissing my cheek before pulling up a chair to sit at the table. "Ben's coming back tomorrow? I love having you here, but he's gone a lot. How am I gonna have my grandbabies." She chuckles. "I can't wait forever."

I pour more coffee in her mug. "He's staying an extra day to play golf. Coming back Monday."

Mom frowns. "Didn't you tell me you guys were having dinner with some clients or something tomorrow?"

"He rescheduled it."

She lowers her coffee cup. "Is everything okay between you two?"

"Of course. Part of his job, I suppose." I turn on the burner under the skillet.

"There's a birthday picnic after church for one of the women from the Benevolence ministry tomorrow. I'll be gone all day. Of course, you can come if you want. You haven't been to church lately, Addy."

"I know, Mom, but I still pray, but he hasn't answered my demands yet."

"How can you say that Addy? Look at everything you have. God's been particularly good to you. Don't ever forget that."

"Why?" I turn from the stove, the spatula dripping batter on the floor. "Is it because God lets you pull me out of the pile of starving children?"

Mom shifts in her seat unable to hold my gaze, her blush a deep red. "No! Because he loves all his children, Addy. All of them."

I flip the pancake in the pan to hide the doubt plaguing me lately. I miss the days when I believed faithfully.

"It's all right, Mom. I'm going to a late party tonight and I'll probably need to sleep in. I'll go with you next Sunday. I promise."

"Oh. You're going out with the girls?"

"With Ninnie. Lisa has other plans. I met this new friend at work. We're going to a live Haitian band party. I've never been to one."

"Is your new friend on staff or was she a patient?"

"No, he's a local Haitian police officer." I put the plate with the pancakes in the oven to keep warm and pour the whipped eggs over the sauteed vegetables.

"What! You're going out with a man?" Her chair legs scrape the floor.

"Ninnie's going. It's not a date with a man." I catch myself before I suck my teeth.

"That's good, Addy. Remember, you're a good Christian girl."

"Mom, I'm a grown woman. I won't do anything I don't want to do. I know what's in my heart."

"I've always trusted your judgement, sweetheart." Mom blesses the food, the way she has my whole life. "Oh, Addy, this is your best yet. Ben's a lucky man."

I shove food into my mouth, suddenly ravenous. "We'll get mani-pedi, too, after shopping today."

The corners of her eyes crinkle like a pleated fan when she smiles. "Addy, how can I say no to such a proposition?"

The mall in Tampa is a nice place to stroll and to part with your money. I lose track of time. We try on dresses, shoes, jewelry. I buy a complete outfit for her with matching accessories and a little black dress for me.

"You spoil me, Addy." She holds my hand as we window-shop, the way we did when I was a little girl. People still stare.

"You're the best mom a girl can have. I'm glad you chose me but if I had the choice, I would have chosen you as well." I drop a kiss on her cheek.

Her eyes swim in unshed tears. "I wish I could have given you a daddy. *Mwen renmen'w anpil.*"

"I love you a lot too, Mom. Let's go home. We both need a nap."

After dinner with mom tonight, I can't get my hair to cooperate, so I fashion it into a French braid and drop it in the middle of my bare back. The one shoulder black dress stops above my knees and hugs my body After dinner with mom tonight, I can't get my hair to cooperate, so I fashion it into a French braid and drop it in the middle of my bare back. The one shoulder black dress stops above my knees and hugs my body like an embrace. I step into my three-inch heel sandals, checking my lipstick in the mirror for the umpteenth time.

The doorbell sounds like a cannon. I skip to the door, hoping mom stays in her bedroom.

"Whoa, you look gorgeous, *Miss* Adele," JR says, his deep voice echoing down the hall.

"Addy, is Ninnie here?" Mom asks, shuffling into the living room. "Oh," she says, gathering the robe around her chest.

"Mom, this is Officer Jean-Robert Vilsaint."

In two steps, JR stands in front of her extending his hand. "Nice to meet you, ma'am."

"Get some rest, Mom. I'll be back late." She opens her mouth. I pull the front door behind us.

JR closes the car door after I pull my leg in. "Are we picking up some girls?" he asks.

"No. Ninnie's meeting us there."

We ride in silence, but it's as if there's another presence in the car. I steal side glances at him. His brown pants and the dark beige shirt tucked inside seem to blend into his skin, making him look almost nude. I hum to the music booming from the car radio.

He glances at me at a red light. "I see you love *konpa* music." He taps the wheel, his head bobbing up and down. "You may be Haitian after all."

"I grew up with it from Ninnie's family next door. I love that rhythm. I feel it in my bones. Must be the DNA."

His head moves in tempo to the music.

# I SHALL FIND YOU

The dance hall in the shopping plaza sits next to a Haitian bakery. Round tables with red and blue tablecloths hug the walls leaving ample space on the floor for dancing. The room is dim with only votive-size candles on the tables. The stage is well lit, and the musicians mill about as they test their instruments. The sounds beat in my stomach. I fight the urge to stick my index fingers into my ears. JR introduces me to a lot of people as his friend from St Petersburg. I grin and nod. Most of the women kiss my cheeks in Haitian custom greetings. People bump into each other. JR leans close to my ear and yells, "I hope your sandals are comfortable. We're gonna dance all night long. What you wanna drink?"

"Rhum Barbancourt and coke," I yell.

He grabs my hand and pulls me along. "Let's go to the bar. Don't wanna lose you in this mob, although it's not possible."

I make a face he can't see in the dimness of the room. The band plays fast and slow songs, but everyone dances with their feet planted like roots as their bodies sway like tree branches to the rhythm in their head, their hearts, their loins. JR's palm on my back burns my skin. Rivulets of sweat run between my breasts. His erection lands on my thigh. I pull away and step on someone's toes behind me who shrieks, "Watch it."

"Keep an eye out for Ninnie," I say to JR. "I hope she can find us."

He nods and pulls me in and whispers, "I'm not going to hurt you ever. I protect and serve my friends."

"Oh, I thought it was the public."

"Well, you're part of the public." He raises his hand and brushes strands of hair out of my eyes. "Your green eyes haunt me."

When the song ends, we walk back to our table. "JR, let's understand one thing. I'm married and I will never cheat on my husband. Me being here is like research for my upcoming trip to Haiti. I want to understand the culture, the people…you know. I appreciate your offer to help. That's all."

"Whoa! Very clear. I apologize if I offended you." He pulls out my chair. "It was never my intention to make you feel uncomfortable." I can't really see the expression on his face. "I do want to help you in Haiti. No strings."

"Thank you, JR. I'm going to call Ninnie in the lady's room." I clutch my bag into my armpit. "I'm worried. She said she'd be here."

JR holds my elbow and parts the crowd with his other hand. He exudes an air of authority people can see and feel. The relative quiet of the bathroom is soothing. I have two missed calls. I hit the voicemail button.

*"Hey Addy, I'm sorry. I'm not going to make it. I'm on my period and the cramps are bad. Enjoy the band. I know you're in good hands with the officer. I hope he's not a gentleman. I want all the details later."*

I pull the phone away from her silly laugh, smiling and shaking my head as if she can see me. That sister.

The party ends after two in the morning. I kick my sandals off and settle into the fabric of the car seat. "That was a lot of fun. I didn't know there were so many Haitians in the Tampa Bay area. How do I find two people in a whole country when I have no idea what exactly I'm looking for?"

"Green eyes," JR says. "Let's get something to eat."

After several cups of coffee and a club sandwich, I open my mouth to speak, and a loud burp comes out. We laugh. "I'm sorry."

"Double dimples," he says.

"What?"

He points to my face. "What to look for in Haiti. Green eyes and double dimples." He laughs. "But seriously, you need to find some info about place, name, date, age, I mean something. Even your PI will not be able to find much without leads. You ever ask your mom?"

I blow air out of my mouth. "What do you think? But there's a locked drawer in the file cabinet I plan to get into tomorrow while mom's at church."

"All these years you live there and now you wanna see what's inside?"

I suck my teeth this time. "It was never locked before. Mom had a safe deposit box at the bank forever which she closed a couple months ago."

"Ask her what's in there? Can't advise you to break into it. I'm a law enforcement officer."

I stop my eyes from rolling as if they have a mind of their own when I'm around this man. "You know the last time I asked Mom about my adoption; she told me how she'd registered with an agency in the US and never received a call. She believed it was because she'd be a single mother. She always thought she'd get a baby in Haiti during her trips."

"Uh-huh! Isn't that reason enough for her to steal one in Haiti?"

"What?" My head swims with all the rhum and coke I'd consumed. "Take me home, JR. I had a wonderful time. Thank you for introducing me to more connections to my birth country. Please come to my birthday party next weekend. You can meet my husband."

At the door, he kisses my forehead. "I had a great time, too, Miss. *Bonne nuit.*"

I lock the door and lean against it, thinking about what JR said earlier about stolen babies. My Christian mom. No. She would never do that. But how far will the urge to become a mother at any cost take a woman?

The sound of JR's car fades away. I kick off my sandals. My feet throb from all the dancing. I halt my steps in front of the room with the file cabinet, barely able to control my impulse to break the lock now. But last time I asked, Mom said there wasn't a note left with me. So, what am

I looking for? I walk inside and pull the handle of the drawer. Still locked. I rub the cool metal of the cabinet like a genie bottle.

"Tomorrow, you'll show me what you hold," I whisper.

# CHAPTER TWELVE

❀❀❀

# KETLY

*September 1980*

Life in Mapou revolves around the many churches that serve as places of worship in good times and shelter in bad. Tall mountains dotted with shacks, huts and mud houses circle the valley like a tight hug. Sometimes I open my arms wide as if I can push them out to make more space. I can't breathe. Since Alice and Raoul dropped me here a few weeks ago, I have not seen a car or a stranger.

I rock the chair to coax a breeze from the morning air. School-aged children run down the road in T-shirts with words in foreign languages, souvenirs from the last missionaries who scour the countryside feeding hungry souls with gospel and killing worms in swollen bellies with pills.

The kids kick rocks barefoot, shoving each other in an impromptu game of soccer. Red dust coats their feet like socks. I sip coffee to moisten my throat. If these kids never leave this village, what will they know of the world? I open the book to read *La dance sur le volcan* by Marie Vieux Chauvet again. I see no bookstores around. I may lose my mind here from boredom and sadness. I miss school. I miss my friends. If Papa hadn't died, I'd be starting my last year of secondary school this fall. Now, how will I ever become a Miss if I don't leave this island?

The door bangs against the wall bringing Matante outside. I put the cup down on the floor and reach for the book again. She places her hands on her ample waist and glares at me.

"Look here, Kekette, I can't read but I know you ain't reading that book you holding upside down."

"You need my help with something?" I ask, stroking the front of the book, and sipping the remnant of the cold coffee in the aluminum cup.

"I reckon, I was doing fine without your help. I want you to help yourself. Can't waste the rest of your life on that here porch. You still got too much of it left."

I look down at my chest to make sure breastmilk is not seeping through my white T-shirt. "I told you…umm…I'm waiting for someone."

She slaps the air with her calloused hand. "Who you runnin' from, child? Five or so weeks ago, you showed up in a car that dropped you here like a sack of charcoal and you still ain't say nothing to me about what you doin' here and why?"

"It's best if you don't know." I can't tell her about Auntie Yvette. "I'll be out of here in December, maybe even before. I promise." I look at the ground as if it can show me the future. "I'll send you money when I get to Paris."

"You goin' where?" Matante lowers herself into the other chair. "Baby, I see so many people here lose land, crops, faith, even family to buy a visa to go yonder. What you sellin' *Pitit mwen*."

"Oh no, it's not like that. Someone special's coming for me. We'll make a stop in Florida, you know where Miami is…" I smile at the blank look on her face. "Anyway, we'll live in France. They speak French there."

She narrows her beady eyes to a razor thin line. "D'you hit your head on the ferry on your way here, baby?"

# I SHALL FIND YOU 85

I shake my head. If I speak, I'll cry. Matante doesn't believe me. Well can I blame her? Do I believe it myself? I stand and shake my legs. "I'm going for a walk. I'll be back soon."

"Stop by Pastor Paul. He's having summer school at the church. You can help a child read and write. You be a good teacher, Ketly"

"I'm going to be a Miss one day, Matante."

"Good. Just be somethin'." She slaps the sheet in the doorway and disappears inside.

I must admit it was a better idea than sitting on my butt daydreaming about Henri and Juliette all day. Volunteering will make the time go faster. Clad in denim shorts and my white T-shirt, I lace up my sneakers after padding my bra with my clean underwear and set out for a walk. The sun plays peekaboo through the dense leaves of fruit trees.

Birds sing and I hum a love song. At the creek, I sit on the ground, crossing my legs under me after pulling a frangipani flower and playing: he loves me, he loves me not with white petals. The flower says he loves me. My heart skips. I cup my hand and scoop cool water to drink before washing the sweat off my face.

At the church compound, the children sit on wood plank benches in a one-room house in the courtyard. They're reading off the chalkboard in a singsong voice. I stand outside the open window and peer inside. About a dozen boys and girls, many I've seen in church the past couple of Sundays, stare at me and stop reading. The board must be under the window. The teacher turns her head and smiles at me.

"Come on in, Ketly."

"Everybody knows everybody here," I mutter under my breath. "I'm sorry…I didn't mean to disrupt." I step into the room.

"I'm Denise. We're done for the day," she says. "I let them go around noon in the summer before it gets too hot. Are you going to help us? Your aunt told Pastor you will."

"Is that right?" I say, feeling annoyed. "I won't be here for long."

"Whatever you can do will be appreciated."

The children run outside yelling, "Au revoir Mademoiselle Denise."

We smile.

"Have a seat," she says.

I sit on the front bench across from her. She talks. I listen. Denise attended the Lycée in Galette and returned to Mapou to teach and to marry André, a local blacksmith. We talk about life on the island, in Port-Au-Prince, in Haiti. Life in general.

Hours later, I make my way back home like a prisoner being returned to solitary confinement. Before I even climb the first step to the porch, Matante comes rushing out of the door, limping on her bad knee.

"Baby, you have a visitor," she whispers.

I stop in my tracks. Goosebumps pebble my sweaty skin. I want to run, but where can I go. Is it Henri? Shadow?

"Wh…who is it Matante?"

"A man. Says he came from Port-au-Prince."

I freeze in place. The sheet hanging in the door moves. I pivot to run. The familiar voice stops me in mid stride. I glare into Alphonse's grinning eyes.

"Hi." He waves.

My knees stop knocking. I glare at him. "What the hell are you doing here? You almost gave me a heart attack," I yell. "I thought it was—" Matante squints at me. "I told you to stay away, Alph. I still have nothing to offer you but my friendship." I press my palm to my chest as if I can slow my heart by pushing down on it. "How did you find me here?"

"I received your note last month. A man took me to Alice's house from the wharf on a moped that brought me here. I showed Alice my carte d'identité. Apparently, she knew who I was." He raises his eyebrows.

"Don't read anything into that." I march up the stairs and hug him, my anger seeping out leaving me empty. "I told Alice what a great friend you have been to me in the city."

Matante sighs. "So, he ain't the man you been waitin' for? The one be takin' you far away." I say nothing to her. "I go make some coffee," she says, before slipping back through the doorway.

I ignore her, too embarrassed about everything in Mapou. I drop my body into one of the two chairs on the porch. Alphonse follows suit. "Tell me why you're here." I grab his hand. "Oh, is it Henri?"

"No. But you need to go with me to Port-au-Prince to see with your own eyes. You won't believe me if I tell you." He shakes his head from side to side. His face, a mask of disbelief. "Perhaps after that…you'll be able to move on with your life."

"Are you crazy? I'm not going to Port-au-Prince. I'm scared. Do you understand that? Just tell me what I need to see."

He covers my hand with his. "I drove Simone to the airport yesterday. She'll be gone for a month." He pauses, staring at the woman going by on a mule. "She went to see Henri. I heard her talking to someone on the phone. She said Henri refused to answer her calls. They have not spoken since she exiled him."

I drop his hands and stand, feeling triumphant. "You see, Alph? Henri loves me and is upset about what his mother did to separate us. He'll come back."

Alphonse looks across the street at the church as if looking for help. I see sadness in his dark eyes. "Let's go tomorrow. You know how much I hate water. I wouldn't have gotten on that ferry if it wasn't *really* important. Shadow went to his village while Simone is out of the country. It's safe."

Later that evening, Alphonse and I sit in the darkness staring at the stars, talking about the unfairness of life.

"I've been driving Simone for over three years now. She speaks openly in front of me as if I'm invisible."

I touch his arm. "I know. She used to let me stand in her office with a long-handled fan for hours in case a fly might touch her skin."

We sigh at the same time and laugh through sadness. "But you know, Alph, the only difference between her and *us* is her money."

Alphonse harrumphs. "Don't forget her almost white skin, green eyes and long brown hair. These characteristics are currency in this country."

"Because people like *us* make it so. We need to value ourselves more." I stroke the dark skin on the back of my hand. "I'm going to be somebody, Alph, with or without Henri. Papa spent hard-earned money to send me to Parochial school in Lasalle. I promised him."

He pats my hand. "For a seventeen-year- old, Kekette, you're very smart. You can do anything."

This morning, before dawn, we are on the wharf. I could hardly sleep last night from the excitement of going to Port-au-Prince. This island is crushing my spirit. When the ferry docks in Montrouis, people shove, and stumble to get off. I slip into one of Matante's floral print muumuu over my clothes, tie my head with one of her cotton scarves and instinctively round my shoulders.

Holding my hand, Alphonse elbows his way across the street. What is it he wants me to see that he can't tell me? My palms are sweating now. Across the street sits Simone's car. It seems like years since I rode in it with her on our way to her department store.

"I'm not getting in her car." I stop in the middle of the street. I hear the honks before I see a car careening toward me.

Alphonse yanks me out of the way and pushes me against the car. "I told you she's gone," he says, trying to hide his irritation.

I'm too tired and scared to argue. I climb into the passenger seat and scoot down just in case. I crack the window down.

"Where're we going?" I ask when I see the edge of the city.

"You want something to eat?"

"We're not on a date, Alphonse," I say, anger coating the words. I'm angry he can't make me love him no matter how hard he's tried. Life would be so much easier for me. But I love Henri. I will never love another man. I cannot. "I'm sorry, Alph."

He takes his eyes off the road long enough to stare at me with a hurt puppy-look. "We're almost there."

"Alph—" I stop when the car enters the cemetery. "Wait! Why are we here?" I sit up to my full height more curious than afraid.

Alphonse stops the car. I'm already out by the time he comes around to open my door. I follow him, intrigued, and spooked. Is Auntie Yvette buried here? Did she forgive me, as she took her last smoky breath? I wipe the tears blurring my vision. We pass old and new graves. I try to read names and dates, but he plunges ahead. I trot to keep up.

When Alphonse stops in front of two shiny headstones, I bump into his back before moving to stand next to him. I read the names and blink to clear my sight. I must be going blind on the spot. The taller one reads: Ketly Murat Beloved Mother 1963-1980. The small one next to it says: Baby Murat Beloved Daughter 1980-1980.

"Alphonse," I say in three syllables. "Wha…what is this?"

"Now you see why I couldn't explain it, Ketly. Simone held *your* funeral service two days ago for her employees. She told them that you went to Lasalle to give birth and you, and the baby died. No one knew who the father was. She brought the bodies here knowing how much you wanted to make Port-au-Prince your home. She invited all your former co-workers to a lavish repast."

Alphonse inhales and shakes his head. "She even cried, when she read the death certificates."

I swivel my head so fast my neck creaks. "Death certificates? But how…I'm alive. My baby's alive."

Alphonse grunts. "Oh Ketly, you're so naïve. You can have whatever you want in Haiti if you're Madame Simone."

"But…but, you know I'm not dead, did you say anything?"

He narrows his eyes at me until I look away in shame. Would I have said something to contradict Simone in front of the public and jeopardize my life, my family, my livelihood? I take several steps back from the headstones to distance myself from this macabre scene. Now I know why Simone went to see Henri. She wants to show him proof that I'm dead. That his new family is gone. I straighten my shoulders.

"You're right Alphonse, I had to see this to believe it."

"Now you can forget about Henri. He won't come back, Kekette." He reaches for my hand. "But I'm here."

I squeeze his hand. "Alphonse, take me to Simone's house. Please."

He blinks several times, as if he can't see me. "Huh? Why…what you want there?"

My stomach churns with nausea. I close my eyes and breathe. "I have something to show Henri as well. But I need to get it from her house."

I climb back into the car and slam the door. I'm ready to fight Simone.

# CHAPTER THIRTEEN

## ADELE

Even though I went to bed after three this morning, I've been awake for a couple hours now. I stay in bed and listen to Mom's getting ready for church. I can't remember the last time I had so much fun. I massage my left foot, a blister sprouting under my big toe. I wish I'd shared this Haitian dancing experience with my husband.

Ben is married to his career and golf as if investment banking and sport save lives. He doesn't serve and protect anyone but the wealthy. Truth be told, I hate those stuffy country club affairs where people flaunt what they own and talk about trust funds and profits.

I yawn and my breath washes the remnant of sleep from my eyes. In addition to the rhum, I was intoxicated by the music, the Creole language, the heat, the food and the way people welcomed me as if I belonged. I flip on my back, just as Mom opens the door with both hands to stop any noise.

"I'm up, Mom. You look lovely." The blue dress I bought her yesterday almost matches her eyes.

"Thank you. I love this dress. Now I wish my hair wasn't so lazy and wimpish." She grins.

"You should have gone to the salon yesterday. I'll fix it."

I jump off the bed and run to the bathroom to pee and brush my teeth. After rubbing styling gel through mom's hair, I brush it away from her face before tucking it back with two of my silver combs.

"Who's picking you up today?"

"Flo," she says, sighing, "and she's always late."

Afraid something might happen to keep her home, I say, "I can take you."

"That would be great. I'll call Flo. Will you stay for service?"

"Oh, no! I'm not going to church. I mean…I'll drop you and you can come back with one of your friends."

"Well, I wish…" A car honks outside. "Never mind. It looks like Flo's on time for once after all."

I close the door behind her and peek around the blinds until the car backs out of the driveway. I rush into her room and start pulling open the dresser and nightstand drawers, my heart beating too fast. I stop and look around. "Okay, Adele, you need a system," I say, grabbing my hair off my face and tying it back with the rubber band around my wrist. I open one drawer at a time and search every nook. Nothing.

Her bedside clock tells me I've been at this for almost an hour. Her closet looms in the corner as if daring me. Grateful for the church picnic, I yank open the folding doors and take in the mountain of shoe boxes on the top shelf. I exhale and reach for the top one. Minutes later, I find a single key taped to the bottom of a red shoe she hasn't worn in years. I sit on the bed, suddenly afraid of what I'll find in the filing cabinet.

It takes two attempts to get the key into the lock. Inside the drawer is a gunmetal gray strongbox. I stroke the dull metal as if it's about to grant my most precious wish. I carry the box to the desk and sit on the chair. I lift the lid and stare at its contents. A yellowed square of pink satin rested on top of several manila envelopes. I bring the piece of fabric to my nose and inhale. The dust tickles my nose. I sneeze. I read the labels on the envelopes starting with the first one. Life Insurance Policy. Burial Contract. House Deed. Will and testament. The fourth one, the last in the pile makes my heart skid. *Adele.*

I replace the other envelopes back in the box. Steadying my hands with resolve, I peel the tape covering the clasp. I take a deep breath like someone ready to jump into an icy lake, before pulling out one sheet of paper.

*Bébé: Juliette born July 14, 1980*

*Miss Marge, please take my baby from Lasalle with you for safekeeping. I love her with all my heart, but I have to protect her from people who want to harm her. In December, her papa and I will come for her. God bless you.*

I close my eyes. "Juliette," I whisper. "Lasalle," trying my birth name and place in my dry mouth. I flip the sheet of paper to look at the back. There's nothing written on the other side. Why did Mom lie about the note or knowing, anything about my parents? Clearly my biological mother knew her and trusted her. What does this all mean? The weight of this discovery pulls my head down until it rests on the desk, and I cry tears of betrayal and hope. I hold the piece of paper that ties me to strangers I do not know, but whose blood runs through my body. "*Miss Marge,*" I whisper. "The person, *my mother*, knew my mom and knew she'd take care of me."

Now I must find out why Mom lied for so many years. Who wanted to harm me almost thirty years ago? My body feels heavy, and sleep lurks around the edges of my gritty eyes, but I know I can't sleep. I must talk to my PI. Although there's nothing new to add, except a confirmed date of birth. I dial his number and tap my foot with impatience.

"Hey, Adele, what's up?" he asks.

"Hi Wilner, I have an exact date of birth of July 14$^{th}$. Have you heard anything new since last week?"

"No, but I'm sending someone to Lasalle this week. Will call when I have news."

I end the call. I need to rein in my runaway mind. I fetch the kit I've been working on and lose myself in threading the needle through fabric until a bird emerges through my blurry vision.

Hours later, the doorbell pulls me from the couch. I rush to open it. "Addy, I'm glad you're here. I forgot my house key. I'm so forgetful." Mom stops in the middle of the living room. "You're crying?"

I shove the envelope toward her hand. She takes it. For the first time in my life, she looks at me with anger darkening her eyes. "You have no right," she says, walking to the sofa.

"You lied to me," I scream. She leans her shoulders against the back of the couch, fear flitting over her face. "Over the years, I've asked you many times if there was a note. *You lied.* You owed me the truth. What else are you hiding from me?"

Mom pulls a wad of tissue from her purse and wipes her eyes. "Now I hope you'll put going there to rest. You see…you see. It's not safe."

"What! No. Now more than ever, I must find out why they never came back for me. What happened to them?" I yell, unable to control my anger. "They planned to return for me." Mom's face turns purple. "How did you find me? I need to know."

"Let me rest a bit Addy. I don't feel well." She grabs a pillow from the couch and presses her face into it. "Never doubt that I love you more than my own life."

"The person who left me loves me, too. She said so. She knows you, maybe well. I sense trust between the lines."

"Addy, honey, I brought you home twenty-nine years ago and I never ask any questions."

"I'm going to Haiti in a few months. Nothing will stop me. You understand?" I sit next to her and take her shaking hands in mine. "Mom, please!"

Her eyes linger on my face like a caress, then she nods, and starts talking.

# CHAPTER FOURTEEN

## KETLY

*September 1980*

At the cemetery, Alphonse opens the car door and slides behind the wheel. I look at him sideways without turning my head. Tears spill over his shirt. What is he crying for? He's not being hunted. He's not missing a child. He's not buried alive. He's free to be. I can't shoulder the responsibility for his love. I want Henri. I want his arms around me, his kisses to swallow my despair, his laughter when I make funny faces. I want the two of us to be with Juliette. To be the family we planned. The one Alphonse wants to steal from Henri. I roll down the window as if the car cannot contain my pain. I hit everything my fists and legs connect with inside the car, screaming and banging my head against the seat. "I want Henri. I want Henri. I want—"

"*Shut up*, Ketly!" Alphonse yells before rolling up the window. He stops the car just outside the cemetery gate, then tries to clamp my mouth shut with his hand. I bite it. He yelps. A woman peddling grilled peanuts leans over to gawk at us. "Stop acting like a child."

I stop with Henri's name caught midway in my throat. I hiccup unable to make eye contact with Alphonse. "I'm sorry." I feel shame. "Alph, I need to go to Simone's house now. It can't wait."

"We can't go during the day. Her neighbors are home watching with nothing to do." He sneers. "We go tonight."

I take a final look back toward the cemetery, leaving my fresh tombstone and Juliette's behind. One day I'll be underground, but not today, Satan. I hum a gospel song to repel Simone's dark spirit. But now she'd told everyone we were dead, she needs to really kill me. I shiver.

We drive for several minutes. "You feel better now, Ketly?"

I shake my head. "I'm scared. I don't know what to do besides hiding from Simone until I can be with Juliette and Henri. He will come, Alph."

"Not when he learns you're both dead."

The words stab me with their reality. "That's why I have to go to Simone's house." I touch his shoulder. "I'm sorry, Alph. Thank you for everything, my friend."

He clears his throat. "I'll always help you, Kekette. I admire your strength and determination for a young person. You're brave. Don't ever lose that."

"Alph, I am a mother. I have a responsibility to my child. I must fight."

People ogle the car in this neighborhood. Skinny dogs bark. Flies buzz over the trash clogging the sewer. He parks in a small clearing on a dirt road. He appraises me with all the wisdom of his twenty-five years in his sad eyes. He raises his thumb. "One, Simone will never stop looking for you." Then his index finger. "Two, I hope Henri returns to at least place flowers on your tombstone." Middle goes up. "Three, you know how many young women he'll replace you—" he stops, perhaps, seeing the horror in my eyes. He shakes his head and steps out of the car, slamming the door. I follow him to one of the many food vendors lining up the street on both sides.

"*Pitit mwen*," the short woman says to Alphonse, her dark skin glistening in the heat of the day. "This beautiful girl must be the Ketly you been raving about, son?"

"Manmie," Alphonse says, looking down at the ground. He blows ashes from two low chairs facing a wide plank of wood nailed between two trees. "Have a seat, Kekette." He bends down to land a kiss on the woman's forehead. "Ketly's just a friend."

I kiss the woman's sweaty cheek and fight the urge to wipe my lips with the back of my hand. "Nice to meet you, Manmie," I say before sitting on one of the chairs. "Food smells good."

The early afternoon breeze fights with the heat coming from the blazing charcoals under a big vat of soup Manmie stirs with a long-handled wooden spoon.

"I'll get you two some food. It's almost ready," she says, placing two cold bottles of Cola Couronne from the cooler on the ground in front of us.

My stomach growls, reminding me I was too nervous this morning before the ferry ride to eat anything. People bring their own containers to buy the soup. Alphonse pulls out a cigarette from somewhere in his shirt pocket.

"When did you start smoking?" I ask.

He shrugs. "It relieves stress."

"Not good for your health, I heard."

He takes a couple puffs, blowing the smoke away from me before pinching the red tip between his fingers and securing the butt behind his right ear. Mamie places two steaming bowls in front of us. We dig into our food almost at the same time, the spoons soon hitting the bottom of the aluminum bowls. We look at each other and smile, the deep furrows of his brow flattening out.

Satiated, I lean my chair against the tree, the two front legs up in the air and close my eyes. I burp loudly before sleep pulls me under with a belly full of food and my head overflowing with ideas. I don't know how much time has passed before the tap on my thigh jerks me awake. Alphonse's arm stops my tumble from the chair when the front legs hit the ground.

"Manmie wants me to take you to the house for a proper nap. We still have a few hours before nightfall to go to Madame… to Simone's house."

I look at Manmie. She's busy scooping food into bowls and cups. Her eyes catch mine. She waves the wooden ladle at me. "It's okay, child." She smiles. "Get some rest."

Her caring face makes me long for Mama. I haven't seen her since the day Miss Marge left with my baby. It's only been a couple of months, but I need Mama to hold me as much as I want to hold Juliette.

I kiss her cheek. "Thank you, Manmie. Food was delicious."

Hours later, I open my eyes, the room is dark, and I hear crickets outside the window. I jump up and run out of the room to use the outhouse. Alphonse's leaning against the railing of the back porch, smoking a cigarette.

"What time is it?"

He peers at his watch in the glow of the cigarette. "It's a few minutes before nine. We'll leave soon. Simone's neighbors don't venture out much after dark. They have everything they need at home."

"Umm… Alph…is it safe?"

He touches my arm. "Nothing will happen to you, Kekette. I'm here."

I can only squeeze his fingers.

Shortly after, sweat dampens my armpits in the cool car. What if Simone's back and Shadow's there with her? They'd kill me and place my body underneath the tombstone for real. Can Alphonse protect us both? I cast a look at his slight frame. His narrow shoulders as he steers the wheel with both hands betray his brave words. He parks at the foot of the hill that leads to Simone's house, and we walk the rest of the way. He opens the side door into the dining room with one of the many keys on the ring he carries with him.

Memories flood the pit of my stomach, filling it with anger that replaces my fright; me standing for hours watching Simone eat while my feet swelled, and my back protested as her granddaughter grew in my belly. I walk straight into her den, sit on the swivel chair, and open the desk drawer.

At the bottom of a pile of mail, I find what I need. A letter from Henri with his address in Paris on the envelope. My hands shake as I pull it out. I sniff it. The faint aroma of Henri's aftershave lingers on the thin paper.

*August 1, 1980*

*Maman,*

*This is the first and last letter I'll write to you. I will never forgive you for tearing me away from Ketly and my child who are somewhere out there and I'm not with them. I love Ketly. I will return for her in December. I want nothing to do with you. Ever.*

*Henri*

I wipe my eyes with the hem of my skirt before taking a sheet of paper and pen from Simone's drawer.

*September 12, 1980*

*My Love,*

*Despite the death certificates, I am well and alive. Juliette was born on July 14th and she's your carbon copy including the green eyes. She is safe. I'm hiding in Terreville. When you get off the ferry, find Madame Alice Portier. She'll bring you to me. Meanwhile, please send me letters in her care. See you soon.*

*All my love,*

*Kekette*

This morning, I mail the letter to Henri before Alphonse drives me to the wharf. He pulls me in for a hug. "I'll get in touch if I hear anything, Kekette." Then he pushes me toward the ferry.

Back on the island, I hoist my bag over my shoulder, shade my eyes from the glaring sun and make my way to Alice's house. I climb the steps and yell, "Ali, Ali…you home?"

Alice comes from her bedroom at the back of the house, holding her baby with one arm over her shoulder while trying to button her blouse with the other. Her pink lipstick matches her skirt. "Well, where you come from?" she asks, looking down at my bag. "Did you have a nice visit with Alphonse. He seems like a nice man."

"I went to Port-au-Prince yesterday."

She stops midway to the living room. "You what?"

"I'm sorry I didn't stop by before, but we would have missed the early ferry. Wait till I tell you what I saw."

Alice calls her cook and asks her to serve papaya juice with lunch. We settle on the sofa in the parlor, and I tell her.

She blinks when I stop. "*O merde!* Good thinking about alerting Henri." She shakes her head. "Simone's the devil. When's his birthday in December?"

"The seventeenth." I try to count the days in my head. "He may come before when he gets my letter. I hope." I squeeze her knee. "I'll miss you."

"I'll miss you, too, Kekette." She pats my hand. "I hope everything works out the way you dream it."

"It's not a dream. Henri and I are going to be together for the rest of our lives with Juliette."

"But…what if you can't find Juliette? Do you know where that woman is? America's a big place, you know."

"I know where she lives," I say, rolling my eyes. "I told you she's in Florida."

Alice snorts. "And I told you how big Florida is. I've really only been to south Florida with Raoul when we visit his sister in Miami." She must see the silent scream on my face. "Don't mind me, sweetie. I'm sure Henri has the resources to find Juliette."

I raise the cold glass to my forehead and roll it over my warm brow. I sip then reach for the sleeping baby in her arms. His smell feeds my hunger and fills me with hope. Henri will find our baby and he'll understand why I had to let her go for safekeeping.

We talk until supper time. Raoul comes home from the Lycée where he's been preparing for school re-opening in October. "Hi, Ketly, how've you been?"

I smile. "I'm great, Raoul. Will be even better soon."

He shares a look with Alice after kissing her cheek. We move to the dining room for the meals. Eddy grabs all the attention. His Papa picks him up and launches him in the air. The boy giggles. When Raoul puts him down, Alice runs her palm over her son's sweaty face and kisses the top of his head. He runs to me and tries to climb onto my lap. I lift him up to my chest, inhaling his little boy's smell of mischief before putting him down.

Later, when I get home from Galette, Matante is already asleep. But there are two people snoring on a mat on the front room floor. Matante has visitors. I'm glad I'm leaving soon. This place cannot hold so many bodies and my secret. I wash up in the back of the house under a brilliant moon, before crawling into bed. I roll my body almost in the fetal position as if to keep my happiness from evaporating into the night.

# CHAPTER FIFTEEN

## ADELE

Mom sips from the glass of iced tea I pour for her from the kitchen, as I lift her swollen legs and rest them on a throw pillow on the coffee table. I sit next to her on the couch. Waiting. She's going to tell me the truth. Finally.

"Thank you, baby." She heaves a deep sigh and stares at the Haitian painting of the little girl washing clothes by a river on the living room wall. "One of my favorite pieces," Mom says, closing her eyes. "Always reminds me of the children. So many of them."

I touch her shoulder, shaking the envelope with the note. "Mom, how…?"

She shifts and turns to look at me. "Addy, after my first medical mission trip to Haiti in 1970 my two passions had merged, nursing and becoming a mommy. There were so many babies. Haitian women must be the most fertile in the world." She smiles. "I learned a lot about the human spirit from Haiti and its people, especially the women."

"So, you went to Haiti for ten years before I was born? That explains why you speak the language so well."

She nods. "I was in nursing school in Boston when I met this Haitian student. We became friends and later roommates. On many occasions I went to Haiti with her on spring breaks and holidays. Helène Macombe was from an elite Haitian family. Later, I'd realize how different she was from the Haitians I cared for at the clinic."

"What do you mean?"

"She was very wealthy; well, her family was." Mom sips more iced tea. "Compared to the people in Lasalle, her family lived indecently well in a country like Haiti."

"What were the people in Lasalle like? You ever see anyone with green eyes?"

"No." She touches my cheek with the back of her warm hand. "The people in Lasalle were for the most part poor, hard-working, un-educated…but grateful. They all wanted better for their children, but life was challenging."

"It's hard to believe that no one knows who I belong to in a small village."

Mom presses my hands between hers. "For years, I went every July for one week of medical mission. Going to Haiti became my annual dose of reality, the salve that healed my aching childless heart. The night before the group was scheduled to return home in 1980, I had lain down on the thin foam mattress on the cement floor of the clinic after saying my prayers when I heard a whimper. I placed my small inflatable pillow over my ear and closed my eyes. I was exhausted from a long day." She lets go of my hands.

She raises the glass to her lips and slurps an ice cube from the tea. "Mom, who was it?" I touch her cheek.

"The whimper turned into full-blown wailing. Unable to ignore it, I opened the wooden window and peered through the darkness using my flashlight. I saw nothing at first and the crying had stopped. I held my breath and waited for Haitian nocturnal symphony. Soon, the drumbeats cascading down the mountains drowned all sounds at times faint and then strong as the wind carried the rhythm. Drums in the countryside delivered news of births, marriages, deaths, harvests, and religious ceremonies. The locals read the beats like paging through a daily newspaper."

"Oh. What did the beats say that night?"

"I didn't know, honey." She shrugs. "So, I peered into the night. The sky, the trees, the ground blended into an impenetrable black ball. Precious resources like kerosene, candles, pine sticks, were used with purpose in Lasalle. As my eyes adjusted, I marveled at the multitude of stars in the invisible sky. They seemed to hang from nothing like exploded fireworks before they reached the ground. I rcmember swatting at something that landed on my face from the open window, and I yelped. The wail came again from below. I looked down."

"Was it me?" My hands moisten. I wipe them on my dress. "Did you see anyone?"

She shakes her head and pulls the yellowed piece of satin from the envelope. "No, Addy, but the brightness of the pink satin blanket broke through the darkness. It moved with the next cry. I stepped outside and directed the beam of the flashlight into a box under the window. It caught the white parts of two shiny marbles. Wet green eyes blinked."

Mom looks at me as if searching for the baby in the blanket. I don't blink this time for fear she might stop talking.

"I picked you up." She scoots closer to me on the couch. "You reached your pudgy hand to my face as if you wanted to say something." She chuckles. "I knew right then that I would *never* let you go. God had given me my child. Perfect with no missing parts. I found the note underneath your body."

"So did you tell the other missionaries?"

"Miss Annette was the director of the clinic and lived in a small house behind it. As I waited for her to open her door, I had to think fast. You looked white. I thought you were white. I told her an American friend wanted me to take you to the US to hide you from her abusive husband until she could escape herself. We planned how she'd board the bus the next day with you, in case someone was watching the missionaries as we left Lasalle. It worked."

"But you did find out more later. Didn't you? Who are my parents, Mom?" I hold my breath.

"I'm sorry, Addy. I don't know…anything else." She gazes at the painting. "I never returned to Haiti after I brought you home three months later. *Never.*"

"Oh." Hope leaks out of my body. I slump against the back of the couch. "Where did you leave me?"

"I left you with Helène who was working at the American embassy in Port-au-Prince at that time while they processed the adoption papers. With her help, I was able to bring you home in October. You know in Haiti one can get things done with connection and money. Not that we did anything illegal. You see in the note; your biological mother wanted me to take you to America." She smiles. "I went to see you in August and September though. It broke my heart every time I had to leave you behind."

"Did I cry when you left?"

"Oh yes! You'd cling to me when I handed you to Helène before getting in the car that would take me back to the airport. I held you the whole weekend when I was there. She would chastise me playfully, because after I left, her staff at home couldn't get any work done from having to carry you everywhere." She leans over and kisses my cheek. "You were a spoiled brat." She grins.

"You're the best mother." She looks away. "I'm going to look for *her*. I'll start in Lasalle."

She drops her legs off the table as she shrieks, "After everything I've told you? I will not allow it, Adele." She grabs my hands as if to keep me home. "You can't go to Haiti. Please, stop this…this obsession. It's dangerous. You read the letter."

"Mom." I raise my voice. "Finding my parents is not an obsession. How can you say that? Besides, that was a long time ago."

"Adele," Mom stomps her foot, "even the poorest Haitian mothers don't abandon their children in the middle of the night. So, you know, she must have been desperate and terrified."

"Why didn't you at least go back the following year to find out why my…I mean the woman who left me never came back to look for me? I believe something…possibly bad has kept them away. I need to find out what. You could have gone back to find her. She trusted *you* with her child."

Mom pulls in her lips into a straight line as if to keep the words from spilling out. "I was afraid that someone would know that I have you. After a decade of missions, I was well known in the village." She heaves herself up from the sofa, her eyes landing on everything in the living room, except my face. "I have nothing else to tell you." She leaves the envelope on the coffee table and shuffles to her bedroom.

Mom knows more than she's telling me. Why? The note is addressed to *her*. My biological mother knew her and wanted her to take me. She cannot possibly be afraid of losing me now. I'll always be her daughter. Now I know my birth parents wanted me back. Since they could not come for me, then I must go to them.

# *CHAPTER SIXTEEN*

❀❀❀

# KETLY

*December 1980*

December seems so far away, although it'll be here in a couple weeks. To kill time, I volunteer at the school and the church in Mapou. I find that I love to teach children to discover the joy of reading and to read the Bible to the adults who cherish it so much. Soon, the church ladies offer to pay me a stipend to teach a literacy class for adults.

In the morning, I fetch water from the river that runs behind our house in Mapou and wash our clothes after fixing breakfast and tidying up the place. I walk to the school and lose myself in the joy of children's innocence.

Most weekends with Alice in Galette, we do our nails, press our hair, and now like her, I wear makeup sometimes just to sit on the porch watching people gawk at us as if we are celebrities or freaks.

"I love this plum lipstick, Ali." I smack my lips together and smile at my friend.

"It looks beautiful with your skin tone," Alice says. "You can have it. Consider it one of your Christmas presents." She winks.

"Alice, why do you suppose Henri hasn't written to me in almost two months?" I scoot my chair closer to hers on the porch. "What if he didn't receive my letter? What if he'd left Paris? What if—" I remember Alphonse's words. Has Henri met beautiful young women in the city of lights? Was I too late in reaching out to him? How long does it take for a letter to travel between Haiti and France? My head hurts from thinking so much.

"Henri will be here this month," Alice says. "Stop fretting."

Back in Mapou, I focus my attention on Victor, a boy who lives next door. Seated around the small table with the lamp between us, I help him with homework, and I tell him stories of faraway places. I study Matante's face as she bends over a tattered piece of clothing with needles and thread trying to add more life into it. She looks up and her gummy smile shrouds her eyes in wrinkles. Her few remaining teeth seem to shift in the jerking shadow of the flame. I can't let Henri see how we live. Matante will say something backward, or worse Henri might mention Juliette. I don't want to ask him to lie. Best I meet him down in Galette. Living in Mapou is like being spit out by the sea and left to rot away from civilization. Not for me. I want to live in a big city and go to school. I want to be a missionary nurse and help people in need. I look down at the homework Victor's struggling with, almost ashamed of my thoughts about Matante and this village. Almost.

In the first week of December, after we let the students out, I pull up the single chair in the room and sit facing Denise's back as she erases the day's vocabulary words off the small chalkboard.

"Denise."

"Mm," she mumbles, not turning around.

"I'm going down to Galette at the end of the week, and I won't be back."

"Oh. What's in Galette?"

I take a deep breath and tell her about Henri coming for me. How Simone exiled him to keep us apart. But nothing about Juliette.

"Ketly, I'm happy for you." She hugs me. "You still have a few days before the seventeenth. Don't forget the Christmas pageant for the kids."

"I know. But…but I don't want Henri showing up here." I look away, unable to hold her gaze.

Denise leans on the rickety desk, her face a blank slate like the board she's just erased. "I understand."

"Denise, I didn't mean—"

She slaps the air with her palm. "You should teach once you're settled into your beautiful life, Ketly. You're a natural."

I hold her hand. "Thank you for everything. But I'm going to be a nurse."

"Same thing. You'll teach and heal. Come see me before you leave. I mean… if you have time, of course."

I say nothing.

On Wednesday evening, while Matante's at church, I start packing. Victor closes his notebook to stare at me, understanding peeking into his addled brain. Minutes later, the door bangs against the wall, shaking the faded picture of Jesus in the cracked frame. She stands in the middle of the room peering at me, hurt glazing her eyes.

"When you were gon' tell me you leavin, Ketly?" she asks. I open my mouth. She raises her hand over her head, and I think she's about to break into testimony. "I had to find out from Denise that you leavin' and not comin' back. Huh!"

I fold and refold the same dress. "You showed up here…what end of July as if you been chased by the devil hisself. I open my door, cause you my brother's child. You told me some crazy tale about some man who be coming to take you away. Now five months gone, I ain't see nobody. You just like the young ones here who spend a bit of time in the big city, and they think they better than everybody, 'cause they seen cars, lights, big houses and folks with all their teeth."

I blink fast, but tears run down my cheeks. It's as if Matante's reading my mind. But who can blame me? Who would willingly want to live here? Nothing wrong with teeth. I refrain from sucking mine. "I'm sorry, Auntie."

"I hope you know what you doin', child, and I pray for you tonight, so your prince show up and whisk you back to fanciness."

Matante lumbers to the back room. I sit in the chair next to Victor and drop my face into my palms in shame.

"Why you're leaving?" Victor asks, with an accusation in his in-between boy and man's voice.

"Go home, Vic. It's getting late."

After he leaves, I move over to Matante's chair and close my eyes. I hope God listens to her prayer tonight and that one day I have lights, cars, house, my diploma, my child and keeping my teeth for a long time. Is that too much to ask?

The next day in Galette, Christmas lights blink from the Catholic church across the park. The police station displays a single string of clear lights with many missing bulbs around its low tin roof. But people flock onto the streets in search of something more than food and essentials. They need *zétrennes* to put under meager trees or under beds for children who never receive gifts throughout the year.

"Hey, welcome back," Alice says, taking my hand and pulling me inside. The moped driver drags my bag onto the porch.

"Thank you, Ali." I follow her to the small bedroom at the back of the house where I've been staying when I visit. The full-sized bed is covered in a bright red comforter with green vines running through it. A four-dresser drawer and a cane-backed chair with a small table complete the furnishings. I jump on the bed and throw a pillow at her, smiling.

"You smile so much your dimples are getting deeper." Alice laughs. "I'm sure gonna miss you. As you can see everybody here acts like they're so old they're about to die, even the women my age. They get married and they think life's over. Of course, I've never been admitted into the *club*." Alice makes quotation marks with her index fingers. "I'm not a native. Apparently, Raoul had many dibs on him." We giggle, then she turns serious. "I'm going to tell you how I ended up here." She closes the bedroom door behind her. "I don't tell people here about me." Alice continues. "Raoul found me in Port-au-Prince. Never knew my father. My mother went to Nassau when I was nine, leaving me with a neighbor who threw me out at fourteen when we never heard from my mama and the money stopped coming." Alice sniffs. "At sixteen, I had a baby daughter and no home. Raoul brought us here. Sadly, my daughter died a month later. I enrolled in the Lycée and he sent me to university in Port-au-Prince to train as a teacher. People talked." She licks her lips. "Raoul never touched me. Frankly, I thought he was gay." She smiles. "He married me five years ago on my twenty-third birthday. Sometimes I miss the city, but I owe Raoul so much. I'm…stuck here, but I feel safe on this island."

"But you love him, right?"

She looks at her red-painted nails for a long time, a diamond ring adorning her short finger. "You're probably too young to understand the cruelties of life, Kekette."

"Raoul's a good man, Ali."

"Yes. He is. But a man can't give you what you want that he doesn't have. You understand?"

I think I do. Like Alphonse. I throw my arms around her neck and sniff her Cashmere Bouquet fragrance. "Let's go shopping for my new dress. Oh, your hair's straight."

"Finally put a relaxer in it. No more hot combs and fighting with the humidity on this island." Alice shakes her hair. "I made an appointment for you."

"I don't have money for that, Ali. And how do I maintain it? Don't you have to touch up new growth every couple of months or so?"

Alice sucks her teeth. "Don't worry. Soon you'll be able to afford to go to upscale hair salons anywhere in the world, right?"

I push my shoulders back. "Yeah! When I'm *Madame Henri*. Tell you what, when you come visit, we'll go together. On *moi*." We laugh for a long time.

Later that afternoon, we hit the town and stop at the few stores that carry dresses. I slip a red ruffle-tier chiffon sleeveless tunic over my head behind a curtain in the store in the center of town. I move a box away so I can see my body in the pitted mirror on the wall. The short dress showcases my long-toned legs. I change into my clothes and walk out with the dress draped over my arm.

Today's finally Henri's birthday. At the end of it, I will have to decide my future. I roll out of bed before anybody else and put on the red dress, I style my newly permed hair, apply makeup and slip out of the house before Alice wakes up to stop me. At seven in the morning, I'm sitting on a bench behind the swaying branches of a big Seagrape tree where I can see everything, an unopen book on my lap. Ferries, private boats, and canoes drop passengers all day. By the time the last ferry pulls in at sundown, my dress is drenched with sweat and tears I didn't realize I'd wept. My stomach growls and my throat aches from dryness. Yet I sit, staring at the inky sea as it blends into the horizon to touch the sky. What if I just walk in? How far can I reach before I go under and disappear with all my pain and shame? I have nothing but some clothes and…Juliette. I have my baby. I can let Henri go, but how does a mother let go of her child?

The touch on my shoulder prods me like an electric shock. I peer through the faint grimy light of the streetlamp at Alice's face. "Let's go home," she says.

We stroll through the streets of Galette. I've never seen so many people on this island in the six months I've been here. They laugh. They sing. They're living life here as a final destination. Not a place one waits to be rescued from.

I stop in front of the two-story building that houses the Lycée. My future is my education. The one thing nobody can take away from me. "Ali, I'm going to complete my secondary studies here. I want to go to nursing school. I'm ready."

She throws her arms around my neck. "Oh, Kekette, that's a great idea. You're a smart girl. You'll be an awesome Miss."

A ray of hope pierces through the darkness in my heart and lightens my steps."

A week later, on Christmas Eve, as I approach the market, someone calls my name. "Kekette, you're still here?" Victor says. "Matante said you were going on a plane. I miss you."

"I miss you too, Vic." I run my palm over his head. He wraps his short arms around my waist. "How's Matante?" I ask, annoyed that nothing's a secret on this damn island.

"Her stomach bothers her. She wants me to pick up some medicine while I'm here."

"I'll pray for her." I wish I had some change to give him. I spent all my money on the red dress.

I stay in the bedroom, staring at the ceiling for a week, wondering why Henri did not come, while I plan my return to school. I didn't even go to church with Alice and her family on Christmas day. I need time and space for myself. Her devoted husband, her cute boys, her happiness needle my sadness. If I'm honest, I am jealous of it all.

A week after New Year's Day, Alice comes into the bedroom and moves clothes and books off the chair and sits down. I lower the book I'm reading down on my chest. "Honey, I'm so sorry to ask you this, but Raoul's sister's coming from Miami with her family next week for his fiftieth birthday. I need the room." She scoots off the chair and wraps me in a tight hug. I blink, trying to understand what she's saying. Where does she want me to go? Not Mapou. Please no. "Raoul will drive you to Mapou later."

She kisses my forehead and leaves the room. I put the pillow over my head and pray God for wisdom and patience. How do I plan a future in Mapou? Everything is coming at me too damn fast.

# CHAPTER SEVENTEEN

## ADELE

The elevator in this senior building is as stubborn as its residents. I jab the up button and tap my foot as if it'll make it come faster. Seconds later, I bound up the stairs. Climbing them to the twelfth floor will be my exercise for the day.

"What a surprise!" Beulah says, pulling me inside her apartment, her eyes scanning the hallway before she closes the door to her unit. "Gladys already rang my doorbell twice to ask what time is Mass today? She thinks it's Sunday. Poor soul."

I follow Beulah into the kitchen and place the shopping bag on the table. Earlier this week, she'd asked me to get her some green and yellow yarn for the quilts our group is knitting for the shelters before the winter. They're more sentimental than practical but the babies love bright colors. "I wasn't expecting you, Addy. Isn't your birthday party today?"

"Not till much later. I was in the neighborhood." She pours orange juice in two glasses for us in her small kitchen, and we sit around the table. "Wish you'd come."

She shakes her head. The salt and pepper wig moves slightly to the left. "There's a band playing downstairs later and this new tenant...Eugene...he asked me to be his date." She giggles.

I clear my throat. "Well, Miss Beulah, what happened to ...umm...Paul. I thought you two were an item."

"Paul's so last month, Girlie." She smiles and the remnant of youth peeks from behind her twinkling brown eyes. "At my age, you take what you want when you want it." She grabs a fistful of air before slamming her hand down on the table with a force that belies her frail physique. "Did you invite your new friend to your party...the one you're traveling with to find your mama? Last week you were all twisted in a knot about it."

"I did, but I hope he doesn't come. I don't want Ben to...I don't know. I never told anyone this, but if I wasn't married, I'd definitely see what's under JR's hood."

Beulah collapses into gales of laughter. I join in. We laugh until tears run down our cheeks. "Well, Addy, back in my days, having a man pining for me added sizzle to my marriages. I hope it's doing the same to yours."

I rub my chin, turning serious. "Ben is...so conventional in the bedroom. I wish he'd...you know—"

"Add more spices to his recipes?" She bats what remains of her eyelashes.

"*Recipe*," I say, making a sad face. "Singular."

"Oh dear!" She grunts and reaches for the bottle of vodka from the freezer and pours some in our glasses. We sip our drinks and talk about past love, passion, and expectations. I hug her hard when I stand to leave.

"Don't do anything I wouldn't do, tonight," I tease.

"I don't know about you, but I'm doing *something*." She winks. "Eugene just doesn't know it yet. He best takes his li'l blue pill."

The sound of her laughter peels off my anxiety and carries me all the way to my car.

Tonight, the light beige hue of my silk dress blends into my skin, the fabric hugging my curves. I run the red lipstick over my lips and smack them together. Even with air conditioning, it's too hot for any more than that and some mascara. The truth is the sweat misting my face is not the July heat but my nerves. I cross the length of the master bedroom through the sitting room perched on roman columns over the swimming pool below. Once more, I wonder how my childhood home can fit into this master suite and still have room for a garden. Who needs this much space to house two regular-size bodies? The doorbell rings and I hasten my steps down the staircase to the foyer.

My husband rushes toward the front door and ushers in Mom and Nadine before closing the massive oak door.

"Welcome, welcome ladies," Ben says, looping his arms through theirs and guiding them toward the family room. "I'll go fix your usual." He squints at mom's face. "Marge did you stay in the sun too long today?" She looks like a bruised tomato.

"I yelled at her from my porch to go inside," Nadine says in her loud voice, patting her forehead with a tissue, long braids framing her round face. "Marge fell asleep in the sun again." She shakes her head.

I hug my mother and Nadine and follow them to the sectional sofa in the family room. Ben walks in with two glasses, but I know one is a diet drink for Mom and the other with the slice of lime perched over the rim, a Cuba Libre for Nadine made with five-star Haitian rhum Barbancourt.

Minutes later, I skip to the door when it rings, wondering if it's JR behind it. The two musketeers glide in. Ninnie seems to collect all the air within her grasp wherever she goes, and Lisa uses only what she needs.

"Hey, hey, happy birthday, Addy," Ninnie sings, enveloping me in her arms. "Man, I can't believe we're twenty-nine. I don't know about you two, but I feel oh, nineteen."

"I know, right?" Lisa says, spitting a strand of red hair out of her mouth. "Seems like we were just in pre-school."

"To think next year we'll be thirty," Ninnie says, groaning. "We're getting old." She taps the top of my head. Hard. "Well, at least you're finally reaching your goal of going to Haiti before thirty."

Nadine glares at her daughter. Ben narrows his eyes at Ninnie. Mom's back comes off the sofa as if her spine is released from compression. A flash of anger overrides the tomato red on her cheeks and replaces it with eggplant purple. Ninnie squints at the three people shooting daggers into her. "What…what did I say?" She glares at the trio. "She's going. So!"

"What are you talking about Ninnie?" Ben asks while staring at me. "It's too dangerous for Adele to go there."

Before I can answer, Ninnie points to Nadine, "Hey Ben, I'll have what my mom's having. And…" He halts his steps toward the bar and turns to look at Ninnie. "Adele's a grown woman. She can do whatever the hell she wants."

I step between my husband and my friend. At the rate those two fight, they should be married to each other. Ben and I don't fight. Although, I hear make-up sex is great, but I wouldn't know. I used to brag about my peaceful marriage to my co-workers until one told me maybe my union lacks passion. It takes strong feelings to disagree, to debate and to come together somewhere in the middle. Ben and I are like two fighters who stay in our corners to avoid hurting each other. I take Ninnie's arm and pull her away from Ben. "Come Liss, let me show you my birthday gift in the garage."

"Nice Jag," Ninnie says, closing the garage door behind her. The heat assaults us with a slap. "The color matches your eyes." She lowers her voice. "Is JR coming? Can't wait to meet him."

I clear my throat. "I don't know. Maybe he won't. Too much pressure."

"What pressure?" Lisa asks.

"I need to tell Ben tonight that I'd bought my ticket to go to Haiti in December and hiring the PI."

"But you've been telling them all since…forever that you want to go find your bios. So, what's the problem?" Ninnie sucks her teeth. "You know, I'd go with you if my beau hadn't surprised me with a trip to Europe for Christmas."

"I know." I open the door. "Let's go back in. Time to eat."

The five-course dinner from my favorite Jamaican restaurant infuses the air with its spicy aroma. The curried cabbage makes my mouth water as the jerk sauce smothering the goat tickles my nose. Ben keeps filling my glass from a bottle of wine I suspect costs more than my weekly paycheck. Tonight, I let myself go.

Ben dims the overhead fixture and lights the six candles in the candelabra on the dining room table. The potpourri of fragrance peels off my tension as I sip my wine. I am glad we had removed two leaves from the cherry dining table to make it cozier. I sit at the head of the table and smile at Ben, sitting at the other end. Ninnie and Lisa are on my right and Mom and Nadine are on my left. Wandering eyes linger at the empty place setting next to my mother.

As I stroll by to go change the CD on the stereo in the den, I lean over and kiss Ben's lips. He tastes like dessert. He kisses the tips of my fingers. My body tingles. I twirl on my way back to the dining room. Ben pushes his chair back and takes me in his arms. My head stops under his chin. I lay my face on his sculpted chest and listen to the rhythm of his heart, closing my eyes tightly as if I could hear his feelings. I lead Ben to sway to the beat of the Haitian konpa, unable to feel the intensity of the night I danced with JR last weekend.

"Ben, you dance like the half Black part of you has been murdered," Ninnie says, laughing and slapping her thigh.

"Shut up, Eugenie," Nadine says. "Look at that love." She shakes her head. "Why can't you find a nice man like Ben. I don't care if he's green or blue, alien or human. Just find a man and keep him."

Nadine's the only person who calls her daughter Eugenie without fear of bodily harm. Ninnie hates the name and when we were kids, she swore to legally change it but once she met her maternal grandmother whose name she bears, she couldn't do it. Doesn't mean she likes it though.

"Mom, this is 2009." Ninnie cuts her eyes at her mother. "I'm a professional, independent woman. I don't need a man to be complete. It's beautiful when it works like with Lisa and Adele. But I'm not the marrying type."

Mom shifts her weight in her chair. I know she's looking for a white flag to throw in the ring between Nadine and Ninnie. As for me, I want to delay the end of the party. I know Ben has something up his sleeve besides this dinner tonight and the new car. I only hope it doesn't interfere with my plan.

"What a beautiful cake, Ben," Mom says. "Did the restaurant make it?"

"Yes. It's a multi-layered cake like my wife." He smiles, walking me to my chair when the song ends. He pulls the chair out for me and kisses the top of my head.

"You can have a big piece, Mom," I say. "It's a special occasion. It's not every day your only child turns twenty-nine." I throw her a kiss and stand holding my glass.

Ben stands next to me and takes my hand. One of the catering staff moves the cake from the buffet to the dining room table along with plates and forks. Ben raises my hand to his lips and kisses my palm. I shiver.

"Addy I'm going to make your dream comes true." My heart dances in my chest. I was wrong. Ben has been listening to me. He knows what I want most in the world. Not this museum, not the expensive car, not the jewelry. He must be going to Haiti with me. I smile and squeeze his fingers. "Honey, I book us a trip to Europe. I know how much you want to go to Italy. We have a bungalow in the Italian countryside. We're going in December."

He smiles as if he's waiting for a drumroll and someone to yell ta-da. I pull my hand back and step away from him, dizzy with disappointment. The doorbell rings.

"Oh, JR," I say, opening the front door so he can enter behind a giant bouquet of white roses.

The triumphant look on Ben's face disappears. I was wrong. Of course, I was. Ben gives me what he wants. He never really sees my emptiness, feels my hunger. The lack of support from the people who should be there for me weighs me down. Suddenly, I want to be alone with my thoughts and my plan.

After introducing JR, I raise my glass and say, "I'm sorry Ben. I'm going to Haiti in December to find my biological parents."

Nadine stops the glass halfway to her mouth. "Addy, sometimes folks don't want to get found," she says, shifting her body toward Mom next to her. "Marge, didn't you tell Adele what—?"

"Yes," Mom yells, stopping Nadine. She grabs the back of the chair to steady herself. "I told Addy *everything*, Nadine. I told you she found the envelope. Right." Mom fans her face with her hand. "I need to go home, Addy. Please," she says, her breath loud as if she's been running. "I don't feel good."

I sit her back down. "Mom, what's wrong? Is it your heart again?"

"I guess, I...I stayed too long in the sun." She stands to make her way to the powder room down the hall. "I...I don't feel well, Addy."

I follow. Just before she pulls the door closed behind her, she covers her mouth with her hand. I lean against the door and listen to my mother retch. I close my eyes and pray. "God, please don't let her end up in the hospital again."

My happiness disappears like a lightning bolt inside a Florida cloud.

# CHAPTER EIGHTEEN

❦❦❦

# KETLY

*January 1981*

The car stops with a lurch in front of the house, spitting gravel and red dust. Matante and the local ladies are shelling peas on the small porch. Victor drops the sisal tray from his lap and dashes down the steps.

"You're back. Kekette's back," he says, pulling me by the arm. "Matante, Matante, look, she's back," he yells as if the old lady's blind and deaf.

"Boy, stop," Matante says. "Give the girl some room." She smiles. "Welcome home, Kekette. Vic, help her with her bags."

Matante acts as if she knew I'd come back. A flash of anger roots me to the ground. But I know, there's no one on this island that deserves my wrath. I'm embarrassed about my past behavior toward people who have tried to support me. It has been a hard lesson to accept that no one owes me anything. Not even the people who took away, my child, my peace, my dreams. I will have to work hard against the past to carve my future here or wherever life happens to spit me next.

Raoul hugs me. "Ketly, I'm glad you're coming down to go to school?" I nod and climb the two front steps.

"Good day, Matante." Raoul greets her from the road.

"*Bonjou, Pitit mwen*," Matante waves at him.

I bend down from the waist and kiss Matante's forehead. "I should have sent word that I was still on the island. I'm sorry."

"Whatever for, child." She drinks from a chipped enamel cup and smacks her lips. "There's food on the table if you hungry. I can use another pair of hands with them peas when you finish eatin'."

Victor follows me inside with my bags and places them on the twin bed I'd slept on in the room I shared with Matante.

"Happy New Year, Vic. Tell me how old you're going to be this year?"

"Umm…I know you told me, but I forgot." He scrunches his face in concentration. "I'm sorry, Kekette."

Matante said Victor was dropped on his head at birth. "Fourteen, Vic. You'll be fourteen this year."

"Will you tell me a story later. Please?" he begs.

I rub his head. "Yes. I will."

Telling stories makes the time go faster for me to see where I am heading. I lose myself in the mundane tasks of daily living. I cook, I wash, I clean, I teach Victor, but I don't leave the perimeter of the house. At the end of January, we sit in the front room like we do every night, me stretching my vision in the moving flame of the lamp to read the books Alice loans to me, while I teach Victor to make words out of letters, he sometimes confuses with numbers.

Matante sips her tea laced with a few drops of *klerin*— the locally made booze from sugar cane—while she mends clothes. In a few weeks,

I'll be eighteen. I start school in the fall. Life surprises us sometimes with gifts disguised as adversity. My dislike for this place is going to help me work hard to find the home that I will build for myself somewhere. And one day I will be equipped to find my daughter on my own merits. After I shoo Victor away, I move my chair closer to Matante's and whisper, "Thank you for taking me in again when I came back last week. I'm…I'm sorry."

She peers at me, kindness brimming in her eyes. "Bébé, I'm sorry your young man ain't come. His loss. You young, Kekette. Don't close your heart." She tilts the cup for the last drop and wipes her lips with her fingers. "You'll meet a young man one day and settle down and raise some babies."

I wince as if she'd punched me. "I have no room in my life for anyone else. Maybe *never*."

"Oh, child," she sucks her teeth, "be patient!"

I stay behind the sheet hanging in the front door, protecting me from prying eyes. At church last week, a woman asked me if I enjoyed Paris. No secret in this place. Matante and the village women sell goods at the market every day for coins to buy what they can't grow, and they gossip for free. I have the house to myself to stare at the walls as if they hold secrets I need to decode.

Two weeks later, I hear the engine before turning toward the sound. My heart flutters. It's Alice's car. Is she bringing a visitor, a letter, or bad news. She was here last week for my birthday. I drop the wooden spoon back into the pot of cornmeal and pull the headscarf off my head, grateful I'd combed my hair this morning. I run my palms over my sleeveless cotton blouse and tuck it into the waist of my denim shorts. Nothing I can do about my red-dusted feet. I scoop a cup of water from the bucket next to me and wash the sweat off my face, patting it dry with the dish cloth and dashing to the front of the house. Alice stands on the porch with a wrapped package in her hands. I scan past her into the empty car and stop in my tracks.

"Hey, I brought books." She pumps the bundle up and down. "I was in the city yesterday and picked up more for you. My sister-in-law left, and Raoul and I want you to come down to Galette."

"Let's sit, Ali." I grab the package from her hand and start ripping the brown paper off. "Thank you so much. You know I can do life in prison or on this island if I have books to read."

"Me, too. They've been my greatest companions." We laugh with longings threading through the sound. "You want me to come get you, Kekette?"

"I'm going to help Denise with the school and in the evening teach adult literacy. I have to work out a schedule. I'd like to volunteer at the hospital in Galette as well. Can you help me with that, you know, get my feet in the door?"

She takes my hand. "I'm happy to see you're settling into life on this island. You can do so much good here for you and others. I'll talk to the hospital administrator. I'm sure they can use free help."

We peek into the bedroom. Matante is snoring. I squeeze my friend into an embrace. "She's resting," I whisper. "Thank you, Sister. I love you."

Earlier, I pinned the laundry on the clothesline. Now I shade my eyes with my hand and follow gray clouds moving in the sky. The air smells like rain. In the kitchen, I squat in front of the fire to finish the meal. Matante's sour stomach kept her home today. I pour the tea I made for her into her enamel cup and stand. My knees creak. At eighteen, I'm already old. A drop of rain falls on my forehead. I run inside and send Victor out to collect the clothes from the line.

I touch Matante's forehead with the back of my hand. "I think you have a fever. I made you some basilic tea with lime."

"Thank you, bébé," she says. "How d'you know I wanted that tea?" She tries to sit up. "Oh, we have another visitor. Did Alice leave?"

"How did you know she was here?" I bury my annoyance into a fake smile. No secret in this place.

"Mm…" She groans.

We both look toward the sound of the motorcycle idling in front of the house. I frown. Is today a visitation day in Mapou? We don't get two of these in a month. Victor rushes into the room with an armful of clothes, his chin resting on a pair of my black panties. I suppress a smile. Boys. I shake my head.

"Kekette, the lady," Victor says, breathing hard and pointing toward the front door, "she looks just like you."

Matante takes the cup from my hand before it hits the ground. In a couple of strides, I stand facing my mother. It's like looking in a mirror. Her ebony skin peeks under the coat of dust on every inch of exposed body parts. The headscarf covers her wide forehead, stopping above her dark-brown eyes. Mama smiles. Small white teeth gleam from violet gum. Henri once told me that my smile made him crave plum, a fruit I've never eaten but he'd promised to introduce me to when we travel. I sigh.

I shake my head as if to wake up from a dream. Mama's still standing there with a cloth bag at her feet, arms open wide. I run into them, and her familiar smell of Palmolive soap and Palma Christi oil are like salve to my raw emotions. I haven't seen her since the day Miss Marge left with my baby almost seven months ago.

"Ma…what you're doing here?" I hug her again. "Are the boys, okay? Auntie Irene? I'm so happy to see you."

"Let's go inside, baby girl." Raindrops bounce on our heads. "Don't wanna catch my death in this rain."

# I SHALL FIND YOU

Mama embraces Matante, who's already sitting in her chair in the front room. "Clara, what a surprise?" Matante says. "We weren't expecting you. Were we Kekette?"

Mama sits next to me on one of the chairs around the table. "Had to come see where my daughter is," she says, stroking the back of my hand. "I missed your birthday last week, and I know you're lonely. Matante, thank you for taking her in and keeping her safe."

"Clara, she my kin," Matante says. "The child showed up here and claimed some man's looking to do her harm and she waitin' for another man to come rescue her. Is all I know. She ain't say much more on that subject since she been here."

"What happened with Henri?" Mama asks. "I've been waiting to see you two in Lasalle since December." She squints at me. "You hear anything?" I shake my head. Words stuck in my throat. "I saw the tall man in dark glasses around our village during the holiday season, not doing a good job of blending in."

"Shadow," I whisper.

"Last week two neighbors tell me a tall man been asking questions about you." Mama sips water from the cup Victor places in front of her. "All they can say is the truth that they haven't seen you since you left for the city." Mama wipes dust off her face with a rag. "At least they don't know you're here. You're safe. These people drove you away from home just because you have a child."

A gasp travels from Matante's lips to land on my face and heat it up. The rain has stopped. The smell of baked earth invades the air inside the house. The chair creaks under Matante's bulk as she sits up straighter. "Wait! Ketly has a child?"

Now it's Mama's turn to shift on the chair for a better look at me. "What! You never told Matante about Juliette?" I bite my bottom lip so hard I taste blood. I sit limp in the chair. "They dug your grave already, Kekette. He's just looking for the bodies."

The room's closing around me like a tomb. I have an urge to run, yet I sit unmoving.

"What's going on, Clara?" Matante asks. "Ketly?"

Mama stands behind my chair, wrapping her arms around my neck and cradling my head on her belly as if she wants to put me back in there, where no one can hurt me. "*Pitit mwen,* you can't come to Lasalle…at least not yet. I promise to come as often as I can."

"Don't worry, Mama. I'm not going anywhere." I stand abruptly, forcing her to step back from the chair's legs. "I'm going to finish supper."

"I'll come help you," she says.

"No. No, you stay and talk to Matante. I'm almost done."

I slip out the back door, past the kitchen, through the orange grove, beyond the tall pine trees. Soon darkness envelops me but it's darker inside my head. I stop at the edge of Matante's property in the cover of the dark and sit under a tree. I need space to think. No one comes looking for me. They know I'll return. I can't run away on a small island.

Two days later, I help Mama climb on the back of a moped. "Give big hugs to Sylvain and Jules." I smile. "I miss my brothers even though they were pain in the neck."

"They miss you, too." Mama hugs me hard. "I can't miss the ferry. Left the boys with Irene, and I don't wanna be gone too long. In case someone is watching the house."

"I know. See you in July like we planned last night," I whisper. "Have a safe trip." I step away from her. "I love you, Mama."

# I SHALL FIND YOU

While I wait to put the plan I outlined with Mama into action this summer, I throw myself back into volunteering in the community in Galette and in Mapou. Two days a week, I walk down to the hospital in Galette. Since I want to be a nurse, I enjoy helping wherever I'm needed. I clean floors, I change bed linens, but I enjoy feeding the newborns in the nursery the most, so their mamas can rest. The other three days, I help Denise in the classroom, and I teach adults at night.

In Galette, I hang out at Alice's house after work before making the trek back to Mapou in the afternoon couple days a week. "That's a lot of walking, Kekette. I wish you could stay here with me."

"Ali, I need to help Matante with supper, the laundry—her health's not good. Besides, I made a commitment to Pastor Paul. I want to keep my word."

"My goodness, when do you have time to do anything else?"

"That's the point, Ali. The busier I am, the less I think and the faster the time goes."

I wake up before the roosters to start with the house chores before walking down the mountain. This island is not my home. But the folks are my people. In helping them, I also help myself.

Five months later, on July first, I pack my good clothes and say goodbye to Matante and Denise this time. No sneaking away. I also pack my official acceptance letter into the Lycée in Galette to start school in October. I'm keeping all opportunities open. The missionaries and Miss Marge will be in Lasalle in two days.

On the wharf, I hug Alice and Raoul, who come to see me off. "Please keep in touch, *ti soeur*," Alice says, waving her hand like a flag.

"I will." I make my way to the bow. My head straight. I am on my way to see the woman who's had my daughter for a year. A mother does not ever forget her child. *Ever.*

# CHAPTER NINETEEN

## ADELE

The silence is louder than the whirring sound of the fan in the high ceiling of our bedroom. I'm still disappointed but I reach over and stroke Ben's back in the dimness of the night light. The many glasses of wine and champagne I drank at my birthday party earlier wash away my anger. I mold my naked body to his under the cotton sheet and reach inside his pajamas bottom. He is limp. I set to work with my wet lips on his back and my fingers between his legs.

Minutes later, Ben switches on his bedside lamp and raises his torso on his elbow. "Why did you lie to me about JR?"

"What do you mean?" I still my hand. "I didn't lie."

"You told me, and I quote. 'Honey, I invited my new friend JR to the party. We met at the hospital. JR's Haitian and a police officer,' he says, mimicking my voice. Using his own voice, he adds, "You never said JR was a man."

I grab the pillow behind my head and sit up in the bed. "What difference does it make? Is it my fault you assume everyone I meet in the hospital's a nurse and female? Everything I said is true."

"Withholding information is the same as lying, Adele."

"Oh, like the way you didn't tell me you were once engaged to Paige before you proposed to me."

"Really!" he says, sitting up and putting his pajamas top on. "You're bringing this up again after what…three years. Leave Paige out of it. It's not like I'm planning a trip with her behind your back."

We're finally having a fight. I'm mad and aroused at the same time. "Since the day we met at the gallery, I told you I want to find my parents one day. JR and I happen to be going at the same time. He offers to assist me in my search. Unlike you. This is very important to me, Ben. Do you even care?"

"Why do you want to go to that… that dangerous place? Can't you just let it go. You have everything here."

I fist my hands and punch the pillow, screaming, my hair flying into my eyes and mouth. "That's the problem, Ben. You don't give a damn what *I want*. I don't want the stupid car, the house, your jetsetter friends. The one thing I want you won't support me to get it. I'm going to do this with or without anyone. Do you understand?"

"Addy." He places his hand on my fists and presses down to stop the pounding. "Let's stop this right now and go to sleep. I don't want to argue."

"Well, I want you to understand what's important to me. We've been married three years, and I still feel sometimes like we're roommates sharing space and a weekly fuck."

Ben yanks on the switch to turn off his lamp. The crystal ball at the end of the chain bounces against the marble base. He flips on his stomach, pulling his pillow over his head. I want to beat his back like the voodoo drums I've read about. I want to have make-up sex tomorrow or the day after. How does that happen if we don't show our feelings when we're upset? I'm tired of holding back. The day we met at that gallery the conversation was about what I wanted and how important it was to me. Why is it that JR gets it from my first sentence and my husband refuses to support me?

I grab my robe at the foot of the bed shrugging my body into it. I cinch the sash and quickly loosen it so I can breathe. With my cellphone in one hand, I rattle the doorknob when I pull the bedroom door shut, knowing Ben is awake. I settle on the chaise in the family room. My phone says it's after two in the morning and there's a voicemail. I hit play and raise it to my ear. My heart skips when I hear JR's voice.

*Hey, Madame, I hope I didn't get you in any kind of ...umm...trouble with the mister. I don't think he was expecting me. Bonne fête encore!*

I close my eyes. Expectations. Why do I expect my parents to want to see me? What did Nadine mean tonight about people who may not want to be found? What if my parents had changed their minds about coming back for me? Well, they'll have to tell me to my face because I'm going to find them.

# CHAPTER TWENTY

## KETLY

*July 1981*

Before getting off the ferry, I change into Matante's long sleeve print dress and gather the extra fabric around my waist with the self-covered belt. The high collar keeps the dress from sliding off my shoulders, but my chest disappears into the folds of the blouse. I tie the wig down on my head with the white silk headscarf, the one Matante favors on Sundays for church. The gray synthetic hair scratches my forehead. Sadness invades my soul when I remember donning Auntie Yvette's clothes to leave Port-Au-Prince for Lasalle a year ago to save myself and my unborn daughter.

"I hope you find your baby," Matante said, this morning as she handed me the dress, the scarf and the wig folded on top of it like an offering. "God didn't see fit to bless me with children, but I can sense your loss. Please be careful."

Now, I pull the scarf down over my forehead and take a seat at the back of the bus to Lasalle. Matante's black laced-up shoes pinch my big toes. I will send her many boxes of clothes and shoes and hats when I get to America. I push the dark glasses up my nose and close my eyes against the dust pouring in through the open windows. The groan of the motor covers my humming until I doze off.

On the ground in Lasalle, someone bumps me hard as I reach for my suitcase from the pile on the sidewalk.

"Sorry, Grandma," the woman says, holding on to my arm as if to steady me.

"It's okay, *Pitit*," I say, rounding my shoulders even more and trilling my voice.

"My son will carry your bag." The woman pushes the boy toward me. "Where you goin'?"

"To Clara's across from the clinic," I say. "She my cousin."

We walk in silence with me, forcing breath out of my mouth loudly. When we reach my mother's house, the boy starts to climb the steps to the porch. "It's okay, son," I say. "Leave it here. God bless you." I smile at the woman. "*Mèsi anpil.*"

The line of people waiting to get inside the clinic snakes around the back of the low-hung building. I enter the house through the back door, knowing my brothers will be at my uncle's house for the week as I'd planned with Mama in February. I store my belongings under the bed and feeling safe in my disguise, I cross the road and push my way through the throng of people blocking the front door of the clinic. My heart beats all over my body while my eyes search for danger. The mission is always the first week of July. Shadow can be here if he suspects the missionaries left with Juliette last year.

"Hey, Grandma," someone says, "you gotta wait your turn. Come on."

In the middle of the room, people sit on benches, lean against the walls, bounce babies in their arms. Occasional moans erupt from the cots pushed in the corners for those who can't stand or sit. A woman with a black eye and bleeding mouth presses a rag over half her face while a man holds her elbow, a look of guilt shading his shifty eyes. Then I hear a raised voice in front of me. I know that voice.

"Sir, I already told you I don't have any information about these pictures," Miss Marge says. "If you see your child's pictures on the board you can have them. I bring them back every year as keepsakes for parents."

I crane my neck over the knot of people shoving each other and my eyes stop on Shadow. My legs freeze as if I am sinking into quicksand. I take deep breaths to slow my heart. No one recognizes me. I relax.

"Excuse me, son," I tap the man in front of me on the shoulder, speaking in a quivering voice I didn't have to fake. "I need to sit down. I don't feel good."

"Oh, sorry, Grandma," he says, taking my upper arm and elbowing the people ahead of him. "Move. This old lady needs a seat." He pulls a young boy from the bench.

I can only nod. I sit a couple feet from Shadow as he towers over Miss Marge. My eyes, peeking over the sunglasses, focus on the single picture of Juliette pinned to the board, her green eyes, a beacon in the crowded room. The photo is of my baby lying on the satin blanket Henri had bought on our way to the hotel on the last day I saw him.

"Where's that kid," Shadow whispers, poking Juliette's picture with his tobacco-stained finger. I strain to hear, wishing the people would shut up.

"Excuse me," Miss Marge says. "I only take pictures. I don't..." Her eyes dart around, "I don't know whose child it is." She reddens and beads of sweat dot her face. "I have to go back to work. I have lots of patients to see."

He grabs her arm. She yelps. I start to get up, then Miss Nadine comes rushing from the back room. "What the hell! Get your filthy hand off my friend," she screams. "Who the hell are you?"

"He's been harassing me about …the pictures," Miss Marge says.

"No," Shadow replies. "Only the green-eyed one."

"Nadine, thank you for coming out here to check on me," Miss Marge says, pushing her friend toward the back room. "Let's get back to work."

Shadow snatches the picture off the board. I stand up so fast, the glasses slide down my nose and bounce on the floor. I swallow the guttural scream bubbling in my chest. People turn and stare at me, including Shadow. I bend down to retrieve the glasses and hold my stomach.

"You okay, Grandma?" the lady sitting next to me asks. "I'll get you some water."

The greasy food I ate earlier threatens to come up. As soon as Shadow ambles out of the room, I limp outside. I see no sign of him, yet I don't cross the street to my mother's house. I sit on the ground among the vendors selling food items to the patients outside. Most will return every day until they're seen on the last day of the mission.

At sundown, the groundkeeper closes the door of the clinic. The people disperse, making their way back to far away villages, cradling cranky babies in their arms. Some walk, some mount braying donkeys laden with bundles, some pull *bourrettes* carrying the elderly and disabled people. I watch Miss Marge and Miss Nadine cross the road to our house. I wait for Mama to give me the signal by closing the window in the front room. When she does, I slink inside the back bedroom.

At first the rain drizzles, hitting the tin roof like popped kernels of corn onto a lid. Soon the wind howls and shakes the house like a seizure. I remove the wig and change into a sundress. With shaky fingers, I take the pins out and let the two braids fall around my face.

"That drink's strong, Clara," Miss Nadine says. "What's for dinner? I'm starving."

# I SHALL FIND YOU

"Food be ready soon, Miss," Mama says. "I'm making oxtails and rice with black-eyed peas I picked today."

"Sounds delicious. I've been thinking about your food all day, Clara. How about you Marge?"

"I'm feeling no pain right now." Miss Marge giggles. "Where are your boys, Clara? And please tell me how Ketly's doing in the city."

"Oh, the boys are at my brother's place for the summer."

From behind the hanging sheet in the bedroom door, I spy Miss Marge pouring more drink into the glasses.

"Marge told me she didn't see Ketly last year either," Miss Nadine says. "I miss her this week. She was always such a big help during our mission. Is she still working in Port-Au-Prince?"

Before my mother can answer, I step into the dancing light of the lamp and cough. The two women blink fast from the table, their glasses halfway to their mouths. Mama stands there with a sheepish grin on her face.

"Ketly?" Miss Marge squints in the yellow flame. "We were just asking about you."

I stride over to the table and kiss each woman's forehead. "I'm home," I say, suddenly filled with the loneliness I know will come when I'll have to leave my family again when I go to America.

"Oh my God, look at you," Miss Nadine exclaims. "You look beautiful. You've gotten taller. Don't you think so Marge?"

"Ketly, I'm so glad to see you," Miss Marge says. "Come on, have a seat, sweetie." She smiles at Mama. "Clara, you sure can spring a surprise. Tell us, Ketly how's life in the big city? Do you go to school. Do you have a boyfriend—?"

"Miss Marge, where's Juliette?" I stop her.

Even the rain slows down to listen. Miss Marge stands so fast her chair tumbles backward. She grabs my shoulders and pulls me into her bosom. The smell of alcohol swabs fills my nostrils.

"Who's Juliette?" Miss Nadine asks. "What are you talking about, Ketly?"

I pull away from Miss Marge and stare into her shiny blue eyes, thinking, she didn't tell Miss Nadine about Juliette? I remember they were neighbors.

"What did you do with my baby, Miss Marge?" My voice rises over the thunder outside.

"She means Adele," Miss Marge says. "I'll explain later, Nadine." She grabs my hands and like crabs we both walk sideways and sit in the chairs. "*Ketly…umm…mwen rélé li Adele Marie Pearson,*" she says slowly in Creole as if it's not my native tongue. "I left her with my neighbor. She has a daughter Lisa, who's the same age. Adele's safe."

"Adele. Marie. Pearson," I whisper. A sob escapes my lips. I don't even know my baby's name. Anger brews inside until the lid pops off. I push the chair back and stand facing Miss Marge. "Why did you change it? You know her name." I scream, my voice lost in the rolling thunder shaking the house. "Her papa chose it before she was even born." I swipe at the tears pouring down my face. "I want to be with my baby. I'm safe on the island, but Juliette will never be. Miss Marge, you have to take me to her."

Mama runs from the back where the smell of roasted garlic invades the room. "Ketly, you need to calm down, bébé. Tell them everything. Miss Marge will understand why you had to let her keep your baby temporarily."

I hold on to the back of the chair to steady myself and I take deep breaths. Two pairs of eyes look at me in confusion and curiosity. I talk about me and Henri. About running for months because his mother wanted to yank Juliette out of my womb. About my Auntie Yvette's murder. How I waited for Henri last year when he turned eighteen and he didn't come. And in the cemetery in Port-au-Prince there are two tombstones with my name and my baby's. Miss marge and Miss Nadine gasp like a duet.

Miss Nadine says, "Simone sounds like a monster, Ketly. I'm sorry about Henri. Maybe he listens to his mother. You're young. You'll meet someone else."

"Why everybody keeps telling me that? I don't want anybody else," I yell. "All I want is Juliette. She's mine. I need you to take me to her, Miss Marge. I have my clothes here with me. I'll make a life in America with my baby. I still want to be a Miss. I can go to school there."

Miss Marge drains her half full glass. "Ketly…it doesn't work that way." The alcohol thickens her accent. "I couldn't even take Adele…umm, I mean Juliette with me when I left last year."

"What do you mean?" I ask. "Where did you leave her? I don't understand."

"Ketly, please let Miss Marge finish," Mama says, sitting on a *ti chaise* in the corner of the room, dinner forgotten. Miss Marge picks up the empty glass and puts it down. She pushes her chair closer to Miss Nadine's like we were teams facing each other. Miss Nadine locks eyes with me for a brief second and looks at Mama as if she's not sure which team she's on.

"Ketly, honey, going to America is not like taking the bus to the next village," Miss Nadine says. "You'll need a passport, a visa and airfare."

"Exactly!" Miss Marge says. "I had to leave Adele with my old school friend Hélène Macombe. She works at the American embassy here. When the bus dropped us at the airport last year, I took a taxi to the embassy and Hélène took care of everything. Still, it took a little bit over three months before I could take my daughter…umm…Adele home."

"You mean *my daughter* was in Haiti all this time?" I lean closer to Miss Marge to emphasize the fact that Juliette is not her child.

"Hush, Kekette," Mama says. "Go ahead Miss Marge."

"Yes," Miss Marge says, "I stayed a week with my…with the baby at Helène's house in Turgeau to start the adoption process."

"Adoption!" The word slaps me with its finality. "I said in the note that we would come for our baby."

"Ketly, there was no other way to take Adele out of Haiti. She had to become *my daughter*." Anger flits across her face turning it red.

I stuff my own anger down. "I'm sorry Miss Marge. I don't know how any of this works. But now we're all here, we can figure out a way for me to reunite with my baby. Please ask your friend to help me get to America. I'll clean your house, I'll cook your meals, wash your clothes. I just want to be with Juliette…*Adele*. We can both be her mother. *Wi?*"

Miss Marge stands like a statue, in silence.

"You know, Marge, maybe Ketly has a point," Miss Nadine says. "It seems like she has to live in fear and isolated from her family here. You can help her get a visa." She looks at me and nods in solidarity. "You can ask Helène to help with the process. Marge?"

"I…I…umm… don't know," Miss Marge stammers. "It sounds like Ketly's more interested in finding Henri."

"That's not true," I say, stomping my feet. "Henri can find me, us, me and Juliette if he wants. But I want to be with my daughter. The picture… Shadow took the picture. I wanted it." I kick the leg of the chair and groan in pain. "Miss Marge why did you put her picture on the board knowing what I told you in the note about her green eyes."

"I didn't mean to," she says. "I gave the stack of pictures to one of the volunteers to display. That one of Adele must have slipped into the pile. I was terrified when the man started asking questions."

# I SHALL FIND YOU

"Marge's an excellent mother, Ketly," Miss Nadine says. "Addy's a happy child. She smiles a lot, with double dimples like yours. She loves her two best friends: my daughter Eugenie who's one month younger and Lisa who's two months younger. We all live on the same street. So, it's as if Adele has siblings."

"Thank you, Nadine," Miss Marge says, sounding tired as if she's said all this herself. "I will talk to Hélène and do my very best Ketly, to help you."

I practically tackle Miss Marge. I throw my arms around her neck and kiss her sweaty cheek. The humidity inside the house smothers the air after the rain. "Thank you so much, Miss Marge. You will always be Juliette's second mama. I'll make sure she knows how important you were in her life."

Her body stiffens for the briefest moment before she kisses my cheek. "Wait," she says, walking to her backpack on the floor. She reaches inside and pulls an envelope and hands it to me. "I brought these for me to look at before I go to bed. I miss my baby so much."

Inside are at least half a dozen pictures of Juliette. I leaf through them over the stingy light coming from the lamp and stare into her bright green eyes. I kiss the top picture, leaving a wet smear on it. The second one shows her crawling toward the camera, two teeth filling her upper gum and the last one must have been taken before Miss Marge left to come here. One-year-old Juliette is standing with one hand clutching the arm of a chair, the other extended forward, a big smile on her chubby face, a lock of curly brown hair resting over her forehead. "I'm coming Juliette," I whisper, pressing the picture to my chest.

Joy floods my body.

# CHAPTER TWENTY-ONE

## ADELE

I tiptoe in the dark after kicking the duvet off my naked body. Ben keeps the temperature in the house at a frosty sixty-five degrees in July. He doesn't like to sweat. I love the heat. It's in my tropical genes. In the shower, I touch all the spots my husband ignored last night despite my attempted ministrations.

The smell of the Haitian coffee wins over Ben's sandalwood scent from his shampoo, body wash and after shave. I drape my towel over the brushed nickel bar on my side of the bathroom. The side with the bidet and my own toilet in the privacy closet. I don't even get to yell at my husband for not putting the toilet seat down. He has his own on the other side.

I put on a pair of brown scrubs with pink ducks quacking all over it and bound down the steps. Ben hands me a cup of steaming coffee and I know it has no sugar but a pinch of cinnamon powder with cream. Ben pays attention to some details like that.

"Thank you, hon," I say, kissing his clean-shaven cheek.

"Wait a minute. You're going to work? It's Sunday." He swivels around on the stool to look at me. "We're going sailing with the Cottrells today. Remember?"

I take a slow breath. "Remember I work one weekend a month, and this is it. A friend covered my shift yesterday for my birthday party. I told you."

"Well, what am I supposed to tell our friends? We've planned this."

"No. You've planned this, Ben. Since we've been living together, you should know my schedule by now, so we're not having this…this fight once a month when I have to work a weekend."

The look of horror on his face is comical. "We're not fighting. Addy, we're having a *conversation*."

"Like the one we should have had before you booked a European vacation without asking me about how it would affect *my* work, or if I really want to go there instead."

A fissure opens in the patronizing smile on his face. "What? Instead of going to Haiti. And when were you planning on telling me JR's taking you there? Was I going to be invited? December's our anniversary."

"I know what December is, Ben and it's five months away." I look toward the microwave clock and know I'm going to be late, but I can't walk away. Not now. I need to get this off my chest. Ben follows my gaze.

"You'll be late for work. We can talk later."

"No. I think we need to finish this." I pull up the stool next to him and sit. "I always wanted you to go to Haiti with me, but you've made your position clear about the subject from the beginning. As for JR, he can help me with his knowledge of the country and his professional skills. I told you last night that I bought my airline ticket and hired a PI before I met him. Besides I still want you to go with me."

He reaches for my hand. "Addy, the day I went to your house to meet your mother, she took me aside when you left the room and said, 'Ben, Addy's all I have in this world, but she also belongs to some people in Haiti that she has always been intent on finding. Except, her life would be in danger. She can never go there." He puckers his lips like a period at the end of a sentence.

"That's set?" I frown. "That's why every time I bring it up you change the subject? That's absurd."

"But…but, how about the warning from our state department urging Americans not to travel to that…place? How unsafe it is."

I raise my hand. "Propaganda! I'm a Haitian adoptee with a past that belongs to me. I need that link. You can't understand, Ben. You're not even trying."

"I don't know much about Haiti except that it's umm…poor, dangerous, I mean people shouldn't go there."

"So, you think the two-second soundbites you hear on the news is all that Haiti is." I move my torso back and almost fall off the stool to peer at him. "Wow! For an educated man you sound so ignorant. I've been reading about Haiti's history since I was a child. Your past as a biracial man is tied to the history of the stolen African people who became Haitian slaves." I slide off the stool. "Learn your history, Ben. *Our history.*" I walk toward the hallway closet feeling angry and dejected.

He follows me. "For almost three decades you were happy to be…an American. Is that man…cop guy…influencing you?"

I spin around so fast; I bump against his chest. I step back. "No one's influencing me or taking me anywhere. I want to do this. I will do it," I scream at him. "You don't know me at all, do you, Ben?"

As I reach inside the closet for my work backpack, he touches my shoulder moving my body to face him.

"Oh, Addy, I made you sad. I'm sorry. What can I do to see those dimples?" He brushes the pad of his thumb over my wet cheek and kisses my closed lips. I can only breathe to calm myself down with arms crossed tightly around my chest.

He kisses my cheek. "I don't want you to be late for work." He pats my butt. "Let me drive you. I'll reschedule with our friends."

"I'll drive myself. And they're *your* friends. Not mine." I sling the pack over my back. "I don't even know the wife's first name."

I swipe my car keys off the counter and head out. I know tonight he will want to make love in the middle of the bed with the lights off. Not on the edge, not at the foot, but in the center to keep the shape of the mattress even, as recommended by the manufacturer, before we move to our respective corners. Ben is good at following rules like that. I am not.

# CHAPTER TWENTY-TWO

❦❦❦

## KETLY

*Summer/Fall 1981*

One of the few things I like about living on the island is the ferry ride. Being on the ocean seems to give me a hint of open possibilities. There are no constraints. The ocean belongs to all of us, unlike mansions behind high walls guarded by lazy dogs. With Alphonse's help once more, I'm now the owner of a passport that will take me to America. I spent most of the money Miss Nadine had given me for the travel documents. I'm going to wait for Miss Marge on the island.

I look at the limitless horizon and remember the conversation with Alphonse this morning on our way to the wharf.

"Kekette, I'm so glad Miss Marge came back this year. That was such a great plan," Alphonse said. "You're so smart."

"I know." I grinned. "I had the idea when Mama came to see me on the island for my birthday in February. I had to find patience, I didn't know I had, to wait for July." We laughed.

"So, she gave you her contact information before she left?"

"No." I paused. "She asked me for my information. I gave her Alice's to get in touch with me when she gets the ball rolling."

"So, she didn't give you her address and phone number?"

"No. Why you keep asking me that, Alph?"

"Did you ask her, though?" He puffed on the cigarette between his fingers, curling smoke rising to his squinty eyes.

I nodded. "Yes! She told me she'll be in touch when it's time for me to go to the embassy for the visa. Her friend, Hélène will help like she did with Juliette."

"Mm-hm," Alphonse muttered. "Well, I'm glad she's going to help you."

As the ferry docks in Galette, I wonder. What was he implying?

Now two months later, I still haven't heard a word from Miss Marge. Before I even climb the first step, Alice says, "Sorry, but still nothing came in the mail this week." She pats the seat next to her on the verandah. "I'll get you something cold. We're going to a party tonight."

"I'm not in the mood." I drop my body into the chair and the weight of the world settles on my shoulders, curving them into my chest. "Why do you think Miss Marge never even sends a note to let me know how things are going?" I rock the chair. "I hope Juliette's not sick or... I wish I'd asked Miss Nadine for her information. What if Juliette—"

"Ketly, stop. You're gonna make yourself and me crazy. You trusted that woman, otherwise, you wouldn't have left your baby for her to take. Right?"

I sit ramrod straight in the chair. Of course, I trust Miss Marge to keep Juliette safe. But will she give my baby back? Trepidation crowds my chest. I struggle to pull in a deep breath. I remember Miss Marge always wanted a baby. Any baby. I shake my head until Alice stops rocking and stares at me. "Kekette, what is it?"

I open my mouth and tell her.

∞∞∞

The front yard of the clinic teemed with mothers holding babies in their arms with more children holding on to the hems of skirts, ends of sleeves with fear of the syringes etched on tiny faces. The older ones ran around the legs of the adults playing tag and the sicker ones sat in the shade of the trees. It was pediatric consultation day.

At age twelve, I started to volunteer and help Miss Annette in the clinic on Saturdays and in the summer. She has lived in the little house behind the clinic since I was born. She took care of pretty much everyone in the community.

"Ketly, I'm so glad you're here," Miss Marge said as I placed a band-aid on the thigh of the screaming toddler she had just vaccinated after handing her a lollipop. "Remember how you wouldn't get off my lap until Miss Annette would come out screaming at us to move on." She laughed. "How old are you now?"

"Fourteen," I said.

Miss Marge hugged the little boy in her lap and kissed his brown cheek. His mother called him to hurry up while she collected the rest of her brood scattered around the yard. A look of sadness clouded Miss Marge's blue eyes as she stared at the children.

"You have kids, Miss Marge?" I asked.

She shook her head. The pile of blond hair on top cascaded down around her round face. "I can't have any."

"Who said that?" I asked, not understanding.

"My body's missing a part," she said, patting her stomach. "Some women have them at will around here. It's…unfair."

"Can you adopt one in your country?"

"Oh, I'm going to get *my daughter* from Lasalle," she signaled a little girl to climb onto her lap for her shot. "It will be so much less complicated."

∞∞∞

Now I sit back down, not even realizing that I'm pacing in front of Alice as I tell her the story. "And a year ago, Ali, I literally handed her the daughter she always wanted."

"And you can't get any information to track her down. You know foreigners come here and do whatever they want. No one records what they do. Yet when I go to America, I have to write my personal information *everywhere* I go. They need to know who you are and what you're doing in their country, but they treat Haiti like one of their states. They keep records on all of us."

"*Records*," I yell.

Alice narrows her eyes at me as if I am mad. "Huh? What are you saying?"

"Ali, I'm going back to Lasalle tomorrow. I think I know where I can get Miss Marge's information."

The ferry trip becomes a great escape. I relish it.


Tonight, after supper in Lasalle, Mama takes the dishes to the back of the house for washing. I barely taste my favorite fish stew she cooks for me. My brothers are coming back next week to start school in the first week of October. I miss them.

"Be careful, Kekette," Mama says, wiping her hand on the hem of her skirt. "I hope you find what you are looking for."

I wait for the moon to disappear behind the thick clouds before slinking to the back of the clinic. I knock lightly on the back window of the small house behind the clinic.

"*Kimoun sa'a?*" Miss Annette asks, her footsteps shuffling along the cement floor before stopping under the window.

"Miss Annette, it's Ketly," I whisper. "I need to talk to you."

"Ketly?" She opens the back door. "Let me put the lamp on."

I follow her inside. She strikes a match. The sulfur odor fills the small space. She holds the lamp over her head to peer at me. She squints; her face is mapped with wrinkles everywhere. "Kekette?" she says, her shoulders dropping down. I pull the wig off along with the glasses. "I thought you were in Port-au-Prince." She takes in my disguise. "What's going on?"

"Let's sit down, Miss Annette and I'll tell you."

When I'm done, the kindness on her face almost unravels me. "So, you see, I know you keep records on the missionaries in the clinic. Please, I need to look in Miss Marge's folder."

"*O Bondié*! I looked after your baby the night you left her at the cinic." Miss Annette limps to the back room and comes out with her reading glasses perched on her wide nose, a set of keys dangling in her hand. She closes her house door behind us. I follow her in a few feet to the clinic. My heart booms in my chest. I will find Miss Marge and Juliette. She probably lost the piece of paper I wrote Alice's information for her. Maybe, she has been waiting for me to reach out. Maybe.

As soon as Miss Annette unlocks the filing cabinet, I yank open the top drawer and shove my hand inside. "Wait, child, I know where it is." She hands me the lamp and pulls up a chair to the bottom drawer and opens it. She riffles through a couple of faded blue file folders and frowns. "Hmm!"

"What?" I ask, moving closer with the light so she can see better.

She pulls folders out now with more urgency and drops them on the floor. "Light that lamp over there," she says, "and bring it here."

I place one lamp on top of the filing cabinet and crouch next to her with the other one on the floor. I open folders reading the names of nurses, camp counselors and teachers I met as a young child over the years. Each file contains name, address, school attended, date of birth, nationality, occupation and phone numbers. My hands moisten in anticipation. Miss Annette moves from the bottom drawer to the third, second and first. She lowers herself into the chair and grunts.

"Her folder's gone," she whispers.

I raise myself up on my knees from my sitting position and scoot closer. "What do you mean gone? You're sure, Miss? Can I look? It's kind of dark."

"Hush, child," she says, reaching out for me. She rubs my back while she talks. "The night before she left a couple months ago, Marge came to my house after everyone has gone to bed and asked me for the key to the cabinet. She said she needed to update her file with new information. Later, she brought the keys back to me and I never checked. I had no reason to. Now it's gone." The older woman taps her chin. "She planned this."

I raise my head from her lap. "She did this after I asked her to help me go to America to be with Juliette. She never intended to." I close my eyes. The weight of Miss Marge's betrayal crushes my spirit.

"I'm so sorry, Kekette. This is sinister. I wish I could help you."

"Let's look for Miss Nadine's file. They're neighbors. I can reach out to her. She gave me money to get my passport." I squeeze my hands together in my lap with hope replacing despair.

Miss Annette dives into the cabinet again. Minutes later, she covers her mouth, her eyes big behind her glasses. "It's gone too. What's going on?"

"Why would Miss Nadine take her file?"

"I believe Marge took it because she knows you can track her through Nadine. This is sinister."

"Miss Annette," I plead, "do you remember anything about Miss Marge's contact information?"

"Honey, you see how many folders I have in here. Marge was one of the regulars, but we have missionaries from everywhere."

"What am I going to do?" I whimper. "How can Miss Marge do this to me?"

She pats my head. "You know she started coming here in the early seventies, young and full of energy and dreams. She seemed to prefer to care for the children, even though I clearly recall she was a surgical nurse. I never question their motives. I welcome the help because the need's so great here. People do this kind of work for many different reasons." She sighs. "Marge often wallows in self-pity about not having children. Unlike me, who embraces every child as if they're my own. Well, I figured if God wanted me to be a biological mother, he'd have send me a husband."

I shift from my position on the floor and wipe my face with the hem of Matante's dress. "I'm not married, and I have a child, Miss Annette."

"Oh, baby, it's not a judgment. I was raised to believe that you don't have children before marriage. I'm old…different times."

"Miss Marge," I prompt.

"Oh yes. Marge asked me on many occasions to identify mothers here she could adopt a baby from. She said it was too much hassle back home for a white woman to adopt a black baby, but she can do it here. I guess she got her wish."

Miss Annette's words hit me like a hammer, confirming my suspicion. They push Juliette away from me further until pain fills me to capacity.

"I only have to wait another nine months before she returns. Now that I have a passport, Miss Marge won't leave here without taking me to Juliette next year. She even changed my baby's name to *Adele*. I hate it."

Miss Annette shakes her head. "I hope you're right, but Marge isn't coming back here. She got what she wanted."

I jump up from the floor to stand over her. "Why? Did she say something to you?"

Silence stretches. Miss Annette stares at the filing cabinet as if she's overlooked something. I wait. "I bet she didn't expect the baby's mother to return asking for her child." She pauses. "And you being the mother, Kekette complicates the situation for her. She *knows* you."

"What else can I do Miss Annette to find Miss Marge?" I stomp on the cement floor until the pain shoots through my knees.

She reaches for my hands and hums a hymn. I close my eyes and join her. We stay like this for a long time. "Miss Annette," I whisper, "you think God's punishing me for having a baby out of wedlock?"

"Oh no, child. God doesn't work that way; the devil does and he's around us in many forms."

"I believe God will bring Miss Marge next year so I can find Juliette." I raise my head and look into Miss Annette's eyes for agreement.

She kicks the cabinet with the toe of her slippers as if to remind me of what is gone from there. "If it's any consolation, Marge will take great care of your baby."

"What? I want Juliette back, not taken care of."

"I'm so sorry." She reaches for my hand. I clench hers like a lifeline. "Let's go. I'll make tea and you can tell me about your life on the island."

Over several cups of citronelle tea with too much brown sugar, I tell Miss Annette about my plan to go back to school in Galette next month to complete my secondary education. How I'm going to apply to the nursing program at the hospital there. Ever since I was a little girl, all I ever wanted to be is a Miss. Nothing else. As I speak the words coming from my head and my heart into the night, it occurs to me that to find Juliette, I will need to find myself first.

The next morning, I am on the ferry, going back to the last place I ever thought I'd go to carve out my future.

# CHAPTER TWENTY-THREE

## ADELE

Days fly into weeks and weeks into months at the speed of life and death when you work in trauma. The weeks after my birthday party were no different. I marvel every day at the ability of human beings to harm each other for reasons I can never understand. Some of the staff call it job security, but I got into nursing trauma patients to help victims of car accidents, heart attacks, broken bones, near-drownings, and such. The stabbings, shootings, beatings filing into the ER like a parade are man-made and have no place in a civilized society. But these almost daily occurrences bring JR to my ER often. His presence distracts me from work and immerses me in my upcoming trip. Mom's almost daily attempts at catastrophic illnesses ramp up my anxiety and guilt.

I sense his presence before I even see his face. JR walks up to the nurse's station and leans over the desk as if he has all the time in the world. My co-worker, Eleanor, seated next to me stops typing and ogles him in his uniform like a vulture breaking its fast.

"*Alo, bonswa*, Addy. You have a minute for a cup of coffee? I want to tell you what I found about Lasalle," he says in Creole. "I'm doing some digging on my own. I have someone in Haiti I trust."

I raise my eyebrows. "*Vrèmen?*"

He raises his own. "I'm a detective, baby."

"*Wi*," I slap my forehead. Eleanor moves her head back and forth between us as if the movement can translate the words for her from Creole to English. "What did you learn?"

"Come on! You have a minute, *Miss*?"

"No. I don't." I hitch my chin toward Eleanor. "She's signing off now. I can't leave." I try to focus my attention on the paperwork in front of me. My heart thumps with anticipation. "Don't go anywhere, JR."

He pouts like a petulant boy. "I'll wait over there." He struts toward the row of plastic chairs in the corner.

Eleanor clears her throat so loudly, all the while I'm praying that an ambulance does not come in. Her beehive hairdo could nest a flock of birds. Her pale gray eyes look young in her sun-damaged face. Like Mom, Eleanor spent too much time in the sun before skin cancer was a concern.

"What did he say?" she asks.

"Oh, he needs to tell me what he learned about…umm…my upcoming trip."

"Un-huh. Why y'all don't speak English?"

I shrug. "Creole's our language."

"He's sweet on you, girl. Watch out."

"Well…I'm not on the market."

"He's a beautiful man, Addy." Eleanor licks her thin lips. I hide my smile behind a stern look. "He has that…yum…bad boy vibe even though he's a law enforcer." She winks. "I'd break the law so he can put handcuffs on me. Wish I was a wee bit younger."

I blush. "Ellie...well, maybe he likes his women a bit...mature. Can you cover me for five minutes?"

"Go, honey." She cackles, shooing me away with her liver-spotted hand.

A stretcher bursts into the unit.

Hours later, I call JR as soon as I have a minute to spare. No answer. At the end of my shift, I open my locker and pull my backpack out, grateful that I have a weekend free of parties from my friends and social obligation from Ben's job. Ninnie's out of town with Dr. Pierre, the longest boyfriend she's ever had, and this is Lisa's seventh wedding anniversary. She reaches the seven-year itch. I'm happy for her.

At home, I kick off my clogs and the cold marble floor cools me off on my way to the kitchen. There's a note on the counter from Ben that he is playing golf with his dad and reminding me of his paternal grandmother's birthday party tonight.

"Goddammit!" I slap my forehead. "I forgot."

In my walk-in closet, I lie down on the silk rug on the floor to do my stretching exercises before my shower. All I really want is to talk to JR. Why doesn't he just leave me a message with the information? He's annoying and inconsiderate. I didn't ask him to dig. Did his person find my mother? I dial his number again.

"Please call me as soon as you have a chance or leave me a message. I do have a social obligation tonight, so I may miss your call. I need to know what your contact found out. Thank you so much for your help." I hit End.

I lace my hands behind my neck on the floor and my gaze stops on the painting of the "Coconut Woman" on the wall. I finally brought it here from Mom's after three years as if I'm not anchored in this house. I love that piece of art. It makes this museum feel like my home.

About an hour later, I set out to select my outfit. Being around Grace always puts me in a competitive mood. It started from the day I met the woman. I still blame Ben, but I suppose I did not help the situation either. Why did he have to propose to me on the day I came face to face with his mother and his ex-fiancée?

I choose a short cranberry silk dress with a boat neck. A pair of beige patent leather sling back, gold dangly earrings and matching bracelet. I towel-dry my hair, and dark brown curls fall pell-mell over my face and neck. I slide a clear headband over my forehead to corral it in place. The smokey eye-makeup accentuates my green eyes. I grin back in the mirror to check for lipstick on my teeth: they shine like pearls. My double dimples always make me wonder which one of my biological parents have bestowed that gift on me. I check my phone for the umpteenth time.

"You look beautiful, Mrs. Barrett," Ben says, rushing into the room, kissing the back of my neck. His sweaty odor mixed with his bold fragrance stirs my body. I start to follow him into the shower.

"I'll be ready soon." He squeezes my butt.

"*Bennie,* we don't have a gift for your grandma. I totally forgot about the party."

"Please don't start, Addy." He shakes his head. "I got something for Grandmother," he yells before closing the shower door.

"Of course, you did," I mutter. The man who remembers everything except his promises to me.

Later at the Barretts, I stand on my toes to kiss Senior's cheek. The butler carries a tray with drinks. We each grab one, except Senior.

"How you're feeling?" I ask. "Following nurse's orders, I hope." I smile but survey him with critical eyes.

I remember my fear last week when I recognized Senior on the stretcher in the emergency room before my training kicked in. The numbness on one side of his face turned out to be a mini stroke.

Senior pulls me in for a hug and kisses my forehead. He turns to a shorter man on his left who looks like him and says, "Little brother, meet Adele, my very competent daughter-in-law."

The man extends his hand. "I'm Cedric. Nice to meet you. Heard so much about you from Senior."

I shake his hand and smile. Grace stares at me from across the room. I stay with the boys.

"I was lucky, Ced," Senior continues, "Adele was on duty. She saved my life. She's quite the trauma nurse."

I swat the air with my hand. "I did not. Make sure you take your medications and don't work so hard."

"Hear that, Ben?" Senior says, taking my left hand in his. "Tell your husband to show up for work for more than a couple of days a week. He thinks playing golf and traveling are in his job description."

I bat my eyelashes at Ben. "You don't go to the office? Don't you have clients who need you to count their money every day?"

Ben bristles. "This is 2009, folks. We have technology now. No one needs to be chained to a desk to manage hedge funds."

"Oh, well, the perks of working for Daddy's firm," I say with what I hope is levity to hide my envy.

Across the big room, I spy Grace in a knot of women whose clothes and jewelry could finance a small nation food supply. The doorbell rings and Paige waltzes in before the butler makes it to the door. Grace races over to hug her and they air-kiss on both cheeks. Paige's golden hair shimmers under the prisms of the chandelier like gemstones. Her eyes scan the room and stop on my husband. She smiles at him. He waves his hand halfway before he lowers it when our eyes meet. Grace and Paige make their way over to our group.

"Cedric, you remember Paige," Grace says. "She's like family. Paige just moved back here from Europe."

"Hi Paige," Ben says. "Why don't I get you a drink?" He rushes to the bar.

Senior still holds my hand. "Paige, you remember Ben's wife, Adele."

"Of course," she says. "The nurse, right?" She smiles but more like a grimace. "We met the day Ben proposed to you. Remember. That was…what a couple years ago?"

"It'll be three years in December," I say.

"Well, congratulations. I left the country before the wedding." Her eyes find Ben coming over with a dirty martini.

I throw my left arm around Ben's neck and rest my head on his shoulder. Paige twirls the end of her shawl in a jerky movement, her face reddening under her tan.

"Ben, I'll see you next week in your office," she breathes the words. "I need to go over my investment portfolio with you."

"If you'll excuse me," I say to the group, pulling away from Ben. "I'm going to see the birthday girl." All eyes train on me. Grace sneers. Paige pouts. Senior smiles. Cedric bows. Ben is silent. I sashay over to the solarium.

I sit next to the older woman with Senior's kind eyes. "Thank you for saving my son's life, Addy," Grandma Barrett says. "Now keep an eye on your man and those two vultures. Grace and Paige are up to no good." She lowers her voice. "Paige cheated on Ben after their engagement. Now she wants back in. That girl's smarter than she looks."

I lean over and kiss her cheek. "I'm not worried, Grandma Barrett."

Perhaps I should be. The tension between Grace, Ben, and Paige is unmistakable. I look around the house and a sense of aloneness grips my heart. Even the man who is my husband laughing deeply at inside jokes between his mother and ex-fiancée seems like a total stranger. I clutch my purse with my phone inside and head to the powder room. Voicemail.

"Damnit where's JR?"

# PART 2

# CHAPTER TWENTY-FOUR

## KETLY

*July 1991 – Ten years later*

Ten years ago, I returned from Lasalle with the news that Marge had taken all the information from the clinic that might lead me to her. Like Miss Annette predicted, Marge never returned; neither did Nadine.

I wave to the old groundkeeper of the hospital as I make my way to work. The island has given me the opportunity to become a nurse. It has nurtured me into a respected, valued and self-sufficient member of my community.

"Bonjou, Miss Ketly," the old man says the same thing to me every day in the past five years. "Have a blessed day, Miss."

"And to you the same." I smile, repeating the same answer. We both have not missed many days of work over the years. We love what we do.

Routines keep me grounded in my daily activities and knowing what comes next in my life. I walk into the dressing room at the back of the hospital and change into my starched white nursing uniform on a hanger in my designated locker. I brush mascara onto my eyelashes and run the lip gloss wand over my lips. I pin my nursing cap to the top of my

# I SHALL FIND YOU

chignon. From the maternity ward, I peek into the nursery and the sight of babies everywhere fills part of the void in my core. I love helping women bring their babies into the world in a safe, sterile, light-filled atmosphere.

"Miss Ketly, *Miss Ketly!*" the unit secretary yells, as she pokes her head into the break room where I stand in front of the coffee pot. "Martine's screaming for you."

I can hear the young woman holler before I even turn the corner. "Hey, Martine," I say, wetting a cloth in the basin next to the bed and wiping her face. The July heat is winning the fight against the ceiling fans churning hot air in defeat. "Today's a special day to have a baby."

Martine closes her eyes and groans, riding another contraction. When she opens them, she says, "Why's today's special, Miss Ketly?"

I smile and remember. *"It's my daughter's birthday."* Instead, I say, "Well, some special people were born on July fourteenth."

"Like who?" She huffs.

"Umm...I don't know, but I'm sure there are plenty. People are born every day, and some become famous, and some are very special to someone else."

Martine tries to sit up. "Ooooh, it hurts," she howls, stretching the words like an elastic band.

I move to the foot of the bed to check her progress. "Come on, Martine, the pain will go away as soon as your baby comes out and you won't even remember it."

"How do you know?" She pants. "You don't have kids."

Every time someone says that to me, my womb spasms with emptiness. "I...I read it in nursing books when I was in school." I tap the bottom of her foot and move down the hall to the next room.

Hours later, before leaving the hospital, I step into Martine's room. A bassinet wedged next to the headboard sits empty while she holds her swaddled baby boy in her arms and her husband beams at them, not sure what to do with his hands.

"Isn't he the most beautiful baby you've ever seen, Miss Ketly?" he says.

"Absolutely! Felicitations to you both, although Martine did all the hard work while you did the fun part." I laugh. "What's his name?"

They look at each other and as if they've rehearsed it, say at the same time: "Mathieu."

"A beautiful name. Have a great night, Martine."

"You too Miss Ketly. See you in the morning."

"I'm off the rest of the week. I have business in Port-au-Prince."

"Oh…okay, come by the house when you return, Miss. I want to make sure I'm taking good care of my son."

"Do come to my monthly Mother's Club when you're up and about, Martine. You, too, Papa. First baby can be scary. You'll meet the other first-time parents." I wave to the family before rushing outside.

Later this afternoon, I get off the moped and say to the driver, "Come back for me in a couple hours."

Matante is in her chair with the needle and thread that had become an extension of her fingers working on a pair of shorts I recognize as Victor's. He comes in from the back with a steaming cup in his hands. I smell her favorite tea lemon fragrance wafting in the air.

"Oh, Matante, Miss Ketly's here." He beams like a full moon.

"Go bring her some tea, Vic," Matante says, smiling. "I wasn't expecting you. Everything okay, Bébé?"

# I SHALL FIND YOU

I peck her forehead and pull a chair next to her. "Everything's fine Matante. I wanted to see you before…I'm going to the city tomorrow for my visa interview. I told you the date. Remember?"

She takes my hand. "I hope you get it. You work so hard and I'm proud of you."

"Oh, Matante, you gave me that kick in the pants I needed to do something with my life. I will get this visa because you helped me. You believed in me." I put my head on her shoulder. "I'm sorry for my stubbornness."

"You were going through your teenage rebellion, Kekette." She strokes my face with her calloused palm. "Go get your baby from the thief. I'll be praying for you. You two will be safe here." She pushes her sleeve up and extends her arm toward me.

I reach inside my workbag and like I do during my monthly visits, I check her blood pressure, her temperature and listen to her lungs, her heart and declare her good for another fifty years. She laughs. Her missing teeth no longer embarrass me.

Over the years, I've built my portfolio to secure a visa from the American embassy. Marge has reneged on her promise to help me get to Juliette, but she can't stop me from making the trip to find her. I'm going to America on the strength of what I have accomplished in the past decade. At almost thirty, I've waited a long time for this day with wisdom that has grown out of hardship. Getting off the moped from Mapou, I walk into my dark and lonely house in Galette with joy in my steps.

# CHAPTER TWENTY-FIVE

## Adele

Traffic is sparse on the bridge to Tampa. I push the Tabou Combo CD into the car stereo, which became my absolute favorite Haitian band since JR gave it to me for my birthday in July. It has only been a couple months, but I play it so much, it's skipping already. I tap my right hand on the steering wheel to the beat of the music, while belting out the lyrics. The windshield wipers seem to go with the same tempo as the melody. I scold myself for not transferring my umbrella to this car. The rain's coming down like fists banging on its roof. I raise my face to the rearview mirror and shake my freshly straightened hair. I'll be damned if I'm going to get this hair wet after spending over three hours and the equivalent of a day's work in cash to make it look this sleek for a day. Ben left this morning, only two days after his return from DC to another business trip to New York.

∞∞∞

Last night, he'd rolled onto his back and said, "Addy, I wish you could join me on my trip, but I know you have to work and wouldn't dream of taking the day off."

I'd pressed my lips together to keep the bad words inside. "Well, Ben, you need to give me more notice. I don't work at my daddy's firm. As a matter of fact, I don't have a daddy."

"Touché, Mrs. Barrett," he'd said. "You know…you don't even need to work."

"Stop, Ben," I said, raising my voice. "I just knew you'd say that one day. I love what I do, and I don't only do it for money. Besides, I told you about my plans for the weekend with the girls. It seems like you never listen to what I say."

Clearly, he forgets I have a road trip planned for Lisa's birthday. Are Ben and I a unit? Do I have to lose myself to another person to be happy? I love Ben but I want to remain Adele Pearson. The daughter. The nurse. The friend. The wife. One day a mother. Do I have to give something up to be all of these? If so, what?

I almost miss the exit to MLK Boulevard from the Howard Frankland bridge. The streaking noise of the wipers on the dry windshield pulls my eyes to the wink of sun peeking from behind fluffy clouds in the sky. I park in a shopping plaza with a nail salon, a Caribbean food store with a money transfer sign taped to the front door, a laundromat and tucked at the very end is a Haitian restaurant. I still put my big canvas bag over my head to thwart off an errant raindrop as I duck out of the car and dash through the front door. JR smiles, waving to me from his booth.

"No doubt, you're Haitian," he says, raising his bottle of Prestige beer in a salute.

I squint at him. "Why?"

"Because Haitians will run for cover from one drop of rain, but not from raining bullets." He guffaws.

"I've never heard anything like that before," I say, sliding into the booth. The tear in the plastic scrapes the back of my thigh below my skirt.

"Ouch," I say, rubbing the spot. The smell of fresh garlic and onions makes my stomach growl.

"I see, I have a lot of work to do to make you an authentic Haitian. The genes help, but you need exposure." He cocks his eyebrows and the sunshine coming through the picture window seems to go through his irises and turn them translucent.

The waitress skips toward us with nothing in her hands. "*Bonswa, m'sier,*" she says to JR in Creole and smiles, showing all her teeth. "*M'se Marjorie. I'll be your waitress.*" She leans into his shoulder to touch the beer bottle, her fingers gliding over the back of his hand. "Want another one?"

The two unfastened buttons of her white blouse reveal the top of her breasts straining against the confines of the fabric. Before JR can answer, she glances at me, and the smile disappears, replaced by a scowl. She nods and says in heavily accented English, "Good afternoon, Madame. What you wanna drink?"

"*Bonswa, Marjorie,*" I say in Creole. "I'll have *Haitian* coffee, please." I lick my lips. "And a Prestige, too. Oh, do you have akra?"

"Ah," she says, turning to a laughing JR, "she speaks Creole. I thought she was Hispanic or something."

"*Non,*" I say. "*Haitienne natif natal, Pitit.*"

"So, where you from in Haiti?" she peers unblinkingly into my eyes as if she can find the truth.

I look at JR, at great loss for words. Where am I from in Haiti? Isn't it the reason why I'm sitting across from this man I met a couple months ago? To find that very answer. I sip some water from my glass and wet my throat.

"Marj," JR says to the waitress, placing his palm on the plastic covered menu on the table. "I'll have another beer while you grab hers and I'll be ready to order for us when you return." He smiles up into her face.

As soon as she is out of earshot, I whisper, "What did you find out, JR? My PI called last night. His person found the clinic where Mom used to work and the house that sits across from it where the nurses ate and drank after work." I place my phone on the table. "See how I'm telling people I'm Haitian and I don't even know where Lasalle is, where my umbilical cord is buried."

His smiling eyes open wide. "Okay! Haitian woman."

"Please tell me what you learn."

"Right. Let's order and I'll tell you what I know so far," he says slowly as if I'm a child about to throw a tantrum.

What if he'd learned something bad? Like my bios are not alive. Maybe I don't want to know until I make the journey for myself. When Marjorie returns with the beers, JR orders many dishes without looking at the menu. I notice she doesn't write anything down.

"How will she remember all this?" I whisper to her back.

"She'll bring what they have." JR laughs. "You probably don't know how long it takes to cook authentic Haitian food." He tilts his head. "It's too early in the day for much."

I smile remembering Nadine teaching me and the girls to cook Haitian food over the years. We'd start with preparing the spices: peeled garlic, onions, celery, sour orange juice, cloves, different types of peppers, salt, vinegar. She'd blend it all and pour it over the pork chunks and let it marinate in the fridge overnight to make grio the following day. The smell of the cooking food was enough to fill us up with anticipation and a taste of what was to come. Nadine complimented me for being the best culinary student of the three musketeers. She was a great teacher.

I make a face at JR across the table. "See, JR. I know how to cook Haitian food. It's in my blood. Nadine is the best cook."

"So, Nadine's been going on mission in Lasalle with your mom, right?"

"Yes," I drag the one syllable. "But the last time she was there was the year before I was born. In July 1980 when Mom found me outside the clinic, you know," I prompt, waving my hand. He nods. "Nadine didn't go because she gave birth to Ninnie that August. Since then, Nadine only went on missions to Gressier which is where her family's from. Why d'you ask?"

Laden with a huge tray, Marjorie places the dishes on the table. "The lambi's not ready yet so I bring you *mori*." JR pulls his lips in, hiding the laughter lurking in his tamarind eyes. "We make the best salted fish in town."

"I have no doubt," he says.

"Oh, we don't have black rice," she continues, "so I'm giving you some *pitimi* with beans on the house. I bring *paté kodé*, and fried plantains. The akra is not ready yet, but I'll bring you some marinades soon." She arranges the plates in front of JR as if I'm not even there. "Anything else you need, *Officer*?" She strip-searches him with her eyes.

"We're good, Marj. *Mesi*." She bats her eyelashes at him. I cough in my hand to hide the smile.

"Call me if you need *anything*." She pivots like a dancer, shaking her backside like a Morse code.

"How did she know you're a cop."

"I've been here in uniform before, but immigrants are weary of the law. Marjorie's got papers."

"How can you tell?"

"She'd be working in the kitchen if she was undocumented. Not waiting tables. They have signals, you know."

And here I am with an American birth certificate and passport. I vote. I have many legal identities, but I'm also an adoptee. I chew a piece of fried pork. "*My grio* tastes better."

"Mm-huh!" JR says, licking his fingers after putting a piece of fried plantain in his mouth. He rubs his bottom lip with his index finger. The AC unit in the window coughs periodically before belching a gust of cool air into the room and releasing JR's musky cologne. I fight the urge to lean over and touch his hand.

I put my fork down. "JR, what's the news?"

He lowers his eyes to my face. "Well, since the only piece of information we have is that your mother is from Lasalle, I decided to start there. Too bad that's not where Nadine went back to over the years. Haitian villages keep secrets, and it takes time to build trust before people will tell you what they know. My friend stopped there a few days ago. He travels the countryside as a water technician for one of the many NGOs taking over the country." JR sighs as he pulls a napkin from the dispenser on the table and wipes his lips and hands. "Yesterday, he called to say, he found the clinic or more precisely where it used to be."

I pull my spine from the back of the booth and lean in, my heart beating loudly in my ears. "What…but my PI said they found the clinic in Lasalle?"

"He's right. It's in the same place but they expanded it into a primary school and built a bigger clinic next door, and he confirms the house across from the clinic as well. Now the woman, Rose who lives there remembers something."

I grab JR's upper arm. "Remember what…who?"

"Calm down, Addy." He pats my hand. "Lasalle's only about an hour by car from Port-au-Prince. My friend will go back. Neighbors corroborated that Rose's related to a woman named Clara who owned the house and had a daughter and two sons. Rose asked him to bring her phone cards next time."

"So, is he going back this week? I can send money if he needs to…you know bribe her."

He clicks his tongue. "No. He told her he's scouting Lasalle for his NGO. She can't know that he's there for info about a green-eyed baby left at the clinic almost thirty years ago because someone was threatened. It would scare Rose into silence. These villagers don't trust city folks."

"But…"

"We're getting somewhere, Addy." The impatience must be painted on my face. "Don't you see? Hopefully by the time we go in December, we'll just drive, walk or donkey over to your biological mother's house somewhere in Haiti."

"Why you say mother and not parents?"

"Because," he pauses to stare into my eyes, "a mother with a husband or the father of her child by her side would *never* abandon that child to save her life. My guess is your mother was very young. Your father might have…you know taken advantage of her."

"What? You mean…as in…*rape*." The word congeals the food in my stomach. "I don't think so. In the note she wrote that she and *my* papa would come back for me."

He still taps his chin with his index finger. "I'll bet my pension, your father's the problem," he says. "Somehow."

"Problem…" I mutter.

"And he has green eyes," he continues, his gaze drilling into mine as if he can see the culprit.

I nod. "Well women have been fixing problems created by men since the beginning of forever."

"But women are so powerful in their apparent fragility that men unknowingly fall into traps we can hardly escape," he replies.

Not letting him have the last word, I bat my eyelashes and say, "What would be the meaning of life for men without women?"

"Indeed," he says.

"*En effet*," I say.

# CHAPTER TWENTY-SIX

❀❀❀

## KETLY

*July 1991*

In my bedroom, I open my satchel and drop the letter from the bank showing my impressive balance, my employment verification letter signed by the hospital administrator, the invitation from Raoul's sister, Suzanne, to stay with her during my stay in Miami, my birth certificate, my passport and the deed to my house. Next, I pull the overnight bag from the closet and start packing.

"Miss Ketly," the voice yells from the doorway. It's Tim-Tim, a teenage boy who hangs around the wharf and brings me monthly letters from Alphonse. "You're home late. I came before," he says, handing me the envelope.

"Follow me." I walk with him to the back of the four-room house. I built it solely to pad my portfolio. Will I spend the rest of my life on this island? I don't know. It all depends on what happens at the interview for the visa. If I bring Juliette back home, this will be the safest place to live. For my daughter, I'll do anything. I grab two coins from under the tablecloth and hand them to him.

# I SHALL FIND YOU

We stand in the middle of the room. "How many babies today, Miss Ketly and what are their names?" It's a game we play.

"Tim-Tim...I don't remember. I have a lot on my mind today."

"Tomorrow, then. Bye, Miss Ketly."

I open the envelope and read. Alphonse is a loyal friend. In my selfishness, I failed in the past to see how he had put his feelings aside to help me leave Port-au-Prince alive. My road to safety has been paved with angels along the way to protect me under their wings.

July brings lots of rain on the island, turning the potholes into mini reservoirs. People hustle to get indoors before the deluge. I look down at the ground to avoid stepping into mud with my new sandals.

I pluck three red hibiscus and a bunch of purple bougainvillea from the hedge that circles the church. I miss the fruit-laden trees of Mapou and its starry nights, but Galette offers year-round blooming and fragrant flowers to make up for all the trees that had to be sacrificed to build a capital city on the island. The Lycée sits across the park, next to the police station. The six policemen on the force play dominoes all day long or chase wayward hogs or chickens reported missing by their owners. Not much crime occurs here in public. Domestic disputes do not concern the authorities, even when the women come to the hospital with broken bones, missing teeth, and hopelessness.

As president of the nursing association, I started the "*Respè Fam*" program last year to empower women to demand respect, equality and access to family planning. Domestic violence charges are now filed routinely. Under pressure from our organization, the policemen have no choice but to chase men too, even if not with the same ardor as a missing pig.

As soon as I step onto Alice's porch, droplets of rain kiss my cheeks. I hurry to get inside and pull the door halfway closed behind me. She looks at the clock on her dining room wall.

"We've been waiting for you to cut the cake," she says.

"I had to see Matante after work this afternoon. I plan to leave as soon as I get the visa and a seat on a plane." I shrug. "I'll sit on the wings if I have to."

Alice pulls me into an embrace. "I pray you get it, Sister."

"I want to bring my daughter back with me, Ali."

At the table, Simon climbs off his chair where a tall blue and pink-frosted cake sits with eleven candles jutting from the middle. He wraps his arms around my legs trying to pick me up off the ground.

"Stop Simon." I laugh, bending down to drop kisses on his head. Lanky fifteen-year-old Eddy ambles over and lifts me up. "Eddy, put me down, boy." I swat his back with the flowers, giggling, hibiscus petals floating to the floor. "It wasn't that long ago I was bouncing you on my knees. Ali, Eddy was what…four when I met you for the first time on the ferry?" We nod at each other.

"No one ever told me who Juliette is," Simon says, pointing at the cake with the words: *Bonne Fête Simon et Juliette*. "I always imagined she was my twin, and I killed her."

I gather the boy in my arms. His softness cushions my heart like a pillow. I hand the bouquet to him and the wrapped gift box containing the silver car. I rub his head with my palm. "She's a special girl who was born in July, too," I whisper in his ear.

"But where is she? Why we never see her?" The pre-teen asks.

"Simon let's cut the cake," Raoul says, walking to the table with a box of matches.

It's after ten in the evening when the boys finally make their way to their bedrooms after their friends leave. "I'll clean up," Raoul says, almost pushing me and Alice outside. Soon he joins us on the porch with tall glasses of rum punch. I gulp half the glass and close my eyes.

# I SHALL FIND YOU

"You know Mama had a recipe for the most potent drink and Mi... I mean Marge and Nadine would come over every night from the clinic for dinner, but I think it was the booze that attracted them the most."

Alice reaches for my shaky hand. "Are you ready, *ma petite soeur?*"

"I'm so afraid of a refusal. That's my last hope, Ali."

"Oh, you'll get a visitor visa," Raoul says, pouring more drinks into our glasses. "You have impressive credentials. Besides Suzanne's an attorney in Miami. She'll help you with bringing Juliette home."

"By the way, Raoul, it took three trips to the bank for that acting president to get my financial information right," I say. "I guess no one from Port-au-Prince wants the job here, huh?"

"Somebody's starting in two weeks, as a matter of fact," he says. "Luc's young and quite excited to come here. He knows he'd never get a position like that at any bank in the city. Dogs eat dogs there."

I tilt my head. "What's he running from?"

Alice lets out her high-pitched laugh. I join in. Raoul tries to look stern as if we're unruly girls and gives up with a smile.

"Good luck with the interview, Kekette," he adds.

"What I need is a husband and a couple of kids to shore up my credentials."

"Well, can't help you with that," Raoul says, walking back inside.

"I guess it would have helped if I had a family here." I lean from my seat toward Alice. "Alphonse wanted to marry me. Maybe I should have taken him up on the offer."

"Kekette, that sounds horrible." Alice peers at me in the diffuse light coming from the ceiling light. The rain drizzles, and a soft breeze blows the mosquitoes away. "You don't mean that."

"I do. At least one of us would have been happy." I shrug.

"How about you? Don't you deserve love and happiness? It's a tough road to marry for convenience, Kekette."

I stare at her. "I have not had sex in a dozen years, Ali." Raoul places the plates with slices of cake on the table next to me and skips back inside pulling the door closed behind him. "No man on this island has ever looked at me with interest. It's as though I repel them. Why?"

"Kekette you're a great nurse and community leader, but I heard rumors that the men are scared of you with all the empowering programs you run here for women."

"Well, I'm never going to find a man on this island, then. I won't stop teaching women to demand what they deserve." I stand after draining the glass. "I'm going to bed." I hug my friend and kiss her cheek before peeling her arms from around my waist and plunge into the night. I stop at the wharf before going home. Small fishing boats with flickering lamps litter the surface of the sea. I peer into the darkness of the water and feel the calm that the sounds of the waves always bring me. On the other side of the ocean is the daughter my heart will never forget.

# CHAPTER TWENTY-SEVEN

## ADELE

It was a quiet shift in the ER today, allowing my mind to somersault between the conflicts raging in my head. Why is it that my husband is not interested in having sex? Since we saw Paige two weeks ago at his grandmother's birthday party, Ben's been moody. Paige left the country shortly before our wedding and I hadn't thought about her, knowing she was on another continent. But the most surprising thing is that I'm not jealous as much as I hate anyone taking something that belongs to me, if I still want it.

"Earth to Adele," Miss Beulah says. "You've been staring at the yarn like it's gonna knit itself. We have to work faster to finish the quilt before Christmas."

"Yes, ma'am," I say, plunging the needle through the square of red yarn.

She leans toward me and speaks loudly despite her hearing aid. "Everything's okay at home, Addy?" She rests her hands on her lap crossing the needles. The other women stop chattering. Beulah glares at them. The clicking sounds of knitting needles fill the circle again. "Been a while since I've been in love, Addy," she now whispers, "but I remember you have to work at it like this quilt we're making. You understand what I'm saying?" I nod. "And don't let anyone else come between you and your husband. Three people in a marriage never work."

I kiss her cheek. She smells of Ivory soap and bergamot hair grease. Her gray afro is thinning at the crown, but her eyes shine with wisdom and mischief. Since I told her about Paige and she'd met JR when he came over to the senior center last week to give me some updates from Haiti that he could have done over the phone, she's been throwing these pieces of advice into our conversation.

"As always, you're right, Miss Beulah. Life sometimes throws you curve balls to see which one you'll chase." We resume knitting.

A bit later, she looks at the clock on the wall. "Don't be late surprising your husband, Girlie."

Ben left for work this morning, before I was even awake. He's training a group of new hires today. He likes to be on time. Last week I was on the last day of my period and Ben always acts like it's the plague. Surprised, he doesn't come to bed in a hazmat suit when I'm menstruating. I chuckle. Now I'm so horny I can't think straight. We're practically still newlyweds; therefore, we should be having more sex than we are. I try.

After my shower, I slip into a pair of thong panties, a red cotton mini dress and red espadrilles. I tease my hair to make it big, apply more makeup than I usually wear, choosing clear lip gloss instead of my regular red lipstick. I plan to lick that boy like a dog happy to see his master and I don't want to paint him red. I spritz another spray of Chanel No. 5 behind my ears, the back of my knees and between my legs. A scent that stirs me and too many memories of my first love. I hope Ben's nose follows the trail. I giggle.

I pull my car into the parking garage of the skyscraper where Barrett Enterprises is located. I take the escalator upstairs to where his office is located. "Hi, Kathi," I say to his secretary. "How are you doing?"

"I'm fine, Adele. Thank you," the petite brunette says. "He should be almost done. You want me to call him?"

"Oh, no it's a surprise."

I stand by the private elevator Ben uses to get in and out of his office. Shortly, with his head down and his cell phone to his ear, he starts to walk past me.

"Hey sailor," I say. "You wanna have a good time?"

He looks up and says to the person on the phone. "I'll call you back…umm…later."

He picks me up and twirls me around. The security guard claps. Ben winds his arm around my waist, and we wait for the elevator that leads to the parking garage.

"I didn't expect you, Addy. What a surprise." He kisses my forehead.

"I have more surprises." I pinch his butt. "I'm going to feed you, but you can have dessert first."

On the third level, I press the keyfob to open the doors to my car.

"What about my car, Adele? Oh, I need to go to the dry cleaners. I have errands—"

"I'll bring you back to pick up your car after dinner, Ben. Stop asking so many questions." My excitement now ebbs and flows.

"Addy, why did you park in the darkest part. It's not safe."

"You'll see," I say in a deep voice, as I slide into the driver seat. Ben gets in and closes the passenger door. As he reaches for his seat belt, I stop his hand and swing my left leg and then the rest of my body over the console to land square in his lap.

"Adele, what…what are you doing?"

"What does it *feel* like I'm doing, *mon amour*?" I murmur, grinding my groin into his. I feel his tentative erection but his face registers shock. He peers into the darkness outside. "I miss my husband...a lot," I whine, sticking my tongue into his ear. He squirms away. He grabs my thighs as if to lift me off him, his hands slide up to the side of my butt.

"Oh, you...you have no panties on."

I kiss his lips. "You like that, bad boy?" I whisper.

"Umm...Adele, let's go home. We have a bedroom, a bed...I need a shower. What...what if someone sees us?"

The more he talks the more I feel myself retreat into this woman I don't want to be. Conventional. Predictable. Rigid. I move back to my seat, start the car, click my seat belt in place and burn rubber out of the garage. Ben grabs the dashboard, throwing side glances at me but says nothing. For that I'm grateful. At the exit, I stop and he jumps out of the car.

Later that evening, Ben climbs on the bed and pulls me into the middle of it. "I'm sorry...umm...I was such a prude this afternoon. I want to make it up to you, Addy."

He kisses the back of my neck, his hands mapping my skin with urgency. The rejection earlier still rankles. I'm used to being chased, not being the hunter. When Ben tries to turn me on my back into the missionary position, I try to resist as my mind takes me to some memories that are too strong to fight.

∞∞∞

It was Andrew, sprawled on my back, his weight squishing me into the sand. The waves crashed over our entwined feet under the stars, while he whispered those racy words in my ears that always drove me to explode before he even got to the last base. I could hear the laughter strangling his words, "Do you like it, *Adelina*?" Andrew nibbled on my earlobe. "Tell me how much, baby. I want to hear it."

"I like it a lot," I cried. "I do. I do. Yes, *I fucking do.*"

Ben stops thrusting into me and through the sliver of light coming from the bathroom nightlight, I see horror on his face and realize I have spoken the words aloud. Ben likes silence and darkness with his sex. I pull my lips into my mouth, like a zipper, swallowing the sexy words I want to say to my husband. I close my eyes and wait for the release that never comes, while everything else escapes my body in a flash, leaving me empty and wanting.

# CHAPTER TWENTY-EIGHT

## KETLY

*July 1991 – Port-Au-Prince*

The cab drops me off in front of the building with an American flag snapping in the early morning breeze. I curb my urge to kneel and pray on the steps as if it can grant my wish before I face my fate inside. The multi-storied structure looms above me. Employees walk up the steps with purpose, looking at watches and skipping the rest of the way. My watch reads eight twelve. I take my place behind the line on the side of the building. My new black shoes with two-inch heels squeeze my feet. I run my palm over the skirt of my cream linen suit, square my shoulders and exhale, trying to remember to do that more often.

"Bonjour, Madame," says the security guard, a bow-legged man with a thick mustache that covers his upper lip.

"Bonjour, Monsieur." He opens the door. I step into the cool foyer. Behind a desk in the middle of the room sits a young woman with skin the color of ripe mangos. Her name tag reads: Siani Bienvenue.

"What's your name, Madame?" Siani asks.

"Ket…" I clear my throat. "Umm…Miss Ketly Elina Murat."

She runs one long red-painted nail down a list on a clipboard and puts a check mark next to my name. She tilts her head toward the hallway. "Have a seat in the Blue Room. Someone will be with you shortly."

The first nameplate on the wall next to a door reads: Meredith Brown. The room's empty. The second nameplate is Sheila Carrey. She sits behind a desk with a mountain of files in a corner of it. Her light brown eyes crinkle at the corner in a smile. I wave and smile back, feeling a slack in the band squeezing my chest. The next room is beige and empty with the name: Mark Fuller on the plate. I freeze in front of the one next to it. *Helène Macombe,* the woman who kept Juliette for almost three months before Marge could get her to America over a decade ago.

The woman I attempted to see twice over the years but was not allowed to without an interview. Without thinking, I walk into the office, and she looks up and squints. Her wavy hair streaked with silver, frames a still-youthful face, but she's almost as white as Marge.

"May I help you?" she says in French, gnawing at the tip of the pen in her hand, a smile fleeting over her thin lips. Maybe my interview is with her. Surely, she'll help me.

"Yes, yes." I try to slow my booming heart. "My name's Ketly, Ketly Murat and…" The smile disappears from her lips; her eyes widen, showing a lot of white around her hazel irises. She puts the pen down and stares at me as if I'm a ghost. "Miss Marge…Marge Pearson said she left my daughter, Juliette…umm…she calls her Adele now, but…she left my daughter with you in 1980 before she could come for her."

"Madame." Helène stands. "I have no idea what you're talking about. You have clearly confused me with somebody else." She walks around the desk forcing me to step backward until we get to the door. "What are you doing here anyway?"

"I have an interview for a visitor visa. I'm going to find my daughter."

"Well, good luck then," she says and closes the door in my face.

I raise my fist to knock. I'm confused. Why did she say she had no idea what I was talking about? I lower my hand. I don't want to be late for my interview or cause a scene. In the Blue Room, people dressed in their best fill three rows of seats. Hope paints us all with the same brush. A woman rolling the beads of her rosary points to the chair next to her—the only vacant one.

"I'm Marie-Marthe," she says. "This is my second time trying to get a visa. I want to go to New York. My son and his wife live there. I can help them with the kids. Where your people at?"

"Miami," I whisper, pushing my back hard against the plastic chair to stop my body from shaking. Why does Helène pretend she doesn't know Marge or Juliette? Clearly, she recognizes my name. I close my eyes trying to decipher the meaning of all this. Every half-hour or so, a short middle-aged woman comes through the doorway and calls someone. Minutes later, the ones blessed with visas peek into the waiting room and smile, wishing the rest of us good luck. Those who are denied drag their bodies outside with their heads down in humiliation. I hum in my head.

"What time was your interview supposed to be?" Marie-Marthe asks. "I came early. Mine's at ten-thirty."

"Ketly Murat," the older woman calls.

I stand.

"Bonne chance," Marie-Marthe says, "I'm praying for you."

I nod. "Merci beaucoup."

I enter the office next to Helène's. The man doesn't look up from the thin folder he's reading from. I pull the envelope with my original documents from my handbag and put it on my lap, pressing down to stop my feet from tapping the floor.

A while later, he raises his head. "I'm Mark Fuller. I'll be conducting your interview. May I please have the documents we requested in our letter to you?"

I slide the package across the desk toward his extended hand. Our eyes meet. I smile. He looks away. He opens the envelope and pulls everything out, placing it on the desk. He flips the bank letter face down without reading it, doing the same with the employment verification and the deed. Hope lifts off my body like green leaves in a windstorm. I wrap my arms around my mid-section. He picks up the invitation letter from Suzanne and nods as he reads the two paragraphs. He turns it over as if looking for something more.

"How do you know Suzanne Rémy?" he asks, still staring at the letter.

"I met her over ten years ago. Her brother Raoul and his wife Alice are very close friends. Suzanne comes to Haiti—I mean Galette every December with her family." I smile. "I'm practically a member of the family."

"You have children, Madame Murat?"

"Wha...?" I swallow a lump. "No...no, I don't have children. I mean, not here. It's a...long story, sir."

"What will you be doing in Miami during your stay?" He asks, shoving all the documents back inside the envelope.

I relax my shoulders down. "Oh, Suzanne has all kinds of fun activities for us to do and there's her fortieth birthday bash."

He hits some keys on the computer on the desk and jots down words on a pad. I crane my neck to see, but it's all in English. I shift on the chair the way I used to do in school when the *pinèz* sucked my blood. It's almost eleven on the clock behind him. On the credenza are framed pictures of Mark with a smiling woman with curly black hair and two boys who look like him. The dog in the middle seems to be smiling as well. Stick figure drawings in orange, yellow, and blue dot the side walls. Suddenly, he looks at me from the computer screen for a brief second.

"Madame Murat, I'm sorry but…umm…we cannot issue you a visa to the US at this time."

The words tunnel into me. Juliette recedes in the distance, getting smaller and smaller. I reach out my hand to grab her and it lands on Monsieur Fuller's fingers splayed on top of the desk. He pushes his chair back, dropping his hands in his lap. My terror mirrors in his eyes. "Madame Murat, you need to leave."

"Monsieur Fuller," I whisper. "Should I return another time?"

He stands but remains behind the desk. "Madame, I don't know what to tell you." He glances at his watch. "I'm…really sorry."

He comes from behind the desk and opens the door. I pull myself out of the chair and blink the tears clouding my vision. At Helène Macombe's open door, I stop, our eyes connect. The corner of her upper lip lifts in a sneer. She reaches for the telephone and swivels around with her back to me. I stumble outside, pushing through the line of people that has grown longer and thicker. Some of them will get a visa today, but one thing is certain, I will never get a visitor visa to America as long as Helène Macombe works at an American embassy anywhere there is one.

On the sidewalk, I hold the folder over my forehead as if to block the sun, but in truth I feel naked standing in the middle of Port-au-Prince without my disguise. I don't have much trust in people. I flag a taxi and climb inside. It's empty. I pray he won't pick up anybody else before dropping me at Alphonse's house. I'm in no mood for small talk. Marge has stolen my baby and I'm running out of options to get her back.

"Excuse me, Madame. This is your stop," the cab driver says.

"Oh, I'm…sorry." I reach for my wallet.

I hope no one's home at Alphonse's mother's house. I want to be alone with my thoughts. Inside, I push the bedroom door open and tiptoe through it, knowing his wife is in the back house Alphonse built before their marriage. They have a boy and she's pregnant again.

∞∞∞

Yesterday, I was full of hope of getting a visa when Alphonse picked me up at the wharf in a rusty Peugot. Simone no longer allowed him to drive her car to his house. Someone reported seeing his wife in the car with their child. She didn't relent, even when Alphonse explained that his son had fallen ill and was unconscious and he needed to get him to the hospital fast.

"Why do you still work for Simone?" I asked him on our way here. "Please don't stay because of me, Alph. This woman can corrode your soul."

"Driving is all I know how to do well. It's not easy finding a job like this here." He honked at a pedestrian. "How many people do you think have cars here and need a chauffeur. But since I'm there, I can find out if she's planning to harm you. You know."

"Thank you, Alph." These words were too small, but they were all I had to offer him.

"On that note, couple days ago, I heard Simone on the phone telling someone that Henri left Paris. Her PI said Henri's been in Africa. And Simone cried as she told that person on the phone that her son has not spoken to her since he left Haiti a decade ago. Kekette, I believe Henri left Paris before receiving your letter."

"Alph, I've always believed that. Well, I lost my daughter. Simone lost her son." I felt no joy in all this misery.

"I guess now that I'm a parent," he said, "Henri's rejection's the ultimate punishment for Simone. She deserves it."

I snickered. "There will never be enough punishment for this killer."

Now I kick my black pumps off, rubbing my sore toes. I move quickly before Alphonse, or his wife returns. I change into a pair of cotton shorts and a matching blouse, strapping my feet into my sandals. I leave a note on the dining room table letting Alphonse know I didn't get the visa and close the door behind me. I buy a pack of cigarettes from the store down the street and walk to the bus that will take me to the ferry. I have my work, my auntie, my friends and my committees on the island. I have a good life to live. But one day I want to look my daughter in the eyes and tell her I did not throw her away in that cardboard box.

# CHAPTER TWENTY-NINE

❀❀❀

## ADELE

The busy workday has left me wrung out and restless. I drive like I'm in a parade through downtown. I don't want to go to that empty house. Before our marriage, I wanted to start our life together in a neutral territory, but when Ben dragged his feet on it, I let the matter drop. I could tell he loved his house. It's in the same zip code as his mother's.

Now I yawn so wide my jaw clicks. The timing of the road trip with the girls couldn't have been better. I need to escape from Ben, the hospital, Mom, JR, the PI. I yawn again, grateful to be off tomorrow. In my line of work, there's no room for too many errors. Saving lives depends on being sharp and present. The sun hovers on the edge of the water casting jewels on its surface. I love sunset.

Later at home, I pull my carryon from the closet and start packing for the weekend. I lift the hanger with the white dress I wore the night I met Ben at the gallery. Too sexy. I spread the fingers of my left hand and contemplate my wedding rings. "I'm not on the market anymore," I mutter. Yet, I fold the dress and put it in the suitcase.

Today, I pick up Lisa first. "Hey, birthday girl," I say. "You're the baby of the group. Wait, so how d'you get in kindergarten with me and Ninnie when your birthday's so late in September?"

Lisa snorts as if the sound's coming from her nose. Kids used to call her the Little Red Pig in school, until Ninnie beat up somebody for it. "Well, Addy, my mom knew somebody who knew somebody," she whispers. "It was all hush-hush."

"Oh, The Kindergarten mafia ring," I whisper back. We laugh until I pull in front of Ninnie's condo, where she's pacing like a sentry.

"Why she looks so mad already, Liss?"

Lisa shrugs and rolls down her window. "Hey Ninnie. I love your dress."

Ninnie bends down and kisses Lisa's cheeks. "Thank you, Liss." She opens the back door and slides in, pulling her bag next to her on the seat. She taps the back of my head, hard. "Why you always appoint yourself the designated driver, Adele?" She sucks her teeth like she's playing a musical note. "I wanted to drive."

"I swear, one of these days you're gonna swallow some teeth. I'm driving because you're a fool on the road and I don't want to die this weekend," I say. "And Lisa doesn't like to drive anyway. So, sit back and enjoy the ride. Oh, and shut up unless you have something nice to say."

"Dang, girl, you're in a foul mood," Ninnie starts with her teeth-sucking, then stops. "What's wrong, Addy? Not being laid enough?" She lets out her deep-throated laugh. "That's why I love me a Haitian man. I think, the tropical heat makes them horny all the time."

"Eugenie Anne Moise," Lisa turns to look at her. "You ever think about anything else besides…you know."

"Fucking!" Ninnie scoffs. "No. Is there anything else besides a good cognac to rid the body of life's daily assault?"

I look at Lisa. We shake our heads. "What's wrong with her," Lisa mouths. I shrug and find an oldies station. We sing along to the music our mothers played when we were growing up in the eighties.

It's a sunny autumn day and I'm in no hurry. I get on US 19 and plan to hit all the small towns along Route 27 and Route 98. The landscape never changes going through Homosassa Springs, Crystal River, Chiefland. Based on the number of churches we drive by, there shouldn't be any sinners left in these towns.

"Man, I'm starving," I say. "Anybody else? We can stop soon." Food always unites us.

On a stretch of Route 98, the treetops from both sides of the street seem to meet in the middle until I drive through, and they part like a green curtain.

"Oooh! Look at that sign," Ninnie says. "City of Mexico Beach. Let's stop here. I need to pee anyway and I'm hungry too."

Lisa closes the canvas bag with the chips, nuts and grapes we've been munching on along the way. "I want some real food, too."

I leave the main road and meander around the town before pulling in front of a wooden shack with a tiki roof. The sign reads: Best Soul Food in Town. We order samples of almost everything on the menu. For two hours, we eat, drink unsweetened iced tea and gossip. We consume enough lard to clog leaks on a submarine, but I've never had greens with crunchy bacon or cornbread with cream of corn oozing from below the top crust.

"Let's make our way to the hotel," I say. I stretch my arms over my head as I slide out of the booth. "I want to swim in the ocean tonight."

A couple of miles from the restaurant, Ninnie's snoring in the back and Lisa's head keeps hitting the doorframe. I hum to the song playing on the radio to stay awake.

At the hotel, we follow the bellhop pulling our luggage through the glitzy lobby with its gleaming marble floor to the registration desk. Our eighth-floor suite overlooks the ocean. I open the French door and step onto the balcony. Lisa and Ninnie follow. We stand in silence for a long time, each lost in her own thoughts. Seabirds fly in formation, free to go anywhere their wings can take them. Many people are limited by politics, geography, laws as to where they can go in the world. An American passport breaks many of these limitations. For that, I am grateful.

# PART 3

# CHAPTER THIRTY

## KETLY

*Summer 1996*

Five years ago, when I returned from Port-au-Prince without the visa, I threw myself deeper into my community. They had given me so much; I wanted to give back as much as I was able.

The smell of the potluck dinner we share at every monthly meeting reminds me that I'd worked through lunch today. I hasten my steps to the parish hall at the back of the church, where my Mother's Club meets once a month. Most of the members also attend our monthly *Réspè Famm* club meetings as well. It seems the more children they have, the less they fight for their rights to have a voice in their relationship. Men on the island want nothing to do with me, when their partners no longer put up with their bullshit. They have been coming to our hospital with "accidents" more frequently than the women do now.

"Hey, Miss Ketly," Martine says. "I save you some of my *pain patate* before these vultures eat it all." She laughs when Eveline yanks on the braid on the side of her head.

"Who you're calling vultures," Eveline teases. "You need to make more. You're so stingy."

"Well, my husband ain't complaining." Martine pats her belly with baby number three.

The women laugh. I can almost see the tension lifting from hunched shoulders, furtive looks, and measured words. They talk, they listen, they share, they gossip, they giggle. They never bring their children. They have learned they're not bad mothers for enjoying time away from their kids. In fact, it makes them better mamas.

Elisia hands me a covered plate of food. I sit in a circle of women of all ages. Some of them can barely read, some have gone to university in Port-au-Prince and come back home to settle down. I've learned so much from this diverse group. I clap my hands after dinner. The room gets silent. "Let's begin," I say.

We go around the table, and everyone checks in with updates on whatever they are working on from the month before. The support is palpable. No room for judgment.

"Miss Ketly, how long I have to wait to get pregnant again after stopping the pill?" Elisia asks. "We're ready for a second child." She beams. Her three-year-old son is striving after a challenging start. She's a fast learner.

"Hey, Elisia, don't let him have all the fun," Martine yells from across the room. The women hoot.

I smile. "Okay, I'll go over it again, Elisia."

Beretta is shifting in her seat, a smile flitting across her beautiful face. She is one of the women who did not go to school much before having her five children. She works hard to give them what she did not have. "You have something to share?" I ask her.

She almost jumps out of her chair with excitement. "My oldest daughter receives a scholarship to go to the city to university." The women clap. Those sitting next to her tap her on her shoulders. "The kids are all doing so much better in school, since their father left. They tell me how happy they are for the peace in the house and that I'm not being battered." She pumps her fist in the air. "I should have had him arrested long time ago."

"Better late than never," goes a chorus of replies.

"Congratulations, Beretta," I say. "You're a super mama."

At the end of the meeting, women walk in groups to husbands, children, boyfriends.

"Thank you, Miss Ketly." Beretta hugs me tightly. "You know my loser husband told all his loser friends you're a ballbreaker. That's why no one here wants to date you."

I hug her back and drop a kiss on her smiling face. I make my way back to my empty house, but I'm full of joy and purpose. A ballbreaker. Huh!


Today I race home to change after work. Vincent, the new professor from Port-au-Prince is coming to dinner and Alice threatens me with bodily harm if I'm not nice to him.

"Alice, you need to stop your matchmaking," I chastise her. "I don't need to be tangled up with a man. I'm fine."

"Come help me set the table." She puts her arm around my waist. "The men will be here shortly." She sniffs my hair. "And for God's sake stop smoking. It'll kill you and repel prospective husbands."

I push her away with my hip. "I know about the killing part, but maybe I don't mind the repellent."

She laughs. "Don't you want to get married, Lil sister?"

"Not necessarily. But I can do with some good quality sex though."

We laugh a lot when we're together. Alice brings the best out of me with her patience and generosity. I throw the wilted flowers from the vase out of the open window and pour the water out. From the full pitcher on the dining room table, I fill the vase and place the bunch of hibiscus flowers I'd plucked from the park in fresh water. I tuck a red one behind my ear and do the same for Alice. She smiles.

"Luc didn't want to come," she whispers.

"By the way Raoul was right, he's competent. I have no complaints with my banking services since he took over."

"He's very qualified and he loves people." She sighs. "A great combination."

"So why didn't he want to come, Ali?" I make eye contact with her. She can't keep a secret. "I mean, he welcomes any excuse to be around *you*."

Alice stretches her neck to look at the entrance to the dining room. The cook and housekeeper are in the back getting the meal ready. She turns up the volume on the radio and pulls me down to a chair. At this rate, we'll never finish setting the table.

"Yesterday, I was at the bank, you know to…take care of some business for Raoul…it was late in the afternoon so there was only one teller and a couple of people in line. Luc came out of his office and called the man before me. Then it was my turn. 'You look ravishing, Alice,' he said, closing the door behind us. The weeks of flirting sizzled in the small space. His fitted suit, the part in his hair that makes him look like a little boy, the muscles underneath…" Alice scoots closer to me and lowers her voice so much I have to strain to hear. "Kekette, I tell you, the heat…I ran my palm over his chest. He took my hands in his and kissed my fingertips one at a time. The fear, the impossibility of what we were doing, fanned hot flames between us. I wanted more; I wanted so much more."

"Oh, Ali." I lean over and we hug. "This is dangerous and…you know I love Raoul. He's a good man and he adores you and the kids…you need to stop before it gets too far—I mean you haven't—"

"No, I'd never do that." She shakes her head. "But what am I supposed to do? If I leave Raoul, Luc and I won't be able to stay on this island. How about my boys? Raoul won't let me have them."

Raoul walks into the room, a big smile on his face. "Oh!" he says. "You're okay, Kekette?"

I wipe my dry eyes to take the focus on Alice's wet ones. "I'll be okay, Raoul." I sniff.

Alice stands." I'll go check on dinner."

Raoul makes his way down the hall toward their bedroom, halfway through, he halts and says, "Oh, I think you'll like Vincent. His uncle was my classmate in Port-au-Prince, and he highly recommends him. I'm glad he agreed to come here to teach even though he plans to emigrate to the US soon…don't know the details, but grateful for the help."

My ears perk up. "Oh yeah! When? How is he getting to the US? So, he's not going to be here long?"

"I only know his sister's in Boston and she's sponsoring him."

"Alice is already trying to set me up with him. I don't want to waste my time if he's leaving soon."

Raoul walks back into the room. "His uncle said he's a nice guy and when I met him in Port-au-Prince last month, I was impressed with his intelligence and ambition."

"Then, I'm looking forward to meeting him."

"Right," he says, looking at his watch and trotting down the hall.

I sit on a chair folding a cloth napkin until it becomes a ball, and I flatten it again on my lap to iron out the wrinkles. It sounds like Professor

Vincent holds possibilities. After all, I'm never going to attract a local. I throw the pile of napkins on the table and walk out to the verandah. I reach for the pack of Comme Il Faut from my skirt's pocket and strike a match. I inhale deeply, imagining the black smoke skipping my lungs. I need to quit.

Soon, I crush the cigarette under my high heel and sprint back into the dining room. Maybe Vincent is the diversion I have been waiting for.

# CHAPTER THIRTY-ONE

## ADELE

The sea water has washed away my anxiety, leaving me relaxed and clear-headed. I wrap my hair in a plush white towel and step out of the hotel shower. I slip into a loose cotton dress and make my way to the living room. Lisa and Ninnie are waiting.

"What took you so long?" Ninnie whines. "Lisa wouldn't let me start until you come out."

I survey the bottles on the kitchen counter. "Ninnie, we're only here for a weekend," I say.

Ninnie rolls her eyes. "What you wanna drink?" She pops open bottles and starts mixing drinks. Lisa and I join her sitting on the stools. The TV show in the background is playing a too-morose beat for the occasion. I turn it off.

Many drinks later, Lisa starts crying while staring into her Vodka gimlet. "Okay, confession time," Ninnie prompts.

Lisa sniffs and takes a swig of her drink. The tip of her nose is as red as Rudolph's. "I think Robert's having an…umm… affair."

"No!" I say, the booze slurring the single word around my thick tongue. "Not *Wobert*."

"Why do you think that?" Ninnie asks in a clear voice. Alcohol sobers her up instead of making her sloppy and maudlin.

"He...he's never home. He travels to Vegas a lot, supposedly opening a new office for the company. When he's home, he's distracted, jumpy and he...he, you know..." Lisa breathes out as though she's been holding her breath.

"Doesn't wanna fu...I mean make whoopee," Ninnie says.

Lisa nods.

"Well, it may not be another woman," I say. "You know Ben's gone a lot, too. I trust him. I never..." I look at my friends, remembering how much I trusted Andrew. Can you really trust a man? I want to believe that you can.

"Maybe he's gambling, Liss," Ninnie says, squinting at her. "If he's in Vegas a lot. Check your finances."

Lisa's eyes open wide. "You think...I'd rather lose all our money than deal with adultery. My mom went through it with Dad. It nearly destroyed her."

"Cheating does hurt," I say. "It undermines our confidence as women. I'd never accept that from a partner. *Ever*! I have no reason to suspect Ben of anything, but Grace's trying everything to get him back with Paige."

"What?" Lisa and Ninnie say at the same time.

"Ben told me Grace forced him to volunteer on a committee with Paige for a Christmas fundraising event at their country club."

Ninnie's mouth hangs open before she closes it to say, "Grace's a bitch, but Ben's a pussy to let his mama push him around like that. *Merde!* Addy, you need to slap Grace silly. Seriously!" She burps.

"Geez! Ninnie, take a breath," Lisa says, sipping her drink. "Addy, what you gonna do? I don't trust exes. Too much history…you know."

"Well, I gave him an ultimatum," I say, "and he resigned from that committee. How would he feel if I was still socializing with…Andrew?" I stretch from the stool. "Ben's smarting about JR and we're just friends."

"Bet, that's why Paige cheated on him," Ninnie says. "Ben's boring as hell."

"I'd never condone adultery," I say. "Divorce is painful, but I believe it provides both parties the respect they deserve. If ever I want to be with…another man, I'd respectfully end the marriage."

Ninnie raises her hand, like we're back in the second grade. "Men and women just can't be friends. You can't sit here and tell me JR doesn't have the hots for you, and you don't feel some kind of way about him." Before I can deny it, even though I know she's right, she raises her eyebrows almost to her hairline. "He do. You do!"

Unable to sustain her stare, I say, "Well…I respect my vows."

"See," Ninnie says, "that's why I keep Pierre on a short leash around the soon-to-be ex-wife. Them vows bind folks."

"Oh, you care now," Lisa says. "I thought it was only…*sex.*"

Ninnie looks toward the balcony. I follow her gaze. Stars wink in the sky. "I don't know, but lately the idea of Pierre sharing space with her rattles me," she confesses. "He spends a great deal of time at the wife's house to *see* the children." She makes air quotes. "This is wife number two; the kids are young." She slurps her drink, a faraway look in her eyes. "Is that love, guys or is it because he legally still belongs to another woman?"

# I SHALL FIND YOU

"Ninnie, you'll know soon enough if it's love," I say, "if you ever lose it."

"Will you marry Pierre if he proposes?" Lisa asks.

Ninnie makes eye contact with each of us and shrugs. That says a lot.

This morning, my mouth is cottony like the puffy white clouds playing peekaboo with the sun in the bluest sky. It's past ten on Saturday morning. I call Mom, then I wake up my friends. We have a late breakfast at a local diner and take off with no planned destination.

Later that evening, my tanned skin glows against my white mini dress. The four-inch heels extend my legs by miles. Lisa's freckles seem to jump off her oval sun-kissed face under her long straight red hair. The green jumpsuit hugs her small frame, making her look like a college freshman. Ninnie sweeps into the room behind Lisa in a swirl of a print fabric as loud as she is. Her braids shine in the light and their beads cling as her long legs cut the distance to the door in a couple of steps. We prance down one block from our hotel to a bar with a live reggae band. The sultry early evening air ruffles my bangs like a kiss. At the door, heads turn. Men gawk. I smile. We still have it.

We flirt with the older men. We drink fruity cocktails. We dance until the band wraps up and they bring the karaoke machine on stage. At three in the morning, the hot bartender walks us to our hotel as we sing off key on the street. He doesn't leave until the elevator door closed, carrying us happy and drunk to our suite.

The trip back home is mostly quiet today, yet we communicate through silence like we've been doing since babyhood. My friendship with these two has filled the gaps in my life left by being an only child with a single mother. They shared their siblings and their fathers with me over the years. This weekend reveals to us that we want more from our current relationships.

"I had so much fun I actually forgot about my problems with Robert for a while," Lisa says. "I wish we could have gone to Haiti as we'd planned for your birthday last year, Addy. Imagine the fun we would have had. Right Ninnie?"

"Tons, sister. Haitian beaches are legendary," Ninnie says. "But now she's going with her friend JR." She slaps the back of my head as she stretches the word friend.

"Stop it, you," I say. "I need JR for the purpose of this trip, but the Three Musketeers will go together after. I need to do this alone. There may be danger."

"Well, he better keeps you safe over there," Ninnie says. "I can't believe that husband of yours wouldn't take you. Ben's such a pussy."

"You introduced us. Remember?"

"Addy, don't remind me. Not one of my best matches. I suppose."

"Wait, Ninnie," Lisa says. "How can you say that? That's her husband. They need time to work out their differences. That's all. A marriage is an unfinished canvass. There's always more to do."

"Look, our experiences, our cultures, our expectations make us unique. Ben grew up confused about his racial identity," I say.

"Especially with a black mother like Grace who wants to fit in so much with her country club buddies that I don't think she lets Ben explore his blackness. The boy totally lacks exposure," Ninnie says.

We shake our heads in agreement. "People want different things in their relationships besides blind love," I say. "What's important for one may not be for another. We shouldn't have to choose all the time."

Ninnie squeezes my shoulder. Lisa taps my knee. They know what I want.

I no longer want to choose between being a daughter, a wife, an adoptee, a friend. I can be all. But if I must choose, my heart is clear as to who at this stage in my life I need to complete the circle that started my existence.

# CHAPTER THIRTY-TWO

❊❊❊

# KETLY

*December 1999 – January 2000*

People around me lament that time passes too fast, but for me it's always an eternity. The island is alive with visitors coming from abroad and Port-Au-Prince for the end of the year holiday. It may not have luxurious amenities to offer, but its verdant countryside, the unpolluted air, the unhurried way in which life moves here attract foreigners and native alike. Christmas decorations litter the island. In the past two years, Vincent has been the diversion I needed. I no longer wait for fireworks to ignite between my sheets, despite the *Bleu de Channel* I sprayed liberally on my skin, his skin, the linens, and the air to trick my body to reproduce old fires. Alas. But having company in the bed fills up holes.

After dinner at our favorite restaurant to celebrate Vincent's long-awaited interview at the American embassy, and the new year, we stroll on the beach inhaling the salt air.

"Honey," Vincent says with hesitation in his voice, "let's start our family before I leave for America. You'll have more help here with a baby…and I'll apply for both of you when the time comes." My hand twitches in his as I fight the urge to push him away. "You'll be a great mother." He raises my hand to his lips and kisses my palm. "You want to have more children one day. Right?"

Grateful for the darkness, I iron the repulsion out of my voice and say, "Vince, I don't ever want to be an unwed mother again. I can wait."

"But, Kekette?"

"Vincent, I won't change my mind about this. There's no rush. I promise we'll have a family later." I peck his forehead with a light kiss.

"I'd marry you today if it wouldn't delay my trip because my sister applied for me as a single individual. But she said spouse and children sponsorship move faster than siblings, so I'll come back as soon as I can."

"Promise?"

"Promise." He licks the back of my hand now. "Of course, I have to work first to save money for the paperwork and my airfare."

"I'm not going anywhere, Vince."

"I want to help you get to America to see your daughter."

"Vince, it has been twenty years, twenty…since I've seen Juliette. I didn't think I could survive without her, but I have. So, I can wait. Maybe she'll even come find me."

He stops walking. I halt my stride and bump into his hip. "Do you love me, Ketly?" He entwines his skinny fingers through mine. "Even a little bit?"

His short stature and bony face do nothing to inspire me to even try in all these months. I've learned over the years that love is spontaneous. It can't be cultivated. "I care for you deeply, Vincent." I cast my sight into the distance over his head, unable to look him in the eyes. "I've always been honest about my feelings."

"True." He runs my palm over his hairless face. "I love you, Kekette. I hope you'll learn to do more than caring for me one day."

∞∞∞

I usher in Y2K with none of the anticipated drama, but Vincent has a visa to emigrate to America. He picks me up and tries to twirl me around in the hospital lobby. We stumble and I grab the counter at the nursing station.

"What are you two celebrating?" the receptionist asks, chuckling.

I pull Vincent outside. One of the pastimes on this island is gossiping. I don't want to fuel the engine today. "I'll be right back," I say to her.

We stand facing each other against the cement wall in the back of the building. I reach for his hands. "Did you make the airline reservation while you were in Port-au-Prince? When are you leaving? I have suitcases you can use."

He lets go of my hand. "What! You want me to leave today? Would that be soon enough, Miss Ketly? I just got the visa. Will you even miss me?" He looks hurt.

"I'm sorry, Vince. You're not being fair. I want to help with the ticket and whatever else you need for the trip." I touch his narrow shoulder. "Don't be mad. Of course I'll miss you. No one to talk about books in bed."

"I'm sorry, Kekette." He raises the collar of his light jacket against the cool January air coming from the ocean. "My sister says February is one of the coldest months in Boston."

"Oh, you'll be fine until I get there to keep you warm." I loop my arm around his elbow as we walk back into the building. "We can move to Florida. Raoul's sister lives in Miami, and she said it's like being here. Sunny, hot, with hurricanes and all."

# I SHALL FIND YOU

Tonight, we stay up talking and planning our future in between having sex. It's as if Vincent needs to store it up for the cold days looming ahead. In the flickering flame of the lamp, the sharp edges of his face soften. I plaster a smile on my face when he reaches for me again and I make all the right noises until he groans and sags like a *poupée twal* on top of me.

"I will come back to marry you, Miss Ketly," he murmurs before sleep pulls him under.

∞∞∞

Two weeks ago, on a clear February day, Vincent left for America. I missed him more than I thought I would. He was a warm body and he loved books. Now Alice rushes into the break room and hands me an envelope.

"Who's it from?" I ask, grabbing it from her.

"I was at the post office. It's from Vincent."

"Let's step outside." I rip open the envelope and motion for her to come read it along with me as we sit on a bench.

*March 15, 2000*

*Mon amour,*

*It's colder than we'd imagined in Boston. When I arrived, there was ice — ice mind you on the ground. I thought I'd never be warm again.*

*Last week I met many Haitians at my English language school. A new friend's going to teach me to drive a cab. I'll be back in December to marry you. I miss you so much, especially at night in my cold bed.*

*I love you!*

*Vince.*

Alice hugs my neck and squeezes hard. I cough. "What, you're trying to choke me to death." We giggle.

The following week, I pack the dress, shoes and hat I bought for Matante and get on a moped. Victor appears in the doorway. He's been living with her since his mother passed away. "Wasn't expecting you till end of the week," he says.

"Hey, Vic." I shake the bag. "I bring her some stuff for Easter."

"She's been under the weather since you left last week, Kekette."

I skip over the two steps into the little house that had given me shelter at a time when I was homeless and hopeless. I still feel shame when I think about my attitude in my ignorant youth toward my lovely aunt who never judges me. The early afternoon sun lights up the shabbiness of the room. Matante's lying in the bed with a wet rag on her forehead. "Oh, Bébé, what a pleasant surprise."

"What you're doing in bed in the middle of the day, woman?" I kiss her on both cheeks. "I brought your Easter outfit for Sunday."

She groans. "My legs can't hold me up no more." She shifts her body, and a whiff of urine escapes from the bed. "My bones hurt, child."

In the kitchen, I boil her favorite bath leaves and have Victor carry the aluminum basin to the bedroom and fill it up with water. I massage her scalp as I wash her hair. We sing old gospel songs. I scrub her skin and rinse it before rubbing lotion all over her body. She moans. I spritz Bien-être eau de toilette on her from the big bottle I brought with me the last time.

"I want to wear my new dress and shoes now, Addy."

"But…Matante they're for Easter, this Sunday. Today's—"

"I know what today is." She glares at me. I shake my head. We smile.

Minutes later, she's dressed in her new outfit with the hat over her newly braided hair. Victor and I help her walk to the porch. We pull her chair out from the front room, and she sits with a smile on her face. People stop to chat and shower compliments about her beautiful clothes.

"Good afternoon, Matante Hilda," a woman from the church says. "Don't you look lovely."

Matante waves timidly. Her toothless smile warms my heart. "My beautiful niece takes great care of me," she says to the woman, while patting my hand.

I tell her about Vincent's letter. How I don't love him but am willing to marry him to see the world beyond this place, and if I can find Juliette in America, what will be the harm? When will the next prospect show up on this island? I promise to treat Vincent with respect and be eternally grateful to him.

I thought she'd fallen asleep until she says, "Kekette, what if your young man comes back one day? Are you willing to still be respectful to Vincent or any other man?"

"Umm...well..." I stammer, blindsided by her questions. And just like that she's unearthed deeply buried feelings I have not examined for so long. Somewhere in the world Henri is living with the belief that Juliette and I are dead. How can I fault him for never coming back to Haiti? We were just kids with no business bringing another kid into this world. Henri has had his closure. I need to find mine. "I really don't know Matante."

"Don't cause someone pain by trying to unburden your soul from yours." She takes my hand. "You have a good heart; let it and God guide you."

Holding hands, we sit like that for a long time. "It's been an eternity," I whisper. "Juliette is a twenty-year-old adult."

"She ain't a baby no more," Matante whispers back. "She may find you before you find her."

The frequent letters from Vincent keep me company on long, quiet nights. Tonight, I keep looking at my watch while the women cut a cake for Beretta's birthday after our monthly meeting. We celebrate everyone's birthday in the group. Some of the women confess to never having a birthday party or sometimes even remembering their birth dates. Now we party with cakes, hats, noisemakers, streamers, drinks and handmade gifts. The women make a racket with the noisemakers, letting their inner child come out to play, where no one looks at them cross-eyed. I smile.

"Happy birthday, my friend." I hug Beretta. "Ok, listen, ladies, I have to go now. I want to surprise Vincent tonight with a phone call on his birthday."

"Go ahead, Miss Ketly," They yell. "Go call your boyfriend."

"When's the wedding?" Martine asks. "I hope I'll get an invitation."

"Hey, Miss Ketly can't invite all of us," Eveline says. "A wedding's a private affair, not a *ra-ra* band."

Beretta raises her hand. "Who made you planner?" She cuts her eyes at her friend. "I hope Miss Ketly gets to go to America to see her daughter soon after her wedding. I pray about it every night."

I escape through the back door, beaming with gratitude. This is my tribe. I plan to invite all of them. It'll be a celebration. I want to have all my sisters with me on my wedding day.

Later, in Raoul's den with one of the few telephones on the island, Alice hovers over the chair as if she can clear the line of static. "*Allo, Allo,*" I yell over the crackling noise. "Vince, can you hear me?"

"Oh, hold on," a woman's voice says. "I'll get him."

Seconds later, Vincent's voice booms in my ears. "*Allo. Se ki—*"

"*Bonne fete*, Vince," I yell.

"Whoa, *Miss* Ketly. What a lovely surprise. How are you? And Alice, Raoul…? I'm so happy to hear your voice. I miss you. I thought of calling you but didn't want to run the bills here."

"Hey, slow down, Vince."

"Oh, the minutes are expensive. I just got home from work. I miss you so, my love."

"You work late. Is it safe?"

"I go to school during the day. So, I drive the cab at night. It's okay. Oh, I opened an account and I'm saving everything to come back as promised."

"I'm so proud of you. I'm counting the days until December. Alice and I are planning the wedding. When will you get here, Vince?"

Dial tone.

In September, no letter came from Vincent. I called early October, his siter said he was working. I was terrified that something bad had happened to him. I've heard all these stories about muggings and stabbings in America.

The second week of October, Alice brings me a letter from Vincent at choir rehearsal. Alice raises herself on her toes to read along.

*Hello K*

**Sorry about last month, but I'm so busy with work and school I hardly have time to sleep.**

*Vince*

"What's going on with him?" Alice says. "He didn't even reply to your request for a wedding date in December. And why haven't you bought a wedding gown yet? The reception hall manager needs confirmation. You know December's a busy time. We—."

"Shut up Alice," I scream.

Two women sweeping the church stop to stare at us. I massage my temples, trying to force the migraine away. I'd written several letters to Vince asking him to let me know his arrival date in December before this curt note from him. I can't deal with more betrayal. Alice rushes toward the exit, going fast on her short legs. I sprint and grab her.

"I'm sorry, Ali. I didn't mean to yell at you."

She pats my arm. "I'm sorry, too, Kekette. I need some air. I'll be right back."

The rest of the evening drags me down with it. Even singing the gospel songs that usually lift my spirit fails to soothe my nerves. What's going on with Vincent? There aren't even enough lines in his missive to read between. My body craves the cigarettes I manage to cut down in half. Alice comes back only when we start to warm up. She stands at a distance from me in the choir pit.

Later, we walk in silence to her house. I smoke almost a whole pack of cigarettes. Alice stays away from me as I lock myself inside Raoul's den with the telephone, urging it to ring. I call twice. The second time, I leave a message for him to call me the following day anytime in the evening. I close the door to the den behind me and take the long way to my empty house, stopping at the wharf.

∞∞∞

Tonight, I stay over to catch Vincent early. At around four in the morning, I tiptoe to Raoul's office and dial. The rotary sounds echo in the room like the thunder of cannon balls. I look up to see Alice standing behind me wrapped in her cotton robe, sleep shrouding her eyes.

"Is it ringing?" she whispers, placing her comforting hand on my shoulder.

I nod. "*Allo.* Yes, it's Ketly." I exhale. "I'm sorry to call so early in the morning, but I need to speak with Vincent."

"He's not here," a woman says, "and you need to stop harassing me with all these calls."

"Where's he? I haven't heard from him in weeks. Is he all right? I'm worried. This is Ketly."

"He moved out the end of October." She sounds tired. "I don't think it's my place to tell you, but he's such a coward. He's living with a woman who's expecting his child. He knows how to get in touch with you, so no sense calling my house anymore."

She hangs up.

The receiver bounces on the tile floor when I drop it. I double over to control the spasms building in my belly. I groan and rock my body back and forth on the swivel chair.

"Kekette, what's going on?" Alice rubs my back through the fabric of my nightgown. "Talk to me."

"Vincent's not coming, Ali."

"Oh, honey. I'll make coffee and you can tell me what he said." She reaches for my hand. I pull it away.

After changing into my street clothes, I open Alice's front door and trudge to the beach. The streets are quiet. Even the birds are still sleeping, perhaps with a partner they love. I was willing to marry a man I didn't love so I can get to someone I really do. Can I be angry with Vincent because he's found someone to make him a papa. I never want any more children. I have long shouldered the responsibility for my own happiness. I will continue. Sitting on the bench, I stare into the inkiness of the water keeping its secrets buried underneath. Like me. I open my arms to the tentative sunrise as if to coax it to show its brilliant face. I hum into a new dawn, a new day, by myself. Juliette is still out of reach physically, but she grows in my heart every day.

# CHAPTER THIRTY-THREE

## ADELE

After a quick shower, I season two salmon steaks and put them back in the fridge and pull two sweet potatoes, a bag of string beans and the makings for a green salad. Another glass of wine dilutes my anger at everybody. My mother for being sick, Haiti for being in my blood, Ben for being selfish and JR.

JR for monopolizing my thoughts. I want to run away from everything. Why can't I have what I want? I didn't go to the college I wanted, because I couldn't go away and leave Mom. I didn't marry the man I wanted because he left me for somebody else. Maybe I became a nurse because that's what Mom always said I should be.

I slap the bowl down on the counter and a crack appears at the bottom. The ringing of the bell pulls me from my wallowing. "Coming, Mom," I yell, walking down the hall to her bedroom.

When she came home last week after spending one night in the hospital for observation, I gave her the bell to summon for help, and I now come over every day after work before going home to spend time with Ben. The cardiac stress test, the MRI of her belly, the ultrasound of her kidney, all the tests were negative.

"Well, what's wrong with her, Dr. Cooper?" I'd asked.

The doctor had narrowed her eyes and shrugged. "Umm…she needs rest. I suppose."

Halfway to her bedroom she rings the bell again. "I'm coming." I grit my teeth.

"I'd like a cup of tea, sweetie," she says. "It's so chilly for November."

"I'm making us salmon for dinner. We've been eating too much fried food this week. Nadine's grio is dangerous."

"Huh, it's good but I've never had grio like Clara's." She immediately raises the book to cover her face but not before I see the red blooming on it.

"Who's Clara, Mom? Is she someone in Lasalle?"

Why does the name sound so familiar? I close my eyes before tapping my forehead hard. In his last report, the PI said a lady named Clara who had a daughter, and two sons lived in the house across from the clinic.

Mom drops the book on the bed and grabs her chest, rubbing and moaning. "Oh, Addy, the pain…I can't believe they can't find what's wrong with me. Let me have some tea, please. I'm cold."

I know she's not going to tell me anything about Clara, but she has just told me *something*. "I'll put the water on. I've hired someone to help you. She starts this weekend so I can train her before my trip next month."

"Adele, I don't want anyone to help me. If you insist on leaving me alone here to go to Haiti, then what do you care if you come back and find me stinking up the place with my dead, decomposing body."

"Oh, Mom, really. Christie is an experienced caregiver. It hurts me you're acting this way."

"Then don't go. Stay."

I pour water from the bedside pitcher into the vase with the dozen roses Ben sent to her at the hospital. "These are from Ben. Remember?"

"They're beautiful. Ben's so thoughtful."

"I'll get your tea." I escape to the kitchen.

I need to work things out with Ben before my trip. Whatever I find in Haiti, when I return, I want to start our family. Lately, our connection seems haphazard.

My phone rings as I pour the water over the chamomile tea bag in the mug. "Hello, JR. What's up?"

"Just checking on you and your mom."

"We're doing good. But it seems every time I plan to go to Haiti, she gets—"

"Let me guess." He pauses. I'm surprised he doesn't say, drumroll. He's so dramatic. "Sick. Yes? She's been faking it?"

"I don't know what to think." I blow air out of my mouth. "Earlier she mentioned someone named Clara. I believe it must be the same person your friend and my PI reference to us."

"Told you, Adele. She's hiding something."

"You know, after our high school graduation, me and the girls planned to go to Haiti for my birthday and snoop around a bit. We even made reservations, then Mom found out," I lower my voice, "and she ended up in the hospital. Okay, so her glucose level was dangerously high. Then four years later, after college graduation, Ninnie booked us a trip there. It was gonna be my search trip and a bachelorette party for Lisa."

"And let me guess again. Marge's in the hospital?"

I nod before I say, "Yes...what's going on?"

"Adele, you know Marge's no longer worried about losing you to some woman who gave birth to you so long ago. There's something she did in Haiti she doesn't want you to unearth."

"No, my mom wouldn't do anything to intentionally hurt someone...I refuse to believe that. I think, even at my age, she's afraid of sharing me with another mother. I'm all she has. My PI is finding out pretty much the same information as your friend. Heard anything more?"

"My friend will call if and when he has something to report, so you might as well fire your PI and save some money."

"Oh no, he might find something else. Besides, this is my search. Something I was going to do anyway."

"I admire your tenacity, Miss."

"Listen, my whole life I've pestered Nadine to tell me if she knew anything about...my adoption. She'd always said, 'ask your mom.'" I tap my chin. "You know, JR, maybe asking her about someone she can direct me to is a better strategy. Like I can ask her about Clara. That will take the focus off mom, if she's protecting her somehow."

"Brilliant mind! You're doing great investigative work, Adele." He laughs and I can see the dimple in his chin. "I'm working tonight, but I can stop by tomorrow afternoon with dinner."

"Umm...I'm picking up my husband tomorrow and...I'll be home more now since I have a caretaker starting soon with Mom."

"Okay. Let me know if I can help in any way. I'm here."

I hold the phone against my cheek, after we hang up, staring through the kitchen window. I can see Nadine's house. I plan to talk to her soon. Mom rings the bell. I cringe. I put the tea in the microwave to heat it up.

At home the next day, the cleaning lady left a trail of lemony scent and a glossy house. I sort the mail into Ben's, mine, and the bills we share. We keep our assets separate. We have a joint account for the house. I put the champagne in the fridge and marinate the steaks before looking at the time. When he called me early this morning, he said he'd take a cab home. I want to surprise Ben by picking him up. No fooling around in the dark parking lot this time. I blush. I made reservation at his favorite French restaurant in Tampa for tonight.

Halfway down the stairs, the house phone rings. My heels echo on the stairs. Soon, we'll be filling it with little Barretts' feet. Well, no more than two. I smile.

I'd left my cellphone downstairs and probably missed many calls. Maybe it's Ben or something with…Mom. I hurry.

"Hello, hello," I say, breathing loudly.

"Is Benjamin home? He's not answering his mobile phone."

"Good afternoon, Grace." I grin. I won't let the devil spoil my good mood. "He's not. May I help you?"

"I can't get either him nor Paige to answer their phones and there's an emergency meeting for the holiday fundraising committee. I need to reach them."

"Oh, Ben resigned from the committee weeks ago." I try hard not to suck my teeth. "You must be mistaken."

She guffaws so loudly I pull the phone away. "Whatever gives you that idea?" She snorts. "*You* must be mistaken."

The dial tone sounds louder than usual it seems, mocking me.

# CHAPTER THIRTY-FOUR

❦❦❦

# KETLY

*December 2005*

December is forever a time to recap at the end of the year and to welcome the dawn of a new one. It's a time to reflect on what is next. It may bring regrets, but there's always hope. Even with all the festivities with my club members, I long for more. For the past five years since Vincent was a no-show for our wedding, I still dread the whole season. Over the years, plenty of male teachers, bank employees had come to the island and left it. City folks don't last too long here unless they're hiding from something or someone. Alice tries to set me up with all of them, young, old, in between. After Vincent, I swear to never use someone's affection selfishly. I have everything I need. What I want can wait.

I crush the cigarette under my heel and walk back into the church for Christmas rehearsal. Alice wrinkles her nose as if I'd try to shove a cigarette into her mouth. Luc left his post at the bank and escaped the island last year, putting a stop to their flirting. Alice projects happiness, despite pining for a man she can't have without breaking up her life like the fragile porcelain set Raoul's mother had given her as a wedding present. Every woman on this island wants what she has. But it seems like life gives us nothing without taking something away.

"Lucille," I say to the pregnant woman standing next to Alice, "you look like you're going to have that baby any minute now. I'm off duty tonight. Okay." We all laugh.

Mama has been spending Christmas with me since Matante passed away in her sleep three years ago. I miss her a lot. Matante taught me self-reliance, empathy, self-love, and humility. At forty-two, I am still a work-in-progress. I am proud of what I have done on this island, empowering women to be better mothers, to demand respect in their relationships, to be financially self-sufficient.

"I hope Baby waits for Christmas Day to be born," Lucille says. "Wouldn't that be nice?"

I thump her stomach like a watermelon in the summer. "Hmm, that's ten days from now…I don't know."

"Well, I can hope." Lucille taps her belly as if to send a message to her fifth child.

Dressed in his three-piece suit and a felt hat balancing over his tuft of gray hair, the choir director seems to float into the sanctuary. Silence blankets the choir loft. He raises his hands. Christmas lights strung inside the church blink rapidly casting a festive pall over the shabby pews. The kids slink outside running to the playground in the patchy grass covered in mud. Darkness seeps through the open windows along with the sudden sound of drizzle. I open my hymnal and breathe. I start to cough. Many of the women turn to gawk, as if I have TB or something else just as contagious. Alice glances in my direction from the front row.

"Don't say it, Ali. I'm trying." I glare at her.

She clears her throat before cutting her eyes at me. The choir starts singing. Twenty-one women join their voices every week in celebration of love to God, but within their various timbre I can hear hope, despair, joy, impatience, doubt, and faith. Always faith. I've delivered babies from most of them and like parents everywhere they want their children to be safe, happy and to know they are loved.

The island, like a box with a tight lid, keeps everyone in. Women snuggle into their chosen or designated roles as wives, mothers, workers, housewives, leaning on each other. They don't seem to need much more. Is it wrong to be curious about what is beyond what we can see? I've always dreamed of exploring the world. It's never enough for me to read about people, places, cuisines, customs, I want to walk the streets on other continents, breathe the air from faraway countries, listen to foreign languages. Some days, I'm choking on the abundance of air on this island. I want to kick the lid off and escape. The singing pulls me back inside the church. My eyes run with tears from suppressing my cough. I can hardly breathe.

"Let's take it from the top," the director says, staring at me with more lines crowding his face with annoyance. "You need to do something about this cough, Miss Ketly or I'll ask you to leave the choir for good."

My mouth opens to rebuke him and instead something is closing my airway. People have no idea how hard it is to quit smoking, when it's the only vice you have that brings immediate comfort. Later, the women collect their children outside and wave to each other as they make their way home. Small groups gather on the playground, on the street, laughing, whispering, and gossiping. Alice waits for me on the bottom step by the side door. She hands me a mint. I take it and nod. We both turn toward the quickening steps getting closer.

"Lucille, are you in labor?"

"No, no, Miss Ketly," she holds her back, four kids pushing each other around her legs. The youngest one's crying. "I'd like you to check Maurice's ear. He been pulling at it and crying all day. He's warm too."

"Ok. Follow me."

Minutes later, Lucille drops her bulk into my wicker sofa. It creaks. I fetch my medical bag and proceed to examine the toddler squirming in her lap.

"Maurice, you like your Christmas tree?" I ask the boy to distract him.

"We put more decorations out this year," Lucille says, tickling the toddler. "Didn't we Maurice?" She kisses his chubby cheek. "My brother's coming next week to spend some time with us."

"Yeah! Is he coming from Port-au-Prince or a neighboring village?" I pull the thermometer from Maurice's mouth and raise it to the light.

"He's coming from New York, Miss."

I almost drop the instrument. "New York?" I say, gazing at her. "So...he hasn't been here in a while?"

"No. He's been gone over twenty years. This is his first trip back. We didn't hear from him for a couple years. We weren't too worried cause he's done that before. But he sends money to help our family, especially our parents." Lucille tries to stand with Maurice and falls back on the sofa and bounces almost like a ball. We laugh. I take her upper left arm and pull. "I feel like a *rekin*." She taps her belly. "Mom's so excited to see my brother she can hardly sleep."

"He's coming alone?" I ask, following Lucille to the front door.

"Oh yeah. He's not married. He has time I suppose."

"Hmm, men have no expiration date." We scoff at the same time. "He must be a nice man. Your family's good folks, Lucille."

"He was a terror as a boy. But they say age brings wisdom." Lucille lifts a sleeping Maurice on her shoulder. "Come over for Christmas dinner, he'll be here by then."

"Thank you, but my family's coming for Christmas. Maybe after." I rub the baby's warm back with my palm. "He has a fever and an ear infection. Stop by the drugstore. You know what to get."

"Thank you, Miss Ketly. You're so generous. You know, you'll like my brother. He likes books and such."

I swat the air. "I'm not looking for a man, Lucille, but I can always make a new book friend."

I hold the door open for her. "What's your brother's name?"

"Rénel," she says.

∞∞∞

In the past decade, my brothers have been living in the Dominican Republic cutting sugarcane leaving Mama alone in Lasalle. They never seem to forgive me for leaving them after losing papa, but I couldn't tell them until much later the reason for my disappearance. I wonder if Sylvain has ever forgiven me.

"Today's absolutely the best Christmas ever," I say as I fix Mama's hair for church after breakfast. Since my cook is on vacation, Mama and I make cornmeal with fresh tomatoes, liver in gravy with lots of shallots and a side salad of watercress and sliced avocado. "Hurry, boys," I yell toward the back bedroom. We don't want to be late for Christmas service."

The red dress hugs all my curves, stopping at my knees. My permed hair falls below my ears in curls that cost me half a night of sleep on account of the tight hair rollers I kept on all night. I peer into the mirror on the living room wall and run the red lipstick over my plump lips. Mama looks at my dress and presses her lips together before saying, "You gon' put something else over this...dress?"

I swivel around in a circle, my heels clicking on the tile floor. "I have a long shawl, Mama. Come on let's go. I'm singing today."

"I'm glad to see you don't smoke as much anymore. A bad habit for a woman," Mama mutters.

I wrap the gold shawl over my shoulders before stepping out on the front porch. Tim-Tim stops mid-run and breathing through his mouth says, "You pretty, Miss Ketly."

"Thank you, Tim-Tim." He hands me an envelope from Alphonse. "Come by later for your *zétrennes*."

I open the envelope.

*Hi Kekette,*

*Sorry I didn't come before Christmas, but my mother-in-law was visiting. I'll see you after your folks leave. Joyeux Noel!*

*Alph*

I poke my head inside the house. "Let's go guys. Choir master will have my head if I'm late."

One of the three taxis in Galette takes us to the church. I pause at the door and scan the crowd. I don't see Lucille's family in the area where they usually sit. I make my way to the choir pit.

When I get there Alice grabs my arm. "You look gorgeous," she whispers. "Been looking for Lucille, too."

"Why," I whisper back, looking at her, at the same time she taps my rib with her elbow and tilts her head toward the entrance.

Lucille and her family, her parents, and a tall man with skin like unpeeled coffee bean scan the assembly. The church is full. I know Lucille's looking for a spot where they can all sit together. Tall Man leans over her and says something. They split. I follow Tall man with my eyes, as he guides Lucille's mother to the second row. People squeeze against each other to let them sit. He wears a red shirt under a charcoal grey suit, with his hair cut close to his scalp. He looks successful.

After the service, people mill outside talking, laughing. Lucille rushes toward my group dragging Tall Man behind her. "Miss Ketly, this is my brother Rénel."

He nods slightly. "So very pleased to meet you, Miss Ketly. Lucille talks about you all night. You have a beautiful voice."

Alice clears her throat so loudly; her husband pats her back a couple times. "The whole choir sings heavenly," Rénel continues with a pinch of laughter seeping into his words, as he extends his hand and shakes Alice's first. "Joyeux Noel, Madame."

"Welcome back to the island," I say, then I introduce my family.

"Thank you, Miss." He bows. "Have a blessed day, everyone." He takes his mother's hand. Such a beautiful gesture. I resist the urge to turn to see more of this elegant man.

After dinner late in the afternoon, we sit around my dining table. Mama fixes her famous drink. I sip and listen to Sylvain.

"You know, Kekette, when you practically vanished, Mama wouldn't say much except you went to Port-au-Prince and I didn't understand why the whole family couldn't be together." He takes a gulp. "We'd just lost Papa, and I felt like we lost you too. I resented the fact that you could go to the city while me and Jules were stuck in Lasalle."

I lay my hand on his forearm. "I understand Syl. I'm sorry I couldn't tell you guys the truth at the time. It was for all our safety."

Jules nods. "I remember seeing the man with the dark glasses even though he tried to hide." He looks at Sylvain. "Remember, Syl?"

"I do. He even talked to us a couple of times. I wish I'd known what he was fishing for. We could have handled him." He flexes his biceps under his long sleeve shirt.

"Well, I'm glad, you didn't, Syl. That man was dangerous. He's a murderer." I gulp a mouthful of rhum punch. "So, how's life in the Dominican Republic? I hope you guys are safe and working on building a future."

I see the pain in Sylvain's eyes before he opens his mouth. "Sister, life is hard for Haitians in DR." He blinks several times. "We're living in hiding too. We can only be in the field. We paid good money in bribes to make it here to be with you and Mama and pray we can slip back in over the border undetected." Sylvain rubs my arm. "You seem to have a good life here as a respected Miss. I'm glad you've found a home."

My heart hurts for all the misery we suffer everywhere. And yes, I found a home in a place that has protected and nurtured me while I fought it for so long.

"I'm so sorry we never got to meet our niece Juliette," Jules says, drumming his fingers on the table. "So, you never met a man on this island, Kekette?"

I stand and drain the drink from my glass. The sun has set over the horizon in a multi-colored sky. "Let's clean up. There's a Christmas concert in the park across from the church. We should go."


The days fly by. We walk all over the island, visiting with my friends, going to church events, and strolling along the beach. I cherish the time spent with Mama and my brothers. I feel less alone. I am part of this clan. Last night we had dinner with my second family. Alice and Raoul may not be blood, but I owe them a lot for making me a part of their own tribe.

Now on the wharf, we hug, laugh and cry. The boys shade their eyes as if looking at the sunrise climbing over the water, but I can see the tears.

"I love you, little brothers." I hug them tightly. "See you next Christmas." They wave.

I throw my arms around Mama's neck and I'm the little girl who needs her mother at times. "I'm still waiting for you to move here, Mama. What are you doing in Lasalle by yourself?"

She plants kisses on my forehead, and my cheeks with her wet lips. "I can't leave the village. What if someone comes looking…for you, you know…" She shrugs. "Lasalle's my home. Maybe you'll come back one day."

I pat her shoulder and gently push her toward the gangplank. "Safe travels, Mama."

I stroll back home, feeling light and free. Lucille wants me to come for dinner today and check on her newborn because she's not latching to feed. I clean all day to kill the time, piling the linen for the laundress to pick up later in the week. I fix some lunch, checking the clock every minute. It seems like the needles never move. By early afternoon, I take some time on my appearance before walking the few blocks to Lucille's neighborhood. Throngs of kids mill in the front courtyard, playing with their shiny Christmas toys. The chickens, goats, and pigeons will enjoy some peace now until the new gadgets break down, run out of batteries or lose their appeal. Their gleeful laughter fills me with joy.

"Hey, Lucille, it's Miss Ketly," her husband yells, poking his head in the open front door. "She was about to send for you."

"Is everything okay?" I ask.

"Something about the baby," he says, shrugging before hitching a big sack over his shoulder and walking away.

I shake my head. He doesn't even know what's going on with his child, but he sure knows how to put them in. What kind of father would Henri have been? He was looking forward to our baby. Is he a Papa now? I wonder.

"Bonjour, Miss Ketly?" says a deep voice coming from the man standing on the porch with both hands shoved into a pair of tight-fitting jeans. A wide smile reveals straight white teeth, his biceps straining against the short sleeve of his red t-shirt. "Please come in."

I take the hand he extends. It's warm and firm. Inside the house, the Christmas tree leans against the window. Branches hang low as if someone has tried to climb them. Toys litter the bare cement floor.

"Is that Miss Ketly," Lucille calls from the back room. "Be right out."

Soon, she enters the living room holding the baby latched to her breast with one hand, while drinking from an aluminum cup with the other.

"Gotta get my strength with this one. She's not a sleeper because she doesn't eat enough. I'm exhausted. Have a seat, Miss." She turns to her brother. "Ren, move the clothes from the divan." She points to the corner of the room. "Put them over there."

Rénel does as his sister asks then sits across from me and crosses his legs with one knee over the other. The red T-shirt stretches over his wide chest. His hair has grown into tight whorls around his long face. He smells of clean cotton. He shares Lucille's wide mouth which now opens in a smile. "My sister says you're the best Miss on the island."

I shift my bottom onto the sofa and heat spreads over my face. "Lucille tends to exaggerate in everything."

"Including having children." He laughs, shaking his head. "She has an army."

Lucille stands from the dining room chair and places the baby in my lap. "I'm done, Ren," she says. "Soon, it'll be your turn." He says nothing. The new infant smell fills me with peace. "And some of us want to have our children before people think we're their grandparents," she continues, laughing so hard, she grabs her crotch and runs out back.

Hours later, after dinner, a couple of drinks and postnatal tips, I push my chair back from the table. "Thank you for a great time, Lucille. Nice to see you, Ren...Rénel."

He stands. "May I walk you home, Miss?"

Weeks later, this becomes our routine. Rénel waits for me every day, in the hospital yard, his right foot planted against a tree trunk with a single red hibiscus in his hand. I look forward to seeing him and I'm surprised to realize that it has nothing to do with him living in New York.

Tonight, he holds my hands in both of his, a faraway look in his eyes. He scoots closer to me on my living room sofa, our entwined hands resting on his thighs. We talk a lot. We read and discuss books. We both love the classics and have read Les Miserables again, so we can talk about it. He's a great listener. It's so easy to share life experiences with him. But I see sadness lurking around his smile sometimes.

"So, when do you go back to New York?"

"I...I don't know yet. I've been away for many years. I missed home. Life in America is...hard." He stares at the single bulb in the middle of the ceiling, as if gauging his words. "I want to open a hardware store on the island. I have a friend who can ship the inventory."

"Oh, so you're not planning on going back for a while. Not even for a visit?"

"Of course, but it'll take time to put everything together and find someone trustworthy to oversee things when I'm...away," he says.

"That shouldn't be a problem. People here are loyal and proud. Something I admire on this island."

"You said you're not from here, Miss Ketly. How did you end up on this island?" He lets go of my hands. I want him to keep them. "We've

# I SHALL FIND YOU

talked a lot about our professional life and future dreams, but I don't know much about your past. You're a beautiful mystery."

It's still painful for me to talk about the past without opening old wounds. "Umm…it's a long story but my papa was from Mapou. You must have been young when you left? Lucille said you spent time in Port-au-Prince before going to America."

"I was young and full of dreams and foolishness. Now in my forties, I hope I've lost the foolish part and kept the dreams. I trained as a mechanic in New York, but when I first got there, life was…difficult." He looks away. "Well, today, I'm in a different place."

"So, after you set up the store, you plan to go back to your life in New York?" I reach for the half-empty pack of cigarettes and the lighter on the side table. I shake one out and flick on the flame. I inhale deeply to calm the craving that makes me unable to concentrate on his words. I squint in anticipation of the nicotine hitting my brain. In only a few weeks, this man is disturbing my hormones in a very sweet way. It has been a lifetime since I've felt this way about a man. He stands, staring at the cigarette in my hand with unspoken disapproval. I take three quick puffs and put it out in the ashtray.

"It's getting late." He raises his arms over his head after looking at his watch. "I should go. Thank you for your time."

"So, will I see you tomorrow?" I ask.

"Do you want to?" He winks.

I stare at his luscious lips before closing the door behind him and leaning against it. "I need to slow down, before I run this man away," I whisper.

I stop to see Alice today before going to work. I need to act fast before someone else grabs this fine man. "Ali, I have a proposition for Rénel. I don't know when the next man with the right credentials will show up here."

Alice squints. "What do you mean?"

"Something Alph said in his last letter about Henri possibly being dead. What kind of mother am I, to not at least confirm that at least my child is alive? Huh!" I blow out air loudly. "At twenty-five, Juliette will understand my reasons for placing her in Marge's care. Maybe she's a mother." I blink fast to stop the tears. "Ali, could you ever let your boys go as if they were never part of you?"

She shakes her head and reaches for my hands. "Oh Kekette, I have to confess that I was glad when you stopped talking about Juliette for years. At least I didn't have to patronize you with answers that can never justify what you've lost. Your bravery makes me feel impotent sometimes."

My hands swallow her small ones. "It's okay, sister. I had to let go of that dream so I could find myself. I never forget her, but her absence motivated me to reach my goals."

"Did Rénel say anything?"

"No, but the single women are drooling over him." I tilt my head back and stare at the ceiling as if a sign will appear to guide me. "Ali, I have a business proposition for him. Might even throw in a bonus in the package." I laugh. "He's very easy on the eyes. I don't want anyone else grabbing him before he helps me."

"Oh, he likes you. I can tell. Will *you* need Bleu de Chanel?" she asks. "I'm going to the city next week."

I shake my head, remembering the woodsy smell of his fragrance. His lean physique. Those lips. "Sistah," I purr. "I won't need Bleu de Channel for *him*."

# CHAPTER THIRTY-FIVE

## ADELE

I place my palm over my chest and fill my lungs with air a few times to abort the migraine galloping my way. Grace's rudeness and Ben's possible betrayal needle my brain. I asked Ben to resign from the committee weeks ago not so much because Paige is on it, but he travels a lot for work already, and I need him to be home more. To start prioritizing our family. I want our children to have the doting daddy I never have. Is my trust in Ben misplaced? Grace must be taunting me with her lie. Why do I let that witch invade my peace?

I grab the car keys off the kitchen counter, my purse, and my laptop bag, in case the flight's delayed. I rush back upstairs for my cell phone and note the time. I must hurry before Ben gets in a cab.

A half-hour later, I freshen up my face in the rearview mirror before stepping out of the car into a well-lit space in the airport garage and locking the door. Maybe I'll ask Ben about the committee tomorrow. No need to spoil our evening with Grace's innuendos. He told me he'd resigned from the committee. Good enough for me.

Over our steak dinner tonight, we'll make resolutions for 2010 to strengthen our marriage. Now that I have a caretaker for Mom, I'll spend more time at home after work and attend more social functions with my husband.

The happiness in my steps propels me up the escalators to the waiting area upstairs. One of the trolleys connecting the gate area to the terminals spits out people who fan about with purposeful steps. Ben's not in that group. The board downstairs says his flight has landed. I crane my neck when another trolley empties out and there is my husband with his arm around Paige's waist, making them look like conjoined twins. He leans over and whispers something in her ear before kissing it. She throws her head back to laugh. When she opens her eyes, they land on mine. As if in slow motion, she stops walking. Someone bumps into her back, pushing her forward. Ben turns to the offender, an angry look on his face. Paige lifts her arm and wraps it around Ben's neck, a big smile on her face before she kisses his mouth. Ben clutches the back of her head for a deeper kiss before moving along. And as if I command him with my shock, he raises his head and our eyes connect.

Time stops. My head buzzes from the thumping of my heart. I step backwards until the escalator railing stops me, then I spin around and bolt downstairs. I sit in my car, not trusting myself to drive yet. I stare at the concrete barrier in front of me as if what I need to do next will appear there like glyphs on ancient walls. Then I remember Grandma Barrett telling me not to trust Paige. But she was wrong. Paige has nothing to do with what I just witnessed. Ben used me to win her back. He's the cheater. Not her.

My phone chimes. It's Ben's ringtone. I hit the steering wheel with the phone and yell, "Fuck, fuck, fuck," until it stops ringing and its innards rain down on my lap and the car floor. I breathe anger in and out as it wraps itself around my long-ago bruised heart that I wanted Ben to heal from Andrew's betrayal. He never did. He never will. It was never his job to do. It is mine.

Why am I not crying over the loss of my three-year marriage? Why do I feel more shame than pain? In many cultures, women are raised to believe we need men. In our quiet and often unacknowledged strength, we carry the load of keeping the social order on our backs, and we don't complain. We endure. And many times, we do it alone.

I leave the garage and drive around, humming the songs on the radio until a calm feeling invades my body. I pull over into a hotel parking on the beach in St Petersburg and check myself in. I sit on the bed and reach for the room's phone. "Hi Mom...umm...Ben..."

"Addy? Is Ben's flight delayed? Where are you?"

"Ben will probably call you. Don't worry about me. I'm fine. We're...he...I need some time alone."

"Adele Marie, you're not making sense. Where's your husband?" Mom yells.

"Mom, I'll call you tomorrow. I love you. Good night."

I call room service for some dinner and open the door to the balcony. The sea air burns my wet nostrils. Staring at the endless ocean, it becomes clear why I'm crying now. I've put my plans on hold for Mom's health, for Ben's ambivalence, for my career, never understanding I'm burying myself along with my dreams into the life everyone thinks I should live. There is never anything stopping me but my own fears of making people uncomfortable. Now I must move forward with what I've always wanted to do.

After a restless night, I make hotel-room coffee and reach for the phone.

"Hey, it's me."

"Adele, where are you?" Ninnie says. "Liss and I have been calling you since last night." She blows her nose like a trumpet. There are tears in her voice. "I need you. My life's falling apart. Pierre broke up with me yesterday." She pauses. "Via email. The asshole. He decided to stay with his wife and work things out *for the children*." She mimics his deep voice. "All the signs were there, Addy, but I ignored them. I logged into his email account; he's been sweet-talking with his wife all along. The prick. Now I know how it feels to be betrayed in love. But I never promise marriage. I...Addy, are you still there? Why didn't you answer your phone...Adele?"

"Because I broke it last night when I saw *my* husband kissing another woman...Paige to be exact."

"What!" Ninnie screams. I pull the receiver away from my ear. "Ben did that? The bastard! What the hell's wrong with men that they think they can do shit like this and get away with it. We need to hire somebody to fuck them up. Yeah. I think we should. You're okay, sister?"

"I'm fine. A bruised ego, and I believe you will be okay, too. These are life lessons put on our path to show us what we're really made of. Remember Ninnie, we're Haitian women. We bend we don't break."

"You're damn right. *Nou sé rozo,*" she says. "I'll let Liss know. We'll see you later."

I give her the name of the hotel.

"Emails," I mutter, reaching for my laptop bag on the nightstand. After only three tries, I log into Ben's account. On December 30, 2007, ten days after our first wedding anniversary, Paige wrote.

> *My lover and best friend,*
>
> *I thought I could forget you by moving to Europe, but I can't. I beg for your forgiveness. You married that woman to hurt me and it's working. Benji, I'm coming back to claim what's duly mine before your charade of a marriage goes too far.*
>
> *Forever,*
>
> *Blondie*

# I SHALL FIND YOU

The same day Ben replied.

> *Blondie,*
>
> *You hurt me. Maybe I married Adele to spite you and my mother who always sides with you, but I'm beginning to develop feelings for my wife. I frankly hoped she'd help me forget you, but I must admit, she's failing miserably. Please stay in Europe. I need more time to figure out what I need to do.*
>
> *Forever,*
>
> *Benji*

I lift the laptop above my head and lower it before I smash it against the wall. Now I'm responsible for his cheating by *failing* to make him forget Blondie. The Prick. I close my eyes as if I can ban the truth from my head and my heart. But I would never have cheated on him. I would leave the marriage first if I'd wanted to be with someone else. He owes me that much. We owe that much to each other.

Sometime later, I open the door after the first knock. Ninnie and Lisa fall into my arms. "I'm so…" they start at the same time. They stop, and we make sounds. A nervous chuckle. A-what's-happening-to-us laugh. I ordered brunch. We drink too many mimosas.

"What you're gonna do, Addy?" Lisa says. "I mean…maybe, the kiss…it's not what you think."

I shake my head. "Liss, I found emails between them going back almost two years. They're together." I press my palms to indicate how close. "The signs were there but I didn't see them because…perhaps I didn't care."

"What?" Lisa's eyes open wide with her blue irises swimming in the sea of white. "How could you not…care?"

"Liss, you remember you and I talking about how there was no spark between these two?" Ninnie says. "We know how Addy can be when she's in love. Right? Remember Andrew? I never saw that fire with Ben."

"Great job, Matchmaker," Lisa says, glowering at Ninnie. "I told you to give her time to find her own man."

"Well, Liss, Ben looked…*fuckable*," Ninnie throws her hands up, "but didn't tell her to marry him. That was *her* decision."

"Ninnie, how are you, sweetie?" I ask.

She blinks several times. Ninnie never likes to show weakness. "Well, you two were right about Pierre. I believe he loved me but loves his children more." She drains her glass and pours more from the pitcher. "Maybe used me to get his wife back, too. *The Salopri!*"

Lisa leans over from the patio chair and rubs Ninnie's back. "Listen, we're still young," Lisa says. "Not even hit the big three-oh yet. You guys will meet somebody worthy of you."

"Well, I think that cop is hot for Addy," Ninnie says, letting out a snort. "He kinda looks like Andrew. Don't you think? Same build. Hope he's not an asshole like him."

"Stop it, Ninnie," I say. "The last thing I need now is an entanglement."

"Mm-huh." Ninnie rolls her eyes. "Keep sayin' that to yourself."

"I'm still married, so I need time to process all of it. I—"

"You're married to a cheater," Ninnie pipes up again.

"Ninnie, let her finish a sentence," Lisa says, swatting at Ninnie's arm.

"Thank you, Liss." I cut my eyes at Ninnie. "I'm filing for divorce. Should be simple. Ben has nothing I want. Wish I could annul the whole affair."

"Speaking of affairs," Ninnie says, "Ben and Pierre deserve a whupping for what they're putting us through."

"Might as well add Robert to the pile," Lisa says, staring at the horizon.

"Wait a minute," I say. "You don't mean…?"

"Oh no, he's not cheating with another woman, but since I took control of our money, he's been stealing and pawning my jewelry to gamble. I finally applied for the bank job I told you guys about a couple of months ago. Mom's coming to help me with the kids for a while." Lisa blows her nose on a cloth napkin. "Being financially independent will allow me the space to make a decision about my marriage."

The waves crash in a whimper on the beach. The temperature has dropped, and a cold wind forces itself between us, goose-bumping our skin. I stand and extend my hands to my sisters. "We're professional women. We want a man when we want a man. He better come straight and right; otherwise, we keep moving forward."

"Damn right!" Ninnie says.

"Damn right!" Lisa echoes.

We clink our glasses, spilling mimosa all over the floor.

# CHAPTER THIRTY-SIX

❦❦❦

## KETLY

*February – July 2006*

We stand facing each other in the hospital yard. With his left arm looped around a low branch of a tree, Rénel smiles before leaning over to kiss my forehead after placing the red hibiscus behind my ear.

"Happy belated Valentine's Day, Miss Ketly." He takes my hand. "Something came up yesterday and I had to meet someone in Montvalle...Came back too late to come over to your house."

"Thank you for the gift." I shake my wrist with the silver bracelet with the amethyst stones he'd left yesterday at the hospital's front desk with the card. "You really shouldn't have. It's too...extravagant."

He opens his mouth wide in a silent cry. "Why? You don't like it?"

I laugh and shove him slightly, my elbow connecting with hard muscles under his tight shirt. "I love it, but that's not the point."

"What's the point, *Miss*?" He looks serious.

I was so worried yesterday that on Valentine's Day, he was meeting a woman somewhere. It scares me the way I think about this man all day.

# I SHALL FIND YOU

"Come on, let's go home," I say instead. The long months of flirting have been smoldering and are now bubbling to the surface. I feel an explosion coming.

"We're still going to the movies later?" he asks.

"Nothing keeps me away from a movie or a book. Although, I've watched this film every year on Valentine's Day."

"I know. It's the perfect movie for the occasion. *Love Story*." He takes my hand before I climb the first step into my house. "What's your love story, Miss Ketly? Everybody has one."

"What's yours?" I pull him inside. "Perhaps we can share stories tonight."

I make lemonade and serve him a glass. Two timid ice cubes melt so fast, it seems like magic. Rénel stares into the glass.

"It'll take some adjustment without electricity twenty-four-seven and an abundance of ice." He groans,

"Welcome to Haiti, American man." I smile, making my way to my bedroom. "I'll be back."

Minutes later, I return to the parlor fresh from my shower and a generous spritz of Bien-être all over my body. I look at the clock and sit next to him on the sofa. We have a couple of hours before the late show.

"You look beautiful," he says, leaning closer. His fragrance wafting from his skin invades my senses. I want to touch his biceps with a hunger that frightens me. I slip my hands under my thighs. He smiles as if he can read my mind.

"You go first." I tap his knee as a prompt, but let my hand linger there.

"Well, I have a seven-year-old son." He sighs. I gasp. "I haven't seen him in more than three years. I wanted to marry his mother, but when her family found out that I was Black and Haitian they threatened to disown her. One day while I was at work, she packed up and left New York with my son. I tried to find her, but my resources were limited and frankly I was…afraid."

I squeeze his hand hard. "*Oh mon Dieu*! That's horrible. People can lose their children in America, too?"

He nods. "Her family's wealthy and…political. I had no idea. She came into the auto shop often where I worked with an old car that was on life support. She worked as a waitress at a diner a couple blocks down the street. We started talking and…" He shrugs. "When she got pregnant with Elliot, we moved into her studio apartment. I asked her to marry me so many times I lost count." He takes a sip of his drink. "Turns out I was the culmination of her rebellion against her white conservative Evangelical parents. In the end she asked them to forgive her, because she wanted to go home. Except she had to choose between me and a life of luxury. She went back with my son." He closes his eyes, tears raining down on his shirt.

I stroke his arm until the skin feels warm under my hand. "Is that why you came back here?" I press down on his hand, angry that he could leave his child when he was already where he could try to find him. "You just give up looking for your son?"

He takes my hand; his thumb stroking my skin. "Your turn."

I look at the pack of cigarettes next to me, but I don't want to pull my hand away. It's as if he's injecting me with a tranquilizer. I open my mouth, close my eyes and tell him everything. How my papa died. The day I arrived at Simone's home and met Henri. The decision to let Juliette go so I could be with her again. My trust in Marge. My exile. My inability to get a visa to go to America. How I tried to use Vincent to get there and the shame and guilt I experienced over it all. How I don't ever want to be betrayed again.

"Now the funny thing is I do miss you when you're not around, but I want to be honest with you." I pull my hand away to light a cigarette. I

# I SHALL FIND YOU

swallow the rising wave in my stomach. I inhale so deep, my lungs burn. On the exhale, I say, "Rénel, I've told you about my daughter. Now I'd like you to help me get to America. As you probably already know, we have to get married. But I'll pay you and we'll divorce once I get there. No strings. I just want to meet my daughter and tell her my truth."

I fold my hands in my lap as if in prayer. He stands so fast; he loses his balance and grabs the back of the loveseat. "I don't need your money. I'm sorry about your daughter." His shoulders slump. "I know you know how I feel about you. You're the ray of sunshine in my life on this…island. I left this place a long time ago to explore life, to make it in America." He shakes his head, staring at the dark sky through the screen of the open window. "I never wanted to live in Haiti again. I thought one day I might visit but the universe had different plans." His gaze lingers on my face. "Now I love the slow pace of this island. This is my home and I'm learning to embrace it."

"But what do you think of my proposition? We can search for our children together and then go our separate ways."

He smiles. "I love your proposition, Kekette, because I love you. If we marry, it has to be for better or worse. Are you ready to do that?"

My heart accelerates. Rénel stirs deep feelings I thought had disappeared along with my first love. "I'm forty-four and I'm not having any more children. I never wanted to, Ren."

"Perfect. I don't want any more children either."

"But…but, Ren, I don't want to get hurt again. We need more time if we're talking about a real marriage."

He cups my face between his warm hands and deposits kisses on my eyelids, my nose, my cheeks, my chin before his mouth travels to my quivering lips. "Do you want to spend more time waiting for the right time, to enjoy your time, Miss Ketly?"

The heat starts from my feet and rises until my whole being ignites. He pulls me to him, my body melding into his. "No better time like this time," I mumble against his burning lips.

He groans as our tongues dance making me dizzy. Coming up for air, he whispers, "I want you."

"How about the movie?" I whisper back.

He pops the top buttons of my blouse. "Let me write you a Love Story tonight, Kekette." He carries me to my bedroom. The man is a superb writer.

In the summer, the smell of ripe mangoes blankets the island. Birds chirp in the flamboyant tree behind my house as if to celebrate the season that brings an abundance of fruits, long sunny days, festivals, colorful flowers and swimming. I flip on my back with my hands behind my head. Rénel strokes my forehead before running his fingers through my hair.

"What. You're playing hooky, too?" I ask. "Don't you have a shipment coming in today?"

"You know, you were right about trusting folks around here." He kisses my lips. "My new store manager is competent, and trustworthy. Besides, your special day is my special day. I'm hanging out with you."

"Well, I plan to stay in bed and read all these books you've been buying me on your frequent trips to Port-au-Prince."

His hand leaves my face and glides over my stomach making its way down. "I love reading with you, and on break time we can have more fun." He nuzzles my neck.

"I always stay home on Juliette's birthday. It's a day for me to remember and to write her story in my mind. This used to be a sad day for me, Rénel. It no longer is."

# I SHALL FIND YOU

"Okay. What can I do to make you *happier*?"

"I am happy." I kiss his neck and lay my head on his chest.

"Well, I have good news. I should at least get my birth certificate soon. So, we can get married. As for my citizenship document, it's up to New York Immigration."

"How did you lose these important documents, Ren? I think we can get married using your American passport. It should have your date of birth and other pertinent information," I muse. "Can we look into that? Let me see the passport."

Rénel pops up from the bed like a wound-up toy. "Why the inquisition? You act like you don't believe me sometimes. I told you I think Elliot's mother took them by accident. I'm going to the city at the end of the week to pick up the birth certificate. I'll check again at the embassy."

"How about your passport?" I say, knowing it's not in the house, since I've looked everywhere except its foundation.

He clears his throat. "Oh, I keep it in the vault at the store. Safer there. I need my birth certificate for another transaction here." He rolls out of the bed and shrugs into his robe, his body sculpted from his daily swimming and jogging around the island. I don't want him to leave.

"I'm sorry, Ren. I'm…just nosy. Come back in the bed."

He tickles the bottom of my foot. I giggle and reach for him. He has long pushed my old longings deep into the recess of my mind where I keep pleasant memories like rolling in the cornfield with Papa, jumping in the lake at my uncle's house, the smell of my baby seconds after she came out of my womb.

"I'm going to the store," he says. "To be continued."

Alone in my bed, I open the window across it and flop back down on the pillow. The book I tried to read earlier had fallen on the floor.

Leaning against the headboard, I gaze into the void of the blue sky, wondering, always, what Juliette is doing on her birthday.

Later that afternoon, Alice comes by laden with food. I haven't eaten all day. "You remember, sister?" I say.

"Yes. I know what today is," she says, hugging me tight in the hallway. "Happy to see you rejoice on Juliette's birthday lately. So long as you both are alive, there's always hope." She looks toward the bedroom. "Where's lover boy?"

I follow her and drop onto the couch, taking the plate, she hands to me. "He left to go to the store. He'll be back. Boy can't get enough." I spoon rice and beans into my mouth. I am starving. "Thank you, Ali."

"On this occasion, I wish I could do more than feed you," Alice says.

I shake my head. "You do enough. I owe you so much."

"Well, finish your food. We're going to get our nails done. I need some face powder…remember, Kekette, you have to fake it till—"

"You make it," I finish. "Except I no longer have to fake anything with Rénel. That scares me, Ali."

She taps the floor with her heels and cuts her eyes at me. "Lucky you."

I am lucky to have found Rénel. I need patience to wait for everything to fall into place.

# CHAPTER THIRTY-SEVEN

## ADELE

Today's my third wedding anniversary. I'd bought gift certificates for me and Ben to spend the day at the spa for the special occasion. Now after meeting with the divorce lawyer this morning, I wish I could leave today and go far away. I let myself in with my key, hoping Mom's napping.

I put my suitcase in the bedroom and shuffle to the kitchen for some coffee. "Addy, you're back," Mom says, startling me. "What's going on? Ben's been calling but won't tell me anything. JR called too and even stopped by yesterday. Said it was urgent. Can somebody tell me what's going on?"

I wrap her in my arms and kiss the top of her head. "I have to call JR back, Mom." I let her go and reach for my new phone in my purse from a chair in the kitchen. "Maybe he found out something more from Haiti."

"What did he find before?" Mom puts her mug down and grabs her head. "Adele, I want you to stop." She bangs the table with her fist. "If you go there, you'll kill me with worries. Why aren't you home with your husband anyway? Isn't today your anniversary?"

Squeezing the phone in my hand, I say, "Ben's having an affair. I'm filing for divorce." I walk into my childhood bedroom and lock the door.

"What! Adele." She jiggles the door handle. "Come out here and talk to me."

JR answers the phone on the second ring. "You're out of town with hubby? Went to the hospital, to your mom's. Where've you been?"

"Busy," I say. "But my PI found out that the late Miss Annette, who was the director of the clinic for decades has family members in Lasalle and someone is going to track them down to see what they know."

"Aha. I was getting to that."

"Then just tell me, JR." My patience is so thin I can see tomorrow through it. I blow into the phone before sitting on the edge of the bed.

"Oh! Well." He coughs. "Anyway, my friend learned from an old lady who lived in Lasalle that Clara owned the house across from the clinic. So now somebody else corroborates her existence. Marge is something else." JR whistles.

"*Clara*," I whisper. "I think she's part of my past, JR."

"So, before Miss Annette, the late nurse your PI mentioned, died, she cried over and over, 'The girl still wants her baby, and the witch stole her child.' Of course, the old Miss had dementia, but the old lady believed the girl never came back because she was pregnant and went to hide somewhere. I bet my pension, Marge knows who Clara is. She knows all the players."

I stand from the bed, pacing the short distance between the walls. In my gut, I know that girl's my mother, and she wants me. All these years, finding her was as easy as making some inquiries by connecting with the right people. Or my mother finding; the courage to tell me the truth.

"Addy, are you still there?"

# I SHALL FIND YOU

"I'm sorry, yes. It sounds like it's her. Can we go sooner, JR?"

"Oh! I thought you wanted to spend Christmas at home."

"Change in plan. I can go anytime you're ready now. I'll even pay to change your ticket."

"Hold on. I can't leave before the thirtieth." He grunts. "Won't get the time off now. We'll find her. So, is your husband going with you?"

"Ben's not going."

"Something happened?"

"Don't want to talk about it. Listen, so we'll go to Lasalle first?"

"My friend said the woman mentioned a Haitian Miss who came with a white one and spent lots of time at Clara's house. Might be Nadine."

"Nadine will be back from visiting her daughter the day after Christmas. I'll talk to her then."

"Great idea. I bet you she knows stuff as close as she is to Marge."

I stop pacing. "JR," I say slowly, "when I was a kid, I used to ask Nadine about Haiti and my adoption. She'd always change the subject. One time she got really exasperated with me and yelled, 'ask Marge.'" My legs are shaking. I sit back on the bed. "She probably knows."

"Why she never talked to you about it? I'm confused. She should be on your side."

"I don't think there are sides in this…situation." I take a very deep breath to clear my head. "You know, I'm going to approach Nadine as if Mom has told me *everything*, and that I'm going to see my biological mother. Not look for her, JR. *See her.* You understand?"

"Yes. I understand, Miss Adele. You're devious. I love it. And don't tell your mom you plan to talk to Nadine."

"Okay. Talk later."

I click End Call and put my head down between my knees to stop the dizziness. Do I know the woman behind the door? Could she possibly know who my parents are and never tell me? All these years. But why? Did Nadine withhold information to protect someone? Who?"

With my phone in hand, I open the bedroom door and snatch my purse from the kitchen table while plucking an apple from the fruit bowl.

"Addy, where you're going?" Mom grabs my arm. I peel her hand off. "Please talk to me."

"Later, Mom. I have to go." I pull the front door behind me.

Several times, people honk for me to move my car forward at green lights. Mom and Nadine populate my head. I open the garage door; grateful Ben's car is not there. I fill several suitcases with my personal belongings. I still feel like an intruder in the house that was never my home. In Ben's office downstairs, I scribble a note wishing him good luck and place my divorce lawyer's card and the new car key on top of the folded sheet of paper. I load up the trunk of my old car with Christmas presents I'd wrapped for my friends at the Senior Center.

The festivities brighten my sour mood. I choose a cupcake and a glass of eggnog and go in search of Beulah. In the activity hall, a group plays bingo, another is wrapping presents at a long table. Beulah's standing next to the piano singing while Olga plays Silent Night. I sit and listen while I lick red and green frosting off my fingers, feeling a sense of peace replacing the confusion.

Later, Beulah and I stroll in the small garden at the back of the building.

"I'm sorry, Addy, about your marriage," she says. "It's a different kind of betrayal than…a boyfriend-girlfriend relationship. I thought my first husband was a demi-god; turned out he was a snake. But the second time around I went in with guardrails." She chuckles. "Turned out I didn't need them. That man taught me to find myself and present it to him when I was good and ready, because he wanted the real me. You understand what I'm saying?"

"Yes, ma'am." I nod. "That's exactly why I'm making this trip. I can't be my true self without finding the truth."

She squeezes my hand with her bony fingers. "Don't ever live for nobody but yourself. That's the only way you can give of yourself to somebody."

We join the karaoke group, and I sing and laugh and gorge myself with sweets. Later, I place the gifts I'd brought under the tree for my knitting partners and escape through the back door.

I feel the beginning of a new life. One I will control. A life that will be complete once I find the people who have given it to me. Hard to believe that it's been only five months since I met JR at the hospital. He's helping me realize a dream I'd held close to my heart since the boy in kindergarten told me I didn't belong anywhere in our small world of Crayola crayons of black, white, brown, green, blue, purple and red. Soon I'll find my roots. Going with JR replaces my long-held fear with a giddiness beyond the search for my parents: I'm going to find me.

# CHAPTER THIRTY-EIGHT

## KETLY

*March 2007*

It has been over a year since Rénel showed up on the island. He loves to drive. On the weekends, we explore the nearby villages. We picnic under fruit trees and next to streams, spending hours reading and making love in the outdoors. It adds spices to an already well-seasoned act with this hunk of a man. But since my proposition to pay him to get me to America, he's pulled away as if he's afraid. Of what, I don't know.

Lately, despite my reassurance that going to America is no longer a condition for me being with him, Rénel seems uneasy around me. I'm running out of excuses to convince him. Since the conversation about the documents, he never mentioned his marriage proposal again. As the saying goes, absence makes the heart grow fonder. So, after clearing some vacation time with my supervisor, I pack a small suitcase, tie it to the back rack of my new moped and head to Mapou. The note I left for him at his store simply says:

# I SHALL FIND YOU

*Rénel,*

*I'll be back in a few days.*

*Ketly*

∞∞∞

Halfway to Mapou, I stop by a creek after plucking dangling mangoes off a tree. I spread a blanket on the ground, reach for the brown bag with my cassava and *manba* sandwich and a banana. After lunch, I lean my back against the tree trunk and close my eyes. The water gurgles and splashes against the rocks in the clear creek behind me. Birds sing and frolic through tree branches. A gray feather with specks of white lands on my nose like the breathy kisses from Rénel. I run the feather over my cheeks, igniting the smoldering fires inside my body for that man. People on foot, on mules, on mopeds go up and down the road. Those who look in my direction wave. Some stare, but for the most part I'm blissfully ignored.

It's a few degrees cooler in Mapou than down in Galette. I hum the way I used to when I lived here with Matante, feeling peace. I wish she was here to advise me, but I know what she'd say. Patience was never my virtue. I breathe the fresh air whistling through the leaves of tall fruit trees and the green carpet of underbrush. Small mud-walled houses sprout at the clearing and among them stands the one room school where Denise still teaches children to write their names and count as high as they can go.

A few yards away, she's squatting in front of her house. "Huh, Kekette," she says, trying to get up from the laundry basin, "what a pleasant surprise."

I help her stand. She wipes the suds on her frock. I pull two chairs from the porch. We sit facing each other. "You didn't come down last month for your check up," I say. "How're you feeling?"

Denise pats her right knee. "Better. The shots help." She sighs and stretches her legs in front of her. A downcast look replaces her usual exuberance. A bunch of kids rush from behind the house chasing each other. I recognize two of them as hers. "Stop running before one of you falls and breaks something," she yells through the swirling dust they leave behind.

"Bonswa, Miss Ketly," the group sings and giggles.

I smile and wave at the happiness and the oblivion of childhood. "Well, I'm surprised hubby didn't drag you down to your appointment. You know how he is about taking care of you."

"Oh, he's upset with me. I won't agree for him to sell some of our land and cattle to pay for a boat ride to Miami." She spits in the dust before taking a gulp from her water cup. "It's dangerous and we have no need for that."

I shudder as I remember once entertaining the idea of going to America by boat. "I agree with you, Denise. Your family is doing well here. It's too risky." I squeeze her hand in sisterhood.

Every day this week I wait for Rénel to show up. I want him to chase me and want me the way I want him. Every night I go to bed, terrified that he'll meet someone else who wants to be his wife and not a business partner. Maybe he changed his mind about not having children and he wants a younger wife. After all, he's the most desirable bachelor around with his status and good looks.

Today is my last day before I return to work. Disappointment coils around my heart and tightens it every time I think about Rénel possibly being with another woman. I pick the black head from the rice in the tray on my lap and throw them on the ground as the baby chicks peck at them and shake their heads before looking for something else. They know what they don't want. They want corn. They will not settle for close enough. "I know what I want, too," I whisper.

Denise looks at me and smiles under the shade of an oak tree. The sound of the moped pulls my head up. He stops at a distance to keep the red dust away from us and swaggers toward me as if in slow motion.

"There you are," Rénel says, taking the tray off my lap and lifting me up in the air and kisses me deeply before putting me down. He tips his cap to Denise. "Good morning, ma'am."

"Bonjour, Rénel. I'm happy to see you on this fine day." Denise winks at me.

I fill my body with his sight, his smell, his laughter. "Alice wouldn't tell me where you are." He kisses me again with his arm around my neck. "Finally, Raoul took pity on me." He hands me an envelope.

"What is it?" With shaky hands, I open it. Inside is a crispy birth certificate. "Oh. You have it."

"More good news. I went to the American embassy. My certificate of citizenship is being processed. I told them it's very important to my wife to be."

I wrap my arms around his neck. I want to marry him to be his wife. My love for Henri has become a ghost that appears unexpectedly but is no longer the steady presence it used to be. I love this man. If becoming his wife gets me to see my daughter, well that'll be the icing on my wedding cake. I giggle.

After coffee and chitchat, I grab my picnic basket and his hand, and we run into the woods frolicking around. At a pond, I cover the ground of a rock-formed grotto with a blanket, holding on to his hand as if he may disappear. He kisses my palm and my fingers. Soon his hands explore my skin as he slides the strap of my sundress down my arms. I shiver in the cool spring breeze facing him in my red bikini cut underwear. We behold each other as if for the first time. The hunger in his eyes fuels my own appetite for lust. He reaches for my panties, and I stop his hands. His breath's coming fast.

"Honey, I'll do anything," he whispers. "Why did you leave Galette? I thought you…were with another man. What do you want, Kekette? Tell me."

I push him on his back and strip his clothes off one piece at a time. I kiss every inch of his taut body as if I want him to remember he can never live without this. He groans when I take him into my mouth. His fingers grab my ponytail like he needs an anchor. When the pressure increases on my scalp, I crawl on top of him and take him inside me. I lift my face to the sun peeking through the leaves, as I ride him hard. Birds stop singing and flitting around as if to bear witness to the gift I offer and I take. I lean over Rénel, our eyes connect. I slow down my movements. He grabs my buttocks and lifts me up and brings me down like an inverted pestle to a mortar.

"Oh, yes, Kekette," he murmurs like a mantra.

My toes curl with the sensation spreading over my body like hot lava. I squeeze my thighs to slow it down. We make love with our eyes, never breaking contact. In one fluid movement, Rénel flips me onto my back on the bed of soft leaves. With my legs resting on his thick shoulders, he thrusts inside me until I yell in surrender. A flock of green parrots lifts off from the branches in a cacophony of wings and squawks, having witnessed my freedom from the memory of all the hurt and the betrayal that have been levied against me.

"Damn, this is so good," Rénel screams with his own release. We collapse; our bodies flushed against each other so that even the breeze can't come between us. "I can't live without this, Kekette.

∞∞∞

We marry the following week. It is just the two of us and Alice and Raoul as our witnesses. After consummating our marriage all week long, tonight, with my head on his chest I say, "Mon amour, we can travel for a proper honeymoon, once we get all your documents. My passport is current. I want to see the world." I tickle him. "Ok, maybe we don't have *world* money." I giggle. "But we can go where we can afford. I'll be happy. What do you think?"

He doesn't answer for so long, I'm thinking he's asleep without snoring for once. "That would be lovely, Kekette. I hope we get to do that. I love you, wife."

I massage his scalp. "Oh, we can see some of the places in Europe from the books we've read. I'd love to visit Notre Dame de Paris, Les Champs-Elisées, La Tour—."

His snoring stops me. I nuzzle the back of his neck and inhale his clean soapy scent. My husband and I are family now. I plaster my body against his hard back and joy pulls me into a pleasant dream.

# CHAPTER THIRTY-NINE

## ADELE

Today, on Christmas Eve, Ben is served with divorce papers. He calls. I don't answer the phone. I have nothing to say though. Mom is at midnight mass with her caretaker. I slip on a red sequined tunic and my high heels sandals and drive over to Ninnie's party. I could have invited JR since he made a point yesterday of telling me he was off tonight, but I don't want to rush into anything. I need time for myself. Besides, he's probably in Tampa at some party with live music and hot girls. Heat burrows under my skin as I remember the night we spent dancing this summer.

"Don't come in sweats, Adele," Ninnie said earlier when she called to threaten me with a curse if I skip her famous Christmas Eve *réveillon*. "I have some real guests coming." Laughing her silly snorting laugh, trying to forget Pierre, just like I'm trying to forget another failed relationship.

At her door, I freeze, when I see JR standing in a corner talking to Ninnie's secretary from work, a glass with amber liquid in his hand. I can't remember her name, but I know she's single. The smile on his face annoys me like an eyelash under my eyelids. He says something to her. The woman moves closer to him and leans her head almost to his chest, cupping her hand around her ear. The bass from Ninnie's stereo beats through my body. Ninnie grabs my arm and whispers, "Mm! girl, look at this specimen. *Officer* JR is a dish." She licks her lips. "I hope you hungry, sister." She bumps me with her right hip.

I stop myself from licking my own lips. "Why didn't you tell me you've invited him?" I squint at her in the dim light of her living room. "Where did you get his number?"

She tuts. "Duh! Sometimes, you can be so dense. He's a local cop. Ain't he?"

"You're conniving, *Eugenie*." I scoot away before she attacks me.

In the commotion, JR looks up and nods at me. He leans over and says something to the woman before striding toward me. Without a word, he takes my hand and leads me to the back porch.

"Why didn't you tell me about Ben?" He closes the sliding door behind us.

"Ninnie talks too much. Why was it important that I tell you?"

The moonlight bathes us as if showing our flaws, our insecurities, all we need to see beneath the beautiful clothes.

"No reason, I guess." He shrugs. "You look beautiful tonight."

For a long time, we talk about my failed marriage, his broken engagement from two years before, our upcoming trip, our professions. Back inside, we dance to Ninnie's generous selection of eclectic music. In the corner of my eyes, I see Ninnie smiling at us, while she disappears into the arms of a new beau I have not yet met.

Much later, back at my mom's house, I fall into a dream filled with all the possibilities in the upcoming new year for my future.

∞∞∞

This morning, I yawn, stretching my arms over my head on the bed. I can hear voices coming from the TV set in the kitchen. In the bathroom, I wash up and change into a pair of clean sweat. Mom and I had exchanged gifts early this morning when I returned from Ninnie's, and she was back from midnight service.

On my way to the kitchen, the doorbell rings. I halt my steps.

"Who's it?" Mom yells from the kitchen.

"Hi, Ben." I open the door wider to let him in. He leans the "Coconut Woman" painting against the wall in the entryway.

"Please, I want you to have it," he whispers. "It was a gift."

I know Paige probably doesn't want that Haitian woman hanging anywhere in her house, staring at her with that all-knowing gaze. I swallow a bubbling laugh.

"Thank you, Ben. Won't you come in? I can make Haitian coffee."

"No! I...I can't face Marge right now. I'm so sorry." He looks at the doormat with the faded Welcome printed on it. "I hope you can forgive me, Adele."

"Nothing to forgive, Ben. We both want different...things."

"I wish you good luck with the trip. I hope you find everything you're looking for."

"Merry Christmas," we say almost at the same time. We smile. I close the door.


The day after Christmas, my packed suitcase and backpack sit in a corner of the bedroom. I keep the door closed. Mom is on a mission to derail me again. For weeks now, she has complained of so many ailments, I lose track. I know her game and I'm not falling for it this time. I will

# I SHALL FIND YOU 271

buy my own place as soon as I return from my trip. Nadine is coming back today from Chicago, and I plan to go see her later.

After an early dinner, I take my car keys and kiss mom's forehead. She barely touches her food.

"Where you're going, Addy? I can use some fresh air. Then we can stop by Nadine's."

I swear the woman can read my mind. "Oh, I'm going to help Lisa with…something. I'll be back soon. We'll go out tomorrow."

She motions to the gift box I have for Nadine in my hand. I close my eyes, wanting to kick myself.

"You're stopping by Nadine?" she asks. "I have something for her, too. I can go with you."

"What…oh, Ninnie will be at Lisa's I plan to give it…umm… to her for her mother. Nadine will be tired from her flight. We'll go tomorrow, Mom. I promise."

I jog to the front door, pulling it quietly behind me, praying she will not walk next door. I park two blocks away from our house and approach Nadine's home on foot like a thief in case Mom's peering at her house from our kitchen window. Ninnie's car is in the driveway. I slip inside the house through the side door which I know they only lock at night.

"Merry Christmas, Auntie Nadine." I hug her after placing the gift box on her bed. "How was your trip?"

"Oh, Addy, I miss that." She touches my cheek. "You guys stopped calling us aunties after you graduated college. You used to call me your black Auntie and Maureen was your white Auntie. Remember?"

"Well even if we don't say it, we still consider you all our Aunties. Right Ninnie?"

She grunts, "Mm-huh," never looking up from whispering on her phone. She's in love again.

Nadine rips open the box, just like Ninnie, eager to see what's inside. These two are so alike. She pulls the silver bracelet I found at a store in Tampa, with the small Haitian flag over the clasp.

"Oh, Addy, it's beautiful." She turns to Ninnie, seated on the chaise in the corner. "Look at this, Eugenie." She swats her daughter's leg off the seat. "Get off the phone. You're being rude. I tell you Addy's the real Haitian." She snort-laughs like Ninnie, slipping the bracelet over her wrist. "Look!"

Ninnie ends the call, snatches a nail file off the side table and attacks two broken nails. Who did she skin last night? I stifle a laugh.

"Speaking of Haitian, I can't wait to leave in less than a week. Can't believe I'm going to *see* my biological mother." I hold my breath.

Nadine's hands still while trying to close the clasp and looks at me. "Oh! Marge told you about Ketly and Lasalle?"

I nod, not trusting my voice while trying to not look away. I paste a smile on my face. "Yeah, *Ketly*. I bet she'll be surprised to see me."

"I bet," Nadine says. "I'm glad Marge broke her silence. She never told me that she'd talked to you about what we learned when we were in Haiti in '81."

"Wait, you and Mom went back to Haiti the year *after* my birth?" I say, moving to sit on the cedar trunk at the foot of the bed. Then I recover quickly. "You know Mom's forgetful lately about…details. Please tell me the whole story in case she might have missed something, Auntie."

"Okay. So, I went back in '81 with Marge. Ketly…*Ketly*…*Murat*." She snaps her fingers. "Ketly lived with her family in the house across from the clinic. Marge and I drank your grandmother Clara's famous rhum punch every night after dinner."

# I SHALL FIND YOU

I moan. *"Clara is my grandmother."*

I nod at Nadine like I already know what she is saying. "Ketly gave birth to you at seventeen, but Marge had known her since she was this high." Nadine splays her fingers above her knees. "So Ketly went to hide on the island of Terreville, because this goon who worked for your paternal grandmother Simone kept coming looking for her and you. Ketly wanted to tell Marge why she left you at the clinic and how she watched to make sure Marge had taken you inside that night and on the bus the next day. You see, Addy, your mama didn't just abandon you. She and your papa…" Nadine taps her forehead with her fingers, "Henri…can't remember the last name. I'm sorry. Anyway, he was seventeen too. They fell in love in Port-au-Prince where she was working for his mother, a wealthy *mulatresse* with green eyes like yours and Henri's. When Ketly ran away before Simone could yank you out of her belly, she exiled Henri to Paris with no money. He never got to say goodbye to Ketly."

I silently whimper.

"But he'd promised her that when he turned eighteen, he'd inherit a large sum of money, and he'd marry her. He picked your name Juliette. Ketly was upset that Marge had changed it. After your birth, Simone erected tombstones in the cemetery and obtained fake death certificates to convince Henri that you and Ketly had died in childbirth. They even killed her aunt."

I gasp and cover my mouth with my hand. Nadine stops talking. Ninnie puts the file down and we both gape at her.

"I'm sorry," I say, "please go on."

Nadine takes a sip from her glass. "Ketly begged us to help her come to America to be with you. From here, she hoped to search for Henri. Marge had a friend who worked at the American embassy in Haiti. *Hélène*…can't remember the last name either. I'm getting old." She shrugs. "Marge left you with her while the embassy processed the adoption papers. Anyway, Marge promised Ketly she'd help her get a visa to come here. I even gave Ketly money to get her passport ready."

I inhale loudly. "What happened? Why do you think she changed her mind?"

"Well, a couple months after our return here, Marge told me that Ketly had contacted her and said, she wanted Marge to raise you and to never tell you about her and Henri. She'd met somebody on the island, and she wanted to start a new life...without you. Marge could have brought her here easily through her friend at the embassy. I'm sorry, Addy."

I stand. "That's not what Ketly said in the note she left with me. It was for *safekeeping,* and she wanted to come back for me."

Nadine frowns. "Ketly said she left a note, but when I asked Marge if she had it when we came back from our last mission, I clearly remember her saying that she'd destroyed it. Hmm!"

"I smell a rat," Ninnie finally says. "Sounds like Marge kept a lot to herself that she didn't share with you, Mom."

Nadine's face clouds over. "You know, over the years, I'd asked Marge many times to tell you the truth, Addy and she'd get upset sometimes and tell me to keep my promise. She'd made me swear not to tell you. She didn't want you to learn that your mama didn't want you. Just last week, she asked me to talk sense into you about going to Haiti because Ketly never wanted to be found. So, I'm surprised she told you..." Nadine stares at me with wide open eyes. "Marge didn't say anything to you. Did she, Adele?"

I shake my head until I feel dizzy and whisper, "No."

She taps her forehead hard. "Henri's last name was Bertrand. I hope you find them when you get to Haiti, Addy."

We smile at each other. Three Haitian women in a room with a secret we each will have to handle in our own way. Why did Mom tell me she'd never returned to Haiti after bringing me home? What is she hiding? What if Mom lied about Ketly changing her mind? Is that what she's afraid I'll find out? In my gut, I knew my mama wanted to come for me. So, now I'm going to her. *To Ketly.*

# CHAPTER FORTY

❦❦❦

# KETLY

*July 2009*

    We settle into our new house. Rénel takes my list to Port-Au-Prince once a month to buy what I want to decorate. We build the house with lots of windows, and I love the sunlight and the salty smell of the island flowing through the filmy drapes I hang in the large living room. He has an easy way about him that attracts people. Rénel now has more friends on the island in a couple of years than I have after living here for decades.

    Six months after our wedding, our daily routine grounds me into my marriage in a way that fulfills my needs. On a day like today, I wish I could forget that I am a mother, the way my husband never mentions his son, as if he doesn't exist. How does a mother pretend her child was never there? Or how can a father?

    On my way to the bedroom to get my book, I pick up the vase off the coffee table and bring it up to my nose and sniff the flowers my husband brings me once a week. He plants hibiscus hedges all around the house when he notices that they are my favorite flower. The sound of his car stops me in my tracks.

"Mon amour." I throw my arms around his neck. "I called you today…umm…I remember it's Elliot's birthday." I raise myself on my tiptoes and kiss his lips. He steps away from me, his eyes hard.

"Why can't you leave things alone, Ketly? Unlike you I've moved on. Elliot's with his mother. I've accepted that I'll never see him again."

I take several steps away from him until the armchair stops me. *"Oh Mon Dieu!* What do you mean by that? How can you just abandon him?" I squint at him waiting for something. He looks away before walking down the hallway to the bedroom. "Well, unlike you, I know I am a parent, Rénel," I yell.

Moments later, he leaves for his weekly Thursday night card game with the local businessmen's association. Later, unable to sleep, I use the new mobile Rénel gave me for my birthday and call Alice. She listens.

"You know, I'm not agreeing with him, but you can be intense, Kekette. I bet he's dealing with his loss in his own way and doesn't want you to remind him all the time. Give him some space, honey. I'm sure he'll go find his son when he's ready."

I swallow my rebuke and instead say, "You don't live with him, Ali. He's extremely content being here, as if he doesn't really want to go back to America to find his son. *Like ever*. Okay, maybe I'm exaggerating, but he's laid-back and I'm afraid if I don't push, nothing will get done. Why can't he go to New York to get the certificate? I suggested it a month ago. He got angry." I shake my head. "I don't know…how can he not want to fight to see his little boy when he has the tool to do it. I…don't understand."

"Kekette, come by tomorrow. Since we got these damn phones, I haven't seen you much. I don't like them."

I smile. "I agree. See you tomorrow."

Tonight, upon my return from Alice's house, we sit on the new swing on our porch after dinner having a drink, my feet nestled in his crotch.

Rénel absently strokes my thigh, and electricity runs through my body. His skin has turned a coppery red from the island sun, making his brown eyes glow. I want to lick him right now like a lollipop.

"I'm sorry I yelled at you yesterday, chérie," he says, his hand creeping higher. "I understand our needs are different. I pray Juliette will come to find you here." I swing my legs off his lap and stand, peering at him. "Not that I'm not going to do everything in my power to help you get to America, but immigration can be painfully slow or sometimes they fail altogether. As much as America doesn't treat us right, we still want to go there, but they don't really want us. We have a home. I never like living over there. There are so many clues your daughter can follow to find you."

I feel dizzy. Did I drink that much? I don't seem to understand what Rénel is saying. I move closer and hold his face between my palms and brush my lips against his. "It's okay, Ren. But that's not what I was saying at all. My daughter *is* a twenty-nine-year adult. I always pray that she's alive, because I don't know for certain. I'd love to know that she's happy…that's all. And maybe she'll find me. But I can't stop thinking about your little boy. He *knows* you. He lived with you. He must be sad not knowing what happened to you. You can fix that. I still miss my papa."

He nods. "Let me go freshen our drinks." He swallows the contents of his glass in one gulp and goes inside with our tumblers.

Later, Rénel lights all the candles casting our bedroom into an amber glow bathing our naked bodies. He unties my French braid and massages my scalp, until all of life's unpleasantness escape through my pores. He sits with his back against the headboard, and I nestle between his legs, my back pressing against his torso. The thumping of his heart beats against my fevered skin. He cups my breasts in his strong hands, running the pads of his thumbs over my erect nipples. I shiver. My body seems to float over the bed. I want him to ground me back on earth with his erection stabbing my back like a knock to enter a sacred place. I twist around within his embrace and kiss his mouth with urgency.

"Oh, Ren, I'm committed to making our marriage work. No matter what. You make me happy."

"Well, I want to *show* you how happy you make me, my lovely wife."

He tickles my neck with the tip of his hot tongue. I giggle and try to escape from him by pushing away from the enclosure of his arms. Rénel pulls me to him and squeezes me so hard against his body, I struggle for breath, yet I don't want to ever leave this cocoon. He opens his legs wide and raises my bottom over them as he enters me. I start to move like a wild buck. He cradles my face between his palms.

"Look at me sweetheart," he whispers, not moving.

I lose myself into his eyes and see unspoken words of love, desire, regret, promise and lust. His gaze burns into mine, daring me to look away. The tension builds in my lower body, and when I come, I whimper like a lost puppy happy to see its mother. I flop onto his chest, spent and wrung out. "Oh, Ren."

"Kekette, I don't ever want to lose you." He rains kisses over my head, as he brushes the hair away from my face. He pushes me gently on my back, never disconnecting with my body. He thrusts deep into me with purpose as if he's searching for the reassurance that we will ride any storm together. Minutes later, my body is slick with our sweat, and we rock to the music in our heart. My husband grabs my hair tightly in his fists. I wince as he pushes in so deep. "I love you, Kekette. I really do."

The next day, the screams coming from the pregnant woman fill the air in the labor room with more hot air. The ceiling fan whirs like it's on life-support. Nothing can spoil my day. I feel anchored and steady, like I can do anything. I look at the clock; I still have a couple hours before the end of my shift. I should have stayed home today to supervise the meals for our first anniversary dinner.

Rénel left unexpectedly early this morning for the city, mumbling about an important business meeting. When I stepped into the living room this morning, a giant bouquet of flowers sat on the dining room table with a card. He remembered what today is.

This afternoon, on my way home from work, I stop at the bakery and buy a small chocolate cake and hurry home to change. Minutes later, when Rénel walks through the door, the smile on his face melts my heart. He places his briefcase on a chair and picks me up.

"Happy Anniversary, wife." He kisses my lips.

"Put me down." I swat at his back. "Go wash up, please."

I set the table while my cook brings the covered dishes inside. The aromas of tasso goat, grilled conch meat, and rice cooked with *djondjon* fill the air. My stomach growls and the buzz from that first glass of wine relaxes my hunched shoulders. Lit candles flicker in the breeze, the flames reminding me of a cigarette. I have not smoked in over a year. My new vice now is my husband's body. I pour another glass of wine from the Igloo cooler; it's a bit warm. Ice melts faster in July.

His cologne precedes him into the dining room. Rénel stands there with his hand behind his back. I stop fussing with the napkin to stare at him. As if in slow motion, a yellow envelope appears. He hands it to me.

"Here's the gift you've been waiting for." I rush him and with shaking hands I untwist the thread and pull a sheaf of papers out. They're in English. I look up at him. "I picked up the certificate of citizenship at the embassy today and filled out the sponsorship application for your permanent visa. I made copies of everything already. I'll drop the original back at the embassy tomorrow. I hope they approve it."

"You did all that today?" Then it hits me. "You want me to go with you to look for Elliot? We don't have to stay there, if you don't want to. We can come back home. Maybe Elliot can spend summers with us here. I hope you find him."

"Okay." He laughs and picks me up again. "I didn't want you to think I'm a deadbeat papa and that I don't want to see my son. I hope they approve my request for you."

"Why you keep saying that?" I throw my arms around his neck and kiss his lips hard. "You go without me if my papers will take too long. I told you I can wait. Trust me, you'll be happier being part of your son's life. It's hard to live with regrets. I spent a great deal of time beating myself for not bringing my daughter here with me. Anyway, did you also get the certificate of citizenship?"

"What?" He pulls away from my embrace. "Oh, I put it and the copy of the application in the vault. Why?"

I throw the papers on the table and grab his forearm. "Don't mind me." I wrap my arms around his waist. "I know you'll do the right thing, Ren."

I don't quite remember eating. I am full of hope, love, excitement, even a bit of guilt for doubting Rénel all these months. He has been thinking about his son, my daughter, me, and us. This is the best anniversary present a wife can have. A husband who listens and cares about her happiness.

"Kekette, come on, let's go to bed." He stands from the dining table and stretches his long torso, reaching for my hand to pull me up. "I want to catch the first ferry in the morning to deliver the application, and we have to celebrate." He winks.

"Oh, I can go with you tomorrow. I no longer need disguise to go to Port-Au-Prince, but I'd love to see Helène Macombe and rub her nose in my happiness. Alphonse said she's still working there."

He lets go of my hand. "Oh no!" Something dances in his eyes like fear. I frown. "They wouldn't let you…umm… inside the embassy. Besides I have a lot of other businesses to take care of in the city. You'd be bored." He reaches into his pocket. "Oh, the delivery guy Tim-Tim gave me this for you."

I see Alphonse's handwriting on the envelope. I place it on the table unopened. I follow my husband into our bedroom.

# CHAPTER FORTY-ONE

## ADELE

I don't remember walking from Nadine's house to Mom's. It's faster than driving my car back. Mom's watching TV in bed. Her caregiver is in the spare room. I pull her bedroom door closed behind me, flip the switch on for the ceiling light and go to stand in front of the TV screen.

"Addy...what's wrong?"

"You have lied to me all these years," I yell, hoping anger will release its grip on my heart. "Don't be mad at Nadine. I tricked her. She thought you had finally developed a conscience and told me the truth."

Mom clutches her chest. I don't move. Instead, I cross my arms over mine. "I wanted to protect you, Addy. You have no idea."

"From what? You knew Ketly since she was a child herself." She flinches and sits up in the bed. "You had no intention of ever bringing her here to be with me and you. Did you? You would never have lost me to her. You may have meant well but that was cruel, Mom."

Her face turns purple. I sway on my feet but control the urge to rush to her, because her eyes are ink-blue with rage. "Why should I have brought her here? It would have confused you and who knows, she might have decided to take you away from me, back to that…that godforsaken place. I couldn't risk that. Can't you understand?" She leans her body forward with her arms extended, as if she wants to grab me. "Ketly probably has a dozen children by now. They have them like flies over there and people who can afford children can't—" She stops. She must have seen the horror on my face.

I close my eyes to avoid looking at her. Fury bubbles in my stomach. I ball my hands as I move closer to the foot of the bed. "So, your mission was never to help the people of the village but to find a way to steal one of their children since they have so many?" Mom scoots back until the headboard bangs against the wall. "She *trusted* you with her child. You lied. You discounted her as if her life, her wish, everything she represents is insignificant to what you…you…the *American* woman wants." I breathe. "I don't think I know you." Her face swims in the tears that pour out of my body. "You never stopped to think about me, about how much I wanted this. You're a very, very selfish woman."

Mom kicks the sheet off her legs and stands, holding on to the nightstand. "How can you say those hurtful words to me, Adele?" she yells back. "I've loved you and given you everything."

"My birth name is *Juliette. Murat. Bertrand.*" I say each name slowly, trying them in my mouth for the first time. "I'm beginning to know who I am now. I need to go find the roots." I close the door behind me.

"Adele Marie Pearson," she screams. "You come back here."

Christie bumps into me on her way to Mom's room. "Is everything ok, Adele?"

"Everything's fine. Keep an eye on her. I'll be out of the country. All the emergency numbers are in the folder I gave you."

Loading my luggage for the trip to Haiti in my car and enough clothes for the next couple days, I check into the same hotel and cry until I fall asleep across the bed.

The next morning, after breakfast downstairs, I sit by the pool looking at the ocean, imagining Ketly Murat on the island of Terreville longing for the child she had to lose to save. Do I have siblings? Dozens of them? Did Henri ever return to Haiti? Simone sounds like a monster. Speaking of monsters, I don't even know how to feel about Mom. I grew up curious about my biological parents, but not because I was lacking in love. I could have found my parents long ago if only Mom had the decency to respect Ketly's and my wishes. How can she decide that our feelings, our needs are less important than what she wanted? Who is Marge Pearson?

I slather sunscreen lotion over my skin and lie down on a chaise in the sun. My phone rings.

"Hi, oh…Mom!" For the first time, I don't want to talk to her. But what if she's sick. "Everything ok, Mom?"

"Addy, I'm sorry. I was selfish, misguided, blind, jealous…" She chuckles, sobs trilling her voice. "Yes, jealous of the poor people who have nothing but are blessed with the most beautiful children. Yes, I wanted one, but Ketly left you for me to take. After reading the note, I was scared that she'd take you back. I loved you too much to let you go but I could have shared you with her. My decision to not bring her here haunted me always, but…but the more time that passed the more I didn't know how to explain it to you or to her. Please…please… forgive… me, Addy…" The sobs chop her words.

"Mom, I'm not going to lie and say I'm not hurt and…angry. Please stop crying before you make yourself sick. We'll be okay. I'll still be your daughter when I come back. Nothing will ever change that. I only want to be Ketly and Henri's daughter as well if they want me to be."

"Yes. Yes. Please come home before you leave. I have a package for Ketly."

I dial JR and leave a message. I spend the day outside filling my new diary with the events of the past few days. I'm no longer married. I have parents with names and a story. I'm a new daughter. I have a clean slate to write new chapters of my life and I'm excited, albeit bruised by more betrayal.

This afternoon, I meet JR in the lobby, and we sit in a corner of the bar. It's almost empty, except for the brunette in dark glasses and blood-red lips who's practically sitting in the lap of the man with a wedding band and a furtive look on his face.

"You want some dinner?" I ask. "I'm starving."

JR keeps staring at me in my sleeveless pink dress with my hair pinned up on top of my head in a messy bun. "You're glowing like a lighthouse in a raging storm," he whispers.

I blush and signal the waiter. I order drinks and appetizers. "I spoke with Nadine yesterday."

JR pulls out a notebook and a pen from his shirt pocket. "Pray tell!"

When I'm done, he closes the book and peers at me in the dark bar. "I'm sorry, but Marge represents what I resent about the way NGO folks go to Haiti and take whatever they want with no oversight."

"Mm-hm!" I grunt. "I have so much to learn."

He flattens his lips. "So, we're basically going to waltz oh—I mean—ferry into Terreville and find Ketly." His face clouds over.

"What?"

"I don't get to use my investigative skills in Haiti to track down your elusive parents." He pouts.

I smile, shaking my head. A lock of hair escapes the pins and falls over my left eye. He lifts his hand languidly and tucks it behind my ear.

I inhale. His fingers burn my skin and stir something inside. I raise my wineglass to my lips, gulp some and say, "Let's order dinner."

Hours later, I yawn so many times after the bottle of wine; JR stands and reaches out his hand. I ignore it. We walk toward the elevator. When the door opens, I stand on my toes and graze his cheek with my lips and whisper, "Good night, *my friend.*"

He runs his palm over my bare arm and kisses my forehead. "Good night, Miss Adele-Juliette."

The door starts to close. I want to follow him to wherever the hell he's going. I lean my head out to look at his tight ass in a pair of faded jeans. He turns at the same time. Our eyes lock. He blows me a kiss over his fingers. I duck my head back inside before the elevator door flattens me like a Cuban sandwich.

My body vibrates all the way up to my fifteenth-floor hotel room.

# CHAPTER FORTY-TWO

❦❦❦

# KETLY

*December 2009*

My impatience drags the workday as if I am doing time at the jail house. Rénel didn't call last night from New York. He must be waiting until he has news. He left to find his son. He promised to take me on trips to America, Europe, and Africa one day. A smile flits over my lips. I'll go anywhere with this man.

After work, I walk to the wharf from the hospital and sit on a bench. I marvel at where the water meets the sky, wondering how long it'd take to get from all these countries from here. I hope he finds his son soon and comes back to me. I miss him already. From time to time, a warm breeze caresses my face, bringing the cries of the seagulls and the smell of salty air in its wake. The chicks follow their mother duck on the pier, and she slows down, turns and quacks, urging them to keep up. She doesn't want to lose not even one from the bunch.

Soon the setting sun sprays the ocean with colorful sparkles of reds and yellows. I check my phone for the thousandth time, to make sure I don't miss a call from my husband. The fight that prompted Rénel's trip to New York still makes me feel bad but not remorseful.

# I SHALL FIND YOU

∞∞∞

A couple of weeks ago, we were seating on the porch after dinner having our nightcaps when I told him a joke, I'd heard at the hospital that day. Rénel usually cracked up at my silly banter, but he'd looked at me and frowned, dark circles framing his eyes. He'd been tossing in bed lately groaning as if he was in pain. Something was troubling him, and I couldn't put my fingers on it.

"Hey! What's wrong?" I tried to tickle him. "That was funny."

He stood so fast; the swing chair almost toppled me to the floor. "Stop it, Ketly. Nothing's wrong. I just have a lot on my mind."

I took his hand and pulled him back to sit. "Listen, go to New York. You have the documents. Don't worry about me. We'll go back when my application is approved. No rush." I touched his chin and turned his face toward mine. I kissed his cheek. "Even if his mother won't let you see him, at least you'll know that you tried, and you'll be able to tell Elliot one day that you went back for him. You understand?"

"Yes. But, I—"

"I don't want to hear it, Ren. Go to New York." He looked away. "You know I won't stop until you do."

He'd nodded. Two days ago, he left for New York.

Now I am waiting for his return. I breathe the salt air until peace lifts the fatigue of the workday off my shoulders. I stand from the bench and stretch before running through the streets, bumping into people, smiling, and waving at passersby. These people have embraced me even when I hated to be here. Now after almost thirty years, this is my home. I'm waiting for Rénel to help me put up the Christmas tree. I hum Silent Night all the way to my friend's house. Alice smiles at me as I climb the steps to join her on the porch.

"Ali, it was fate that put you on the ferry with me so long ago. I know I was stubborn and difficult at times."

"You think." Alice bats her eyelashes. We laugh. "Kekette, you're tougher than you're giving yourself credit for. You inspire young women on this island. You're loyal to those you love. You're a fighter. Heard from Rénel yet today?"

I swat at a mosquito buzzing in my ear. "Not yet. Last time we spoke he said it was snowing in New York. Can you imagine? He had an appointment with a family lawyer today. He'll call soon." I reach for the phone in my pocket and place it on the table between us.

"He'll see his son. The law over there works for both parents. Unless he was determined to be unfit. He'll see him." Alice reaches for my hand and pats it. "Listen, I'm going to the city tomorrow for my eye appointment, remember. Come with me. We can do our Christmas shopping in Port-Au-Prince. That'll be fun."

"Wish I could, but I gotta work. We're always short-staffed in December." I sigh.

"Too bad," Alice says. "You need anything?"

"I need a drink, Ali. I'm so nervous about Ren. I have no doubt he was a great papa to his son. I pushed him to go. I hope he won't be mad at me if he comes back…without seeing Elliot."

Alice stands. "I'll get us drinks."

I take a deep breath to chase my lingering jitters. Later, I grab my work bag. "I need a bath, and a bed. I was hoping he'd call me while I'm here. You have better reception, Ali."

But Rénel doesn't call tonight either. What is going on? Did he see Elliot and his mother? I sit up in bed. Oh. Is he coming back to me? What if Elliot's mother wants Rénel now? But we are married. I toss in bed until dawn pushes the night away.

# CHAPTER FORTY-THREE

## ADELE

JR switches seats with me on the plane in Miami. Since the jet takes off, my heart's beating so fast I feel faint. I open the magazine I bought at the airport terminal and just glance at the pictures of beautiful dishes, people, and sites. I can't focus on the meaning of words. When the pilot announces our upcoming descent into Port-au-Prince, I press my face to the window. From Miami to Haiti is only a ninety minute-flight, and it's taken me almost thirty years to make the trip.

Earlier, I opened the two thick manila envelopes Mom gave me for Ketly and inside were copies of every event of my life along with pictures: First day of school, Report cards, awards, graduation pictures, diplomas, Girl Scouts badges, dance recital programs, prom photos, nursing pin, wedding pictures and invitations. *Everything*. I don't know when Mom thought she was going to give these to Ketly, but she said she wanted to share all this with her somehow. I can't wait to tell her about each and every one of these milestones in my life that she's missed. I pray that I find her. What if Ketly had left the country?

The airport is small and there are too many people vying for a place to stand, sit, and get their luggage. A trio band made up of two men and one woman dressed in *karabella* attires plays an upbeat folkloric song on tall drums while the woman sings. The walls display Haitian paintings of smiling people, green vegetables, yellow fruits, blue sky and mountains with bold colors.

"Sit over here and don't move." JR almost pushes me into a white plastic chair. "I'm getting the luggage and will come back for you after I get the car."

Two days ago, I told my PI, I no longer needed his escort in Haiti before sending him a final payment. I have JR.

I hug my backpack to my chest to control the shaking from my excitement. People walk at a brisk pace trying to get outside. Two female airport employees dressed in navy blue pleated skirts and red checkered short sleeve blouses almost stop in front of me.

"*Sé yon blan*?" the tall one asks, frowning. "Look at her green eyes?"

"I don't know," her companion says, "her skin's kinda light brown, and she's got long curly hair, but I don't think she's white." She shrugs. "Maybe."

"Mm-huh…the money people," Tall one replies.

"You're both wrong," I say in perfect Haitian Creole. "I'm not white. I'm *natif natal* Haitian."

They stare at me as if I was a spirit. They bump into a group of people coming in the opposite direction. I snicker.

"What's so funny," JR says, pulling our suitcases behind him.

"I think I'm gonna have fun here." I laugh.

"Well, I hope so," he says, leering at me. "I plan to."

The city confuses me. I don't know where one house begins and another ends. People and cars compete for the narrow streets as if in a dance with honks blaring in a beat. I roll down my window and inhale the air pungent with ripe fruits, fried meat, scorched earth. The scent of my home. Where my umbilical cord is buried.

# I SHALL FIND YOU

Did Ketly walk these streets when she lived in Port-au-Prince? The air fills the car with the smell of food I grew up eating at Nadine's house, yet it's different. I breathe deep and hold it to imprint it on my brain. Once we leave the bustle of the city, the air is cooler in the early afternoon sun.

"We're in Petion-Ville," JR says. "You want to meet my mom?"

"Please take me to my hotel for a shower. How'bout later?"

"You bet. She'll have dinner prepared for sure."

"We're leaving for the ferry early tomorrow, right?" I say. "How far is it?"

JR reaches over and squeezes my hand. "Relax, I'll get you to the island tomorrow even if I have to swim with you on my back."

I punch his arm, grateful to have him along on this journey. It's as though I've known him for five years instead of five months. This trip is setting my life on a different trajectory. It's sobering to realize that no matter what happens at the end of this adventure, I will not go back to America the same woman I am at this moment. I will go to the island of Terreville. I will go to Lasalle. I will set foot on the soil where I was born. I will not rest until I find my people.

It's going to be a long first night in Haiti.

# CHAPTER FORTY-FOUR

## KETLY

*December 2009*

Today, even the birth of five babies on my shift couldn't make the day go faster. I wish I'd gone to Port-au-Prince with Alice. Waiting for that phone call from Rénel is the most excruciating thing I've ever had to do. Is he all right? Why did I push him so hard to find Elliot? I should have let him make that decision himself. But I want to spare him the regrets that have plagued my existence for too long. Something must be wrong with the telephone lines on this island.

At around four this afternoon, as I'm finishing my daily notes, I hear her voice before I see her face.

"Where's Miss Ketly?" Alice asks the receptionist. "I need to see her. It's important."

"Alice!" I wave to her. "I'm here. Everything's okay with your eyes?" I take her arm and lead her to a triage room down the hall. "What did the eye doctor say? You look...scared."

"I saw Rénel in Port-au-Prince," she blurts out. "He's not in New York."

# I SHALL FIND YOU

I drop her arm like hot charcoal. "What! No! Ali, your pupils were dilated, right? You must have seen someone who looks like him. My husband is in New York to find his son." As I say these words, I feel the floor opening under my feet as if to swallow me whole.

Alice swipes the tears from her still wide-open eyes as if the expression is etched forever on her face. "I spoke with him, Kekette." She grabs my hand, and we fall together on a faded brown vinyl couch wedged under a small window. She hiccups. "I'm so sorry."

Something in my center shifts with every breath, threatening to unravel my body and let it fly away like the seagulls. I can't let that happen. I close my eyes and hum my favorite hymn until my heart only beats in my chest. What is Rénel hiding from me? Why such a monumental lie? When I trust my voice to utter words, I whisper, "Maybe he's married to Elliot's mother. That's set. He and I are not…umm…married. He's afraid to face her." I pull Alice to her feet. "Let's go. I know where to find the answers."

Alice trots after me in high heels to catch up. "Where we're going?" she asks as I head toward the business district. "Slow down, Kekette."

"To do something my gut told me to do long time ago, but…I'm doing it tonight."

"What…?" Alice yells, breathing loudly.

Dusk sneaks in early as people mill about getting ready for the end of the year holidays. At the back of Rénel's store, I pick up a big rock and slam it twice onto the padlock. Wood chips rain down as the door flies inward and hits the wall. I flip the light switch in the back office and rush to the front of the store. I yank a display hatchet from the wall and walk back to his office where Alice cowers in fear.

"What are you doing, Ketly?"

"Come on, Ali. We must hurry before blackout."

I swing the hatchet once before the master lock flies off the safe door. I sit on the floor in front of a pile of paper and bundles of money. Alice joins me.

On the very top is the original application for a permanent visa request I signed sixteen months ago. The application Rénel said he'd delivered to the American embassy in Port-Au-Prince to obtain my permanent residency. Alice touches my shoulder. The single lightbulb in the ceiling flickers.

"We really need to hurry," she whispers. "Won't have light for too long."

I toss aside the envelopes labeled store leases, inventory lists, orders, account receivables, payroll. At the bottom, I pull the last manila envelope and untwist the thread. I empty its contents on the floor. Rénel's Haitian passport assaults me. I dig in, looking for the American one I suddenly know won't be there. The top sheet is a letter in English addressed to Rénel dated October 3, 2009. I stretch my back, releasing the tension binding my body and hand the letter to Alice.

"Read this one Ali. It's dated six weeks ago." I hold my breath, wishing I could read English.

Alice scans it and says, "It's from a lawyer in New York, and it says the case is closed and there isn't much he can do about finding Elliot."

"Oh, no! Why didn't he tell me?" I pull more papers out. Alice reads and drops sheets on the floor while I watch her without blinking and then she screams before clamping her hand over her mouth.

"What! Damnit, Alice. Tell me?"

"Rénel spent two years in prison in New York. The court gave full custody of his son to his mother and terminated his parental rights." She flips the page. "*O Bondié!*"

"*Ki sa?* Is he a murderer?" I grab the letter from her hand and stare at the strange words that are altering my life. "Read it again, Alice. You must be confused with the translation."

"Ketly." She reaches for my hands and lowers her voice as if to soften the blow. "He didn't have a *green card*. Rénel was undocumented in America. He was deported back to Haiti after a roundup from immigration at the garage where he worked. He can't go back."

The weight of this betrayal hammers my head into my shoulders. I close my eyes to stop the room from spinning. I hum and sway until I feel Alice's hand on my back. "Kekette?" The light goes off for a few seconds.

"Let's go Ali. I need to get far away from here."

"To where?" Alice wrings her hands. "Don't do anything foolish, sister."

Alice's footsteps follow me all the way home, while she pleads for me to slow down. Standing in front of the house I've shared with Rénel, it becomes clear what I need to do.

"Ali, I'm going to Mapou to figure out what I need to do next. I need to get off this island for some respite." I groan as if I'm carrying a heavy load. "I can't stay here. I don't want to ever see Rénel again. He could have told me the truth. It's not like he killed someone."

"Oh, Kekette, I'm so sorry." Alice cradles my head to her bosom, sitting on the front step. "You know there's a stigma to being deported. He was probably ashamed and concerned about how people would treat him. Come spend the night with me."

"Thank you, Ali." I kiss her cheek. "I need to be alone tonight. We'll talk tomorrow."

A week later, on a cool December morning, the sun winks at me in greetings behind the mountains in Mapou. I left Galette after finding out Rénel has never gone to New York. He lied about everything. Maybe he never loved me. It seems like anything that brings me joy must be taken away from me. My phone shows one solid bar and no missed calls.

The honk of the car pulls me from behind the house. "Kekette, Alice's here," Denise yells.

"Be right out," I yell back, rolling my eyes and laughing at my friend. Like who else can it be in a car? How many of those travel the rocky terrain to Mapou? To go where?

We sit in a circle in the yard. "Ali, have you seen Rénel in Galette?" I ask. "I'll have to go back to work eventually. I don't want to see him. *Ever!*"

"His sister told me Rénel went to the Bahamas. He has friends there. Two of his employees are buying the store."

I look at one than the other. I'm grateful I am not alone to process this latest betrayal, but I have the template to forge ahead once more. My life is not defined by who sleeps in my bed. I will sleep alone again. I will perhaps one day sleep with somebody, but it will always be on my terms.

"I'm sorry, Kekette," Alice says. "We're here for you."

We talk about our marriages. I have some good memories with Rénel because I know what real love feels like in giving and receiving. Once again, I will have to learn to heal and to move on. "As long as I have breath," I yell, "I will survive." I pump my fist up in the air. "Listen, I'm going to spend some time with my brothers in the Dominican Republic. I need a change of scenery."

"Great idea," Alice says. "Oh, Alphonse called me this morning. He's been trying to get a hold of you."

My phone shows one solid bar. "I know. Alph probably wants to plan his annual visit with me. I'll call him."

"I don't know," Alice says. "This morning, he said it's urgent."

I shove my feet into my sneakers, touch the phone in my pocket, grateful Denise now has a generator to keep it charged. "I should call him back. I hope his mother is ok. She wasn't feeling well according to his last letter." I run to the back of the house for better reception on top of the hill, holding the phone in my hand, and looking for a second bar. I hear footsteps behind me. The trees blur like a green curtain rustling in the wind. On top of the first ridge, I stop and dial Alphonse's phone. The loud beating of my heart covers the faint ringing of the phone.

"Allo, *allo*, Alph…"

"Kekette," he yells, his voice coming in and out. "Henri's coming tomorrow. I tried to call you. Simone had a stroke. Her doctor was able to convince Henri that she won't last long." Alphonse speaks the spotty words fast. "Henri called and I heard Simone say, 'Son, please come. I have a secret to confess that will change your life.'"

My legs shake so much, I lower myself to the ground and squat. "Alph…"

"Henri's coming," he shouts. The call drops.

"Henri's coming," I yell. I throw my arms around Alice's neck while she pants at the foot of the hill. "Henri's really coming," I say before she asks.

"Good." Alice squeezes my hand. "You two need to talk."

All these years I waited to hear Henri's coming and now I'm afraid. Will he blame me for losing Juliette while I'm still safe and alive in Haiti? Will he understand the sacrifices I'd made and the weight of the guilt I carry to protect our daughter?

"Henri will be in Haiti…soon," I whisper to myself.

That night, I sit under the stars while Denise tends to her family. How can I sleep tonight? Do I go see Henri or should I wait for him to come find me? A calm comes over me. I realize I no longer need to run, to hide, to seek, to deceive, to hurt. The Marges, Simones, Shadows and Helènes of this world exert power over people like me, but the universe sometimes shakes itself out as if from a slumber and drops everyone where they need to be. I'll be in my spot in Galette. Waiting.

# CHAPTER FORTY-FIVE

## Adele

Before seven this morning, I'm in the hotel lobby waiting for JR. The smell of Haitian coffee buoys me before I even take the first sip. I'm skipping breakfast because last night JR's mother said the sea is rough in that channel. Besides, I'm too nervous to eat. Tears of joy and relief pool behind my eyelids.

"You slept okay?" JR asks, leading me to the car outside.

"I'm not sure, but I'm ready to meet my mama. I hope she's on the island. I don't know what my next move will be if she's not."

"We'll cross that bridge if we get to it." He takes my hand. "Speaking of bridges, I wish they had one over that water."

"Oh, you're not scared of water, Officer JR. Are you?" I jab his side with my elbow. "You can swim, right?"

"You'd be surprised to know that many island folks can't swim." A sheepish grin creeps across his face. "I had to learn on the force to pass basic training."

"Wow. That's wild." There are so many things I still don't know about island culture. This man will be a great teacher. "Well, I hope Ketly can come back here with us tomorrow. It's New Year's Day. She most likely has a family…everyone can come." My hand twitches in his warm palm. My face hurts from smiling. "How fitting. A new year. New beginning for me and her." I look up into his tamarind eyes. "I'll need your help to get to Simone. She's the only one who can lead me to my papa, unless if he's with Ketly."

"Sounds like a great plan." He flexes his biceps. "I'm ready for my assignment, *Miss*."

I smile.

Every second on the ferry takes me closer to the woman I hope will be as happy to see me as I am to see her. I close my eyes and fill my lungs with the air she'd breathed for almost three decades in hiding because she gave birth to me.

A couple hours later, on the wharf in Galette, JR seems as lost as I feel. It's New Year's Day. I hope to have Soup Joumou somewhere later. All my life, I've had that soup on January first at Nadine's house. She always says that Haitians all over the world eat that soup on that day to celebrate Haiti's victory in 1804 over France to become the first free black republic. People move with purpose. I take in the park across from a church with rusty swings but vibrant with hibiscus, and bougainvillea. A short man runs up to us.

"I'm Tim-Tim. Who you here to see?" He peers into my eyes, his own bulging. Sometimes, I forget they're bright green.

"I'm here to see Ketly…Ketly Murat," I whisper, suddenly afraid.

"Oh, you must want Miss Ketly. Wait right here. The cab will be back soon. Tell the driver to take you to Madame Alice."

"Thank you. How—?"

# I SHALL FIND YOU

The man takes off running. I exhale. Ketly is here. My mother is here.

Soon, a beat-up black sedan pulls up. "Tim-Tim says you need to go to Madame Alice?" the driver says.

"*Wi m'sieu*," JR says, pulling me along.

My feet weigh a ton, but my heart wants to fly out of my chest. *Miss Ketly*. She must be a nurse like me. We climb inside. The car moves. My heart beats everywhere in my body. I hold on to JR's hand and squeeze hard. "I'm scared."

He leans over, kisses my forehead, and whispers in English. "I'm here. I won't let anything happen to you."

When the car stops in front of a blue house with a long front porch, I see Tim-Tim talking to a beautiful woman in a yellow dress. I step out of the car. We stare at each other.

"*Juliette?*" the woman whispers.

I know I'm looking at my biological mother, finally. On her face are the dimples she has given to me.

"*Manman*," I whisper.

# CHAPTER FORTY-SIX

❀❀❀

# Ketly

*January 1, 2010*

Today, Henri's arriving on Haitian soil. What will he do when Alphonse picks him up at the airport and tells him what really happened all these years ago? Will he go see his mother or get on the ferry? I take my seat on Alice's porch, hair coiffed to fall in curls around my face, yellow dress pressed and hugging my curves, feet encased in high heels. People slow down, and stare.

"*Bonne année*, Miss Ketly." They say more as a question than a greeting. I wish Matante Hilda was here. I wish Auntie Yvette was here. I wish Mama was here.

After reading a sentence three times, I close the book and take a sip of my cola. It was flat, but the sugar settles my stomach. Alice comes in and out of the house to check on me as if I may sprout wings and fly away. I pull the letter that was waiting for me at Alice's from the pages of the book and read it again.

# I SHALL FIND YOU

*Dear Kekette,*

*Don't ever doubt that I loved you. I still do. I was ashamed to tell anyone about my situation. I was intimidated by your strength. I have left Haiti, perhaps to never return. I will file for divorce and set you free. I hope you find Juliette one day. Please forgive me.*

*Rénel*

The day is cool and sunny as it ushers in 2010. Sleep sits heavy on my eyelids. I fight, but I must have dozed off. The heavy breathing following the sounds of feet hitting the asphalt pry me awake.

"Miss Ketly," Tim-Tim huffs, holding his side, "there's a woman with green eyes asking for you at the wharf. She with a man. Told them to wait for the taxi. I hopped on the back of a moped to tell you. You look nice, Miss."

I stand, my left ankle twisting as my heel catches between two planks. "Thank you, Tim-Tim." I shade my eyes, looking in the only direction the taxi can come. "Ali, *Alice*, come out here," I yell.

"What is it?" She wipes her hands on a towel. A smudge of blue frosting smears her cheek. She's hardly aged in the thirty years I've known her. She's making her boys' favorite chocolate cake. They're coming with their families to visit. Alice and Raoul dote on their three granddaughters wishing the boys had stayed on the island, instead of living in Port-au-Prince.

"Some man is here…umm…with Simone, I guess. I don't know. Tim-Tim says…" I pace the length of the porch. "Oh My God, I thought Simone was too sick to live. What's happening Ali? Is it Shadow?" I grab Alice's shoulders to stay upright. "Go wake up Raoul, please."

"Who's here?" Alice pats my arm. "Sit down, Kekette before you fall."

"Tim-Tim saw them at the dock. They're here." I wrap my arms around her shoulders and hold on tight.

We both watch the black car chew the feet of road to stop in front of the house. A tall man steps out of the passenger seat. His tamarind eyes look briefly toward the porch and ahead and around before he opens the back door. I let go of Alice. A young woman with skin like the setting sun comes out. When she stares into my eyes, my torso leans forward like my feet are glued to the floor. Her green eyes blink and she stumbles over the steps and falls into my bosom.

"Juliette?" I whisper.

"Manman," she whispers back. The word I have craved for the past three decades fills all the holes in my heart dug by deceit.

A couple of hours later, our eyes dry, we stare at each other as if we never want to blink, lest someone wakes up and it's a cruel prank. Sitting between Juliette and JR, I take my daughter's hands in mine.

"I tried to come to you for almost thirty years," I sob. "I really did."

"I know, Mama Ketly," she says in Creole. "Mom…umm…and Nadine told me the story." She leans over and kisses my wet cheek. Juliette talks about her childhood, the profession we share, the end of her marriage, her hope for a brighter future. "Do you know where…my papa is?"

"He's on his way to Haiti. I haven't seen him since before you were born. I can't even understand how you both return to me at the same time. Let me tell you about all the many ways I have tried to come find you."

Hours later, I take a sip from the glass of water Alice has placed on the table in the middle of our circle. JR stands and turns to face the street but not before I see his eyes swimming in unshed tears.

# I SHALL FIND YOU

"Oh my God! I still can't believe Mom did that to you." Juliette blows her nose on a tissue. "It's hard for me to believe she has caused you so much pain. It'll take some time for me to reconcile the woman who raised me with so much love to the person who could do this."

"In all my anger, Juliette, I never lost sight that Marge saved your life by getting you out of the country. I have no doubt, given the opportunity, your grandmother Simone would have placed our bodies in the graves she'd dug. I have forgiven Marge long ago so I could heal, and you must do the same, *Pititfi*."

She nods, a smile lifting the corner of her mouth which looks like Henri's. "*Mesi, Manman*," she says. I run my hand through Juliette's curls and the silkiness of her hair brings back memories of playing with Henri's. "Can we go back to Port-au-Prince today?"

The hours march on while we talk. "We'll go on the first ferry tomorrow, my daughter. The last one has already left the island. Today's a holiday."

We sit down for a lunch of generous amount of soup Joumou. Juliette and I want to hold hands even while we eat. I'm afraid to blink and find out it's a dream.

The next morning, after breakfast, JR places our suitcases in the trunk of the taxi.

"Please be safe," Alice whispers in my ears. "I'm so happy for you. I'll miss you."

"Thank you for your friendship and sisterhood." I squeeze her. "I will be back. This island will always be my home. Happy New Year."

Now the sea churns and rocks the boat hard enough to threaten to bring my breakfast out. I wave to Alice and Raoul until they disappear like a dot into the bright island sun.

∞∞∞

Sometimes later, we climb into the car JR had left at the dock yesterday. "We're going to the hotel, to wait for Papa." Juliette says, kissing my cheek. "We have so much to catch up on. JR will join us tomorrow."

"Oh, he's not staying with us?" I ask.

JR stares at Juliette, a teasing smile flitting over his handsome face. "He's staying with his mother," she says.

I call Alphonse as soon as the car pulls onto the road. No answer. I breathe the air of true freedom in the city for the first time after years of hiding. But I never feel any safer in my life. Nothing and nobody can hurt me now.

Alphonse calls back while we're having lunch on the pool deck of the hotel. I've never set foot in any place like this in Haiti before. I try not to gawk at the rich people.

"Madame, *Madame*," The waiter clears his throat before I realize he's addressing me. "Would you like another Perrier?"

"Yes. Thank you." I smile at him. "Happy New Year, Alph." I plaster the phone to my ear over the din of many languages spoken by noisy patrons.

"Happy New Year, Kekette," he says. "I talk Henri into going to see his mother first, although he wanted to come to you. Simone won't…last too long and I think it'd be good for him to see her before…She needs to tell him herself what she's done. Be good for both of them."

Tears build in the back of my eyes for not being able to love Alphonse the way he wanted and deserved to be loved. "As always, you're right. Alph, you'll never know how much I love and appreciate you, my dearest friend. You're one of my angels."

"Thank you, Kekette. I'll bring Henri to you as soon as possible." Alphonse clears his throat. "He's sad about Juliette."

My fork clutters on the porcelain plate. My hands are shaking. "Alph." I exhale. "I'm at the Hotel Le Villa with Juliette."

"Wait a minute," Alphonse says, "Juliette! How…how, I mean when…?"

I laugh. "I know, Alph. I can't believe it either, but my daughter is here. Don't tell Henri. Let's surprise him."

In the hotel suite, Juliette and I sit facing each other on the couch. We talk, laugh, cry, and laugh some more. We sort through the envelopes Marge has sent and Juliette tells me about the stories behind each event in her life. Shortly after six in the afternoon, the hotel phone rings. Juliette lifts the receiver from the side table.

"Allo," she says, sitting upright. "Send him up. Thank you."

We look at each other, walk to the door, and open it. Down the hall, even the thick carpet cannot muffle the hurried footsteps. The tall man with skin burned to honey by far away suns stands a couple feet from the door, blinking. Long hair streaked with gray, frames his chiseled face with wisps escaping the ponytail. Our eyes lock before his turn to Juliette's. He frowns before they open wide to take in the image of himself. He opens his arms and crushes us both to his chest.

"My family," he whispers.

Arms wrapped around each other; we trot sideways into the suite. Standing there in the middle of the room, none of us want to let go. The fragrance of Bleu de Chanel floods me with memories. I feel the tremors from my chest before my legs buckle. We kneel on pillows in the living room floor and cry our different yet similar losses and blessings. My tears flow from gratitude and peace. My fingers dig into Henri's and Juliette's backs, knowing I may be hurting them. They lean closer into me as if they, too, need to go back inside me as my baby and my lover. We rock in a fluid circle, our heads touching, the silence broken by sniffles, and the loud presence of undying love. When we look up, darkness pushes against the window. Henri kisses my cheek with his wet lips, then kisses Juliette's forehead.

"I'm so sorry…for everything, my mother has done," he says.

When we step away from each other, Henri sits in the wing chair facing the loveseat, where Juliette and I hold hands and tell our stories one more time. Henri's face contorts as the tales unfold. He sobs.

Soon it is his turn. He picks up the phone and calls room service with an order for drinks and snacks. He pulls a handkerchief from his jean pocket and wipes his face. A flash of anger turns his eyes into a deep green.

"Kekette, when I left you at the hotel that day, I drove to school for soccer practice. At the end of the session, Maman was waiting with Alphonse. She asked me to accompany her to the airport because she'd be gone for a few months for medical care. I thought nothing of it. We've done that before. I was focusing more on all the free time I'll have to spend with you." He smiles at me. "At the airport, after many tantrums, and threats, she put me on a plane for France. It was six months before my eighteenth birthday, at which time I'd inherit the money that would set me free from my mother. Then in July while I suffered because I knew you were coming into the world," He leans over to pat Juliette's hand, "I received a letter with copies of death certificates from Mother telling me you both had died in childbirth. My world ended. I had nothing to return to Haiti for. I took off."

Henri opens the door and lets the server in with the cart. He fixes drinks, plates of food, and hands them to us. I take a big gulp of wine and a small bite of the flaky pastry on my saucer, urging him with my eyes to continue. "If only I'd received your letter, Kekette before I left France. I would have been back here in a heartbeat. All this pain…" He wipes his eyes with the napkin and sips his cognac. "I traveled all over the world.

Maman's PI couldn't keep up with me. Ten years ago, I married this kind woman in Kenya."

I put my glass down to avoid sloshing my drink all over my lap. "Tarika was a teacher," he continues. "I started teaching and loved it. Life was simple. We raised goats and chickens. We had a small garden, but we couldn't have children. Then three years ago, Tari died of breast cancer after a two-year battle. I took off again. I only came back to Haiti because, Dr. Ambroise, who was a good friend of my father and whom I respect, convinced me that she's really dying. I came because I wanted to tell my mother in her face how much she'd hurt me."

Henri kneels in front of me and reaches for my hand. "I hope you never for a second believed I'd abandoned you. I thought about you every day, feeling responsible and guilty for your death."

I raise his hand to my face and rest my cheek in his palm. "I told everyone who'd listen that I believed in my gut you never received my letter."

Juliette scoots closer to me, our thighs pressing. "When I started on this journey, since I understood that I was adopted, I pictured this day," she says. "I will go home, but I'll come back as soon as I arrange some time off with work. You guys will be tired of me."

"Never," Henri and I say at the same time. We laugh and hug our daughter tightly.

# CHAPTER FORTY-SEVEN

❦❦❦

## ADELE

Time flies too fast when you just find your parents after a lifetime of separation. Two days after I met Papa, Simone passed away. After the funeral service today, he moves into a suite at our hotel, and I haven't seen Mama Ketly the rest of the day. I never had a chance to peer into Simone's evil green eyes and ask her why.

This morning on our way out of the city, Papa files a report at the police station against Shadow for murdering Aunt Yvette and terrorizing Mama Ketly for decades. The coward is hiding. The drive to Lasalle gives me time and space to sort out the emotional turmoil mixed with so much joy that assault me daily since arriving in Haiti. I feel raw and open. Yet full.

We drive through poster-card sized towns with vibrant vistas. It's the first week of the new year, people are jubilant and hopeful. We stop and drink juice from the coconut fruit vendor at a roadside stand. The smell of grilled coffee fills the air. I sniff. My mouth waters. "I wish I could have some of that coffee," I say, swallowing my saliva.

"Stop the car, JR," Mama Ketly says.

We pile out and stroll in the direction of the undulating smoke carrying the aroma of fresh coffee.

"*Bon' année, auntie*," Mama Ketly says to the older woman stirring the pot with coffee beans in a cauldron. She sits inside a hut with roof and walls made of braided palm fronds.

"*Bon' année, pitit mwen.*" The woman blows ashes off a couple of low chairs. "Sit. I'll get you some. I just made it."

I cry and laugh with joy. The strong and sweet coffee anchors me to the land and the people I came from. I watch my parents pour hot coffee in the enamel saucers and drink. I try it, instead of blowing on it to cool it off in the cup.

"You're drinking coffee, Haitian style, Addy…umm…I mean Juliette," JR says.

"It's alright, JR. I'm Adele. I'm Juliette." I smile at my parents sitting so close to each other. "I know who I am now."

A bit later, I stand in front of the house where Mama Ketly grew up. JR holds me tight as I cry. A pair of hands belonging to my parents strokes my back securing me in a triangle of love. The curtain parts and an older woman who looks like Mama Ketly runs down the steps and grabs me, squinting into my eyes.

"Kekette, is this…is this, *O Bondié*." She drops down on her knees on the dirt road. "My grandbaby. Welcome home, Juliette. Come on in. I'm gon' make coffee and drinks."

While everyone is inside, enjoying Grandma Clara's famous punch, I stare at the structure across the street where the old clinic used to be. I picture Mom in her youth caring for the children and her deep desire to be a mother. Her lies and the pain she caused Mama Ketly for so long can't be justified. I will learn to forgive her.

We eat. We laugh. We cry. We laugh more. We drink that delicious punch. I drink more coffee. I delight Grandma Clara about life in

America. I promise to return and spend many days with her. She hugs me with the joy of finding a long-lost treasure. I hug her back with gratitude."

Back in the city, we spent a lot of time at JR mother's house. She's funny, kind, and unselfish like her son. He waits patiently in the background and lets me sort out my feelings about everything that has happened so rapidly in my life.

Tonight, in JR's childhood bedroom, I lay on the bed with the dog-eared photo album laughing at pictures of him and his siblings. I can hear my inseparable parents in the living room downstairs laughing at Madame Vilsaint's jokes.

"You were a cute kid." I tease.

"Oh! How about now?" JR tries to pull the album from my hands.

I hold on, laughing and pushing my torso back into the headboard. He falls forward landing on my chest. I scoot down further under him and kiss his lips with a famine that gnaws at my whole body. "I'm happy, Officer Vilsaint," I whisper.

"Oh, Miss Juliette-Adele, I've loved you since the day I saw you in the ER." He snakes his hand under my tank top. "I want you so badly. I can barely sleep and eat." He runs his palm over the silk fabric of my bra. I gasp.

"Tomorrow you can spend the night with me at the hotel." I wink. "I have a birthday present for you." I place my palm on his chest to keep some distance between us. My body's on fire. I want that man. "You can show me how badly, Detective Vilsaint."

"Aww. You remember, it's my birthday tomorrow." He kisses me with resolution, his hand searching with precision. "Why leave it for tomorrow?" He groans, placing my hand over the bulge in his pants. "Addy, I can't wait." He moans.

"Well, Officer—" I reach for him.

"Hey, kids come down for lunch," his mother yells from downstairs.

He opens his mouth in a mock scream. "It's gonna be a long wait." He pulls me off the bed. "I'm not leaving this island in two days without tasting its best fruit."

My body vibrates.

Later, at the hotel, I toss and turn in bed waiting for daylight to bring me JR.


After lunch today, I kick the water in the pool with my feet making a splash. My parents share a double hammock like they're joined at the hips. They whisper, they kiss, they giggle like the seventeen-year-olds they once were. I slather sunscreen on again after swimming a few laps.

"Where's JR?" Mama Ketly asks.

"Oh, it's his birthday today. He's having lunch with his mother. He'll be here soon for the poolside barbecue and the live band later."

"He's such a kind man and I can tell he's crazy about you. Papa and I can't wait to be Grandmère and Grandpère." She pokes his side with her elbow.

"I agree," Papa says, standing up, his green eyes lighting up his face. "I'll be back, Kekette." He kisses her lips. "Going to get my phone from the room."

I smile at her. "You sound like Mom Marge."

I'm not sure where my mother fits right now while I'm in Haiti bonding with my biological parents. It'll take time, but I know I have room in my heart for all of them.

"It's all right, Juliette. Marge's your mother, too. I'm grateful for the great job she's done raising you. I refuse to hold anger in my heart any longer when I can use the space for more love."

"That's beautiful and true, Mama. So many people have wronged you."

"And I have wronged some as well, Juliette. I'm not proud of some of the things I've done. But I've learned to recognize my shortcomings and to emulate and appreciate goodness in others."

I walk over to my manman and climb into the space my papa has just vacated. We tumble down to the ground and laugh with our arms around each other. I can't recall ever feeling such deep happiness.

My face opens wider in a permanent smile that has not left my face since I landed in Haiti. I kiss Mama Ketly's beaming face. I am home.

# CHAPTER FORTY-EIGHT

## KETLY

Frolicking on the pool deck with my daughter reminds me that she will leave me soon. How do I let her go? I feel like I'm losing her again. I can't wait for her return already.

Juliette kisses my forehead and stands. "I'm going to the restroom. I'll be right back, Mama."

"Don't be long *Ti chérie*." I miss her every time she's out of my sight.

She smiles and waves.

Minutes later as we peruse the menu for lunch, Henri strolls toward us and sits between me and his daughter under the umbrella.

"Guess what?" He brandishes his phone as if the information will spill out of there.

"What, Papa?" Juliette asks.

"The French ambassador calls me while I was upstairs. He heard I'm back. We met at university in Europe many years ago…well, anyway, he invites us to a gala tonight at the embassy. We can all go."

"Oh, I can't," Juliette says. "I promise JR to spend…umm…special time with him on his birthday this afternoon."

We look at each other and smile. "Great," Henri says, "It'll be me and the woman I never stop loving." His sheepish grin blooms over his reddened face. "Kekette, I'll follow you anywhere. You'll never be out of my sight ever again, if you want me.

"I've always wanted you, Henri."

"Let's go on a world tour and get married, Kekette. What do you say? I don't want to lose more precious time."

Henri kneels before me like he's making a proposal. The one-word answer clogs my throat. I squeeze his fingers, raise his left hand to my lips and nod. I'm afraid to jinx myself and I'm back on the island as the teenager I was, hiding and living in fear.

"We'll start in Paris, Kekette." He touches his daughter's cheek. "Juliette and JR can join us in Europe."

"Yayyy!" our daughter yells, clapping her hands. "Sounds like a lot of fun."

I gaze at him as if he has spoken in a foreign language. "But…but I'll need visas. Umm…I have a valid passport but…"

"*Mon amour*, I can get you visas to every country you want to visit in the world," he says as if it's the easiest thing in the world.

"Even America?" I whisper.

"Even America, my love."

The sobs cleanse my soul, preparing it for the love of my child and the man I have always loved. Holding their hands in mine, I breathe deeply and behold two pairs of green eyes.

"My beautiful family," I whisper.

# CHAPTER FORTY-NINE

## ADELE

The early dusk embraces the night like a lover. The torches keep the pesky mosquitos away, but the nocturnal sounds of the cool January day roll down the mountains invading my heightened senses. The band is setting up on the stage under the star-studded sky.

JR called me over an hour ago. "Addy, a group of cousins surprised me with a visit for my birthday, laden with cakes and presents."

"Well, how sweet. Take your time. I'll be here *waiting*," I purred.

"Not sweet. I wanted to scream at them to leave after about an hour. All I want is to be with you. I'm on my way. Your folks with you?"

"Nope. They left an hour ago to a dinner at the French embassy. They want to get married and travel all over Europe. So, I'm all by my lonesome But there's a guy ogling me though."

"Then I'll bring my gun." I giggled. "See you soon, Addy." He breathed the words. They tickled me everywhere.

Now I jiggle on the chair to the beat of the music under the paper lanterns, my eyes on the door JR will walk through. Minutes later, he stands there in a warm brown polo shirt, cream pants and a smile that envelops me in its heated promise. I push my chair back and shimmy toward him. JR picks me up and twirls me around, our lips connect as if we will never part again.

We move to the rhythm of the music on the dance floor. My head rests on his chest with my arms wound around his neck, his body like a magnet pulling mine ever closer to paradise. Our hearts beat to the same rhythm of anticipation. JR is setting me ablaze.

"Let's do what your parents are doing?" He nuzzles my neck.

I tilt my head to gaze into those tamarind eyes. "What, go to the French embassy dinner?"

He shakes his head from side to side, trying to look stern. "I want us to go steady, Addy. I'm never letting you go. I'll wait for you for as long as you need. Let's go places together." He kisses my eyelids with lips like butterfly wings. "What do you say, Miss?"

I grab his hand, and we bound toward the elevator. The room key falls twice from my shaky hand as I try to open my room door. He presses me to him inside the room. "Addy, I asked you a—"

I swallow the rest of the words in a kiss that slows down time, erases the past, shows me the future and promises bliss. "You'll have to *make* me say yes, Officer." I pull the shirt out of his pants and run my palms over the peaks and valleys of his stomach. "Can you do that, *Detective*?" I lick his lips.

"Oh, Baby girl," he swoons, squeezing my body to his. "I'm going to make you say many, many, *many* words tonight." JR picks me up and wraps my legs around his trim waist as he carries me to the king-sized bed.

Hours later, with a sore throat, a mellowed body and a promise for more, I scream the one word to that man many, *many* times: *YES!*

# THE END

## Share Your Thoughts

I hope you enjoyed *I Shall Find You*. If so, please take a few seconds to write a positive review. Love you for it!

## I Shall Find You

## Island Sisters

It can be found on all online bookstore:
https://www.mickimorency.com

Visit my Website: https://www.mickimorency.com/
And sign up for my newsletter to get all of my latest news:

Email: mickimorency@gmail.com

Facebook: https://www.facebook.com/micki.morency.1

X: Twitter: https://twitter.com/mickimorency

Instagram: https://www.instagram.com/mickimorency3588/

Goodreads: Micki_Berthelot_Morency

Made in the USA
Monee, IL
13 June 2025